WHEN WE'RE BROKEN

SHAWNA HOLLY

THREE SPARROWS
PUBLISHING

First edition published 2024.
Three Sparrows Publishing
Boerne, TX

ISBN 979-8-9879662-6-6 (paperback)
ISBN 979-8-9879662-5-9 (ebook)

Cover Design by Esther van Bokhorst-Beentjes, Meraki Cover Design

*For those who know what it means
to live a thousand lives
before finding who you're meant to be...
and for those still searching.*

AUTHOR'S NOTE

This is a story centered on trauma, life, love, and loss. It is not a story meant to glorify trauma or mental illness. Nor is it meant to say that we all experience these aspects of life in the same way.

If you are currently experiencing any form of distress or crisis and are located in the U.S., please call or text 988 to reach the national Suicide & Crisis Lifeline.

For those who prefer them, a full list of content warnings can be found on the last page of this book.

PLAYLIST

1. "Heading South" by Zach Bryan
2. "Lady May" by Tyler Childers
3. "Kiss Me In The Dark" by Randy Rogers Band
4. "The Kind of Love We Make" by Luke Combs
5. "Beautiful Things" by Benson Boone
6. "Shake the Frost" by Tyler Childers
7. "Something in the Orange" by Zach Bryan
8. "Leave Me Alone" by Logan Michael
9. "Wicked Twisted Road" by Reckless Kelly
10. "Must Be the Whiskey" by Cody Jinks
11. "Stone" by Whiskey Myers
12. "23" by Chayce Beckham
13. "Coal" by Dylan Gossett
14. "In My Arms Instead" by Randy Rogers Band
15. "Lose Control" by Teddy Swims
16. "Porch Light" by Josh Meloy
17. "I Remember Everything" by Zach Bryan, Kacey Musgraves

PLAYLIST (cont.)

18. "You Should Probably Leave" by Chris Stapleton
19. "Chasing After You" by Ryan Hurd, Maren Morris
20. "Alabama" by Cross Canadian Ragweed
21. "Interstate" by Randy Rogers Band
22. "Die A Happy Man" by Thomas Rhett
23. "Joy of My Life" by Chris Stapleton
24. "Please Don't Go" by Wyatt Flores
25. "A Life Where We Work Out" by Flatland Cavalry, Kaitlin Butts
26. "Letting Someone Go" by Zach Bryan
27. "Hell of A Year" by Parker McCollum
28. "Religiously" by Bailey Zimmerman
29. "The Night We Met" by Lord Huron
30. "Spotless" by Zach Bryan, The Lumineers
31. "Starting Over" by Chris Stapleton
32. "Cover Me Up" by Jason Isbell
33. "Tennessee Whiskey" by Chris Stapleton
34. "The Painter" by Cody Johnson

PROLOGUE

The world bathes in a hazy orange glow, as the sun rises over rooftops, willow oaks, and loblolly pines. There's nothing extraordinary about this particular Alabama sunrise, other than the man I'm unexpectedly enjoying it with. It feels like it's been a lifetime since we've sat side-by-side on this rickety wooden swing. The last time I saw him, I was thirty-seven years old, and it's been twenty years...where has the time gone?

Glen places an arm around my shoulders and passes me a cup of coffee. Holding the warm mug in both hands, I push off with my bare toes, and the swing creaks as we rock back and forth, back and forth.

"So, what do we do now?" he asks, staring at slow-moving clouds.

"Aside from sleep? It's been a long time since I've pulled an all-nighter. I'm exhausted."

He smiles. "Yes, aside from that."

"First, I need to call into work. I'm too old to go in on no sleep. Then, I suppose we have to talk to Jenna. Tell her everything." The thought of it makes my stomach turn.

"She's not going to like it, Cat."

"She needs to know the truth about her parents. We've kept it from her long enough."

He sucks in a deep breath, then lets it out again. "Of course she does. I'm just sayin' she's not going to like it."

"Well, lucky for you, it's up to me to tell her." Reaching out to touch his cheek, I smile. "When I woke up yesterday, I never imagined that twenty-four-hours later, we'd be rockin' in this old swing on the front porch, watching the sunrise."

"Me neither," he says. "I honestly thought you'd throw things at me and slam the door in my face."

"No, you didn't."

"No, I didn't." He smiles again, then stands. "I'll let you rest. Call me later?"

I nod.

He kisses my forehead before descending the porch steps, two at a time, and climbing into that old truck. As he leaves, he swerves from one side of the road to the other, in pure joy—just as he used to, decades ago when we were so young and full of hope.

That afternoon, I call Jenna, telling her it's time she knew the truth about her father. Three days later, I fly to Texas, hug my grandkids goodbye as they embark on a camping trip with my son-in-law, and sit face-to-face with my daughter—wondering where I'm even supposed to begin.

1981

1

CAFETERIA FOOD & MIDDLE FINGERS

Mama lost both Daddy and John Lennon in a single week, providing my first introduction to grief. In my almost seventeen years on Earth, I'd experienced nothing like it.

There's something about witnessing a parent come undone that's disturbing to the core. Watching your life's anchor upended and tossed on the waves, carried away on the tide like it weighs nothing at all, brings doubts—and a primal fear—about *everything*.

Lennon was taken first. Mama sobbed on the sofa for three days. I felt her sadness in my bones, and they shook and rattled from the power of it.

Daddy went next, and she never shed a tear.

Four months passed, and I never saw her cry. My brother didn't cry either.

The tears were all mine.

When I sat my tray on the table, a familiar laugh traversed the cafeteria. Looking up, I saw Liza at the center of what was once my closest group of friends at that godforsaken school, in the-middle-of-nowhere Asher, Alabama.

Liza stood tall and pretty in lavender—her signature color—which perfectly complemented her golden-blonde hair and warm, peachy skin.

She laughed again, and for a moment, I thought she may actually glance my way. Not daring to risk it, I cast my eyes back down, wincing at the shit-brown Led Zeppelin tee I opted for that morning and reminding myself it did my olive skin no favors.

"Hey—uh, I'm Glen." The unfamiliar voice saved me in the nick of time—just before I lost myself in the *my best friend ditched me* self-pity again.

Glancing over my shoulder, I saw a cute, but abnormally tall boy with somewhat shaggy, sand-colored curls hovering with a lunch tray. I nodded, turned back to my food, and poked a finger in the cold, rectangular cheese pizza.

"And you are?" he asked.

I let out my breath more forcefully than intended, and with a second glance, saw his shoulders drop. Realizing I'd hurt the feelings of the one person in the school who'd spoken to me in months, I replied, "Catherine."

"I'm the *new guy*, I guess. Can I sit here?"

"It's not my table. You don't have to ask permission."

He crossed to the opposite side and sat directly in my line of vision. Meeting his eyes, I noticed they were a dark shade of blue—like the deepest part of the ocean on a sunny, cloudless day. I felt my cheeks grow hot and re-focused on my tray.

"Thanks—I think?" He gave a funny look, like he'd never seen a girl be less than enthusiastic about being graced with his presence before.

God, he's one of those.

Even if I was wrong and he didn't expect every girl to swoon at his presence, I gave it till end of day for him to discover who I was and join everyone else in staying far, far away. Or worse, maybe he knew, and he'd been sent to my table as a sick, twisted joke.

I couldn't stand the thought of it. "I'm not hungry. Table's all yours." I grabbed my tray, dumped its contents into the trash, and tossed it onto the cart before exiting the cafeteria.

Liza's laugh followed me, bouncing from the walls and surrounding me, like a tornado surrounds everything lying motionless in its eye. I quickened my pace, seeking refuge from the storm.

Upon entering the musky library, I heard, "Looking for anything in particular today, Catherine?" Ms. Williams, the librarian, stared with eager eyes.

"Only a place to hide, as usual."

She looked at me with concern etched upon her bronzed, angular face. "Did you eat?"

"Lost my appetite." I blew my feathered, auburn bangs out of my eyes and looked down, noticing fluorescent pink gum stuck to the side of my clog.

"Follow me." She marched to the desk and reached for something inside a drawer. "This'll get you through." Sliding a granola bar and peanut butter crackers across the desk, she smiled, then grabbed a stack of books to re-shelve.

"Thank you."

With a nod, she headed for the romance section.

I snagged a tissue from a box and squatted, determined to handle the gum situation with discretion, before the kind librarian took notice.

Out of thin air, a pair of legs in blue denim, attached to feet in blue and white Osagas materialized. Looking up, his height, in addition to his also-blue tee shirt, brought forth childhood memories of *Gumby* on the television.

A giant, muscly Gumby. Only blue, rather than green, from head to toe.

I plucked the gum free and crinkled the tissue in my fist as I stood, knowing full-well there was no reason for that kind of boy to be in the library at lunchtime. "Are you following me, Glen?" I gripped that nasty wad of stranger-gum like my life depended upon it.

"No, but—do you *want* me to be following you, Catherine?" he asked in a mocking whisper, with a twinkle in his eyes.

Determined to provide zero ego strokes to the dimwitted oaf, I didn't answer. Instead, I dropped the tissue in the trash, grabbed the snacks, and set out to find a quiet place to be alone.

"Look, I'm not following you...and I thought you weren't hungry!"

Ms. Williams cleared her throat in warning.

"Shh! Jeez, this is a library, in case you're unaware!" I shout-whispered in his direction.

He took two long strides, stepping within normal library conversation distance. "I came because my truck's running rich and I need a book to fix it."

"I don't care enough to pretend I know what that means."

"It means the air-to-fuel ratio is—"

"I also don't care enough to *learn*." I pulled a book from a shelf and made my way to a beanbag in the corner.

He stood still, seemingly at a loss for words, which brought forth a tiny ember of guilt for not giving him the time of day. "Non-fiction's over there." I jerked my head, pointing him in the vicinity, then flipped to the first chapter of the book.

"Thanks. Nice meeting you." Then, he turned and mumbled, "I can see you're a lot of fun to hang out with," as he walked away.

Pompous ass.

And just like that, the guilt was gone.

⸺❖⸺

"Catherine, this is your stop."

I looked up to meet the bus driver's eyes in the long mirror, then out the window to the big green electrical box that was, indeed, my stop. Closing my book, I made my exit.

She shut the door behind me, then pulled away and stopped with a screaming squeal at the next corner. After tucking the book into my backpack, I started the walk home.

Traveling over dandelion-filled cracks in the sidewalk, I thought of how I used to make this walk with Bo—before Daddy died. Since then, given he was a sophomore with plenty of friends who drove, he rode with them to avoid being alone with me. I was a junior who rode the bus alone—pathetic, really.

Approaching the house, I heard the lawn mower before I saw it.

God, not again.

Mama pushed it up the incline of the yard, then pivoted and struggled to hold on as it rolled back downhill. At the bottom, she wiped her brow with a towel draped over her shoulder, looked up, and saw me standing at the bottom of the drive.

"Mama, you just cut that grass two days ago!" I yelled over the sound of the engine.

"Huh?" She cupped her ear and squinted her face. "I can't hear you! And if I shut this damn thing off, I'll never get it started again!"

I sighed and made my way into the house as she pushed that beast of a machine back up the hill.

"Why do you let her do that?" I asked Bo, who was sitting spread-eagle on the sofa watching a *Brady Bunch* re-run.

"Do what?"

"You should be mowing the yard, Bo, not her." I threw my bag on the table and pulled a grape soda from the fridge.

He shoved a handful of sunflower seeds into his mouth and changed the channel.

"Why do you think she's obsessed with the yard all of a sudden?" I asked him.

"Same reason she's obsessed with washing the car and winding the clocks, I guess. Now, shhh."

"And changing the lightbulbs, caulking the tub…She's never done those things before. Daddy always did—"

I gasped, as suddenly it all made sense.

Bo spit shells into a cup, then changed the channel again.

"Haven't seen Liza around lately," Mama said, scooping green beans onto her plate.

"Neither have I," I replied.

"What's that about?"

"I don't know, Mama. Liza is Liza. She does what she wants."

"Have you had a falling out?" She plopped mashed potatoes next to her green beans.

I watched in horror as juice from the beans made direct contact with those heavenly potatoes. *Ruined.* "Not that I'm aware of." I focused on my plate, the wallpaper—anywhere other than the travesty of Mama's comingling of juicy and non-juicy foods.

"What she means is, Liza isn't the stick-around-af-ter-your-best-friend's-dad-dies kind of friend," Bo piped in.

I threw my napkin at his face, honest-to-God wishing it were a coconut cream pie.

"Is that true?" Mama asked.

I cut a bite of fried pork chop and chewed slowly, hoping to choke on a piece of gristle to buy myself some time.

"Catherine, is it true?"

"Nobody knows how to stick around after something like that, Mama. It's not only Liza."

"Bo's friends still come around."

"Bo's friends are assholes who wouldn't understand tragedy if it hap-pened directly to them, much less a friend."

Bo pointed his fork at me as the wheels spun in his head to compute a witty comeback. Instead, he shrugged his shoulders and took another bite.

"Watch your language at my dinner table, please."

"Sorry, Mama," I replied.

"We'll invite her family over for a barbecue," she said.

"And how would we do that? None of us know how to get the da—"

Mama shot a pointed glare.

"—dang grill started," I finished.

"Then I'll add that to my list of things to figure out," Mama replied. "Now, pass the salt."

⸻ ◆ ⸻

The following Sunday, Liza, her younger sister, and her parents were in our back yard while Mama cussed under her breath, discarding unrecognizable carbonized chunks of meat into a garbage can she'd positioned next to the grill. She'd wait until Liza's parents weren't looking, then flip the burned portions into the can with a subtle flick of the wrist.

"Laurel, might I help?" Mrs. Mason asked Mama.

"What, you know how to—" Mama lowered her voice to a whisper. "—barbecue?"

"I know the basics. I can show you, if you'd like."

"Oh, please, Anna—show me!" Mama removed the elbow-length kitchen mitts she wore for fire defense and thrusted them toward Mrs. Mason.

Mrs. Mason held them like a dirty diaper, then set them on the beer cooler. "Your problem is your fire's too hot. See these?" She pointed to two silver dials. "When they're open, that's a lot of air getting in, and your coals are gonna get real hot. If you close them, halfway or even all the way, the temperature decreases."

"*Oh*," Mama said. "I wondered what those doohickeys were for!"

Mrs. Mason laughed. "You'll have this down in no time."

"Catherine, fetch me another plate of patties, will ya?" Mama asked.

As I walked by, she tapped the trash can with the toe of her loafer and cleared her throat. I picked up Mama's *bin o' shame* and carried it inside and through to the garage, stopping in the kitchen on the way back.

The screen door slammed, and Liza entered. "They sent me to see if you need help."

"Sure, I guess." I pulled the bowl of seasoned beef from the refrigerator, then washed my hands at the sink.

Liza did the same, then we silently formed patties and placed them on a plate between us.

"How many do we need? Seems like a lot," she said.

"We better use it all." I grabbed another hand-full of the freezing cold mixture, rolling it into a ball.

"I'm sorry, Catherine," Liza said.

Smooshing the ball into its proper patty form, I placed it on the plate with the others.

She turned to look at me. "I've never lost anyone. I didn't know what to do—or say."

"For *four months?*" I blinked away the tears as best I could.

She hung her head and reached for another handful. "I'm sorry."

"Liza, you lead the group. When you turned your back on me, they all did. I lost my dad, my best friend, and every other friend I had—*in a night.*"

A tear rolled down her cheek, and she wiped it away with a shrug of her shoulder. "What can I do? How can I make it up to you?"

I turned toward the sink and washed my hands while she stared from behind, waiting for an answer I didn't have.

On Monday, I crept toward the cafeteria, dreading running into Liza. Mama often said I was wise beyond my years, but this wasn't something I could just forget and go right back to shopping for records and hoop earrings at the mall. Liza disappeared when I needed her most, and I didn't know how we could come back from that.

I fought my way through the hallway as people laughed and teased, complimented each other on their outfits, and coordinated after school plans. They talked about graduation and prom, their jobs, and on and on.

So much to talk about—and none of it involving a dead parent.

Eyes glued to the faded and scuffed red and white checkered floor tiles as I maneuvered around the crowd, I desperately wished to camouflage myself into the ecru cinder block walls and lockers. When I entered the cafeteria, I saw no sign of Liza. The clock ticked loudly on the wall as I gathered my tray and silverware, then waited for the line to move.

"Hi," Liza said from behind me.

I didn't answer.

"Can I sit with you?"

"Grilled cheese, please," I said to the whisker-faced lunch lady behind the glass.

"Same for me," Liza added.

Making my way down the line, I opted for fruit cocktail, corn, and chocolate milk. Liza did the same.

"Catherine, can I sit with you?" she asked again.

"Sit wherever you want."

She followed me to a table, and we sat facing the cafeteria doors. When the other girls entered, they smiled and waved at Liza, then turned to each other with whispers when their eyes landed on me.

"You see? I'm not some freak show, Liza. My dad *died*." I tore the rock-hard grilled cheese into pieces, just to have something to do with my hands.

"I know, and I'm sorry. Tell me what I can do, *please*."

I wanted to forgive her. I wanted my old friends back. I *didn't* want to be forever known as *the girl whose dad died*, and I knew it would be one long summer—and a hell of a senior year—if things didn't change. But things *had* changed, and there was no going back.

"I don't know, Liza. Not yet." I stood, noticing Glen leaning against the wall, surrounded by smiling, hair-twirling girls. After taking care of my tray, I retreated to the library—hoping Ms. Williams had more granola bars in that desk.

Exiting the bus, I again began my homeward journey alone. Just as I noticed a family of birds land on the telephone wire, an old truck in a stomach-turning hue of olive-green barreled past me. It reeked of gasoline and made such a noise, the birds and I both had an instinct to fly.

In the seconds it took to pass, a hand appeared from the passenger window, casually—but emphatically—giving me the middle finger. And I could swear that hand belonged to my brother.

I watched as the truck parked in my driveway and Bo climbed out. My stomach lurched and flipped in one lightning-quick motion when Glen exited the driver's side.

You've got to be kidding me.

When I reached the yard, I focused on the front door, hoping to avoid their attention.

"Oh, hey, *Library Girl*." Glen popped the hood on his truck.

I trudged up the yard.

"Bo, you didn't tell me *Library Girl* was your sister," Glen said, head tucked beneath the hood. He lifted the bottom of his shirt to wipe a bead of sweat from his face and gave me a wink and a smirk as he did it.

My cheeks flushed and *hated* myself for it.

"Didn't know you'd met." Bo gave me a confused look I would've assumed was full of questions, if I thought my brother could think at all.

Entering the house to their amused laughter, I bounded upstairs to my room and flopped onto the bed. Staring at the ceiling and its layers of peeling paint—goldenrod yellow being the room's current color, then sea-foam green beneath that, then baby doll pink—I wondered what color Mama would choose next.

Why is he here?

And why did he rub me the wrong way, anyway? Was I annoyed because he expected me to fawn over him the way the other girls did? Or was I simply repulsed by him, physically?

A vision of that bare stomach flashed through my mind. *No, it certainly isn't that.*

Maybe it was being an outcast, with no one left to trust, that had me on edge—some ingrained sense of self-preservation. Every friend I had vanished when Daddy died. There's no way someone like *him* could be the one to look beyond what happened. Right?

The truck's engine revved twice, Bo and Glen exchanged *hell yeahs*, and I heard Van Halen blasting from its stereo speakers. And in that moment, I somehow knew that for better or worse, things would never be the same.

2

CHOCOLATE CAKE & CONFESSIONS

In the weeks that followed, it seemed Glen was always at my house, as he and Bo tried to correct his truck's *running rich* problem.

When the sun got too hot, they moved inside to drink all the sodas, eat all the chips, and hog the TV; never missing Bo and Luke Duke on Friday nights. Then they returned to that old truck, searching for its cure. I hid in my room, listening to records and trying to avoid them.

At school, I did my best to ignore him...and the girls who so desperately wanted to be with him...and the boys who would have given anything to *be* him.

"Why are you here?" I plucked up the courage to ask, as Glen gulped water in the kitchen on a Saturday afternoon, while my brother was bent half-naked over the engine of his truck.

He set his glass on the counter. "Bo's good with engines and I'd like to see mine fixed."

"So, once it's settled, you'll be out of here?"

"Maybe. I've sorta gotten used to the asshole. Why? You have a problem with us being friends?"

I took the last sip of my ice-cold lemonade, which I had made just enough of for myself. "I might."

He stepped so close I felt his breath on my neck. "I think that's 'cause you think I'm a bad influence. But the question is, *on who?*" He placed a hand at the small of my back, and a rush of staticky warmth traveled through my bones.

No, no, no—this is not happening.

Not with that asshat, who couldn't find his way around a library if his life depended on it, and who was also my brother's friend. I held little loyalty to Bo, but the fact Glen could *be* friends with him was warning enough for me. And if Glen thought *he* was the bad influence? Then he either didn't know Bo, or my instincts were spot-on, and I needed to stay far, far away.

"That's not a question at all, actually, because I'll be *thrilled* when that old clunker of yours is fixed and you're no longer spending *your* time at *my* house." I tossed my cup into the sink.

"Hmm," he said. "Guess we'll see about that."

⸻ ◆ ⸻

"Yes, Kitty, meatloaf's fine. See ya soon." Mama hung up the phone, then realized she'd tied herself up in the cord. "Oy," she said, picking it up again and spinning in place to unwind herself, as her nursing shoes squeaked on linoleum.

When she slammed the phone back onto the cradle, a tiny *prrrring* sounded, and she froze—unsure if Aunt Kitty was calling back or if she hung up too hard. She waited for another ring that didn't come, then grabbed her purse from the counter.

"I got offered an overnight shift and I can't pass up the money. Kitty's bringing dinner." She kissed my forehead.

"Okay," I said, staring through the window. It was Glen who was half-naked then, and the way the sun radiated from his rounded shoulders had me begrudgingly mesmerized—a fresh development since that afternoon when he simply reached out and *touched* me.

"You okay?" Mama gripped her purse in one hand and keys in the other.

"Yeah. Have a good night."

"Catherine, have you made up with Liza yet?"

"Mama—"

"You're seventeen, going-on-thirty, and you need her." She looked out the window and spotted Glen crouching low to the ground, taking a swig from a giant thermos. "And I'd rather you be needing her than—" She nodded toward him and cleared her throat.

Feeling like I'd been caught red-handed, I snagged an apple from the fruit basket. I knew Mama had a point, but it had been weeks since Liza apologized, and I'd been the one who shut *her* out since then. I didn't know how to make it right.

"Your daddy's only been gone a few months. The worst of it isn't likely to be behind us yet." She stepped forward, taking my hand. "I know you don't have experience to draw upon, so I'm just going to tell ya: It may get harder, before it gets better."

"Something to look forward to?"

"You know I won't sugarcoat things for ya. Give Liza another chance. You're going to need her. Well, if not her, then—*someone*." She glanced back out the window and her eyebrows turned pointy as the worry lines between them deepened.

"Christ, Mama, I'll call her. And quit lookin' at him like that. I can't stand the sight of that boy."

"Hmm," she said, tossing me a skeptical glance, and kissing my forehead again. "I'll be home around 7:30 in the morning. Try not to burn the place down."

Being Mama's childhood best friend, Aunt Kitty often brought dinner, more so after Mama was on her own. That night, she stayed just long enough to invite Glen to join us.

The thought of it made me want to crawl into a hole in the wall and seal myself in from the inside—*a self-inflicted fate of Fortunato.*

I made it upstairs with my plate as they entered. Kitchen cabinets, drawers, and the refrigerator door banged shut a thousand times as they prepared their plates. Then, the air buzzed with electricity as the TV came on, and the banging was replaced by scraping forks, soda burps, and arguments over what to watch.

I dug into Aunt Kitty's meatloaf, which was covered with the sweetest ketchup sauce I'd ever experienced in my life. Even with the door closed, though, their voices carried, and I found myself curious. I turned off the light, cracked open the door, and slunk down against the wall.

"Screw TV. Let's hit the Piggly Wiggly. Maybe Tina will be there, eh?" Bo must've included a punch with his suggestion, because they thumped around on the floor, wrestling like Labradors over a bone.

"All right—I give," Bo groaned through what sounded like gritted teeth. *A headlock maybe? Impressive.*

"Do you think she'll be there? Or maybe—" Glen said.

"*Janet!*" they voiced together.

The front door slammed, then Glen's truck peeled out of the driveway. *Did they even eat? Morons.*

When I finished my dinner, I tiptoed downstairs. On the way to the kitchen, I grabbed their plates from the coffee table, turned off the TV, and the house grew eerily quiet. The sky loomed dark through the windows, and I suddenly felt very alone, but also like I was being watched.

You're crazy. No one's here. They're gone.

I cut myself a piece of Aunt Kitty's chocolate cake. Somewhere, a car backfired, and I damn near jumped out of my skin. I took a deep breath to calm my pounding heart.

What if I called Liza, like I told Mama I would?

Moving to the phone, I tortured myself with each slow spin of the dial and held my breath as it rang.

"Hello?"

"Liza—it's Catherine. Can you come over?"

She took an agonizing moment to respond. "I'll ask."

"Okay," I whispered.

I heard muffled voices, then she came back on the line. "I'll have to stay the night. I can't drive too late alone."

"Mama's working a night shift. Is that okay?"

"Yeah, fine. See you soon."

I did all I could to make the house feel less like something from a horror movie. I turned on lamps and the TV, grabbed blankets for the sofa, and put a pot of oil on the stove for popcorn.

Just as I placed the popcorn bowl onto the coffee table, there was a knock at the door. Peering through the curtain first, to be sure it was Liza, I opened it.

"Hi." She carried a backpack on her shoulder and her sleeping bag in her arms.

The relief I saw in her eyes brought me to tears.

"Why are you crying?" She dropped her things and gave me a hug.

"I'm just—glad you're here."

She smiled. "Mama said it was too late at first—but she gave in. I didn't tell her *your* mama was workin' though, or she would've changed her mind real quick."

"Guess we shouldn't get into any trouble then." I picked up her things and led her inside.

⸻◦⸻

Turns out, when you stop fending off your best friend, you can fall right back into the very rhythm you were working so hard to avoid.

Come 2:00 in the morning, we had finished an impressive portion of Aunt Kitty's cake and caught up on all the important things we'd missed since Daddy died. Well, I'd caught up on all *her* important things, and I think she came to understand my life was frozen in time.

"Why did you invite me over?" she asked.

I twisted the fringes of a blanket around my fingers. "I'm tired of it all, I guess. Of fighting with you, of Bo being an ass, of the way everyone looks at me and whispers about me at school. I want to move on."

"I'm sorry about everyone at school," Liza replied. "They'll come around once there's something new to talk about. You know that."

"Maybe. It's hard, though, being ignored and avoided, but also knowing they're talking behind my back. How is it possible to both be shut out completely *and* the center of attention?"

She shook her head. "I don't know...because we're assholes?"

I propped an elbow on the back of the sofa, burying a hand in my hair.

"Why did you call me *tonight,* though? Did something happen?"

"Not really. Mama went to work, and Aunt Kitty brought dinner. Then Bo and Glen took off to the Piggly—"

"Glen? *The new guy?*"

"He's friends with Bo. It got so quiet when they left." I glanced toward the window. "It's so dark out there, and I felt like someone was peekin' in. I guess I freaked out."

"I don't like being home alone either, and my parents don't even work nights."

"Mama didn't use to work so many nights, not before—" I grabbed another handful of popcorn. "Well, she works more of them now. Pays better than day shifts, she says."

"When do you think they'll be back? Piggly's long closed by now."

"Who knows? But isn't it unfair the boys get to run all over town, at all hours, and the girls are locked away when the streetlights come on?"

"Well, not *all* girls. Who do you think they're out there *with?*"

Our eyes met and hysterics erupted. Maybe it was the sugar, the early morning hour, being in the house alone together, or some combination of all that and more, but we giggled like twelve-year-olds again. And it was just the thing I hadn't even realized I'd been missing.

⁂

Amid our fit of laughter, we must've missed Bo's knocking. Now, he *banged*.

"Jesus Christ!" I hopped over the back of the sofa and turned the deadbolt to let him in.

"What'd you lock the top one for? I don't have a key for that one!" Bo stumbled inside, kicked off his boots, and flopped into the chair. "And look who's back! *Liza Jane!*"

Bo gave Liza a mischievous grin, and she threw popcorn at his face. He scooped a few pieces off his lap, tossed them into his piehole, and chewed with his damn mouth wide open.

"God, Bo, you're drunk," I said as Glen entered, giving me a wink hello.

Who the hell taught that boy to wink? That should be a hangable offense, really.

"I suppose you're just as bad off?" I searched Glen's face to know for sure.

"Nope, just him. He struck out with Janet and took it pretty hard." He cocked his head to the side and grinned at Bo, who I knew would be dead meat when Mama got home.

"You need to go." I attempted to lead Glen to the door.

Looking down at my hand on his arm, he smiled. I turned him loose.

"Mom thinks I'm sleeping over. I can't go home now. She'll have a heart attack!" he said.

"Then sleep in your precious truck then!"

"Catherine, you're so *loud*," Bo said. "He can crash on the sofa."

Liza looked at me with wide, terror-filled eyes. "Catherine—"

"Shit! Shit, shit, shit!" I said, with a stamp of my foot.

"What the hell is going on?" Glen asked, bewildered.

"*Her* mama doesn't know *our* mama is working. She doesn't know there are no parents here. And now a drunk brother and his homeless friend have arrived!"

"I'm not homeless—and why do you *all* call your moms *Mama?* It's really confusing!"

I turned to stare him dead in the eyes. "Where the hell are you *from?*"

"Chicago?" he answered with a confused face.

Well, that explains a lot.

"*Lord,* help me..." I sat on the sofa to think. "Bo's going to bed. He'll sleep well past noon, like he always does, and Mama will be none the wiser. You," I said, pointing to Glen, "will be gone before we wake up. As far as Mama will know, we were asleep before you got back."

"Yeah, it'll be like I was never here," Glen said.

"If only," I replied.

And he stood there, still as confused as ever.

———◆———

"Mama's going to kill me," Liza said.

"It's in God's hands now." I threw the blanket back and slipped under the sheet.

Liza unrolled her sleeping bag next to my bed. "You know, I find it charming you're only religious when it suits you."

"Isn't that the way? Or have I been doing it wrong all my life?"

She laughed, then laid on top of her still-zipped sleeping bag. "It's so damn hot in here. Wish we could crack the door or somethin'."

"We need to be locked in tight when Mama gets home or we'll *both* be in deep shit."

She flipped onto her stomach, pulling the back of her shirt up to her neck. "What do you think really happened with them tonight?"

"Bo drank too much and did something stupid, like always."

Liza chuckled in a sleepy, sugar-coma sort of way. "Do you think they'll always be so dumb?"

"Probably."

"Hmm—"

It grew quiet, then Liza's tiny, wheezy snores filled the room.

Thank you for bringing her back to me—even if I am only religious when it suits me.

⁎

I dreamed of red, white, and blue popsicles and cheesy hot dogs on the beach. Of sun and sand so blinding, I could barely see the seagulls hopping around my feet, taking shade under the umbrella and searching for scraps to eat.

"Catherine," I heard. "Wake up."

I felt a nudge on my shoulder. Opening my eyes, I saw a silhouette I didn't recognize and instinctively threw an elbow, making contact with something much harder than expected.

"*Ow, fu—*" He folded over with both hands on his knees, taking slow, deep breaths.

"Glen? What are you *doing* in here?" I pulled the sheet up to cover myself, unsure if I fell asleep with my shirt pulled up to keep from burning alive.

Pulling himself upright, he asked, "Can we talk?"

Liza rolled from back to side and smacked her lips.

"Get out of here!" I looked at the clock, saw it was 4:30 in the morning, and heaved a sigh of relief that Mama still wasn't due home for hours.

"Please?"

"Get *out* of my room. I'll be out in a minute."

He left as quietly as he came.

That boy better be experiencing a cardiac event, I swear.

I yanked the sheet off my bed, wrapped myself up, then tiptoed through the door. He caught me by the elbow as I exited.

"What is the *matter* with you?" I asked.

He turned me loose and gestured toward the stairs. In the living room, we sat, and I waited for an explanation.

"I'm sorry I scared you. I didn't mean to." He brought his fingers to his cheekbone, where my elbow made contact, and somehow winced and sniggered at the same time.

I held his gaze without blinking, waiting for him to go on.

"Catherine, do you like me?"

I gasped in shock, horror, and humiliation.

"I mean, you don't *hate* me, do you?" He folded his hands together and picked at a hangnail on his thumb.

Weeks of him in my house, crowding every room. Teasing me like I was the little sister, rather than the older. Flirting in the same brutish way he did with every girl in our class, then looking as if he might punch a hole in the wall when I didn't swoon right out of my pants. And he had the nerve to ask if I *liked* him?

When he raised his eyes to mine, butterflies took over my stomach. He wasn't teasing me then—he meant it.

I took a deep breath. "No, I don't hate you. I may *loathe* you a little; find you somewhat *abhorrent*...but I don't hate you."

"Look, I know I'm not smart like you. I don't always get your jokes or references—"

"Insults, you mean."

"Yeah, those too," he said with a half-smile. "But I think I like you."

Now I was the one experiencing the cardiac event.

"What?" Surely, I misheard him.

"And I'm wondering if you might like me too?"

"I, uh—" I scooted back on the sofa, putting the tiniest bit more distance between us. "I barely know you. And what I do know of you, well..."

His head fell as he wrung his hands. "I see."

"You're my brother's friend. Isn't there a law against that or something?"

He leaned back, clasping his hands behind his head. "You're right. I'm sorry I woke you." He tugged at the blanket we were sitting on, as if he were ready to crawl beneath it and never come out again.

Damnit.

"Look—all I said is I don't know you. I can't like you if I don't know you."

His eyes met mine and the twinkle I saw that first day in the library appeared, just the same. "Should we get to know each other then?"

"You aren't *getting to know me* tonight, if that's what you mean!"

He laughed and shook his head. "Obviously not. But maybe we can hang out soon?"

I ran my hand through my bangs and rested my elbow on the back of the sofa to support my tired, bemused head. "I guess that would be okay. As long as you know I can still decide I don't like you."

He smiled and gave a nod. "Of course you can."

3

COMFORT BOOKS & PAC-MAN

"What the *devil?*" Mama shrieked.

I rushed over and cracked the door.

"What's going on?" Liza asked, half-awake.

"Shh—Mama's home."

She jumped up and joined me.

"I'm sorry, Mrs. Fraser. I didn't mean to scare you," Glen said.

"What the hell are you doing on my sofa?" Mama yelled.

"I—uh—it was late when I brought Bo back last night. He said I could sleep here."

"With my *daughter* upstairs?"

"I don't know, ma'am. I haven't seen her."

"God almighty, Glen, go home before I box your ears!"

"Yes, ma'am."

The door slammed.

"What do we do?" Liza whispered.

"Get back in bed!"

Two seconds after we resumed our sleeping positions, the door flew open.

"Liza!" Mama said.

Liza lifted her head sleepily. "Hmm?"

"Guess the whole neighborhood's havin' a sleepover while I'm workin' my ass off, huh?" Mama huffed, then flung the door open on her way out. It bounced off the doorstop and halted, half-way open. Jiggling the knob on Bo's locked door, she yelled, "Robert Daniel! Open this door!"

It squeaked open.

"What?" he grumbled.

"Why was that boy sleeping on my sofa? And what is that god-awful stench? You been drinkin' again?"

"No, Mama, I—"

"Don't lie to me, child! I'm a nurse, for cryin' out loud!"

I heard footsteps coming our way. Then they stopped and traveled back towards Bo. Mama headed our way again, growled in frustration, and stopped in the middle of the landing. "Both of you, out here, *now*."

It felt like walking the plank, but I went.

"This won't happen again, ya hear?"

"Yes, ma'am," we said.

"You're grounded for a week. And Bo, I swear, if I see that boy in the next month, I'll be meetin' him with your daddy's rifle. Got it?"

"Yes, ma'am," he replied.

"Tell Liza to go home. I'm gonna lie down. I'll leave a chore list in the kitchen."

We nodded, and Mama gave a "Hmph!" before stomping down the stairs.

"Way to go, little brother," I said.

"Shut up," he replied.

⸺ ◆ ⸺

By the time Mama woke and padded downstairs, we'd scrubbed toilets and baseboards, vacuumed bug bits out of window frames, dusted ceiling fans, and weeded the garden. Mama's chore lists were a barometer by which one could judge how mad she was, and given this wasn't a dishes, sweeping, and laundry type of list, I'd say she was pretty darn mad.

She filled the coffeemaker with water and a dozen spoonfuls of Maxwell House, then moved to the table, pulling her robe tight around her waist. "Ya'll come sit."

We took our seats, being careful not to drag the chair legs on the floor, which set her off even on the best of days.

"You know you messed up, right?" she asked.

"Yes, ma'am," we said.

"And you won't do it again?"

"No, ma'am," we said.

"Good. Now, I think I messed up, too."

I looked up to meet her eyes, confused.

"Your daddy made the rules, and he was mostly the one to enforce them. I don't think we've discussed what's allowed while I'm at work because he was always here when I wasn't. I'm sorry if you didn't know the expectations. Did y'all get into any kind of trouble?"

"No," I answered.

"Okay." Mama drummed her fingers on the table. "I will say it's nice seeing Liza around again. And the house looks great. Now, run upstairs and find something to do while I have my coffee."

We exploded from our seats, not daring to loiter long enough for her to get any more words in. As I passed by, Mama gave my hand a squeeze.

⚬

Monday morning, Liza picked me up for school. Her parents bought her a lemon-yellow Chevy Chevette a couple months after Daddy died, and it was the first time I'd ridden in it.

I slid into the passenger seat. "This is cozy—and cute!"

"It's not a Mustang, but it'll do," Liza replied as she backed out of the driveway. "So, how much trouble are you in?"

"I'm grounded for a week, and we had to do a ton of chores, but it wasn't so bad. Glen's banned from the house for a month."

"Me too?"

"I don't think so. I think this is one case where we should be glad we're not boys. Bo definitely got it worse than I did."

"I can't believe she didn't call my parents." Liza halted at a stop sign.

"You're basically one of her kids. She doesn't know Glen like she does you. Which, speaking of Glen—"

She looked at me for the half-second she dared to take her eyes off the road. "What happened?"

"Nothing. Well, *something*, but not what you're thinking."

"Out with it then!"

"He came into my room."

"While I was *in there?*"

"Yeah. He scared the crap out of me and got an elbow to the face."

"What did he want?"

"He—told me he *likes* me."

"*What?*" She whipped into the parking lot, taking the first spot she saw. "Tell me everything."

"Okay but walk fast." I exited the car and met her around the back. "He asked if I like him too."

"Do you think it's true? Or do you think he hoped he'd get lucky?"

"He seemed like he meant it."

"Oh my God!" Liza said as we entered the building and the first bell rang. "Tell me more at lunch!" She disappeared into the crowd.

"That's a bummer," I heard from behind me.

I turned and saw Glen, wearing jeans and boots, just like my brother. A barely visible purple bruise rested high on his cheekbone, and I felt the slightest tinge of pride.

"What?" I asked, trudging down the hall.

"I hoped *we'd* have lunch together."

"Not today, sorry. Gotta go!" I weaved around the slow walkers in my way, unsure if it was being late that had me moving so fast, or the awkward *morning after* feeling that arose at the sight of him.

It didn't take long to figure it out. It was definitely both.

<hr>

"What are you going to do?" Liza dipped a chicken nugget in ketchup.

"I have to hang out with him, right? I told him I would."

"You don't *have* to do anything. Do you *want* to?"

"I really don't like him, Liza. He's arrogant, flirts with everyone, and I doubt he's ever read a book of his own free will."

"Then there's your answer."

I pried open my milk carton and took a swig. "But—"

"But?"

"There's something about him I can't figure out. When we were talking on the sofa, he seemed almost—*human*."

"Oh, those *human* boys will get ya every time," she joked.

"You know what I mean, right?"

"Yeah. You're wondering if there's more to him...somewhere." She twirled her hand in the air like she was reaching into the ether.

"Yeah."

"Well, I suppose there's no harm in hanging out. He can't go to your house, so you'll only see him at school. It'll give me a chance to size him up. My douche-radar is the best at Asher High."

I snort-laughed, sucking milk up my nose. "Ah, that hurts!"

Liza laughed and took another bite. "Where is he, anyway? I'd think he'd be here, trying to get your attention."

"In the corner with Susie James."

She peeked over her shoulder and spotted him. "She's practically sitting on his lap!"

"This morning it was Ally Monroe who had him leaned up against the lockers. *Ally!*" I went for another drink, but my stomach turned. I placed the carton back on my tray.

"Maybe he was drunk or stoned, and doesn't remember it," Liza said.

"He remembers. He found me this morning and asked to have lunch. I said no."

"Then his pride's hurt, and he's showing off. They all act the same dumb way, I swear."

"I can't eat another bite. Wanna go to the library?" I stood, and through the corner of my eye, saw Glen distance himself from Susie James.

"Nah. See you in gym." She took her tray and joined our old group of friends at the center table.

———— ◆ ————

I headed straight for the book I knew I needed. *Where The Sidewalk Ends* may be juvenile, but it was my comfort book. Pulling it from the shelf, I hugged it tight against my chest.

As I came out of the aisle, the library door opened. Glen spotted me and a smile spread across his face. I proceeded to the back of the library to find a table.

"Figured I'd find you here," he said. "Bored with your lunch date?"

I sat and cracked open the book.

"Can I join you?"

I didn't answer, but he pulled out a chair anyway.

"You have a terrible habit of asking permission to *be* in public spaces," I said, skimming the words I knew by heart.

"Should I be more rude next time?" He smiled again. "Why do you come here? It's not really a place your friends hang out."

"Exactly."

"So, you're hiding from them? Why?"

"You ask too many questions."

"I thought you said we could get to know each other."

I closed the book, unsure if I should leave, or let him in. "*Why* do you want to?"

"I told you, I like you."

Opening the book again, I asked, "Do you read?"

"I *can* read."

"But *do* you read?"

"Comics, sometimes."

The bell rang, so I stood. "Take this one." I handed him my most beloved book. "It was written for five-year-olds, so I'm sure you can make your way through it. Even has pictures."

I headed to class, leaving him sitting at the table, staring at the cover.

⚹

"Mama, what are you doing now?"

Head tucked inside the fridge, she said, "The light's out. I'm trying to pull out the bulb but can't get the damn cover off. Did you glue it on?"

"Why would I do that?"

"I don't know! You were always playing with the glue when you were little. Thought maybe you did something to it."

"I didn't glue the cover on, Mama."

The phone rang, and I answered it, expecting Liza.

"Hi," Glen said.

"Are you calling for Bo?"

"No."

Silence filled the line, and it was very, very awkward.

"I read that book," he said.

"In one day?"

"Well, yeah. It's a bunch of nursery rhymes; not quite the deep literature I expected you to enjoy."

"They're poems...and that's the point. You don't have to think too hard unless you want to. You can enjoy the silliness."

"Which is your favorite nursery rhyme?"

"My favorite *poem*, from that book, is *Ickle Me, Pickle Me, Tickle Me Too*," I answered.

"I thought that one was sad. They were gone, lost forever."

"Or they were free."

Silence on the line.

"Is that what you want? To be free?" he asked.

I couldn't answer that with Mama in the fridge, so I asked, "Which was your favorite?"

"I liked *Listen to The Mustn'ts*."

"You would," I said with a laugh. "It's all about defying authority and social conventions."

"Or it's about being true to yourself...and hope."

"Aha! Got it!" Mama held the light bulb cover up in victory, then unscrewed the bulb. "I need to call the hardware store to see if they have these in stock."

"I have to go," I told him.

"See you at lunch?"

Mama moved closer, tapping her watch.

"Yeah, see you then."

Two weeks later, Liza said, "I have an appointment, so I can't babysit you two at lunch today." She gave a teasing grin as she parked.

"What do you think of him, though?"

"I kinda like him. He's a bit spacey, but they all are. And he seems interested enough."

"Two weeks of lunches and that's your full conclusion?"

"You want a book report?" She opened her door and climbed out.

I did the same and leaned against the car with my arms folded across its top. "Liza, really. Is he a douche, or not?"

"I don't know! You're the one with the gift!"

"For the last time, I'm not psychic. Now, what's the split?"

"I'd say 60/40."

"Sixty-douche or sixty-not-douche?"

"Not," she replied. "Now let's go!"

Making our way toward the school, he found me, just as he'd found me every day since that first phone call. And like every other day, my heart skipped a beat.

"Mornin'," he said to the two of us.

Liza smiled, then bounded inside, leaving us to walk alone.

"So, do you think your mom really meant a month?" he asked.

"She definitely did."

"But you're not grounded anymore, right?"

"Uh—no, not grounded."

"Maybe we can do pizza at the arcade then? Friday?"

"Are you asking me on a date?"

"It's only a date if you let me pay. If you buy your own pizza, we're hanging out. No different from the cafeteria."

"Well, okay then. And yes, I'll bring my own money."

He smiled. "That's progress, I guess."

"Meaning?"

"The day we met, you didn't want me breathing the same air as you."

He was right. Now I struggled to fall asleep at night, as my brain poured over every time our knees had touched beneath a table or he'd brushed a piece of hair over my shoulder. I longed for him to breathe the same air I did, and when he didn't, I looked for him. I always looked for him.

"I'll meet you there," I said. "Mama says you are to come nowhere near our driveway."

He laughed and took off in a sprint, sliding through his classroom door as the tardy bell rang.

Friday night at the arcade was a bad idea. It overflowed with people, and though we snagged slices of pizza, there was nowhere to eat it.

"Wanna go outside?" he asked over the loud music—REO Speedwagon, I think—and screaming conversations.

I nodded, and he led the way.

"Over here." His bicep twitched when he gestured toward the sidewalk, and my cheeks grew hot.

We sat, leaning against the building. He went for a bite, did that mouth breathing thing when it burned his tongue, and I laughed.

"Hi, Glen," Ally Monroe sing-songed with a smile as she passed by.

He nodded without looking up and took another bite.

"You're not friends anymore?" I asked.

"Never were."

I wondered if he said the same thing about me when I wasn't around. "Are we friends now?"

"I think so, but I still don't feel like I really know you. You don't talk about yourself much."

"Isn't it good manners to not talk about yourself too much?"

"I guess, but sometimes would be okay."

"What do you want to know?"

He stared across the street. "What happened with your friends?"

I took my turn to stare into the distance. "It got weird after my dad died."

"What did?"

Shifting my weight to relieve the pressure on my tailbone, I said, "They sort of...left me behind."

"Stopped talking to you?"

"Yeah. I don't blame them for it anymore, though. They didn't know what to say and Liza leads all of them. She didn't know what to say either, so they sort of disappeared."

"But she's around now. The others haven't come 'round?"

"Liza invites them to sit with us or hang out after school, but..." I looked down at my plate.

"Man, that sucks."

"Well, when everyone thinks your dad died in a bloody forklift accident, they don't really know what to do with that."

"That's not what happened?"

"You've heard it too?" I asked, and he nodded. I took a deep breath and wished I could be anywhere but there, telling that story. I still had night-mares of what it must've been like. Nightmares where I had a front-row seat to my father's death.

"You don't have to tell me, if you don't want to."

I set my plate on the ground. "He worked at the metal factory outside of town. A forklift trainee ran into a shelf stacked with pallets. It collapsed, which led to more shelves collapsing, and when Daddy tried to move out of the way, he stumbled. He hit his head on something, which led to a bleed in his brain. They did surgery, but he died anyway."

He took my hand—something he'd been doing more lately, and which always took my breath away—and a tear rolled down my cheek.

"How did the rumors start?" he asked.

The absurdity of the answer made me laugh, and he stared with a blank expression, waiting for me to share it.

"Well, it was Ally Monroe," I said.

"Ally?"

"Yup."

"Why would she do that?"

"Because she's evil?"

His expression remained unchanged.

I sighed, ran my fingers through my hair, then worked through a tangle at the ends. "She's never liked me. She bullied me all through sixth grade. In middle school, she became boy crazy, and pretty much left me alone. But her dad works at the factory, so I think she may have known about it before I even did. By the time I went back to school, she had made up this gruesome lie—for no reason other than to make my life hell—and they all believed it. People literally made way for me in the halls...like if they came too close, they'd be infected with some sort of parent-killing disease. No one knew how to talk to me after that, including Liza."

"Why didn't you tell people the truth?"

"Nobody wanted to hear the truth. They were too invested in the lie Ally told them, and I could barely admit to myself that my dad died, much less talk about it."

Another tear fell and that time, he wiped it away.

"And your mom?"

"She works more now. When she's not, she does all the things around the house he used to do. She never sits *still*. I don't think she's even cried."

"What a nightmare—all of it."

"Yeah." I picked up my pizza and took a bite. "I just can't wait to graduate, get out of that house, and away from that school."

"Where will you go?"

"Anywhere is better than there, with Mama not making any sense, and Bo being a jerk for no reason."

"I'd say he has a reason."

"I lost my dad too, and I don't treat him like garbage."

"People handle things differently. Your mom's response is to do whatever it is she's doing. Yours seems to be to run away from it all. His response is something...different."

"I guess." I took another bite. "You know, you may not be the dumbass I thought you were."

"Thanks?"

Standing and tossing what was left of my pizza into the trash, I said, "I need another slice. I can't eat it once it's cold, *bleh*."

"Weirdo," he said as he stood. "Let me buy. Then, we'll play Pac-Man. I have the high score!"

"No, you don't."

"You'll see for yourself: 'G-DAWG', that's me."

"Of course it is."

4

PSYCHOPATHS & MAGIC FIELDS

After that day at the arcade, Glen and I spent nearly every day together after school. We talked about all the unimportant things people talk about while getting to know each other, but we shared the hard things, too.

I recounted stories about my dad, like how he and Mama used to kick us out of the kitchen so they could cook together. How he'd win us armfuls of stuffed animals at the county fair. How he went to every school play, dance recital, and game we ever had.

And I told him about the nightmares.

He wasn't afraid to listen, to ask questions, to wipe away tears when they came. He was so unlike the other kids in our school that I'd spent most of my Sunday morning lying in bed, wondering what he'd been through that made him so different. When I eventually went downstairs for a late breakfast, I found Bo sitting at the table.

"What's going on with you and Glen?" he asked, shoveling Froot Loops into his face.

"What do you mean?" I grabbed the Frosted Mini Wheats from the pantry, took a bowl from the cabinet, and poured my cereal.

"You're always together. He's given up on his truck because of you, ya know."

"I didn't tell him he couldn't work on his truck." I pulled the milk from the refrigerator and poured into my bowl.

"When is he supposed to do it? I don't think you'll be out there fixin' it with him."

"So, you're mad he's hanging out with me, and not you?"

"I'm not mad. I just want to know what's going on."

"We're getting to know each other." I placed the milk carton back in the fridge.

"You've been getting to know each other for a while. What else do you need to know?"

"Bo, come on."

"No matter how long you spend *getting to know each other*, he'll never be who you think he is, Catherine." He shoveled another bite.

"What does that mean?"

"It means you only know what *you* see of him. You don't know what he's like when you're not around."

"And what is he like then?"

"Let's just say he doesn't shy away from the attention from the girls."

"What girls?"

"All of them!"

My heart sank.

"If that's true, why wouldn't you have said something weeks ago, Bo?"

"Because I thought once he'd had his fun with you, he'd leave you alone."

"What does *that* mean?"

"You know exactly what it means. And I'm surprised he's still hanging around, if you catch my drift."

"Bo! I have not done what you think I have...not that it's any of your business!"

"Ah, *that* explains why he's still hanging around."

"So, you think—"

"Yup. Go on and get it over with, so I can have my friend back, already."

"God, you're an ass! You're wrong about everything!"

"Am I? Or have you just not figured it all out yet? You're way too good for him, anyway."

"He's not good enough for *me*, but he's good enough to be *your* friend?"

"You and I are not the same and you know it."

"Boy, do I ever." I tossed my bowl of uneaten cereal into the sink and left the house with a slamming door.

Ten minutes later, I rang Liza's bell, out of breath.

"Hey!" she said, upon answering the door.

"God, I wish I had a car!" I wiped the sweat from my face with the back of my hand.

"Why didn't you call? I would've picked you up."

"Bo pissed me off, and I left."

"What now?" She led me inside, to a chair at the kitchen table.

"He said—Liza, he said—" The words choked my throat, my eyes filled with tears, and before I could stop it, I began sobbing into my hands like a child.

"Hey, what did he say?" She moved close and hugged my shoulders.

"He said a lot of things! That Glen is only spending time with me because he wants to fool around, and I should let him, so he'll move on, and Bo can have his friend back. That Glen isn't who I think he is. That he still hangs out with other girls. That I'm too good for him and I should call it off. Hell, what *didn't* he say?"

"God, your brother is a psychopath!" She plopped down into a chair. "Do you think any of it's true?"

"I don't know! I was grounded for the first week, I don't have a car to hang out with people after school, and I wouldn't want to, anyway. How would I know?"

"I can ask around. Or we can start going to the Piggly; see what it's like."

"And what? Hide in the bushes with binoculars?"

"If that's what it takes, then yeah."

"No, Liza. I don't want to spy, hang out with people who don't want me around, ask questions, or snoop behind his back."

"Then what *do* you want to do?"

"We haven't made anything official. He's technically free to do whatever he wants, and I can't say—or feel—any kind of way about it."

"Oh, you're definitely *feeling* some kind of way about it," Liza said, twirling her hair.

"I need to talk to him...figure out what we are. Whether or not we're...*together* together."

"So, your options are to either have *the talk* or go undercover to see for yourself? I think I'd rather hide in the bushes."

⚬

The next day, Glen picked me up for a basketball game. After parking, he shut off the truck and reached for his door handle.

"Wait," I said.

He turned to look at me and pulled his hand back onto his lap.

"Glen—is this a date? A real date?"

"If you want it to be," he answered.

My heart skipped a beat. His expression was so hopeful and earnest, I had to look away. "I think I do." I pulled my left hand to my mouth and bit a hangnail.

"Then it's a date." His smile lit up his whole face. "Are you ready to go in?"

"No. I mean, not yet."

"What is it?"

"You remember when I said we could hang out, but I could still decide I didn't like you?"

"Yeah."

"Well, I've decided."

"And?"

I turned to look out my window. "I like you. A lot."

"I know," he said, taking my hand.

I faced him again. "What do you mean, *you know?* You're a cocky SOB, you know that?"

His laugh told me he was both proud and amused. "Yes, I know that too."

"Well?"

"Well, what?"

"Do you think...we could be more than just friends?"

"I think we already are," he replied.

"I mean—"

"Look, Catherine, if you're asking me to be your boyfriend—"

"I'm not—"

He rested his hand on the side of my face and stroked my cheek. "Then my answer is yes."

"Oh."

"So...is that what you're asking?"

"Yes." I squeezed my eyes tight, hiding from the embarrassment of the conversation. It felt like kindergarten, and I'd just handed him a note saying, *check yes or no.*

"Okay, then. That's what we are."

I sighed in relief that I'd survived the ordeal and reached for the door, but he placed a hand under my chin and turned my face to his. Then, he looped that arm around my hip and pulled me in so close I heard every breath he released.

His eyes roamed over my lips, then up to meet mine. "Can I kiss you, Catherine?"

I sucked in a sharp breath as the anticipation clawed at my insides. "Okay."

And kiss me, he did.

———— ❖ ————

"You and Glen are really a thing now, huh?" Liza asked.

I tucked the phone under my chin, grabbed the long, wound-up cord, and disappeared into the laundry room. Sitting on the floor, I ran the cord under the door and closed it. "Yup."

Just the mention of his name brought back the memory of us in that truck—*and that kiss*—and I felt my face grow hot.

"Are y'all going to the bonfire?" she asked.

Liza's sister said something in the background, then Liza yelled, "I'll be off in a minute!"

"I think so. You gotta hang up?"

"Yeah, she's buggin' me for the phone."

"I have to get my chores done anyway or Mama won't let me go anywhere."

"I'll see you later tonight then."

"Yup, bye." Returning to the kitchen, I hung up the phone.

"I wish you wouldn't do that to my cord. I've replaced it twice already," Mama said, entering with a toolbox in hand.

"Sorry, Mama. What are you doing with that?"

"Sink's drippin' underneath." She took a seat on the floor.

"And you're going to fix it?"

"I'm going to try. We'll see how it goes." She opened the cabinet door, inspected the plumbing, then pulled a wrench from the toolbox.

"Can't we call a plumber, or Uncle Charlie?"

"If they can do it, I can do it. Used to watch your daddy fix it all the time. It's the same damn leak we've had since 1972. Go get me a towel, child."

I retrieved one of Daddy's old work towels from the laundry room and handed it to her.

Mama dried the pipe, then stared intently, waiting to catch that traitor of a drip.

"Can I go with Glen to the bonfire after my chores are done?"

"Fine with me. Keep an eye on Bo, though. That boy always finds his way into trouble."

"Okay." I turned to leave the kitchen, but only made it half-way.

"Catherine?" Mama asked, with her head still stuck beneath the sink.

"Yes?"

"You and that boy—I know things have gotten more serious."

I held my breath and squeezed my eyes.

Oh, God, here it comes.

"I know you know where babies come from—so don't be stupid."

"*Mama*—" I whined.

"You know what I mean. So, don't be stupid."

"Yes, ma'am. I won't be stupid."

"Get on with your chores then, if you actually wanna go."

I turned and took two normal steps toward the stairs, in attempt to hide how mortified I was, then ran the rest of the way to my room.

Mama gave a hearty laugh, alone in the kitchen, as I closed my door.

◆

I'd been watching for Glen, in hopes I could somehow jump into his still-moving truck and avoid a meeting between him and Mama. Or worse—him and Bo. But a girl can only hold it so long, and I heard him knock just as I flushed the toilet. I gave my hands a quick scrub and exited the bathroom to see him on the stoop, cap in hand, greeting my mother.

"Hello, Mrs. Fraser," he said.

"Hello, Glen. Come in before you let all my cold air out," she replied.

"Mama, we really need to go."

"Nonsense. The boy will come in, we will chat, then you will go."

I gave Glen an apologetic glance, but his eyes danced with confidence. It was a look that said he'd done this a thousand times, and I didn't know if I felt reassured or concerned by it.

Mama moved toward the sofa and beckoned for us to join her. As she took her seat, a suspicious hissing noise erupted in the kitchen, followed by a loud *pop!*

"What on Earth?" Mama jumped up and Glen and I followed her into the kitchen. She opened the cabinet under the sink to find water everywhere; the big, curved pipe disconnected.

"Mama, what did you *do?*" I pinched my nose against the putrid smell filling the room, and Mama did the same.

"I fixed the damn leak! That's what I did!"

"Do you know where the main water valve is?" Glen asked. "We need to shut it off."

"Near the hot water tank in the garage," she answered.

I led Glen into the garage, pulled the chain to turn on the light, then pointed to the water heater. He located the valve and turned it until it was tight.

"Let's go check out your mom's handiwork," he said with a smile.

"Did you find it?" Mama asked when we re-entered the kitchen.

"Found it." Glen squatted next to the sink, reached in, and picked up a broken piece of pipe. "Mrs. Fraser, come take a look."

Mama walked over and squatted next to him.

"This is the flange that holds the pieces of this P-trap together. There should be one here and here." He pointed as he spoke.

"Yeah, it had a leak, so I tightened everything with a wrench and put sealant on the joints," Mama said.

"You have to be careful not to overtighten though. And sealant won't help if the crack is on the inside."

"Oh." Mama's shoulders slumped in defeat.

He picked up the curved piece of pipe and inspected its inside. "There's a ton of gunk in here and it's corroded, too. So, the crack got bigger, the pressure built up inside, and it blew the pieces apart." He pointed to the water at the bottom of the cabinet. "This water sits in the bottom of the curved pipe. It's supposed to be there, to keep the sewer gasses from coming into the house."

"Is *that* what that smell is?" I asked, with my nose and mouth covered with my shirt.

"You need a plumber," he said.

Mama stood. "Thank you, Glen." She crossed the kitchen and pulled the phone book from a drawer. Flipping through the pages, she found a number, then picked up the phone.

We moved back to the living room while Mama made her call.

"Your poor mom," Glen said.

"Yeah." I looked at him in genuine wonder. "Hey, how do you know all that? You're seventeen, for crying out loud."

"My dad, I guess. He knows a lot about a lot of things. I used to help him."

He'd never mentioned his dad before, and I realized I knew nothing about him.

"You kids get going. That's all the excitement there'll be around here today. Plumber's on the way." Mama waved a white dish towel of surrender in the air.

⸺⟡⸺

He parked on the dirt at the edge of the field, where everything that made Asher a community happened: live music and festivals, farmer's markets and county fairs, 4H competitions and livestock shows, weddings and after-prom parties, too.

Sometimes it was a place of happiness and new beginnings. Others, it was where everything went wrong: spouses caught cheating behind the mirror maze, drunken brothers assaulting dishonest carnival game workers, and once, a veteran who mistook the *whiz! bang!* of fireworks for bombs in Vietnam.

Maybe that's why the hair on my arms stood on end whenever I went there. That field was a doorway to what could be the best or worst day of your life, and you never knew which it would be.

"You okay?" Glen took my hand in his.

"Yeah, fine. Can we sit for a minute though?"

He shut off the engine but left the radio on.

I kicked off my sandals and shifted, so my head rested on his lap and my bare feet hung out the window. "I've realized something," I said, enjoying the warm breeze between my toes.

"What's that?" He trailed his fingers across my bare shoulder and down my arm, then back up again.

"I don't know why you moved here, what happened to your dad, or what your mom does for a living. Will I get to meet her soon? Is there some reason I shouldn't meet her?"

"That's a lot of questions."

A knot formed in my stomach. I feared I'd intruded or assumed everything between us to be more than he did. "Well, you can pick one."

"My dad is still back in Chicago, I think, but I don't know where. I have a half-sister, Robin, who's a month older than me. After we were born, my dad spent his time between the two families. Didn't seem to bother my mom too much. My sister would stay the weekend or a couple weeks each summer, and I would stay at her place too. It was a weird, messed up arrangement, but it worked."

I sat up straight to look at him. "Your dad had two families?"

"Yeah."

"Was he married to either of them?"

"No."

"Well, what happened?"

"One day he left and didn't come back. He took boxes and suitcases, which he'd never done before, so I knew he was gone for good."

"And you don't know where he is? Isn't he at your sister's house?"

"I went there a few weeks after he left. There was a for-sale sign in the yard and the house was empty."

"He left without telling you where he was going?"

"Yeah," he said, cycling through the radio stations and pausing at Aerosmith. "Then one day, I came into the kitchen before school, and Mom said I wasn't going to school. She said we were moving to Alabama—I have an uncle here."

"Did you at least get to say goodbye to your friends?"

"No. By lunchtime, the movers were packing up our furniture and by dinnertime, we were on the road."

"God, that's awful. I'm so sorry." I ran my fingers through his hair and paused with my hand resting at the base of his neck. His skin was hot and damp, and that beautiful, rich color all boys who spent too much time in the southern sun seemed to have at that time of year.

He took my hand again. "I'm not." His deep blue eyes met mine, and he pulled me closer.

"You're not?"

"Well, sorry for my mom, yeah. And it sucks he chose them over us and disappeared, but I'm not sorry to be here." He ran his knuckle from my temple, down to the tip of my chin, then lifted it gently and stared into my eyes. "Can I kiss you again?"

A nod was my only answer, and I hadn't even finished it before his lips found mine.

5

BONFIRES & BENCH SEATS

Two loud, fast bangs sounded from the hood of the truck. I jumped to the far side of the cab and slipped my feet back into my shoes, fully expecting Mama to be the source.

"You lovebirds going to make it to the bonfire?" Liza smiled and turned toward the field.

I saw the lopsided grin come upon him and knew he was considering a more entertaining option. "Well?" I asked.

"I guess we have a bonfire to get to." He took my hand, opened his door, and pulled me out after him.

Walking toward the crowd of people who'd gathered, I looked back toward the cars and saw many of them filled with people just like us, snuggled together across bench seats, soaking up every quiet moment they could; lost in their own world before re-entering ours.

"What are you smiling at?" He looked over his shoulder, searching to see what I saw.

"Just people. This is going to be the best bonfire yet, I think."

A lightning bug crossed our path, blinking once, then again. Another seemed to chase it, then they were tangled in what appeared to be an intricate dance.

"What do we do now?" he asked.

"S'mores!" I led him to the Girl Scouts' tent, then said, "Two, please," to the adorably freckled girl standing behind the table as I dropped a donation into the jar.

She handed me two brown bags, each filled with supplies for four s'mores each, same as it had been since I went to my first bonfire when I was two years old. You never think you'll want four, but somehow, beneath a dark canopy speckled with twinkling stars, the air thick with bonfire smell, and folks gathered around acoustic guitars, there was always room for one more.

"Now we go claim our sticks!" I said.

"Sticks?"

"What do you think you roast the marshmallows with, ya dummy?" I elbowed him in the ribs, and we set off toward the Boy Scouts, where we chose two roasting sticks.

"So, the girls provide the sweets, and the boys provide the sticks? Sounds about right," he said with a chuckle.

"God, only you could make this into something dirty."

"Nothin' dirty about it, Cat." He gave me a wink.

I felt myself blush and looked away. He'd started calling me Cat during our lunches together at school, and while I wasn't sure how I felt about it at first, I eventually found myself longing to hear it again...and again.

"Ya know, I used to hate it when you winked at me like that, and I didn't care for being called *Cat*, either."

"And now?"

"They've grown on me." I pulled him in close and looped my arm through his as I noticed the mayor preparing to set the massive pile of brush ablaze. "It's time!" I pulled him to the center of the field, where we joined the circle of people buzzing with anticipation.

"Ten, nine, eight..." the mayor yelled as he held a flaming branch up high, and the crowd joined in counting.

"Make a wish," I said, closing my eyes. When I opened them again, I saw Glen had closed his, too.

"Seven, six, five, four…"

Glen's eyes were still closed.

"Three, two, one!"

All at once, the crowd erupted in cheers and yelps as the mayor tossed the branch onto the pile and the flames took hold. Glen wrapped his arms tight around my waist and lifted me from the ground. He spun us in circles as I giggled, then planted a long, fiery kiss on my lips, my body still suspended in mid-air and pressed tight to his. We were smashed together like peanut butter and jelly—no, like ooey gooey marshmallows and melted chocolate—and for a moment, the world disappeared.

"What was that?" I asked with a laugh once I'd found solid ground.

"It felt like a southern New Year's Eve or something. A kiss seemed appropriate, don't you think?"

One look around is all I needed to realize we'd become the stars of our own little show. Mamas squinted their eyes and shook their heads in disapproval. Dads stood with legs spread wide and arms crossed over chests, as if saying, *that would never happen with my daughter*, while all their daughters stared, whispering in excitement, and wishing it would.

I leaned toward him and whispered, "Look at all these scared mamas, all wondering if their sweet daughters are next."

He arched a brow. "If only their sweet daughters were as innocent as they let themselves believe."

"And how would you know they're not?"

"Just a hunch is all. Just a hunch." And there was that wink again.

——◆——

We were roasting our second marshmallows when Liza appeared and said, "Hey, I gotta pee. Come with me."

I turned to Glen and said, "Be right back."

"I'll be here." He took my roasting stick and held it with his, rotating them over the fire.

Liza stopped a few feet from the portable toilets, then turned to face me. "I'm not sure if I should tell you this or not, but—"

"Tell me what?"

"Well, Ally Monroe's not too happy seeing you two making out."

"We're not making out!"

"Whatever you're doing, she doesn't like it."

"So what? It's not like they were ever together."

"Well..."

"Well, what? Glen said he hasn't dated anyone since moving here."

"I don't know if they *dated*, but they definitely did—*something*."

That tiny seed of doubt I'd stuffed away when Glen became my boyfriend resurfaced and suddenly, I felt light-headed. I squatted low to the ground, then sat. "What's she saying?"

"She's just—running her mouth." Liza shifted from foot to foot, clearly uncomfortable and holding something back.

"Liza, what's she *saying?*"

She sat and picked at the grass between her legs. "She's bragging about all the times they've been together...and in quite clear detail. Says she doesn't know what he's doing with a *damaged prude* like you, and that she gives it a week before he's back tapping on her bedroom window."

"*Damaged prude?*"

Liza hung her head and gave a little nod.

"Tapping on her window?"

She nodded again.

"Are you saying they had sex?"

"According to her, yes, and more than once."

"When? Do you know when?" I jumped to my feet and my heart pounded an irregular rhythm in my chest.

"That's the thing—according to her, the last time was a few days ago."

"*What?*"

"After the basketball game," she mumbled, staring at the ground.

I sucked in what felt like all the air in the world, then managed to choke on nothing at all. "The game—the night we decided to—become a real thing..."

After he took me home? After we spent twenty minutes snuggled up, whispering secrets in the dark cab of his truck? What was it, one final goodbye-lay since he'd committed himself to a *damaged prude?*

"I need you to take me home," I said.

She stood. "Now?"

I nodded. "Tell him I'm sick—throwing up or something—then, I want to go home."

Liza pulled her keys from her pocket and handed them over. "I'll be quick."

Nodding, I wiped the tears from my face and made my way through the crowd.

⸺⬦⸺

Forcing myself between two young moms with babies on their hips, I heard a commotion.

"What the hell, man?" The voice sounded angry and confused—and it belonged to Glen.

"Yeah, *what the hell*, asshole!" The unmistakable voice of my brother responded, then he let out a loud grunt, and I heard someone fall to the ground.

Keep an eye on Bo. That boy always finds his way into trouble.

For the thousandth time in my life, I wondered how Mama always predicted these things.

I weaved through the growing crowd of onlookers, as moms ushered children back to the bonfire, bribing them with more s'mores when they whined about *missing all the fun.*

As I reached the front of the crowd, Glen stood and dusted off his jeans. "What's your problem, Bo?"

Bo moved two steps closer to Glen, bringing them nearly nose-to-nose. "My problem is that your *old* girlfriend is blabbing her mouth to anyone who'll listen, and your *new* girlfriend—is my sister! I told you to stay away from her. I knew you could never be good to her. *I knew it!*"

"Dude, I don't know what—"

Whatever Glen meant to say never came out, as Bo pulled back his arm and landed a solid punch right on Glen's face.

Glen fell to the ground, his hat taking flight and landing in the dirt. He gave his head a little shake, then came back to his feet. "You sure you wanna do this? That's the only shot you're gonna get, man."

Bo charged toward Glen, wrapped his arms around his chest, and attempted to force him to the ground, but Glen was bigger and stronger, and came out on top. As Glen brought his fist back, Mr. Schmitty, the corner store owner, stepped forward. He pulled Glen to his feet by his collar.

"That's enough, boys. Sort this out elsewhere," Mr. Schmitty said.

Glen stumbled free of his grasp, retrieved his hat, and shoved it onto his head backwards. Turning to face Bo, he said, "I've done nothing to your sister. Nothing!"

"Tell us something we don't know," I heard from behind me.

I spun around to face Ally, and her entire entourage burst into laughter.

"Let's go." Liza took my hand, and my eyes met Glen's for a split second, as she pulled me away.

"What the hell was that?" Liza asked, tires squealing as she cut the corner onto Elm Street.

"Jesus, you tell me!"

"He's freaking hot though, right?" She made another turn.

"What? Who?"

"Glen! I think it was the backward baseball cap or something, but *good Lord!*"

"You're not serious?" I asked, trying to read her face.

"Yes, I'm serious! *Dang,* girl!"

The laugh escaped before I could rein it in, then grew as she joined in and pretended to fan herself with her hand. But as we pulled into my driveway, it all came rushing back. "I don't know what to do," I told her.

"I think you wait for him to come to you."

"Then what?"

"Figure out the truth. Or...whose truth you believe anyway."

"What would you do if Ally is the one telling the truth?"

Liza leaned back in her seat and stared out the window. "I think it would depend on what I wanted from him. If I knew I was graduating in a year and had no intention of seeing him after, I'd keep him around—but only if he kept that damn hat backwards." She fanned herself again, then gave a little smile.

"And if you—wanted more?"

"Do you want more?"

I did want more...I wanted *all* the more. But I also knew how stupid it would sound to admit that after what just happened. I gave up on finding a suitable answer and looked away.

"Yeah, I thought so," Liza said.

"If you think the hat's hot, you should see him under the hood of that truck." I turned to her with a tiny grin.

"Gah!" Liza pounded her fist on the steering wheel. "Call a girl next time, yeah?"

Mama placed the newspaper down on her lap and said, "You're home early."

"Yeah." I started climbing the stairs to my room.

"Where's your brother?"

"Probably icing his fist on a cold beer in a truck bed full of girls," I replied over my shoulder.

"*What?*" Mama sighed, picked up her paper again, and spoke more to herself than to me. "Can't say I'm surprised. You know what would be surprising? If that child came home one Saturday without needing to ice *somethin'*."

Just as I made it to my room, I heard pounding on the front door. I stopped to listen as Mama opened it.

"Who do you think you are, bangin' on my door?" Mama asked.

"I'm sorry, Mrs. Fraser, but—is Catherine home?"

"Hello, Glen. How are you this evening?" she said, to make a point.

"Oh, uh, good evening Mrs. Fraser. May I speak with Catherine, please?"

"I don't know if you may speak with Catherine, but I will ask her." Mama closed the door, then walked up to meet me on the landing. "Do you want to see him?"

"I'm not sure."

"You don't have to. I left plenty of boys standing on the doorstep in my day. If he's worth your time, he'll come back."

She was right: He would come back. So, we could either have the conversation, or I could lie awake all night worrying about having it the next day.

"I'll talk to him."

Mama turned back toward the stairs. I started to follow, but she waved me off. "Not yet. Make him sweat a little, at least."

"Good grief, Mama."

"Well? I assume he deserves it?"

I shoved my hands in my pockets. "Probably."

"All right then." She returned downstairs alone, then opened the door. "She'll be a minute. You can wait there." She closed the door again and clicked on the TV.

Intending to count to sixty, the night replayed through my mind, and I grew more and more angry. I gave up at forty-eight, headed downstairs, and opened the door.

"Cat, I'm so sorry."

I took a seat on the top step, and he sat beside me.

"What are you sorry for, exactly?"

"That's not how I expected our night to go." He pulled off his cap and bent the bill between two hands.

"Is it true? About Ally?"

He took a deep breath, and said, "What about her?"

"God, you're going to make me say it?"

"I need to know what you're asking, Catherine."

"I'm asking what happened! I want to know everything."

He looked down between his feet. "We hung out, and we messed around, but it was before we were together, I swear."

"Did you have sex with her?"

"Yes," he answered without hesitation.

My heart sank, and I felt like I'd forgotten how to breathe. "After the basketball game?"

"What? No."

"She says you did."

"Well, it's not true."

"What happened then?"

He stood, moved down the stairs, and paced on the sidewalk. "I went to see her, but nothing happened."

"Glen! You asked me to be your girlfriend hours before that—" I stood, and my knees felt weak. "—and you went to see her after you left my house?"

He bounded up the stairs and attempted to take my hand, but I pulled away.

"Cat, she's lying. I knocked on her window, and she told me to climb in, but I didn't. I realized I was stupid for going there, told her I couldn't see her anymore, and left. That's the truth!"

My eyes filled with tears, and I turned away to hide my face.

I will not let him see me cry.

The door opened and Mama said, "Y'all need to say goodnight now."

"Goodnight, Glen."

"Catherine—" He reached out for me, but I was already gone.

"You wanna tell me what that was about?" Mama asked, scooping Neapolitan ice cream into two bowls at the kitchen counter.

"How much did you hear?"

"All of it, of course." She licked the scooper, then tossed it into the sink.

"Why did you snoop?"

"Because I'm your mama, that's why." She returned the ice cream to the freezer, joined me at the table with the bowls, and slid a spoon my way.

"He got into a fight with Bo. Well, Bo started it."

"I thought they were friends?" Mama curated a spoonful of ice cream containing all three flavors at once, then savored it like she's never had ice cream before.

I used my spoon to separate the flavors before starting with the strawberry. "They were."

"What were they fighting about?"

"Me, I guess."

"You? What about you?"

"I don't want to talk about it, Mama."

She took a long, hard look at me. "Catherine, I know you think I'm a hundred years old, but I'm not. I'm *thirty-seven* years old."

"I know how old you are, Mama."

"I remember what it was like when I found my first boyfriend."

I squirmed in my seat, wishing I could pass out on command.

"He was tall, like Glen. Handsome like him too."

"Mama—"

"Shh—just listen." She took another bite before going on. "For six months, my world revolved around that boy. It ended as quickly as it started, and I thought I would end right along with it. I thought I loved him. Of course, after meeting your daddy, I knew I never loved him. I was infatuated with him, and certainly drawn to him in some hormonal, biological way—"

"Oh, *God!*"

"But it wasn't love. I won't say a seventeen-year-old can't feel love, because I know it can happen. I saw it with Kitty and Charlie. What I'm saying is, it's hard to tell if it's love when you're in the middle of this...phase of it. So, rather than getting all wrapped around it in your head, trying to figure out if it is or isn't, take one day at a time. Do you enjoy spending time with him?"

"Yes, I do."

"Then do it. If a day comes when it's not feeling right for you, come home, then try again another day. If you notice many days have gone by where you haven't enjoyed it—or you have—then you're closer to figuring it out and one day, you'll know for sure."

"It's not a question of *love*," I said. "It's more a question of *trust*."

"Well, it's him you're in a relationship with, not Ally Monroe, right?"

I nodded and pushed away my bowl.

"So, maybe you owe it to him to put your trust in him until you have some sort of first-hand experience that leads you not to. You're a smart girl, and you have a strong intuition. You'll figure it out. Besides, we all know what sort of girl Ally Monroe is. She's the last kid in this town I'd ever trust."

I laughed a little because she was right.

"But—and this is a huge but—always trust your instincts. If your gut tells you someone isn't worthy of your trust, you can walk away. What does your gut tell you about Glen?"

"I want to trust him. I wasn't there, so for all I know, he's telling the truth."

Mama nodded.

A car door slammed outside, and Mama peeked through the kitchen curtains. "Run on upstairs because Bo's home, and I don't plan to be quite so soft with him."

I stood, and she pulled me in for a hug.

"Thanks, Mama." I headed for the stairs but stopped midway. "Maybe don't be too hard on him," I said, gesturing toward the door Bo was about to walk through. "He stood up for me, Mama."

She tilted her head, then her eyes widened once she pieced it all together—my finding out about Ally and Bo and Glen fighting. She nodded. "All right, child. Now *get*."

6

SHOOTING STARS & CICADAS

Nico's Pizza smelled of garlic and sweaty boy-feet.

I chose a chair facing the window, and Glen took the booth across from me. He sunk into it so far, I could see over the top of his head, and it made me a bit happy to feel like I'd have the upper hand in the conversation.

"I figured we should try pizza somewhere besides the arcade, since we ended up on the sidewalk last time," he said.

"Nico's is better anyway, even if it does smell like feet."

He laughed. "I think that's parmesan cheese you're smelling."

"No, it's definitely feet."

"You think they're back there flinging pizza dough in sweaty gym socks?"

I shrugged.

The waitress brought our drinks, then said, "Pizza's coming right up."

"Thank you," Glen replied.

Once she'd gone, he leaned forward with something to say, then leaned back again, like he didn't know where to start. I decided to let him off the hook, for both our sakes. I'd overthought the whole thing to death already and really just wanted to put it behind us and move on.

"Okay, I came here intending to make you squirm—to watch you suffer before I said we're good." I pulled a straw from its wrapper and placed it in my cup. "But I think I'd rather forget about it."

"Forget about...the suffering part? Or the *we're good* part?"

"The suffering."

"Thank God! What I told you was the truth, Cat." He looked at me with eyes pleading to be believed.

"I know."

"You do?"

I nodded. "Ally would do anything to make me miserable. I'd be crazy to believe her over you."

He reached across the table and took my hands in his. "Just so we're clear...I'm never going to another bonfire again. You're on your own for those."

That made me laugh. "They were less dramatic without you around, that's for sure."

"Me? That nonsense was instigated by *a girl* and *your brother*."

"Have you talked to him since?"

"Saw him at the Piggly a couple days ago. Can you believe he just *what's up*-ed me, like he *didn't* assault me with a hundred witnesses?"

"I can. He has the emotional depth and attention span of a toddler. He gets mad, then he gets over it."

The waitress brought our pizza, and we pulled steaming hot slices, stretching them above our heads, twirling up the cheese, and piling it on top.

"Are you over it?" I blew on my scorched fingers.

"Yeah, I don't really hang on to that stuff either. Plus, my Uncle Rudy is short a few men at work. I'll help him till school starts, and I thought Bo might like to make a few bucks, too."

"My brother? Do actual work? Good luck with that. What kind of job is it?"

"He lays brick and stone—for new construction and landscaping."

"You know how to do that?"

"Some. I told you, my dad could do almost anything, and I helped a lot. I'll learn the rest. I'm a quick study."

After dinner, we headed to the parking lot. Walking toward the truck, Glen squeezed my hand. When he did, I realized I'd been anxiously waiting to get a sense of where we stood. Lying in bed at night, washing my hair in the shower, staring at the back of the cereal box—through it all, I'd wondered if it would be the same between us, or if everything good went up in flames with that bonfire.

I snuck a glance up toward his face, and found the answer I sought, as an indescribable sense of peace settled deep within my bones.

We drove to the outskirts of town, and he pulled off the two-lane highway onto a dirt road. The truck bumped and rattled, and I gripped his leg with every squeal. Darkness surrounded us as we drove deeper into the trees, and Billy Squier sang through the radio. It was chaotic and exciting, and I loved every second.

He cut a hard right, the back of the truck swung wide, and he spun the wheel to set us back on a straight path. When he pressed hard on the gas, I choked and gagged on noxious fumes of gasoline.

"Still haven't gotten that fuel mixture right. Workin' on it, babe." He gave me a quick peck on the temple.

"Where are we?" I asked.

"County Lake. You've never been here?"

"Not that I remember."

"It's the best spot around to see shooting stars."

"I can see shooting stars from my back porch."

"Oh, you're in for a treat." He grinned and shoved his foot onto the gas pedal again.

We reached the water's edge, and he whipped the truck to the left, so we faced away from it. Then he threw his arm across the seat behind my head, looking over his shoulder as he backed up. Suddenly, I floated not in the stench of gasoline, but in the dizzying scent of—him.

He cut the engine off and threw open his door. "Coming?"

I peered into the darkness. "It's scary out here. We're in the middle of nowhere!"

"Aw, come on, Cat. There's nothing to be afraid of, unless you're scared of me?"

"You don't scare me, boy."

"All right then." He held his hand out for me to take.

When I grasped it, he pulled, and my butt slid right off the seat. He caught me at the small of my back, then pulled me up into his chest. Our faces were so close, I saw his in double vision.

"I don't think I need to ask permission, since I didn't at the bonfire, but can I—"

"Shut up and kiss me, Glen."

"Yes, ma'am." He spun his hat from front to back and pulled me in closer.

When our lips met, his grip tightened around my waist and I felt each finger's placement on my body, like a five-pronged lightning rod digging straight into my skin.

His hand slid upward over my arm, and to the back of my neck where he took hold, fingers laced through my hair. Then, with a strength of will I could never find, he pulled his lips from mine and bent at the knees to look me in the eyes.

"Oh, Cat, honey...you've got it *bad*," he said with a crooked smile.

Unable to move a muscle, I said, "I have no idea what you're talking about."

He leaned in again and gave a playful bite at my bottom lip. He held it between his teeth for a second, until I gasped, unable to recall what to do with the air in my lungs. My whole body grew weak when he let go, and once again, he steadied me.

"Okay, you've made your point." I gave him a little shove, then pulled my hair to one side, smoothing it again. "Mama's gonna take one look at me and think I've been up to no good."

He twirled a wavy tendril around his finger. "You look fine. Come on, let's sit."

Walking to the back of the truck, he lowered the tailgate, then offered a hand as I hopped onto it. As he sat and scooted in close, a shooting star blazed across the sky.

"Did you see that?" I pointed toward the sky.

"There!" he said, pointing at the same star. "I told you! When was the last time you sat on your porch and saw a shooting star two seconds later? *This* is the place for shooting stars."

"How did you find it?"

"Went for a drive on a Saturday, right after we moved here. Saw the dirt road and decided to see where it led. Been coming here ever since."

"Do you fish?"

"Sometimes. Haven't caught anything, but I don't mind. I like the process of it; the stillness and quiet."

"Doesn't sound quiet to me," I said, referencing the chorus of cicadas emanating from all around us.

"What *are* those damn bugs? Or are they frogs? And why are they so loud?"

"You've never heard a cicada?"

"Not before moving here. I can't believe people *choose* to live down here. I've never seen or heard so many bugs in my life."

"Wait until you see one up close. Some are as big as your fist!"

"Oh, hell no. Nope, nope, nope," he said, shaking his head.

"Now who's scared?"

"Bugs the size of my fist? Damn right, I'm scared. That you *should* be scared of."

Another star raced from one end of the world to the other.

"There!" we yelled and pointed together.

"Let's count them," I said.

"Most I've seen in one night is thirty-four."

"You have not! Thirty-four?"

"Yup."

So, we sat, we talked, and we counted—neither of us finding the willpower to climb back into the truck and go our separate ways. At least, not until we'd made it to thirty-five.

"What time did you get in last night? We may need to set a curfew now you've got places to be," Mama said, while pouring her mega cup of coffee.

"A little after midnight, I think."

"Well, since you're nearly grown, and it's summer, I guess that's okay. Midnight then—the new summer curfew."

"Yes, ma'am." I poked around inside the fridge, in search of orange juice.

Mama watched me for a moment, then sighed, and reached behind the milk. Retrieving the juice carton, she held it out for me to take.

"How did you know?"

"I've been your mother for seventeen years. I know what you're looking for."

"That's a really crazy superpower, you know."

"You'll have it too one day, assuming you decide to have kids."

I suddenly felt panicked at the direction of the conversation. *Abort! Abort!*

I poured my juice, returned the carton to the fridge, and beelined for the stairs.

"Where do you think you're goin'?" Mama asked.

Shit!

"Did you need something?"

"Yes, a conversation. Come sit." She pulled out a chair for me at the table, then pulled one out for herself. "Where did you go on your date?" She took a sip of the hot coffee, which was yet another superpower. Mama could drink boiling water straight from a kettle.

"To Nico's," I answered.

"And then?"

"Uh, to the lake to watch for shooting stars. We counted thirty-five! Can you believe it?"

"What lake?"

"County Lake, I think? I don't know the name, but that's what he called it."

Mama let out a loaded sigh. "I know the one."

"You've been there?"

"Used to go with your daddy when we were dating. It's been a hotspot for teenagers since long before you were born, ya know."

"Really? I've never heard anyone talk about it and there wasn't anyone—"

Oh no.

"Wasn't anyone else there last night?"

"Mama—"

"No, I get it. This is the part of your babies growing up that you're warned about, but you're never prepared for. A year from now, you'll be on your own. And you've never given me reason not to trust you, or to think you'd make poor choices, so until you do—here we are." She tugged at the sleeve of her robe. "I wish your daddy was here, though. It would be nice to have someone to help me figure all this out. I feel like I'm making it up as I go along."

"I think we're all making it up as we go along, Mama."

"Hmm—" She took another drink, then looked down into her cup. "Catherine, I'd like to take you to the clinic for birth control pills."

"*What?*"

"It doesn't mean you have to have sex; not until you're ready. But it would be good to be on it, so you're protected when the time comes. Also, whoever you have sex with needs to wear a condom. Pills won't protect you from disease."

"*Oh my God.* Sometimes I really hate you're a nurse, Mama."

"Why? Because I can talk about s-e-x and educate my children?"

"*Oof,*" I said, burying my face in my hands.

"I'll schedule for next week because, well, I know how *interesting* summers can be, with all that freedom and everything. They'll have condoms, too. So, we'll grab a bag of those."

"A *bag?*"

"Just to be safe."

"And for Bo? He needs them more than I do."

"Yeah, for him too. Lord, help me, he'll be the first to make me a GiGi, I know it."

"Are we done? Can I take my juice and hide already?"

She laughed, then waved me off.

I ran up the stairs to my room, crawled beneath the covers, and buried my head under the pillow.

Damnit to hell, I forgot my juice.

There was a knock, and the door squeaked open. Feeling a tap on my shoulder, I peeked out from under the pillow to see Mama holding my cup. She handed it over, then turned to leave.

"Thank you," I said.

"Mm-hmm," she replied, as she shut the door.

"It was so bad, Liza! I swear I thought I would die." I grabbed a pair of Liza's shorts from the basket, folded them, and added them to the stack on her bedroom floor.

Liza laughed so hard, she rolled onto her side in tears. "When do you go?"

"Tuesday, and she's going with me!"

"It could be worse. You could get pregnant," she said, returning to an upright position.

"We're not having sex!"

"Not yet." She raised an eyebrow, twirled a pair of underwear around her pointer finger, then burst into laughter again. "If you don't think it's obvious what's on both your minds anytime you're in a room together, then you're delusional."

"What are you talking about?"

"Sparks! Fireworks! Tension, baby! The air is thick with it!"

"Jesus, you need a job—or a hobby. You're insane."

"We'll see. I bet you don't make it till the end of summer."

"Wait—you mean until school starts back, end of summer? Or autumn solstice, end of summer?"

She shrugged. "You tell me. And who says, *autumn solstice?* You read too much."

Just then, Liza's gaze turned toward her bedroom door as we both heard footsteps outside it. She jumped to her feet and flung it open. "Come back here, you little snoop!" Liza ran down the hall, chasing after her sister, screaming, "You heard nothing, Lori Anne! Nothing!"

Tuesday morning, I was so nervous, I couldn't eat. By the time Mama came downstairs, my cereal had turned to soup.

"Come on, now. It won't be that bad. Eat," she said.

"I really can't."

"Goodness, you girls and your dramatics. I don't recall ever putting on the show you do over every little thing. I'll make eggs."

She cracked and scrambled eggs, cooked them, and threw cheddar cheese on top. Then she set a plate of them on the table, pulled a bowl of mixed fruit from the fridge, and brought that over too.

"Now, eat." She walked back to the stove, dished out a helping for herself, then joined me. "Goodness—coffee." She started to get to her feet.

"I'll get it," I said. "Thank you for breakfast." I stood and fetched her coffee.

"Sure! Maybe the nurses will even give you a lollipop when you're done, honey." She gave a teasing wink, and I knew she said it to make me laugh, but it didn't help. "Oh, lighten up, Catherine. There's only one time in your life when your mother gets to take you for contraceptives. This is a milestone for you! Maybe I'll put it in the baby book!" She laughed out loud at her own joke.

"Haha," I said, unamused, as I started on my eggs.

"I need to run by the hardware store after. There's a hole in the back fence that needs mendin'. Chicken wire should do it."

"Did we not learn anything from the pipe situation, Mama?"

"I can surely hammer some wire into wood, don't you think?"

"If you say so." I took another bite, trying to determine the best way to ask what I wanted to ask. "Mama—why do you feel you have to do everything on your own? I'm sure Uncle Charlie could help with the fence."

Without missing a beat, Mama said, "Because I am a widow, not an invalid."

I stopped chewing mid-bite and looked up to see her face. It was the first time I'd heard her refer to herself as a widow, and the word carried more weight than I thought it would.

"What?" she asked with a mouth full of strawberries.

"Nothing, I—" There were no words to describe what I felt for her in that moment. It was sadness, heartache, and even pity, which I knew was the last thing Mama wanted.

"Are you okay?" She rested her fork on her plate.

"Yeah. What time do we need to leave?"

"In about twenty minutes. You'll be ready by then?"

"Yeah, I'm ready."

———— ◆ ————

Apparently, moms bringing daughters for birth control was standard procedure in our town, and I'd never felt more relieved to be just another name on an olive-green file folder. A weight check, a few instructions and warnings, a chance for me to ask questions (which I didn't), and one prescription scribbled on yellow paper later, and we were done.

"You'll schedule a check-up for next year at the front desk. No need to come back until then, unless you have troublesome side effects." The nurse was young, thank goodness, and kind.

"Thank you," Mama said before leading me to the lobby.

As soon as we entered, I saw her. "Oh, God, *no*—"

"What is it?" Mama looked around for the source of my current drama. Then she spotted her. "Ally Monroe!"

"Shh!" I spun around, hoping that if I couldn't see Ally, she couldn't see me.

"Hey, Catherine. Funny meeting *you* here," Ally said, loud enough for the world to hear.

"Mama, hurry up!" I hissed through gritted teeth.

Mama drummed her fingers on the counter to get the receptionist's attention.

The woman turned to us. "Checking out?"

Mama nodded. "Catherine Fraser."

"Give me one second to check the notes." She searched the countertop for her glasses, then placed them on the tip of her nose. Thumbing through the folders, she said, "Fraser, Fraser...I don't have a Fraser."

"It may still be in back," Mama said, trying to speed things along.

"I'll check." She disappeared, then returned with a folder with my name on it. "Here we are."

Skimming the notes, she muttered, "Mm-hmm," showing her acknowledgement of their contents. "Contraceptive consults are covered by your insurance, so there's no payment due today. Just take the prescription to the pharmacy, and they'll get you set up."

Oh, God! Did she say that out loud?

"And here is the—uh—*bag* of barrier contraception you asked for. It's more than we usually give in samples, but the doctor said it was okay."

Mama snatched the bag and turned to leave. I followed on her heels.

"Mrs. Fraser, we need to schedule Catherine's checkup for next year!"

"No need to take up any more of your time, Miss," Mama replied. "We'll do it by phone. Have a great day!"

Ally leaned into her friend, whispering behind her hand. They giggled, and as the door closed behind us, erupted into full-on laughter.

"Mama?" I whined.

"I know, child. Just keep walkin'. And whatever you do, don't look back."

7

PROMISES & PARKING LOTS

Thanks to Ally, I was the talk of the Piggly Wiggly social club for three days, and it only took Glen one to hear the news.

"Who told you?" I swatted at a mosquito.

"Everyone, I suppose." He laughed, and I wanted to punch him in the face.

I wondered if that *I can't get enough of him, but I also want to inflict bodily harm upon him* feeling would ever go away?

"It doesn't mean I'll have sex with you."

"I know that."

"Then why do you look so damn happy?" I batted at the mosquito again, cursing their magnetic attraction to my blood.

"You have to admit it's kind of funny."

"I don't find it funny at all!"

"You don't?" He kissed my neck, just behind the ear.

A shiver ran down my spine, clear to my toes, which involuntarily curled toward the night sky.

"That's not fair. I can't be mad when you do that."

"I know that, too." Tilting my face to his, he kissed me softly on the lips. Not a flame-inducing kiss, like so many we'd shared, but a gentle one. Then he scooted further into the truck and leaned against the cab. I, of course, followed his lead.

"How many do you think we'll see tonight?" he asked.

"I don't know. The moon's pretty bright and it's cloudy."

"Oh, ye of little faith." He took my hand in his.

"Matthew," I said.

"What?"

"It's from the Bible—the book of Matthew."

"That is definitely a book I haven't read."

"Well, don't feel too bad about it. Plenty of church-going people 'round here haven't read it either."

"Catherine!" He leaned forward between his knees, dropping his head as he laughed. It was a full, hearty laugh—the kind I didn't get from him often but had recorded in my brain and sometimes heard in my dreams.

"It's the truth!"

"You're terrible," he said, still laughing. "The worst."

"Am I? I think Ally Monroe's the worst."

"Oh, no...we're not going there again." He stood and hopped over the side of the truck.

"What are you doing?"

He reached into the cab and turned on the radio. Then, he held out a hand. "Dancing."

I stood, sat on the side of the truck bed, and swung my legs over. He steadied me by the waist as I jumped down. "This really is a cool truck," I said, as he pulled me close, and we swayed.

"Baby, you ain't seen nothin' yet."

"Got big plans, do ya?"

"Yup—and I don't mean just for the truck."

I looked up to see him staring out over the water. "I would've doubted you a couple months ago, but I see it now. You're more clever than you let on."

"Took two months to figure that out?"

"Well, you do an excellent job of hiding it."

He chuckled, then held me tighter. "I don't come from much, and I won't ever get into Harvard, but I'll make something of myself, Cat." He kissed the top of my head. "You'll see."

June disappeared in a blur of nights at the lake, pizza at Nico's, Pac-Man at the arcade, and waiting for Liza to get off work at her new job at the grocery store.

"Why don't you work here?" Liza punched .89 into the register for eggs.

"Will you stay after school starts?"

"Maybe. Or I'll try the Piggly. Things are way more exciting over there than at IGA, that's for sure." She punched in 1.75 for milk and .35 for bananas. "Three dollars, fourteen cents, with tax."

I handed her four dollars, and she provided my change.

"See? So easy, a baby could do it," she said.

"I'll think about it. See you tomorrow."

Exiting the store, I shaded my eyes and searched for Glen. He pulled out of an aisle, stopped beside me, then leaned across the seat, popping open the passenger door.

"Ma'am," he said with a smile.

I scooted to the middle, placing the groceries in the seat next to me. "Liza wants me to work here."

"You don't see enough of each other already?"

"Apparently not," I said with a laugh. "It would be nice to have spending money, though. Things are tight at home since Daddy died and senior year is expensive."

"You're right about that." He put the truck in gear and gripped my thigh as he drove.

I flipped through the radio stations, settled on The Eagles, then rested my head on his shoulder as he took me home.

There's nothing Alabama folk celebrate more fiercely than American independence—aside from *The Birth of Our Lord & Savior,* of course.

Liza picked me up as the sun reached that magical point when the world bathed in twilight, dotted with lightning bugs and the slow appearance of evening stars. I watched the blur of trees through the window as she drove.

"I talked to the manager," she said. "He's desperate for a stocker and said you can start next week."

"But I didn't apply."

"He said he's known you since you were born, that your mama shops all the time, and he knows you won't be any trouble. So... *please?*"

I sighed, bit my thumbnail, then said, "I mean, I could use the money..."

"Yay!" Liza said, bouncing in her seat. "We are going to have *so* much fun!"

"Only if you promise not to leave me for the Piggly! And I'll need a ride sometimes."

"You got it," she said with a squeal as she turned up the radio.

The trees caught my attention again. Whizzing by so fast, I couldn't distinguish one from another, much less spot individual branches or leaves upon them. Suddenly, it felt like time was passing just the same; so fast the days, weeks, months were blurred together, imperceptible for the individual bits of magic they were.

"Do you think it's weird this could be our last Fourth of July in Asher?" I asked.

"What do you mean?"

"We could be anywhere next summer."

"No big plans here," she said.

"College?"

"God, no. I'm trying to talk my parents into a year off, then maybe junior college."

"What would you do for an entire year off?"

"Work, save money, maybe spend time at the beach."

"With me, of course, because that sounds amazing," I said.

"Nah."

"You're gonna ditch me?"

"Catherine, you're the ditcher in this scenario. You're smart and can do anything. You'll be the one leaving *me*. I'll make sure you know where to find me, but if I come up missing, the first place to look will be IGA or Pensacola Beach."

"I'll pass that along to the cops investigating your disappearance."

"Unless I've robbed a bank or something...don't tell them where to find me if that's how it plays out."

"If you rob a bank, I'll be the brains behind the operation. I'll be wherever you are."

"Ha! Isn't that the truth?" Liza laughed, then pinched my cheek. "Like Bonnie and Clyde."

I smiled, then forced a frown. "Wait—which of us is Bonnie and which is Clyde?"

Liza's laugh filled the tiny car as she pulled into a parking spot. "Come on. Hot dogs and hot *guys* await!"

—◦—

Glen never got off work before dark, so he arrived after we did, jeans covered in mortar and a bit smudged across his cheek too. He walked up to me, looking like some grown-ass man, crossing his yard after a hard day's work, eager to join his woman for a cold drink on the front porch.

I smiled at how vividly I could see it, then snapped back to reality when he leaned in to give me a quick *hello* kiss.

"How was work?" I asked.

"Brutal. When does this heat ever end?"

"Not until October. You're stuck with it."

"Lucky me."

Liza appeared with two hot dogs. "Hey, Glen. I didn't know you were here yet. I didn't get you one."

"No problem. But do you think there's anyone around who'd offer a tired teenager a cold beer?"

"Plenty of guys in the parking lot who'll help you out," Liza answered.

"Here's hopin'," he said. "Anything for you two?"

"Mama would kill me," I replied.

"I'm good," Liza said.

I watched him as he went, the way his dirty jeans clung to him in all the right places, not going unnoticed.

"Mm-hmm," Liza mumbled as she took a bite.

"What?"

"Like I said, end of summer."

I threw her a *shut your mouth* sort of face as she giggled and chewed.

"Does it bother you he drinks?" she asked.

"Who doesn't drink, besides us?"

"Good point. Why *don't* we drink?"

"I tried it once—Daddy offered a sip of beer when I was little. Bo and I were playing in the driveway while the grownups sat around being boring."

"And you didn't like it, I imagine. Beer's nasty."

"I spit it into the grass and ran inside for water. They were still laughing when I went back outside."

"Rude," she said. "I had a Boone's Farm at a party."

"What's that?"

"Some sort of sweet strawberry flavored drink—a wine cooler, I think. It was better than beer, I'll say that."

The music started and songs fitting for the holiday, like "America the Beautiful," "Sweet Home Alabama," and "American Girl" had an immediate effect on everyone there. People held their drinks high and danced, anticipating the first whistling *zoom* and ground-shaking *boom* to start the main event.

"He's going to miss the fireworks," I said.

"We've got at least two more songs." Liza devoured the last bite, then dragged her hand across her face to wipe it clean. "You gonna eat that?" She gestured toward my hot dog, and I handed it over.

"I'm gonna find him. Stay here so I don't lose you too."

⚬

It didn't take me long to spot him, but when I did, I stopped in my tracks.

What the hell?

Illuminated by the headlights of a parked car, stood Glen and Susie James.

And before I could stop myself, I thought, *well, at least it isn't Ally Monroe.*

How effortlessly it crossed my mind took me by surprise. Did it mean that I didn't mind if he drank beer with other girls under the stars, so long as it wasn't Ally he did it with?

I ducked behind a car and watched. Snooping wasn't something I enjoyed, but I'd much rather witness whatever this was, than to rely on details relayed through the Telephone Game.

Susie leaned in close to Glen's ear, cupping the back of his neck. He smiled as she pulled back, looking into his eyes.

Then the headlights turned off and everything went black.

Damnit!

Squinting in the dark, I tried to determine if it was two shapes I saw—or if they'd come together as one.

The first *scream, bang* of the fireworks erupted and under their bright white light, I saw Glen walking toward the field, alone. I let him get far enough ahead I wouldn't be noticed, then found my way back too.

"There you are," Liza said. "Told you he'd make it back in time!"

I sat between them. Glen held a beer in one hand and placed the other on the ground behind me to support his weight as he looked up to the sky. The full length of his arm ran along my back, and I wasn't sure if it radiated heat from a day's work in the sun, or if the heat rose from my own skin at his touch.

Was that same arm wrapped around Susie in a secret kiss a moment ago? Around Ally after the basketball game? Who else has he held with those arms while they also held me?

I don't know, and I don't care.

That was the answer, plain and simple. I knew him, and he knew me. I knew he wouldn't touch a cheeseburger with mustard or onions; that he preferred to wake up early, rather than sleep late; that what happened with his dad bothered him more than he let on; that he missed his sister and friends. I knew he wanted more for his life than anyone expected him to achieve.

I knew he loved me.

And I knew then, even if I'd never fully known it before, that I loved him, too.

◆

The next morning, Liza called.

"So, what happened when you went to find Glen?" she asked with her mouth full. She was always chewing on something, it seemed. "You came back looking so pale, you glowed in the dark."

"I couldn't find him, so I came back."

"Hmm," she said.

"What?"

"You're a horrible liar."

"Liza, I don't want to talk about it."

"So, there *is* something to talk about."

"No, there isn't. I have to go."

"*Sure* you do." She sighed in that exaggerated way she always did when she wanted to be sure I caught it—and the meaning behind it. "Do you need a ride to work?"

"No, Mama's off today. See you there." I hung up the phone and headed to my room.

Flipping on the stereo, I grabbed my favorite pink blanket I'd had since birth, and curled up in bed, wondering why I didn't just tell her.

Then it hit me.

I didn't tell her—I wouldn't tell her—because if I did, she'd have questions, and I'd have to admit I did too. And I didn't want to have questions. I didn't want to have to justify or explain anything, not even to myself. I simply wanted to be *Glen's girl*, wrapped tight around him like moss on a tree, growing with him as he grows, living off the same damp air, finding relief in the same cool rain...growing in the same direction, reaching for the sun.

⸺◆⸺

After a slow morning at work, followed by a short lunch break, I endeavored to set up a display of charcoal briquettes in front of the store. The sidewalk steamed, the bags weighed nearly as much as I did, and I sweated like a pig as I pulled one at a time from the pallet and placed them in a pyramid.

It seemed really unfair that Liza stood behind the register, twirling her hair and smacking her bubble gum—bored out of her mind—while I did the hard work alone.

"That's it," I mumbled.

If the boss wouldn't ask her to help, I sure as hell would. I headed for the door, but before I got there, I heard a familiar rumble. Scanning the parking lot for him, I smiled.

Can't even stay away for a whole work shift, huh? Now who's got it bad?

When I spotted him though, he'd pulled into the Piggly across the street. He backed into a parking spot, then hopped out of the truck, high-fiving the guys and nodding to the girls in that irresistible way he always did. Someone handed him something—a drink, probably. He lowered the tailgate and hopped onto it.

My heart sank, and my blood boiled at the same time.

There's nothing wrong with him hanging out with friends. Get a grip.

But then I saw Ally, and any cool left within me evaporated. She jumped onto the tailgate and scooted in next to him.

I lugged another bag onto the pile, blinking back tears I refused to cry. Reaching for another, I tossed it onto the pile too, glad I hadn't made it inside to ask for Liza's help. She didn't know what I'd seen, what thoughts and feelings had popped up inside me. They were mine alone, and I could cast them aside as quickly as they came. Like it never happened.

I continued pulling bag after bag, sucking in a deep breath with each lift and forcing it—and every thought in my head—out with each toss. When finished, the display looked more like a toppling Christmas tree than a pyramid, but I felt strong, like I could do anything.

Was that all there was to it? Could fear, doubt, insecurity—all those things no one ever wants to feel—just be tucked away somewhere in a dark corner of the brain, like replacing a book on a shelf?

Apparently so, because the urge to look back across the street disappeared. When Glen picked me up after work, I slid right into the truck. When he kissed me, I felt nothing but the here and now. No charcoal briquettes, no Piggly parking lot, and no Ally Monroe. Just the two of us snuggled close on a bench seat, driving toward the sunset, longing for more. Always *more*.

⸺ ✦ ⸺

By the end of July, I ran the register, managed lunch breaks, and made the weekly schedule. Liza had grown less chatty at work and sulky when we hung out, and I suspected she was upset I'd been given more responsibilities than she had. Glen continued to impress his uncle and regularly oversaw jobs on his own while he worked elsewhere.

It felt odd that we were doing grown-up jobs and making grown-up money. It made me dread going back to school and being pulled from the real world, back into hallways crowded with people who were only interested in gossip and Saturday night pasture parties.

"I quit," Liza said, as we laid on towels in my back yard, slathered in olive oil, with lemon juice in our hair.

"Quit what?"

"IGA."

I lowered my sunglasses to see her face. "You *quit?*"

"I'm bored of it. And school's about to start, so what's the point?"

"You said you wouldn't leave me!"

"I said I wouldn't leave you for the Piggly. Trust me, I have no intention of working there or any other grocery store anytime soon."

"It's not that bad, Liza. You work the register. It's not like you're stacking charcoal."

"What does that mean?" She sat up and leaned back on her hands, practically begging for a fight.

"It means there are worse jobs."

"Well, I don't want to do that one anymore, so I quit. Walked out last shift."

"You *walked out?*"

"I was just standing there like a statue and got to thinking about every-thing I could be doing, but instead, I was waiting for somebody interesting to walk through the door. No one interesting ever walks through that door, by the way. No one."

"I can't believe you walked out. What are you going to do now?"

"I thought about working at the diner or Nico's, but maybe I'll go to the beach until school starts. Remember my cousin, Valerie? She moved to Pensacola a few months ago and invited me to visit. Seems like a good place to end the summer, don't you think? You should come with me!"

"Liza, I'm not quitting."

"But we'd have so much fun!"

I laid down on my stomach, turning my face from Liza.

"Think about it, at least," she said.

"Have fun in Pensacola."

"Catherine—"

"*What?*"

"You know Glen will be here when you get back. Or if he's not, then at least you'll know—"

"Know what?" I sat up to see her face again.

"I'm just saying, if you have doubts, maybe you'd gain some clarity if you went away. Left him to his own devices to see what he does."

"I don't have doubts, Liza. Not one." I grabbed my towel and left her alone in the yard.

It's what she wanted anyway, to be the only one left lying in the sun.

8

MELTDOWNS & SINATRA

"What will you do without Liza?" Glen asked as he brought sodas and chips from the kitchen.

"I don't know...whatever *will* I do?" I shifted my eyes to his.

"Hmm...maybe Liza should *stay* in Pensacola." He set the snacks on the coffee table and dropped to his knees between my feet.

Keep your feet on the floor, and you'll never do anything you'll regret later.

Mama's advice was becoming increasingly hard to follow. Especially as he placed his hands on either side of my head, buried his fingers in my hair, and stole a kiss.

I wrapped my legs around his waist, pulled him to me, and heard a soft grunt as his kiss deepened. Breaking away, I leaned my head back to breathe. He moved to my jawline, neck, collarbone, and shoulder, then re-traced his steps, ending back at my lips where he started.

I could lose myself in him for hours—I knew, because I had.

But not in my mother's living room.

"Glen—"

He pulled back, placing his hands on the sofa on either side of my hips.

The door opened and Glen jumped onto the sofa, somehow grabbing a soda and popping the top in the process.

"Oh, *come on!*" Bo said, stomping up the stairs.

When his door slammed, I laughed so hard, I cried. "You! How did you do that?"

"What are you talking about, woman?"

"The soda! How—" I couldn't finish the sentence, I really couldn't.

Glen gulped his drink, eyes fixed on the TV. "Worst timing, *ever.*"

The way he sat there, legs spread, and cheeks flushed, I was both dying at the hilarity of it and quite enjoying the obvious power I held over him. I scootched closer.

"What's this?" I pointed to the TV, still giggling.

"Who the hell knows?" he said with a laugh. "Pass the chips."

I tossed the bag onto his lap.

"That reminds me," he said, tearing open the bag. "My uncle still needs help at work. Any reason I shouldn't ask Bo?"

"Nope, but he won't last."

"Not as grown up as you are, huh?"

"Meaning?"

"Nothing bad. Only that you've changed."

"How so?"

"Well, you don't seem to care what your old friends think anymore. You don't seem so sad about your dad. You like your job. And me, I think you like *me.*"

"I definitely like you." I wrapped my arm around his and squeezed tight.

"Well, what if I said...I think I *love* you?"

My brain ceased to function as I stared.

"Cat?"

I moved my palm to his face and leaned in. He kissed my forehead and paused there, placing a hand behind my head.

"Then I'd say, I think I love you too."

⚬

Four days later, we'd just finished dinner and were at the lake, dancing beneath the stars. As he pulled me closer, positioning his lips near my ear,

I could hear every breath he took. I could feel his heartbeat within his chest, pressed against mine. Closing my eyes, I lost myself, not in the song's rhythm, but in the rhythm of *him.*

"Promise we'll always do this," I whispered.

"Dance?"

"Dance *here*, under these stars, next to this old truck."

"I had hoped for an upgrade someday. This old thing can't run forever. Takes a lot of effort on my part."

I looked up and saw his playful grin. "Always this truck. You're not allowed to get rid of it, ever."

"All right, always this truck."

When he led me to lie in the grass, I rested my head in the soft spot between his chest and shoulder. "What happens after high school? I want to be wherever you are, always."

"We have a year still. We'll know the next step when we see it. It will find us, Cat."

"How do you know?"

"Because that's how it works. It's just one opportunity, one decision after another."

"Until someone dies."

He leaned his head up to see my face. "Where'd that come from?"

"Mama didn't make a decision that led to Daddy dying. Some things just happen."

"But none of that can be predicted or prevented. Just...enjoy the moment, Cat. It'll be over before we know it."

I realized then that I hadn't thought about Daddy in a while, not for more than a fleeting moment, anyway. I'd sorta shoved the grieving daughter aside and focused on everything else.

"Hey...where'd you go?" He lifted my chin, finding my eyes in the dark. *I'm here. If I'm lucky, I'll always be here.*

Because my fights with Liza never lasted long, she dropped me off after work the next day. When I got home, Mama was mowing the yard again, while Bo sat on the sofa stuffing his face with Little Debbie.

"Can't you do something useful?" I asked on my way toward the stairs. "It's a thousand degrees outside, but *she's* cutting the grass, and you're watching TV."

"I don't see you cutting any grass," he said. "And Glen's picking me up to meet his uncle."

"About the job?" I faced him with one foot on the bottom step.

"What do you know about it?"

"I know it's hard labor, and I bet you won't last a week."

He stood and crossed the room, stopping just in front of me. "Should we also bet on how long before your panties are around your ankles, or has that ship *finally* sailed?"

A loud *smack* split the air, and Bo grabbed the side of his face. It wasn't until I felt the sting in my hand that I realized it was me who'd done the slapping.

"You *bitch!*" He lunged for me as Mama entered in grass-covered overalls.

"What the hell is going on here?" she yelled.

Bo halted, glaring at me with rage-filled eyes.

"And why are you calling your sister a bitch? I heard that clear out on the porch!"

"She hit me!" he yelled.

"I'm sure you deserved more than she gave. Wanna tell me what you've done, so I can settle the score?"

"What? You're—" He looked at her.

"I'm *what*, child?"

He looked back to me. "God, I can't wait for you to get out of this house!" He bolted for the door, slamming it behind him.

"What was that?" Mama asked with hands on hips.

"I *may* have insinuated he has no work ethic and wouldn't last a week at that job."

"And that insult deserved a slap to go with it?"

"No, but his offer to bet on how long it would take Glen to get my underwear off did."

Mama gasped as her hands fell to her sides. "I'd say it did." She walked to the kitchen, giving me an *attagirl* pat on the back as she went.

When Bo and Glen returned, Bo ran straight to his room.

"Well, he's hired," Glen said, before giving me a peck on the cheek. "Wanna get something to eat?"

"Told Mama I'd eat here. Why don't you stay? She went to town but shouldn't be gone long."

"Yeah, okay."

We moved to the sofa and flipped through the TV channels, choosing some black and white show I'd never seen. I dozed off, then woke when Mama's car door slammed. Five minutes later, she still hadn't come inside.

I looked toward the door. "What's she doing out there?"

"Offering us privacy?"

"Never." I stood and looked out the window. "What the *hell?*"

He joined me, and we stared at Mama in the driveway with her head bent beneath the hood of the car.

"Should I help her?" he asked.

"No, I'll go."

Mama looked up when she heard the door close. "I see Glen's here."

"Yeah. Can he stay for dinner?"

"Fine, but there'll be no dinner if I can't get these damn bolts off."

"What are you doing?"

"The car battery keeps dyin' on me. It's been jumped in town twice now. So, I got a new one."

"Why didn't they just change it there?"

"Because I told them not to! It can't be that hard...I just can't get the bolts off." She leaned into it with her full body weight that time, but it still didn't budge. "They're rusted tight." She tried again.

"Mama, really, can we maybe—"

"Catherine, I—can—*Ow, shit!*"

"Mama!" I rushed toward her.

She lifted her right hand and blood streamed down her wrist. "I'm fine. The wrench slipped, and I scraped it. Bring the first aid kit, will ya?" She wrapped her hand around the wound, then raised her arm over her head.

I ran up the steps and through the door.

"What happened?" Glen asked.

"She's trying to change the car battery and hurt herself. Why won't she let someone help her with—*anything?*" I pulled the first aid kit from under the bathroom sink, then yelled, "Bo!" up the stairs.

He appeared on the landing. "Why are you yelling?"

"Mama's trying to change the car battery and she's hurt herself. You need to help her!"

"I can help her. It's simple, really," Glen said.

"She'll be embarrassed if you do it. It has to be Bo."

"She'll be embarrassed, no matter who it is. Let him do it," Bo replied.

I dropped the kit and took the steps two at a time to reach him. "Bo, I swear to God, if you don't help her, I'll knock you down these stairs."

"Okay! Jesus, what is *wrong* with you? *And* her?" Bo said, gesturing toward the yard. "You've lost your damn minds!" He descended the stairs, then exited into the yard.

"I really could've done it," Glen said, as we watched through the window.

"Whatever she's going through is getting worse. I don't know what to do."

He wrapped an arm around me as we stared.

A moment later, Bo stalked back inside. "I offered. She said no. Leave me alone." He disappeared to his room again.

"For Christ's sake," I said, moving back outside. "Mama, you have to let Bo help you."

"I don't need his help!"

"You're hurt!"

"And where's that first aid kit, huh? Did you bring it, or did you just come out here to remind me of *all the things I cannot do?*"

"Mama, I'm trying to help."

"You're *children*, Catherine! It's not your job to help me! I—am—your—*mother!*"

Her eyes locked on mine, and I couldn't look away. I stood, tethered to the concrete, unsure what to do.

"Damnit! *Damniiiit!*" Mama yelled at the top of her lungs as she fell to her knees and dropped the wrench to the ground.

I noticed a man and woman come to a sudden stop on the sidewalk and stare. I saw the neighbor's curtains pull back a few inches, then close again.

They were all watching.

"Let's go inside." I took a tiny step toward her.

"Don't—*touch me!*" she screamed at the sky with her eyes pinched closed.

Wiping tears away with the back of my hand, I said, "Mama, please—"

She opened her eyes, and they instantly landed on mine. Despite the intensity of her gaze though, she didn't see me at all. She looked *through* me, toward something—or someplace—I couldn't see.

Someone on the sidewalk said, "Laurel?"

I didn't know who it was, and I knew better than to turn to find out.

Mama's eyes shifted to her left, eerily robot-like, at the sound of her name. Then she dropped her head, noticed the blood streaming to her elbow, and stood. "Fine. Let Glen do it. I'll pay him. Don't ask your brother again." She turned and walked to the house.

I followed her through the door.

"You're on your own for dinner," she said, as she went to her room.

"What do I do?" I asked Glen an hour later as he dried his hands on a kitchen towel.

He leaned against the counter, crossing his feet and arms. "I don't know."

A door squeaked upstairs, then Mama appeared with a basket on her hip. She walked toward the laundry room and stopped half-way there with her back to us. "Is it done?"

"Yes, ma'am," Glen replied.

"Thank you. Catherine, there's money in my purse. Pay the boy." She continued to the laundry room and began transferring clothes into the washer. Each step—scooping the detergent, pouring it in, setting the dials—took twice as long as it should have. Then, she appeared to sleepwalk back to her room.

Sitting on the porch, my stomach growled. "Cereal for dinner?"

"Sure," Glen replied.

I went to stand, then sat back down. "Is she having some sort of mental breakdown? I know the nurses she works with. Should I call them?"

"I don't know if—hey, can you call your aunt? Maybe she can help."

"Aunt Kitty!" I sprung to my feet and threw open the door, only to find Mama was already on the phone.

"Yes, Kitty. Okay." She hung up and carried the clean laundry to the sofa, where she folded each piece, still operating in slow motion.

I looked to Glen, shrugged my shoulders, and pulled out every box of cereal we had. "Pick your poison."

We chose, and sat quiet as church mice, eating and watching Mama make glacial movements as she folded.

Just as I scooped the last bite, the door flew open, and Aunt Kitty ran inside. "Laurel! What the hell? I thought you were dying!"

Mama looked up with tears streaming down her face. They were the first tears I'd seen her cry since Lennon died.

"Oh, you *are*. You poor thing. Let's go lie down," Aunt Kitty said, guiding Mama upstairs.

Mama's sobs and wails could be heard so clearly from where we sat, we could have been standing in the same room. Bo came downstairs and rounded the corner, looking at me with the same face he had when he was five and we saw the neighbor's dog hit by a car. He was terrified, worried, sad—and completely freaked out.

"I can't stay here," I said, placing my bowl in the sink.

Glen did the same and followed me toward the door.

I turned to see Bo, looking lost and alone. "You wanna come too, jerk-face?"

He ran out the door and hopped into the truck bed.

Glen took my hand. "Cat, what do you need?"

The answer was simple. "I need you to take me away from here, now and forever. Just take me away."

"I will take you anywhere you want to go." He pulled me in and held me tight, my silent sobs spilling out in sync with Mama's, traveling through the walls.

He kissed my hands clenched together in his, then opened the door to the start of my escape.

———❦———

Climbing Glen's porch steps, I realized I hadn't even met his mom yet. "Are you sure this is okay? How will she feel about you bringing us here because our mama's gone crackers?"

"We don't have to tell her that part if you don't want to. She'll let you stay, no matter what." He led us inside and to the kitchen.

"Glen?" Her shoes clacked on hardwood as she approached. When she appeared, her eyes went to me as she said, "Well, hello!"

"Mom, this is Catherine."

Ms. Lewis stood a few inches shorter than Glen and at least a head taller than me. With her deep blue eyes and sleek, black hair—which reached the mid-back of her glittery navy-blue cocktail dress—she looked like she'd stepped out of a movie screen, right into that kitchen.

"It's so good to meet you!" She wrapped me in a tight hug.

"Thank you, Ms. Lewis," I said with the air she'd yet to squeeze from my lungs.

"Call me Janine." She turned to my brother. "Good to see you, Bo."

He nodded and dug into the bags of food we grabbed on the way there.

"Brought you a bacon burger, Mom." Glen found it and held it out for her to take.

"Thank you, but I have to run." Snagging her handbag from the countertop, she headed for the door. "Two sets tonight, so don't wait up. Make yourselves at home."

I glared at Glen, silently demanding he ask permission for us to stay. He followed her into the living room, and I went with him.

"Is it okay if they stay here tonight? Things are kinda weird at their place right now. I'll sleep in the den with Bo, and Cat can take my room."

"Fine with me. If there's anything I understand, it's *weird*." She kissed Glen on the cheek, said, "Love you," then left.

I peeked through the curtain as she searched her bag for keys. "Is she humming Sinatra?" I whispered.

He laughed and pulled me back toward the kitchen. "Probably."

Turned out, Janine spent her nights crooning the songs of Ella Fitzgerald, Dinah Washington, Peggy Lee, Dean Martin, and the like. She traveled to neighboring counties to perform in bars, clubs, restaurants, and corporate events.

"Why doesn't she perform here?" I snuggled into Glen's side on the sofa.

"Says it's too small of a town. She doesn't like seeing neighbors doing things they'd rather no one know about, then facing their wives in the grocery store afterward."

"How sordid could Asher-folk be?"

"You'd be surprised."

"When does she get home?"

"Usually around 3:00 in the morning."

"And you're just here by yourself?"

"Yup, unless Bo's here." He nodded toward my brother, watching TV in the den. "It's not bad, though. I like being alone."

"I wish I could hear her sing. I bet she's amazing."

He stood and held out his hand. "Come on."

We crossed the kitchen, turned down a hallway, and came to a door, which he opened. He stepped inside, motioning for me to follow.

"Is this her room? Should we be in here?"

"She doesn't mind." He flipped through a crate of records. Pulling one, he placed it onto a record player, turned on the power, and set the needle.

A low, velvety voice crawled out of the player, building volume and depth with each sultry line. I sat in the room's only chair—an oversized, golden-yellow one positioned near the window. Glen sat on the floor, leaning against my legs.

"This is her?"

"Yup. She recorded a few demos years ago, when she still had hopes of making it to New York or Hollywood. Now she listens to them, with a drink or two, when she's had a bad day. Mom's a pretty happy person, so she doesn't pull them out often."

I stroked his hair as we listened. Daddy used to like this music, and it made me wonder which song was his favorite.

I also wondered whether Aunt Kitty had talked any sense into Mama, or if this would be our life going forward; running away, looking for some-where to hide when she descended into madness.

I couldn't do it. I just couldn't.

As if sensing my worries, Glen stood and leaned over me. "Can I kiss you, Cat?"

"Yes, you can kiss me, dumbass. Why do you even ask?"

He grinned. "Well, come on then," he said, pulling me up. "I can't kiss you with my mom in the room. It's just weird."

9

FOOTBALL & BABY BUMPS

That was the first of many nights I spent at Glen's, sleeping in his bed—engulfed in the intoxicating scent of him—while he slept in the den. It was torture sleeping under the same roof and not *feeling* the warmth of him.

Aunt Kitty and Uncle Charlie visited every day after *the incident*, filling in to do all the things Mama no longer could. Some days she hummed, watched the birds, and commented on the weather. Others, she barely spoke. We walked on eggshells—tiptoeing around her—and it was exhausting.

When Liza returned from Pensacola, we sat in her living room watching *Bewitched* as she told me all about her vacation. I knew I should tell her about Mama's breakdown, Bo's jack-assery, and how Daddy's death had cast a shadow none of us could escape; leaving me desperate to get away from that house, which sucked the life out of all of us one tiny drag at a time.

But I couldn't. She'd never understand. So, I turned up the volume when the commercials ended, and Endora popped into the scene. Endora had always been my favorite.

⎯⎯◆⎯⎯

"You did what?" I asked in total disbelief.

"I made the football team," Glen answered casually, taking a sip of the beer Janine kept stocked in the fridge.

"You play *football?*"

"I have since I was ten, and I was driving Bo to camp and tryouts all summer, so I tried out, too. What's the big deal?"

"I'm just surprised, I guess."

"You'll come to the games, right?"

"Of course I will! What position will you play?"

"What do you know about football positions?" He gave a skeptical sideways glance.

"This is Alabama. We *all* know football positions."

He chuckled and said, "Receiver."

"*You're* a receiver?"

"Why are you so surprised?"

"I'm not—I mean, I don't—"

"I'm messin' with ya, Cat. I didn't tell you because football is on a whole different level down here, and I didn't know if I'd make it."

"So...my brother is quarterback and *you're* his receiver?" The scenario was laughable, considering their friendship was more on-again/off-again than any romance at Asher High.

"He's only quarterback because the senior QB didn't make the grades to play. And I am *one* of his receivers."

"Jesus. This may be an exciting year after all."

"Considering trying out for the cheerleading squad?"

"Hell, no. You're out of your mind."

Laughing, he pulled me in for a kiss. "Yeah, didn't think so."

That week, in addition to learning my boyfriend played football, I also discovered I'd been promoted to shift manager at IGA. When I found out, I called Glen from the break room.

"Hello?" he said.

"You're not going to believe this."

"You made the cheer team?"

"Glen!"

He laughed. "Well, what?"

"I've been promoted...and I get a raise!"

"Congratulations! What will you do with all that extra money you'll be rollin' in?"

"I'm going to save it."

"For what?"

"For us."

"For us?"

"For an apartment or something. Some place that's ours." I sucked in a deep breath, realizing we'd never talked about moving in together after graduation. "Wait—is that presumptuous of me?"

"If you're asking if I'm in, the answer is yes. I'm *all in*, Cat."

That conversation prompted a new routine. When things got crazy at home, we shopped for sheets, towels, kitchen utensils, bathroom rugs—anything small enough to be stashed away without drawing attention.

"You really should do this with Liza," Glen said, lifting his cap and scratching his head. "You keep asking about things I know nothing about. What the hell is *chartreuse?*"

I picked up a potholder. "*This* is chartreuse. And I want to shop with *you.*"

Truth was, I couldn't shop with Liza, because Liza couldn't know. She'd think I was crazy, and that wasn't a conversation I wanted to have.

"Or I could wait in the truck..."

"It's not that bad, is it?"

"Well, it's not *great*." He shoved his hands into his pockets.

"Fine. Wait outside. I'm almost done, anyway."

He gave me a peck on the cheek, then headed for the exit. I turned down the next aisle to peruse bathroom accessories.

"Catherine?"

Freezing with my hand outstretched, I turned my head. "Aunt Kitty!" I positioned myself between her and my cart, hoping to block her view of its contents.

"What are you doing here, sweety? Does your mama need something?"

"No. Uh—I mean, yeah—a new soap dispenser for the bathroom." I grabbed the first one I saw and tossed it into the cart.

"She could've asked me for it. I'm sure you have better things to do, right?" She smiled that knowing, Aunt Kitty smile.

"I don't mind. It's kind of fun to look around. I grabbed a couple things for my hope chest, too. You know the one Mama gave me when I was twelve? To save things for when I get my first place?"

Please remember the hope chest.

"I remember. Uncle Charlie made that hope chest, you know."

"Right. Well, I should get going. I'm due at work in an hour, so..."

"Okay, hon." Aunt Kitty started to back her cart out of the aisle, then stopped. "Catherine?"

"Yes?"

"I know things are difficult at home, but your mama misses you. Maybe come around more often?"

My heart sank when I realized what she meant: that I spent my time everywhere but at home, and it hurt Mama's feelings. But two days ago, I heard housewives at IGA discussing how Mama *blew a gasket* at the bank when she couldn't remember the passkey to her account. There's no way in hell I could return home to that again.

I smiled and said, "Yes, ma'am," to appease her.

"Have a good day at work." Aunt Kitty vacated the aisle, leaving me wondering what she'd come down it for.

Placing the soap dispenser back on the shelf, I moved toward the check-out, pretending I didn't notice when Aunt Kitty returned to the aisle we just left.

"She'll tell Mama, I know it."

"So? You don't want her to know?" Glen asked.

"God, no! She'll lecture me in that way she does that makes me feel small and immature; like I'm five. You haven't told *your* mom, have you?"

"Yeah, I have. There's not much I don't tell her, Cat." He turned into the IGA parking lot.

"Park somewhere. I'm not ready to go in yet."

"You're going to be late."

"Just park."

He parked, then turned to look at me. "What's this about?"

I stared at the one dark cloud in the sky, watching it move closer by the second. "I don't know."

"Well, think about it a minute."

I evaluated my current state. *What was I feeling?*

"I think I'm afraid she'll be disappointed in me, and Mama is *scary* when disappointed. She says things that leave you feeling tiny and...angry. But she's always right, even if it takes a while to realize it."

"And?"

"I'm afraid she'll say I'm being stupid, and she'll end up being right."

"Ah, I see."

"What do you see?"

"It's me you're unsure of."

"No, I—"

"Cat, you *would* be stupid if you weren't even a little unsure."

"It's not *you*. It's all of it. Will we make enough to support ourselves? What kind of life will we have? Will I regret not going to college?"

"You can go to college. Not everyone moves into a dorm and takes eighteen hours a semester."

I nodded to show I heard him.

"And as far as money goes, we already make what many adults around here support a whole family off of. We'll be okay."

I nodded again.

"We have a year, Cat. Let's see how it goes."

I placed a hand on his cheek.

He leaned in, touching his forehead against mine. "Now, get your ass inside before you get fired."

The sky illuminated with a bright flash of lightning. Booming thunder split the air, and the heavens opened, dumping rain like someone had upturned a bucket over our heads. He started the truck, drove me to the entrance, then kissed my hand as we said goodbye.

⸻ ◆ ⸻

The first day of school was unremarkable, aside from Susie James showing up with a baby bump, and everyone speculating who the father was.

"Who do you think it could be?" Liza asked at lunch.

"Who *couldn't* it be would be the easier question."

"Do you think she'll ever tell?"

"Do you think she really knows?"

"Catherine!" Liza laughed and popped the top on her soda.

"It's a fair question."

Liza picked up her sandwich. "You don't think it could be—" She jerked her head toward a table of football players—at Glen, in particular.

"Liza! What the hell?" I tossed my sandwich onto the tray, suddenly having lost my appetite.

"If she's showing, she's a few months along, right? It could've happened before you were together."

I did the math in my head, and hated that Liza wasn't wrong.

"Are you going to ask him?" she questioned.

"What am I supposed to ask? *Hey, did you happen to knock up Susie James sometime last spring?*"

"Maybe not like that. Ask if he used a condom or something. A question that could be just you wanting to know what you're getting yourself into."

"Mama has been freaking out about some new disease she read about. She's been nagging me to *use protection*, even though I've told her a thousand times I'm not having sex."

"Use that. Tell him she's lecturing you, and you want to know if he's used protection."

"*Ugh.* I hate this place."

The bell rang, and as everyone moved toward the cafeteria doors, I saw Glen's eyes lock on Susie James and travel straight down to her protruding belly.

Damnit all to hell.

⚬

I didn't work up the nerve to bring it up until Friday night, when we were sitting in his den, playing *Space Invaders*.

"So, this is going to be weird, but I need to ask you something," I said when alien invaders reached the bottom of my screen, and I'd lost my last life.

He took the joystick and started a new game. "Okay."

"Mama read something at work that has her freaked out. She keeps bugging me about...using condoms to prevent infection."

He exploded a row of aliens without a word.

"So, it got me thinking. Have you used condoms when you...well, you know..."

"Huh?" The red UFO flew across the top of the screen, and he jerked the controller, aiming to blow it up for bonus points.

"When you have—or had—sex, did you use a condom?"

He looked at me as his cannon detonated. "Are you asking about Susie?"

"I'm asking if you've used protection."

"No, I think you're asking if I got Susie pregnant." He dropped the joystick in his lap and leaned back on his hands.

"I think we should be open with each other, is all."

And I also thought no one should ever doubt that boy's intelligence again. He didn't miss a damn thing.

He picked up the joystick and began a new game. "Yes, I've used protection. Well, there were a couple times I didn't, but it was before I moved here. I always did with Susie."

"Oh. So, you did sleep with her then."

"Why did you ask that question if you didn't even know?"

"I mean, I figured, but I didn't know *for sure*."

"Do you really want to get into all this, Cat?"

"I don't know. I think so?"

"Well, when you decide for sure, we can talk."

His cannon exploded again. Tossing the joystick to the floor, he disappeared to the kitchen.

⸻ ◆ ⸻

"Bo, tell me you didn't get that girl pregnant." Mama stood in front of the TV, blocking his view.

"It wasn't me," he said, trying to see around her.

She crossed her arms over her chest. "How do you know?"

"Because I wouldn't touch Susie James with a ten-foot pole. Catherine should probably ask her boyfriend, though."

Mama's jaw dropped, seemingly coming unhinged. She marched toward me, and I heaved a huge sigh. Pushing me into a kitchen chair, she took the one across from me.

"What's he talking about?"

"I don't know, Mama. What's he ever talking about?"

"Catherine, did Glen have unprotected sex with Susie James?"

"Jeez, you don't beat around the bush, do ya?"

"Catherine!" Her eyebrows were squished together, her worry lines fully entrenched between them.

"Okay, okay! No, he didn't."

"You asked him?"

"I did."

"Well, that was mature of you. And you believe him?"

"Why does everyone keep insinuating I shouldn't trust my boyfriend?" I stood and headed toward the stairs.

Mama took me by the arm, holding me in place. "Sometimes, child, we become so entranced by everything around us, we can't see what's staring us in the face. That's all."

Oh, the nerve of her, lecturing me on being blind to reality, when she couldn't even see what she'd become.

"I can see just fine, Mama, *trust me.*"

She took a deep breath. "Why did that feel like an insult, directed at me?"

"Because it *was!* For Christ's sake, can't you see how we tiptoe around you, never knowing who you'll be that day? Will you garden and bake cookies? Or lock yourself in your room and sob through the night? Will you laugh at a cheesy line in a TV show? Or scrub floors until your fingers bleed? Will you go to work? Or call in and spend all day in bed? It's too much, Mama!"

"I'm sorry if how I'm handling the loss of my husband is too much for you, Catherine."

"Is that what this is? I don't even know anymore!"

"Because you're never here!" she yelled as she stood.

"Why do you think that is? Between you and *him*—" I threw my hand toward Bo, who stood from the sofa and left the house with a slamming door. "Who would want to be here, huh?"

Mama sat back down in her seat. "Then leave, Catherine."

"What?"

"Leave."

"And go where?"

"To Glen, I suppose. We both know it's what you want; why you're counting down the days till graduation and shopping for home goods."

"Aunt Kitty told you—"

"Of course she told me."

I sat at the table and dropped my head into my hands. "Mama, I just can't do this anymore."

The door opened and Aunt Kitty entered with a casserole dish. "Dinner's here!" Closing the door with her foot, she pulled her sunglasses to the top of her head.

"I'm not hungry," Mama and I voiced in unison, as Mama went upstairs, and I walked out the door Aunt Kitty just came through.

⁂

The setting sun created golden ripples on the lake as they approached the shore, then pulled away again in a hypnotic rhythm.

Glen leaned back on his hands and crossed his legs at the ankles. "I'm sorry, Cat."

"For what?" I picked a blade of grass and wrapped it around my finger.

"*Space Invaders.*"

"Oh."

"I handled that all wrong, and I'm sorry. I'll tell you anything you want to know."

I looked out over the water, determining if there was anything I *really* wanted to know. "Do you love me, Glen?"

"You know I do." He put an arm around me and pulled me closer.

"Then I don't need to know anything else."

He tilted my face up to his. "I mean it, though. I'll never treat you that way again. If you have questions, I'll answer."

"Okay." I maneuvered so my legs were draped sideways over his, and he cradled me to his chest. He rocked back and forth and all the questions I had, but would never ask, cycled through my brain in an endless loop.

But none of it mattered. All that mattered was we were crazy about each other. Never in my life had I experienced a physical *ache* when separated from anyone else—aside from losing Daddy. Only Glen. And never had I wished I could hit some cosmic pause button and stay exactly where we were—together, always.

I'd lost my dad, the mom and brother I knew and loved, all my friends...and even though Liza came back around, things weren't the same. *What else was left that really mattered?*

There was only him.

———— ❦ ————

The next week, the school buzzed with chatter. Apparently, Susie James tossed a cup of something into Matt Gardener's face at a party over the weekend, and the world discovered who the father of her baby was. Susie wasn't in school on Monday, and rumor had it she wouldn't be back.

"She's transferring to some school even further in the boondocks than this one." Liza ran her fingers along the spines of a row of books in the library. "Can you believe it?"

"It's always the girl who gets sent away. The boys stay and pretend like nothing happened." That was an understatement. Some wore it like a badge of honor, proving they were *a man now.*

"Horse shit is what it is." Liza plucked a book from a shelf.

"Agreed."

"I'm going on the pill," she said, glancing at the cover of the book, then placing it back on the shelf.

"Are you with someone?"

"No, but I'm damn sure not ending up like Susie when I am. No babies for me." She picked another book. "Are you and Glen…"

"No."

"Huh—I never thought he'd last this long. He probably makes you feel awful about it, too. Are you sure he's not gettin' it somewhere else?" She flipped to the first page of the book.

"Liza!"

"What? Don't tell me you haven't wondered the same thing!"

.Of course I had, but I'd made my decision: I didn't care. We loved each other, and he was *my way out.* And he'd never once pressured me to have sex. I'd never felt unsafe, uncomfortable, or unloved. Maybe he wasn't someone people pictured as the waiting type, but that didn't change how I'd experienced our relationship—whether Liza believed it or not.

"You're out of line," I said to her.

"We're best friends. I'm never out of line."

"You sure about that?"

Shock blanketed her face. "Which part?"

I hadn't meant for it to be a statement with a double meaning, but since she pointed it out…"Both," I said.

She stared, mouth gaping wide. "Well, then." Placing the book back on the shelf, she headed for the end of the aisle.

"Liza," I called after her.

She paused, then turned to face me.

"Truth is, I don't care. I love him. If he's—" I flipped my hand into the air, indicating something I hoped wasn't there. "—with someone else, I don't want to know. Ever. Promise me you'll never tell me."

"What the hell is wrong with you?" She took a step toward me, and I backed up to maintain the distance.

What was wrong with me?

I was a girl who'd lost her daddy; tossed into a sea of sadness without knowing how to swim, while her own mother drowned right beside her. A girl whose world imploded, and who instantly became acutely aware of every whisper and stare. Whose best friend and brother abandoned her in her darkest hour. And who somehow met a boy who, inch-by-inch, brought her back toward the light.

Couldn't she see?

I knew she couldn't, so I simply said, "Promise me, Liza."

She stared, trying to make sense of something she couldn't possibly understand. "I'll never promise you that. Never."

10

VICTORY & WANT

That day in the library seemed to have been the end of my friendship with Liza. However, with football in full swing, her absence went largely unnoticed. I spent my days working or watching the guys practice, and Friday nights yelling from the stands. By joining the team, Glen had found his place in the Asher High social hierarchy and brought me along with him. I wouldn't say I'd made new *friends*, but I'd determined which football girlfriends were safe to sit with at lunch and during games.

"You sure look good out there," I said to Glen as he exited the locker room after practice and led me to his truck.

"Do I?" He pulled me close and squeezed my ass.

"As a *player*, dumbass."

"I prefer my interpretation."

"Well, maybe you're not wrong there either," I said, running my fingers through his hair, still wet from the shower.

I saw the crooked grin, heard that low growl I'd come to love, and *man*, was it getting harder to pull myself away from him. I didn't even know why I did anymore. At first, I didn't know him well enough to give him that part of me. Then, I wanted to be sure I loved him. It was also pure defiance for Mama putting me on the pill, embarrassment from Ally telling the entire school about it, and fear that Glen would think sex was inevitable because of it. Now—I honestly didn't know.

"Let's get out of here," he said, opening the truck door.

I climbed in and scooted over.

"Where do you want to go?" he asked.

"Paris. New York. London."

"I don't think I've got enough gas in the tank for that, Cat. Maybe next week." He gave me a wink.

"The lake then. That's always my second choice."

He started the truck and pointed us toward the outskirts of town. When we arrived, he cut the engine and sat quiet and still.

"What is it?" I asked.

"What happened with Liza?"

I sighed and crossed my arms. "How do you know about that?"

"I'm dumb, Cat, not blind."

"Please. You only play dumb when it suits you."

"So?"

"I don't know. Things are just—different." I focused on my hands, pushing back the cuticle on my thumb. "She's so self-absorbed. She says whatever she wants and doesn't give a damn how it makes people feel. And she doesn't work for anything! Her parents give her everything, so why worry about keeping a job? Her one goal after graduation is to become a beach bum in Pensacola!" I sighed, grateful to unload those very real feelings, but also knowing there was so much more I couldn't say.

"She's seventeen."

"So are we!"

"She hasn't experienced anything like what we've been through. She hasn't lost a parent or watched her mom struggle. She's a true seventeen-year-old, not one who's seventeen-going-on-thirty."

I wouldn't admit he was right, but I didn't have to think very hard to know he was. "Sometimes I wish you really were just dumb."

He laughed, then opened his door and pulled me out, digging his hand into my back pocket as we walked toward the water.

"I think you came along at just the right time," I said as we sat in the grass. "How'd you do that?"

"Fate? God? Serendipity? Karma?"

"Eww—to all that."

"Eww *to God?* Watch it, or the sky will open and rain fire upon us both."

"Meh, God and I have a complicated relationship."

"I may not understand girl friendships, but that, I get."

"How *do* you think it happened? You showing up just in time, saving me from my downward spiral of loneliness and self-pity?"

He shook his head. "You froze me out at first, remember? But then, you chose to let me in, and here we are. If you didn't want to be saved, you wouldn't have been. You saved yourself, Cat."

"I saved myself?"

"You did."

"Huh."

He pulled my legs over his lap, twisting my torso toward him. Then, he took my face in his hands, and the world disappeared in a kiss.

⊷

When he walked me to my door, he pulled a leaf from my hair with a cocky smile.

"Shit! Are there more? Mama will kill me if I look like I've been rollin' in the hay all night."

"Hay?"

"It's an expression. Check me over." I spun in a circle.

"All clear," he said with a smile.

Grabbing his shirt with two tight fists, I pulled him in for one more kiss. *God, I never wanted to let him go.*

He came up for air, tucking my head into his chest. "You keep kissin' me like that, Cat, and we're gonna have a problem."

"What kind of problem?"

He leaned in close and whispered, "The winding up naked in the bed of my truck kind."

My whole body went weak and hot. A hunger I'd never known grew inside my chest. Tilting my head towards his, I went in for a second kiss, which sent explosive, crackling fireworks down my spine—and judging by how he gripped my hips, his too.

"Jesus—go inside, troublemaker." He released his hold.

Once inside, I watched through the window as he drove away. He yanked the wheel back and forth, making the truck dance; a boy on top of the world.

A laugh escaped my lips, and I brought my fingers to them, remembering what it felt like having his on mine.

"I hope he doesn't drive like that when you're with him."

I jumped what felt like three feet into the air and spun to face her. "Mama! Have you been there the whole time?"

She was sitting at the table with a mug of coffee in one hand and a novel in the other. Placing the book face-down, she said, "Yup."

Was she watching through the window?

"Well, I'll lock myself away and die of embarrassment now, thanks." As I walked toward the stairs, she cleared her throat and pulled out a chair.

I sat, as she silently commanded, and waited.

She took a sip before beginning. "I want to know your plan."

"What plan?"

"I know you have a plan to—get away from this house, from your brother, from *me*. I deserve to know what it is."

"There's no plan, Mama. Not a fully formed one, anyway."

"Then tell me what *is* formed."

I vacillated between wanting to come clean and feeling like she'd baited me into a conversation we weren't ready for. It felt like a trap, but I had to say something. "I know now."

"Know what?"

"When you told me to take it one day at a time, to see if there are more good days than bad, to learn if I love him—well, I know now."

"I see. And what does that mean?"

"After graduation, we're going to get our own place. I make good money at the store, he does well working for his uncle, and we'll be happy. Mama, I just want to be happy."

"Then what?"

"Hmm?"

"What happens when the debt piles up? When you get sick, and the doctor bills come? When you get pregnant?"

"Mama!"

"Well? What then, Catherine?"

"Then we'll pay the bills. We'll nurse each other back to health. We'll raise our child!"

"You think he'll stick around through all that?"

"What does that mean?"

"Catherine, people in this town talk—a lot."

"And?"

"There's a very good chance that boy will break your heart."

The growl that erupted as I leaped from my seat took even me by surprise. Mama startled visibly, then composed herself with another drink of coffee.

"What happened to trusting him until I have reason not to?"

"That was before I knew your plan." She answered calmly, like her calmness would somehow bring me back down to earth.

"So, you'd rather I stayed here? I can't live like this, Mama! You've changed, Bo's changed, there's nothing left here for me anymore! Every bit of joy, laughter, everything good in this house died the day Daddy did. *You* died the day he did."

Mama's eyes went wide, then returned to normal with a long, slow breath in and out. "I don't want you to stay here. I want you to go to college."

"With what money?"

"You'll get a scholarship. You're smart enough."

"I won't."

"Of course you will."

"This semester hasn't started off great, and I don't see it getting better. There will be no scholarships."

"What do you mean?"

"I *mean*, I'm failing! I can't focus. All I think about is Daddy dying, you struggling just to live, Bo not speaking to me anymore, fights with Liza, work stuff—old friends who won't even look me in the face! So, yeah, I'm failing—at all of it!"

"Catherine—"

"Don't. Unless you have a way to bring him back and make this all okay, just *don't*."

"I told you it would get worse before it gets better. This is the *worse*." She walked toward me and gripped me by the shoulders. "It will get better."

"When?"

Her expression offered no answer.

"It will only get better when I save myself. And I want more than—*this*, Mama." I shook free from her grip and headed for the stairs.

—◦—

Friday night, it was a full house as Asher played Rock Springs, the primary rival in our football division. Homecoming mums were everywhere, girls of the court awaited their moment to shine, and red and black balloons and streamers were tied to every surface.

After the national anthem, the announcer said, "Let's welcome the Rock Springs Hornets to Tipper Field, ladies and gentlemen!" Unenthusiastic applause sounded as the opposing team entered through the tunnel. Then, he said, "Asher High! Arrrre yooooou *readyyyy?*"

A chorus of cheers, stomping feet, and air horns erupted. The bleachers trembled and rocked. When I didn't think it could possibly get louder, cheerleaders unrolled the "Panther Pride" banner, bobbing helmets of pumped-up football players became visible over its top, and every person in the crowd *lost* their mind.

"Scooch over, Catherine! Here come's my boy!" Janine, decked out in school colors and with broad stripes of black grease under both eyes, booty-bumped me down the bench and pulled an air horn from her purse.

Ozzy Osbourne screamed, "All aboard!" through the loudspeakers, and the team burst through the banner with the first riff of the electric guitar in "Crazy Train."

"There he is!" Janine yelled and pointed.

My eyes followed her finger, and I spotted Bo, front and center, with Glen just to his right. The players raised their arms to pump the sky, begging the crowd to give more.

And the crowd did not disappoint. I knew Alabama football was special, and I'd been to games before, but none had compared to this. Whatever *this* was had to be seen to be believed.

After the coin toss, an anticipatory, "Goooo, Panthers!" came from the crowd, synchronized with our kicker's run-in and point of impact with the ball. Rock Springs called a fair catch.

"How can you do this?" I asked Janine.

"Do what?"

"I've seen him play before, but this—this is nerve-racking!" An indescribable sense of dread—or alarm—settled within me. Given that my boyfriend paced the sideline, eager to face-off with ego-fueled football players twice his size, I had a pretty good idea why.

"Ah, that's just homecoming jitters. But it's like any other game, sweetheart. Those boys know what they're doing."

I made it through both teams' first possessions, then excused myself to the restroom as the scoreboard changed, showing us up, 7-3. Locking myself into a stall, I sat on the toilet still clothed, and prayed that Glen wouldn't be good enough to play college ball.

I wouldn't survive it.

A communal "Ohhhh!" sounded from the crowd, and I listened for any hint of what it was about. Hearing the name Trevor Knightly, I sighed in relief. I liked Trevor, but I was sure glad it wasn't Glen's name I heard.

The bathroom door opened, and a group of girls entered. One took a stall, and I assumed the others were primping at the mirror.

"Are you going to the party?" one girl asked another.

"Nah, I'm still grounded. They only let me come because it's homecoming."

"That sucks. Maybe I can ride with Ally."

"She's not going. Says she has *big plans* for Glen Lewis afterward."

I sucked in a breath, as my heart seemed to stop mid-beat.

"Those two again?"

"Apparently."

A toilet flushed, and that girl rejoined the others. They discussed who would be at the party, whose parents were providing beer, how long it would take for cops to show up—then, they left. I washed my hands at the sink.

Ally Monroe.

Big plans.

Why couldn't it be anyone but her?

And how could he be with her when he was always at work, at football, or with me?

It didn't make sense.

The announcer rambled numbers with increasing excitement, then the crowd erupted as he said, "Touchdown, Panthers!" and "Crazy Train" played again.

⸎

"You missed it!" Janine yelled when I returned. "Didn't I tell ya you have to hold it till the end? Bladders of steel, my girl!"

"What happened?"

"Bo and Glen are an amazing team! It was a perfect pass and a clean catch, right in the end zone." She gave me a high-five.

By half-time, we were up, 21-3. Homecoming festivities began, then ended with a newly crowned king and queen. Two lightning-fast early third quarter plays put us within 20-yards. The excitement and tension in the crowd was palpable.

Bo took the snap, felt a bit of pressure, and launched the ball toward the end zone. Glen leaped simultaneously sideways and vertical, twisted his entire upper body, and elongated from head to toe. Nabbing the football with his fingertips, he made what should have been an impossible catch as a gargantuan Hornet tackled him with a helmet to the rib cage, arms wrapped around his knees.

The crowd gasped when Glen landed with a sickening *crack*.

I jumped to my feet, but people were gathering around him as he lay motionless. I couldn't see a thing.

"That's pads, not bones. We couldn't hear bones from here. Sit down." Janine pulled me back to the bench.

"Is he okay?" I looked at her face, seeing a mixture of both calm and crazy. It was that look all moms got when they were worried but trying to stay strong.

"Thirty seconds or less, son." She started counting under her breath.

"Why are you counting?"

"Twenty-two, twenty-three, twenty-four…"

I stood again, trying to get a better view, and she pulled me back down.

"Twenty-seven, twenty-eight…"

On twenty-nine, Glen came to his feet and rejoined his team, to the relief and cheers of the crowd—even the Rock Springs side of the stadium.

Janine's shoulders relaxed, and she gave a smile.

"What was that? The counting?"

"He knows he has thirty seconds to get up. Anything over that and I'm stormin' the field. Football players don't like it when their mothers take to the field—it's *embarrassing*. If he takes a hard hit, he uses the time to find his breath, but he's always up before Mom counts to thirty."

"Okay, but how hard did that guy hit to leave *Glen Lewis* on his back like that? It makes my skin crawl just thinking about it!"

"That's why we don't think about it, Catherine."

After a 28-10 victory for Asher, the crowd dispersed, and our boys jogged to the locker room.

I waited, tucked under a tree, sitting on the grass. I knew it wouldn't be the first place he looked for me, but *technically*, I wasn't snooping. Sure enough, the moment he appeared, Ally pounced.

She wore a burgundy floral dress with an open sweater, tights, and cowboy boots. Her hair, curled and flipped to perfection, bounced as she walked—and worked for his attention.

I watched his face as she approached. His eyes were everywhere but on her—searching for me—and it drove Ally crazy. When he couldn't find me, he turned to her, and I held my breath.

This was it. It would all go very, very right…or very, very wrong. And I suddenly realized why I'd felt such an overwhelming sense of dread before Glen even took to the field.

Ally went to place her arms around Glen's neck, but he caught her wrists in his hands and shook his head. Turning her loose, he walked away. She followed, taking his hand from behind. He flicked his wrist free and waved her off without looking back.

I waited until she huffed and puffed and stalked away, then I jogged to catch up. He looked side to side, still searching for me.

"Hey, there, dumbass."

He turned and ran to me, lifting me from the ground, and I felt weightless.

Absolutely weightless.

⸻◦⸻

"Are you hurt?" I asked, as we lay on a stadium blanket at the lake.

"Nah, I'm fine."

"I can't imagine being hit like that. I've never even been slapped."

He laughed. "That's not surprising."

I gave him a light punch in the arm, then rested my head on his shoulder. "You sure you didn't want to hang out with everyone else?" I certainly didn't want to, and I knew Ally would be waiting for Glen at whichever after-party he showed up at, but that didn't mean I wanted to keep him from celebrating victory with his team.

"There's nowhere else I want to be, Cat." He brushed my hair away from my face.

The long, humid days of summer had gone, and the first signs of autumn had arrived: The breeze felt cooler; the sky seemed clearer; the cicadas had quieted; and only crisp, calm peace remained.

"It's so quiet," I said.

"Want me to turn on the radio?"

"No, I like it this way."

He squeezed me with the arm wrapped over my side. Snuggling into the warmth of his neck, I moved my hand to his hair.

This time when he squeezed, it seemed like he clung for dear life. He moved his hand from my rib cage to my waist and held tighter still. Something in his grip seemed different this time. Contentment? Love? *Need?*

Whatever it was, I felt it too.

"Glen?"

"Hmm?"

I struggled to find the words. Then, I realized, there were no words to say what I felt. Sitting up on my elbow, I leaned in close with my lips hovering over his, and we laid tangled in a web of pure, unbridled *want.*

"Cat—"

I brought my lips to his, and he weaved his fingers in my hair, pulling me in so tight we couldn't even move our mouths. We were pressed together motionless, but with every nerve ending in our bodies aching for someone to be the first to move.

He was asking me a question—and giving me the moment I needed to discover the answer.

The realization *zapped* me at my core like a bolt of electricity. My whole body shuddered, and every hair stood on end. He had wanted me before, even if he'd never pressured me to do anything I didn't want to do, but this time was different. Because this time, I wanted him too.

Whether it was the excitement of the big win, seeing him so clearly rebuff Ally afterward, the chilled stillness of the autumn air and the gentle waves lapping at the shore, or knowing he had grown to be as much a part of me as the books I read, the solace I found in quiet corners of the library, Asher bonfires, or Aunt Kitty's chocolate cake...I knew I wanted him. All of him.

I threw my leg over him, and his face followed mine as I moved, our lips locked tight, and eyes still closed. When I seated myself atop his waist, he set me free and exhaled a slow, controlled breath. His eyes flashed open and stared deep into mine, still asking that same question.

I leaned forward, pressing myself into him, laying my head on his shoulder.

"Cat—" he said, with a shaky breath and a heavy hand on my head.

I lifted my face, positioning my lips at his ear. "I'm ready now."

He grabbed me by the shoulders and pulled me back up to sit. His eyes searched mine, and I nodded my head, then leaned in for a kiss.

He found the hem of my shirt and tugged tentatively, still asking permission. I raised my arms and let him take it.

Then, we were free—as we lost ourselves in the *more* we'd been waiting for.

11

CANDY NECKLACES & RUIN

"What is *this?*" I asked, standing in Glen's garage and staring at the ugliest piece of furniture I'd ever seen.

"It's a couch, or at least, I thought it was when I rescued it off the curb. It's not a couch?" He gave a teasing smile. "We'll have to clean it, of course."

"We'll have to fumigate it!"

He sat on the sofa and pulled me onto his lap. "Fine. I'll clean *and* fumigate it."

Hugging his neck, I said, "This is the sweetest thing you've ever done."

"Snagging a free curb-couch that reeks of cigarette smoke and may or may not have had mouse droppings under the cushions is the sweetest thing I've done?"

I sprung from his lap, landing against a stack of boxes. "It did not! Tell me it did not!"

Smiling, he stood and took my hands. "Someday, you can pick whatever couch you want, Cat, but it's a start." He gave me a peck on the lips.

"What does your mom think about all this?"

"She's excited for us. She did ask if you were on birth control, though."

"God! Why is that always the first place their minds go?"

He laughed again and said, "Lessons learned, I guess?"

"What did you say?"

"That you had it covered."

"Glen!"

"Have you forgotten most of the town knows you're on birth control?"

"I'd like to."

"You worry too much about what other people think. None of it matters, Cat. None of it."

※

Janine worked on Halloween, so we decided to dress as farmers and hand out the mountain of candy she bought at the Piggly.

Most of my clothes were at Glen's now. I'd snuck them over, one bag at a time, since Mama pretty much ordered me to *leave already.* I went home once or twice a week, to avoid the official moving out discussion, but she knew. Mama always knew.

I'd taken over Glen's bedroom, as his things shifted to the den. Even though Janine approved of our post-graduation plan, neither of us dreamed of attempting to share a room in her house. It was an unspoken boundary we'd never cross.

However, Janine worked more nights than not, and it brought a surreal feeling we were on our own already...complete with takeout dinners, cozy movies, walks around the neighborhood, and plenty of time to enjoy all the hot and steamy activities I'd only dreamed of just weeks before. It was so perfect, it didn't even seem *real.*

When Janine was there, we cooked, tended to the porch plants, and folded laundry together. We played cards and listened to records. She told stories about Glen and Chicago, and I kept her in the loop about how things were going with Mama. She even helped me get caught up with schoolwork, and for the first time that semester, I wasn't so worried about my grades.

She had become a sort of second mother to me, which made me feel both grateful and sad. Growing close to Janine made me miss Mama.

When I dared to go home though, I was reminded how much Mama was no longer Mama, and Bo was no longer Bo. Each time, I returned to Glen's relieved and grateful to have found a safe place in my crazy world.

While searching for my cowboy boots for my costume, I heard a tap on the door. Glen entered the room barefoot, in tattered jeans cut jagged at the calf, a half-tucked patchwork shirt, straw hat, and a red scarf tied around his neck.

"Oh, wow," I said, doing my best to keep a straight face. "Can I come with you?"

"What? Where?"

"I—uh—I just want to ask the wizard if he'll give me a brain too."

"Oh, I see. Haha, very funny."

"I mean, it still works—a farmer and a scarecrow."

"I *am* a farmer. What are you talking about?"

"Is that what farmers in Chicago look like?"

He came at me low, tackling me onto the bed. Then he flipped me onto my back, straddled my hips, and dug into my ribs with his fingertips.

"Not fair!" I yelled, struggling to catch my breath.

The doorbell rang.

"Ooh, they're here!" I shoved him off me, lunged for the closet, and searched frantically for the still missing boots.

It rang again.

"They're going to leave," he said. "I'll get the door."

"I don't want to miss the cute costumes—it's my favorite part!"

"If we don't answer, they'll tell their buddies we're not home, and there'll be no more trick-or-treaters."

I saw a pointy, embroidered piece of leather poking up through the pile. "Aha! Found one!"

He shook his head and walked to the living room. When he opened the door, *trick-or-treats* and one tiny *smell-my-feet* filled the air.

Oh, how I love Halloween.

By 10:00, we'd flicked the porch light off, and all the tiny goblins and Indiana Joneses went home to sleep off the sugar high.

"That was fun." I flopped onto the sofa, lifting the candy necklace I wore around my neck for a bite. "These things are genius. It's just there for you whenever the craving strikes."

"Unless you're a germophobe," Glen answered.

"What?"

"Think about all the bacteria on your skin; all the crap floating through the air. What if someone sneezes in your direction?"

"Eww, gross!"

"I prefer a good smoke," he said, placing a candy cigarette between his lips.

A bank vault safeguarding treasured memories opened as he placed his fingers around it, pulled it away from his mouth, and blew invisible smoke.

"Oh, wow."

"Don't tell me you don't like candy cigarettes. Every kid likes candy cigarettes." He took another pretend toke.

"No, it's just—Daddy used to buy them for us." I picked up the package and flipped it over in my hands. "My favorites were the bubble gum ones."

Glen squeezed my hand. "Does it make you feel better to talk about him? Talking about mine just makes me feel worse."

"I haven't tried much, I guess."

"You can if you want."

I pulled my knees up to my chin, wrapped my arms around them, and leaned my head onto his shoulder. "He would pick us up early from school sometimes, for no reason. He'd have a day off and take us to a movie, or a park, or for ice cream.

"One time, Mama was pissed. It was state testing week, and we missed a half-day of tests. I don't think that's what made her angry, though. It was that when the school called, she didn't know what to say. Mama doesn't like to be made a fool of, in case you haven't noticed."

"Nobody enjoys feeling like a fool."

I opened a box of Bottle Caps and popped an orange one into my mouth, savoring the tart fizziness of it. "I miss him so much. But it's just as hard to *not* talk about him as to talk about him, I think."

Glen put an arm around my shoulders. "What else?"

"Do you want the big things like Easter and Christmas? Or the tiny things I find odd to even remember?"

"Whatever you feel like talking about. We've got all night."

⁓⊙⁓

November flew by in a whirlwind of school, work, and *Glen*. Before we knew it, Mama had prepared a Thanksgiving feast fit to feed all of Asher, while Janine offered a non-traditional meal of chili and cornbread with a side of college football on the TV.

"We'll do my house first, then skip out before dessert. Then we'll come here for the 2:30 game and be ready for round two by the time it ends. Just don't stuff yourself on Mama's sweet potato casserole. That's always everybody's number one mistake."

"Noted." He slammed the hood of his truck and leaned against it with crossed arms. "I want to talk to you about something."

"Uh-oh."

"Not *uh-oh*." He pulled me in to lean against him. "It's about this truck."

"You're not getting rid of the truck."

"As you've so clearly stated. But if I'm going to keep her—"

"It's a her?"

"Of course it is. And there are things I need to take care of before graduation."

"Like what?"

"She needs new tires, and routine things like an oil change, spark plugs, and an air filter. You'll be driving her too, and I don't want you stranded on the side of the road."

"Aww, aren't you considerate?"

"Well, you might not like this next part."

I turned to face him and cocked an eyebrow.

He shoved his hands in my back pockets, and said, "I'd like to get her painted, and if I can afford it, maybe new bumpers and wheels."

"So? New paint wards off corrosion and an early death in a scrap yard, right?"

"I like the way you think, but also, money put into the truck is money not saved for our place and everything that goes in it."

"I see. Then start with the necessary things, and after we're settled, use what's left for a makeover. What color will she be?"

"Flat black and chrome—*so much chrome*." His eyes danced at the thought of it.

"Sexy. I like it."

He pulled me in tight with a squeeze of my ass cheeks. "Watch it. Or we won't make it to dinner."

Purely to be ornery, I leaned in and nipped at his ear. "Hope you're hungry," I whispered as I turned and walked away.

We made it to Mama's after a stop at the lake and a quick check for leaves in my hair. The air inside was thick with the heavenly scents of brown sugar, cinnamon, and melted butter.

Mama yanked and pulled at the giant turkey, attempting to pry it loose from the too-small oven's grip.

"Can I do that for you?" Glen asked her.

"I suppose. Need to give 'er a good basting." Mama offered him the oven mitts.

Aunt Kitty washed vegetables at the sink as Bo and Uncle Charlie watched TV. Freeing the turkey from the oven, Glen's biceps strained against his tee shirt in a way that made my stomach flip.

"What can I help with, Mama?" I asked, attempting to halt the indecent thoughts racing through my brain.

"We've got it covered. Go sit. Maybe open a bottle of wine for when the Masons get here."

"*Liza's* coming?" Panic swelled within my chest and suddenly I felt a massive headache coming on. Liza and I hadn't spoken in three months—how could Mama not know?

She didn't take her eyes off the turkey. "Is that a problem?"

"No, I just—didn't know."

"I thought she'd tell you, seeing as I never know where you are these days, and couldn't possibly tell you myself." She went in again with the baster, which made an unappetizing *slurp* sound as it sucked broth from the bottom of the pan.

Right. Mama didn't know about Liza because I never told her. The one time I might appreciate Bo running his mouth, and he didn't. *Go figure.*

"Red or white wine?" I asked her.

"White, of course," she replied.

Walking through the wide arch leading into the formal dining room, I saw Mama's holiday china, Thanksgiving centerpiece, and fancy candlesticks beautifully displayed across the table. It looked exactly as it had every other year of my life.

Only, this year, Daddy won't sit at the head of the table and raise a glass to all he is thankful for.

Tears sprung to my eyes, and I dashed for the bathroom. Inside, I leaned against the door and took deep breaths, hoping to will the tears away. The tightness in my chest intensified until the pressure became too much and I thought I might explode. Grabbing the hand towel, I buried my face in its softness, and sat on the edge of the tub. Then I let the feelings come in a torrent of muffled sobs.

Tapping on the door, Glen said, "Cat, are you in there?"

"Give me a minute." I moved to the mirror and wiped the mascara tracks from my cheeks.

When I opened the door, he pushed me back into the bathroom, shutting it behind us.

"We can't be in here together," I said.

"Are you okay?" He took my hand.

"I'm fine."

"Do you want to talk?"

"No."

"Cat—"

"If I do, I'll cry again, and I can't cry anymore today. Not here."

"Okay." He held my face in his hands and kissed my forehead. Then he opened the door, gesturing for me to exit first.

When I did, Aunt Kitty appeared. Her mouth fell open in a capital O, then she took our hands, leading us into the dining room.

"Catherine, you know I love you, but your mama is hanging on by a thread in there. So respectfully, I ask, what the hell are you doing?"

"We were talking, Aunt Kitty. I needed a minute to—"

"Actually, I don't want to know. Can you *please* just help me get her through this day? Thanksgiving was your daddy's favorite...It'll be a miracle if we can get her to dessert!"

"Okay," I said.

"Thank you, sweetheart." She turned to leave, then called over her shoulder, "Don't forget the wine!"

I turned to Glen and whispered, "Didn't I lose someone too?"

He pulled two bottles from the wine cabinet. "I've got these. You get some air."

I couldn't risk going through the front door, and the only other way out was through the kitchen, so I tiptoed upstairs to my room and closed the door behind me.

All my favorite things glowed in the soft, mid-morning light: The wall of framed posters Daddy helped me hang, the net of stuffed animals I'd collected since I was born, the corkboard with ticket stubs from movies and concerts with Liza, the books I'd curated my whole life.

It was my room, still as it was when I last left it, but it was also different. It felt like the air had gone stale, or I'd walked into an abandoned house that no longer belonged to me at all.

All at once, I heard a crash in the kitchen, a shriek from Aunt Kitty, and a *what the hell* from Bo. Throwing the door open, I dashed downstairs and saw Mama standing with oven mitts on her hands and the roasting pan turned upside down between her feet.

"I burned my arm and just—" Mama's lip quivered as she stared at the ruined Thanksgiving turkey on the floor. The broth from the bottom of the pan had splattered across the kitchen, painting cabinet doors, the refrigerator, and Mama's shoes and pants.

"Mama, your legs and feet. Are they burned?" I asked, moving closer.

"I, uh—I don't think so." She tilted her head down to get a look but stood firmly in place.

"I'll clean it up, Mrs. Fraser. Maybe you should put something on your arm," Glen said.

She handed him the oven mitts. He put them on, then picked the roasting pan up off the floor. When he did, a wide strip of melted linoleum came up with it, just as the Masons arrived.

Mama gasped and brought a hand up to cover her mouth. "Philip laid this floor," she said to no one in particular. Wiping away tears with the back of her hand, she cleared her throat. "Well, I guess that's that." She left the kitchen, walked upstairs, and took herself to bed.

<hr>

We didn't have Thanksgiving dinner. Aunt Kitty suggested the Masons come over another time, and they set a record for how quickly dinner guests can come and go.

Bo stormed out of the house, acting like the world *owed* him a Thanksgiving dinner, and the rest of us scooped the food that hadn't been dropped on the floor into storage containers. Aunt Kitty then ushered Uncle Charlie and us out the door, insisting she'd stay with Mama for the night.

Glen drove us to the lake. We didn't speak. Once he parked and turned off the engine, we continued sitting in silence, watching the birds soar over the water.

"Will it ever get better?" I asked, not knowing if I'd spoken to him or God or the universe.

"I don't know, Cat. I hope so."

Tears fell as I lowered my head.

He wrapped an arm around me and pulled me in close. "I want you to know I understand why you're in such a hurry to graduate, to move in together."

I nodded.

"But Cat, I have two things I want to do, and I need to know they're both all right with you." He tilted my head up and looked into my eyes. "First, tomorrow I'm going to fix your mom's floor. Then—" He leaned in and gave me a tiny peck on the lips. "I'm going to ask you to marry me."

My head gave a reflexive, involuntary shake of incomprehension. "What?"

"I know your motivation for living together is to get away from all—*that*." He motioned back toward the city. "And I'm fine with that, so if you want to say no and just live together, I'll still be a happy guy. But I love you, Cat, and I want to marry you."

"Is this a—a *proposal?*"

"God, no. Not after the morning we've had. I only wanted you to know one's coming, so you can think about it."

"I don't need to think about it."

"Yeah?"

"Yeah."

⸻◦⸻

It had been ages since I'd talked to Liza, but still, she deserved to know. So, I pulled her into the library at lunch and wasted no time getting to it.

"I'm going to marry him, Liza."

"Is this a joke?" she asked in a tone that sounded both doubtful and alarmed.

"I don't expect you to understand, but I thought you should know."

"My God, you're serious."

"Yes."

She took a step forward, then stopped and buried her face in her hands. When she looked up again, her eyes were desperate and pleading. "Look, I know you're ready to get away from your family, but he isn't your way out! There must be another way."

"I'm sure there is, but this is the way I choose."

"Let's get an apartment together. I'll get a job, and we'll decorate the place, go to parties, meet new people. It'll be everything we always wanted. Just you and me."

"Because you've been so reliable over the last year?"

She took a deep breath. "I know I haven't been the best friend, but I'll keep trying. Eventually, I'll get it right, *right?*"

"I'm not changing my mind, Liza."

"I just—I don't understand. Don't you care about the rumors? Where there's smoke, there's fire, Catherine. You're smart. You *know* that."

"No, I don't care about the rumors, Liza! And I told you that three months ago!"

"I know you don't honestly feel that way."

"That's where you're wrong. He loves me, I love him, and that's all I need."

She stepped closer. "If you do this, I can't be there when you make that mistake. I won't do it."

"Great. I'll save you the trouble of an RSVP." I grabbed my bag and headed for the door.

"Catherine! Please!"

"Bye, Liza."

Stepping out into the hallway, I knew I should feel some sort of loss about throwing our friendship down the drain, but all I felt was relief in knowing that it was done, and she was one less person I had left to disappoint.

1982

12

SPILLED BEANS & BUNGALOWS

Christmas, New Year's, and Spring Break passed, and I counted down the days till my birthday, graduation...and June 7th—the day we'd secretly set as our wedding day.

I didn't know why I hadn't told Mama we were getting married, aside from the fact that I hardly saw her anymore, and it didn't seem like a conversation you had when coming and going. Besides, she knew we planned to move in together, so I didn't see how eloping could make anything worse. There was no money for a wedding, anyway.

I'd spent the last two nights at home. The last thing I wanted was *you're never here* drama from Mama on my birthday. I didn't expect there to be much of a celebration, but one thing was certain: Aunt Kitty would bring cake.

Mama knocked on my bedroom door, pushed it open, and sat on the bed. I placed my bookmark inside *The Collected Poems* by Sylvia Plath and waited.

"Happy birthday, sweet girl," she said.

"Thank you, Mama."

She placed her hand on my leg and gave a little sniffle, fighting whatever emotion stirred within her. "I wish your daddy was here."

"Me too."

She pulled her hand back to her lap. "It's been hard for you, I know, and I'm so proud of you. I haven't been the easiest to live with, but with Kitty and Charlie's help, I think I can see the light at the end of the tunnel."

I nodded.

"Grief's a real *bitch*, yeah?" she asked.

"Yeah."

"It would kill me if you left our home angry or upset with me, and I know you'll leave soon. I'm not mad about it because I understand. Some days, I'd like to drive far away from here, too. I get it." She wiped her face with the tissue she'd taken to carrying in her pocket, now that she'd been emotionally uncorked. "I guess I want to be sure we're alright."

She was right about Aunt Kitty and Uncle Charlie creating a light at the end of the tunnel. *This* was my mama, not the chaotic mess we saw on Thanksgiving or on any bad day before that. It had been a slow progression, but an obvious one.

"We're alright, Mama. And for what it's worth, I don't blame you for anything."

She muffled a sob with her tissue. "Well, I do. I wanted so badly to be strong for both of you; for things not to change any more than they had to. I wanted to somehow make up for what you'd lost. I knew I couldn't take his place, but damn if I didn't try."

"I know."

"Sure as hell learned my lesson, didn't I?"

I wasn't sure what to say, so I said nothing.

"Well," she said, getting to her feet. "I know your plans are set, but you're always welcome here. I won't try to tell you how to live your life, but you'll always have a home here, Catherine."

For a split second, I wondered if I should tell her I wasn't just moving out—I was getting married. One look at her face though, and I couldn't do it. This was the first real conversation we'd had in months, and judging by the puffiness of her eyes, she was a wreck about it. I couldn't ruin the moment; not on my birthday and not when it would only make her feel worse.

So, I said, "Thank you," and stood as she wrapped me in a hug.

"I'll call Kitty and see what time she's bringing cake. Any requests for dinner?"

"Whatever you decide is fine."

"Chicken pot pie it is."

"My favorite."

"I know."

⸺◈⸺

"Catherine, get a move on!" Mama yelled from downstairs.

"I'm coming, sheesh!" I shoved my feet into shoes and grabbed my purse from the dresser. Catching my reflection in the mirror, I paused.

This was really happening. Graduation day had come, and in one week, I'd be married. Butterflies coursed through my stomach, and I felt like I needed to lie down.

Get a grip and go get this done.

I threw open the bedroom door and headed downstairs.

"Look at you!" Aunt Kitty stood from the sofa and took me by the shoulders. "Just yesterday I was holding a bawling baby in the hospital and now, here you are, all grown up." She wiped a tear.

"Aunt Kitty, please, don't make me cry."

"You're right. It's a happy occasion. No tears!" she said.

Bo came down in jeans, a tee shirt, and old sneakers.

"You're not going dressed like that!" Mama yelled.

"It's graduation. It's not like she's getting married," he quipped back.

The room went quiet, and all eyes turned to me.

"What?" I asked.

"Just go change!" Mama said with a flick of her wrist and a point toward the stairs.

He grumbled, disappeared, and returned minutes later with dress pants and a collared shirt.

"Better. Now, let's go!" Mama shooed us all out the door.

Aunt Kitty and Uncle Charlie sped away in their blue Caddy, and we climbed into our car.

"Looking forward to meeting Glen's mother. What's her name again?" Mama asked.

"Janine."

"What a pretty name."

"Wait until you see *her*."

After names were called, pictures were taken, and all the tears were shed, we found Glen and Janine. Of course, I'd known where he was all morning—I always knew where he was.

He approached with a triumphant smile and gave me a light peck on the cheek. Then he turned to Mama. "Mrs. Fraser, this is my mom, Janine."

"Nice to meet you. I'm Laurel." Mama offered her hand.

Janine ignored Mama's outstretched hand and embraced her in a stranglehold of a hug. "It's so good to finally meet you! I'm so sorry my work hours are nuts. I feel like this should have happened months ago!"

Janine's enthusiasm was off the charts and Mama stared at me over her shoulder with a *what is wrong with this lady* face.

"Yes, well, my hours are a bit nuts too, so I understand," Mama replied, still wrapped in Janine's squeeze.

I stifled a laugh, took Glen's arm, and said, "I'm starving."

Mama wrestled herself free. "Kitty made enough for everyone, I think." She turned to Janine. "Why don't you join us?"

Janine's face lit up with her smile. "We'd love to! We'll follow you. Er—well, I guess my son knows where he's going, doesn't he?" She gave a hearty laugh and the rest of us, aside from Bo, joined in.

Mama threw another look of disbelief my way and I returned it with a *be nice* one of my own.

On the way home, Mama said, "You weren't kidding about Janine. She looks like a movie star!"

"And she's a singer. Can you believe it?"

"What kind of singer?"

"Jazz mostly. She's amazing."

"Of course she is. Wow." Mama shook her head.

"Be nice to her, Mama. She's very sweet."

"I'm sure she is. Why wouldn't I be nice?"

"I don't know. Just throwing it out there, just in case."

On our third bottle of wine, and with Aunt Kitty's buffet nearly picked over, Janine said, "I'm so glad to have finally met you, Laurel. I feel like we're family already—and I guess after next week, we will be!"

My heart stopped in my chest. I mean, I knew it hadn't *literally* stopped, but it damn sure felt like it. My eyes went straight to Glen, who ogled his mother in mortified disbelief. Casting a look around the room, I saw *everyone* staring in disbelief—mostly at me.

"Excuse me, what?" Mama mumbled with a mouth full of cheese.

"Oh no, did you not—" Janine looked from Mama to Glen to me, then back to Glen. "Oh, Glen—*really?*"

"Catherine?" Mama looked to me for an explanation.

When I didn't offer one, she turned to Glen. "Glen?"

"We were going to tell you," he said.

"When?" Mama stood. "When were you going to tell me you were *marrying* my daughter?" Her hands moved so fast through the air with every word, I could barely see her face through them.

Janine shifted in her seat, then stood, placing a hand on Mama's arm. "Laurel, they only told me because they needed Glen's birth certificate. I assumed you knew as well. I am so, so sorry."

Mama gave Janine a long, not-very-friendly look, then turned to me.

"Mama, please—"

"Please what? Are you asking for my permission? It's too little, too late for that, I'd say." She placed her hands on her hips, gave both of us a hard look, then stormed out the front door.

"Goodness," Aunt Kitty said. "That was quite the surprise. I'll talk to her." She left in pursuit of Mama.

Bo sat at the kitchen table with a smirk on his face I wanted to slap right off, and Uncle Charlie popped open a beer. He wasn't one for words anyway, but right then, he was plain stumped. He pulled out a chair next to Bo and sat.

"I thought she knew!" Janine said to Glen. "How could you not tell her...and not tell *me* you hadn't told her?"

"We wanted to wait until after graduation, but clearly that was a bad idea." He looked at me and said, "We should have told her."

I nodded, still at a loss for words. The truth was, I didn't know how Mama would take the news, and I just wanted one day of good memories to look back on before ruining everything. I didn't want to not be on speaking terms with my mother at graduation. I couldn't do that to myself—or to her. Though, I suppose, the bigger truth of it was...I was afraid.

"Welp, I'm going to check on my girls while you—uh—handle yours," Uncle Charlie said, as he patted Glen on the shoulder and disappeared into the yard, beer in hand.

Bo leaned back with an evil grin, shoving snacks into his mouth like he was watching one of his damn TV shows.

"Will you ever grow up?" I asked him.

"If this is what growing up is, then *hell* no. You can have all that."

———— ◆ ————

It took a full day for Mama to process what happened. Then it took at least a half dozen instances of her entering the kitchen with an open mouth and something to say, then shaking her head, and leaving again...before she finally took the seat across from me, dropped her head into her hands, and said, "Okay, Catherine. I have nothing to say but *okay*."

The next day, Glen and I drove to the last three rental properties on our list, knowing that if one of them didn't work out, we'd be living at Janine's until new ones opened up.

As we pulled into the driveway of the third property, feeling restless and defeated, I looked across the yard to the red front door...and it was love at first sight. I threw open my door and ran straight up the steps to give the old landlord a hug. I hadn't been introduced to the man yet, but I loved him. Well, I loved his *house*, which meant I loved *him*.

It took one hour for us to tour the place, ask all the questions, sign the papers, and for the money to change hands. We left that day with keys in hand, and the most amazing feeling of hope, excitement, and accomplishment crept into my heart.

Then June 7th arrived.

Our wedding was at the courthouse, with Aunt Kitty, Uncle Charlie, Janine, Mama, and Bo present. As promised, I did not invite Liza.

The day started with rain showers, which Aunt Kitty swore was good luck, but then it transformed to hot and humid, with clear-blue skies—as June in Alabama should be.

My dress was white with tiny gold flowers, an off the shoulder neckline, and a flirty ruffle around the bust. I was quite proud of finding something new, which I bought with my own money, and which could be worn all summer long. It was perfect.

Minutes before our appointment with the justice of the peace, Mama pulled me to the side. "Give me your hand." Tying one of Daddy's baby blue handkerchiefs around my wrist, she said, "It's a peace offering. For kinda freaking out when Janine spilled the beans."

"Kinda?" I replied with a smile.

She shrugged. "It's also your something old, something borrowed, and something blue."

"Thank you, Mama." I leaned in and kissed her cheek.

"Yeah, yeah—go on, you have a boy to marry." She hugged me, then turned me loose as something behind me caught her attention. Her mouth fell open, and she said, "Well, I'll be damned."

I spun around and saw him.

Lord, help me.

His hair was trimmed and styled so his curls fell just right, as he stood there grinning like something from a dream in dark blue jeans, a tailored white button-up shirt, navy blue tie, and brand-new boots—the church kind, not the work kind. I suddenly felt very self-conscious, almost childish, as I realized there was not an inch of *boy* about him. That one was all *man*.

Aunt Kitty whispered in my ear, "He cleans up awful nice, doesn't he? *Woo-ee!*"

"Yes, ma'am. He sure does," I said with a smile.

He smirked and shook his head because, well, Aunt Kitty's whispers were not as discreet as she believed them to be. Then, Janine handed him a bouquet of purple irises and baby's breath.

Crossing the room in long, confident strides, he held them out for me to take. "I know you said you didn't need flowers, but Mom insisted. She put them together herself."

Crying before we'd even started, all three women rushed at once, offering handkerchiefs and pleading for me not to ruin my makeup.

When Janine turned back to Glen, she pinned an iris to his shirt and smoothed a wrinkle. Then she gave a teary-eyed smile before finding her way over to Mama.

Glen leaned in and whispered, "Are you ready?" sending a shiver down my spine.

As if I could ever answer anything other than *yes, forever yes.*

⚬

After finger-foods and champagne at Mama's, there was no dramatic, rice-filled sendoff or honeymoon to get to. Instead, we loaded the last of my things into the truck and said what felt like a thousand tearful goodbyes.

"Mama, I'm not moving to Timbuktu," I said.

"Forgive me if I'm not ready. It all happened so much sooner than I thought it would." She wiped her face, then gripped me in a hug like she never wanted to let go.

"Well, you know where we live!"

"I do. Still can't believe y'all can afford that big house. Are you sure I can't gift you a little check to help for the first few months, at least?"

"We'll be fine. Save it for Bo...maybe he'll need it for college."

"Pfft! We'll see about that," she whispered. "Well, maybe the car, then?"

"What? *Your* car?"

"I'll be shopping for a newer one soon, anyway. Maybe I'll pass it along to you as a combined graduation and wedding present."

Not sure if she was serious or not, I replied, "Now, *that* I would take," before giving her a kiss on the cheek.

"You ready to go?" Glen placed an arm around my waist.

"Ready."

"I'm not," Aunt Kitty chimed in from the front porch, where she'd sat to compose herself. She stood and made her way over to us. "I won't say goodbye. Just give me a hug."

I reached toward her, and she said, "You too, Glen. You're family now. Get in here." He smiled and joined us for a hug. "Now you may go," Aunt Kitty said.

"Not yet," Janine piped in. "I want one of those, too." She came forward, and it was group hug number two.

I laughed at how silly it all seemed; everyone acting like they'd never see us again. All except Bo and Uncle Charlie, who were sitting spread-eagle and cross-legged on the porch swing, watching the crazy crying women from afar.

When I caught Uncle Charlie's eye, he stood and joined us. "Catherine, love, I'm so happy for you, but you need to go on and get out of here before you dehydrate all these poor women." He leaned in and offered his hug, too.

"Thank you, Uncle Charlie. Take care of my mama."

"Always," he replied with a tiny salute.

Bo, still sitting on the swing, gave a wave before chugging the last of his champagne. Knowing it was all I'd get from him, I accepted it as a token of kindness rather than a slight, and waved back. Then, for good measure, I blew him a kiss. He scrunched up his face and mouthed, "Eww."

Glen laughed, then took my hand and opened my door. I climbed inside and scooted to the middle, as I always did. He waved one last time, then slid into the driver's seat. As we pulled out of the driveway to begin our new life, I turned backwards in the seat and waved, waved, waved...to all I left behind.

⚬

Our house was perfect; a creamy white, single-story bungalow. I took full credit for securing the place, due to the kind old landlord having a sweet spot for any young lady who reminded him of his own perfect daughter.

He said he'd wanted to sell it for years, but his wife wouldn't hear of it. He promised once he'd won her over, we'd be the first to know.

Unpacking the last of the dishes Mama gave us from her own kitchen, I looked around and took notice of the gorgeous, soft afternoon light. With windows wrapping around two sides of the kitchen, there wasn't much upper cabinet space, but more natural light than two people should ever be allotted in their starter home.

I added *plants* to my shopping list, below *toilet paper, kitchen towels,* and *bleach.* I'd hang them in the windows; create my own secret garden.

The back door opened, and Glen came through it, covered in dirt.

"What do you think you're doing?" I shoved him back outside.

He gestured to his soil-covered clothes. "I'd hoped for a shower."

"You're not coming in here like that, sir. Kick the dirt off your boots and leave 'em outside. I just mopped this floor for about the twelfth time today."

"Yes, ma'am." He winked and removed his boots. "Anything else I should remove while I'm out here?"

"Yes, now you mention it. Your shirt."

He pulled the shirt over his head and tossed it to the ground. "Anything else?"

"Your breeches. There's a lot of dirt on those breeches."

Without batting an eye, my beautiful husband unbuttoned his jeans, let them fall to his ankles, and kicked them to the side with a socked foot. "Anything else?" he asked with a raised brow.

"Well, the socks, naturally."

He pulled those off, too. "And now?"

"That'll do. We don't need to give the neighbors a free show now, do we?"

He growled and charged inside, sweeping me off my feet and throwing me over his shoulder like a sack of potatoes.

I giggled, screamed, and kicked my legs. "Put me down, ya brute!"

He gave a hard *smack* on my ass and carried me straight to the bathroom, where he deposited me in the shower.

"Well, this isn't what I meant."

"Isn't it though?" He dropped his underwear and flipped on the shower, with me still standing fully clothed inside it, and now soaked to the bone with the freezing cold water.

"Dumbass!" I screamed through chattering teeth.

"I'm going to need you to stand very still, Mrs. Lewis, while I strip you naked and make you regret, with every fiber of your being, *ever* calling me *dumbass*."

1983

13

CHAMPAGNE & CHEMISTRY

Leaving work with steak, fresh veggies, potatoes (and all the trimmings to add on top after they're baked), and a chocolate cake, I headed home to cook. It was our first anniversary, and I wanted to celebrate in a way Glen would appreciate: with his favorite meal...and sex. Lots of sex.

Time and time again, well-meaning people had teased and warned about the inevitable end of *the honeymoon period*, but I saw no end in sight. It had been the best year of my life. Every morning, I woke with the man of my dreams, and every night I drifted off to sleep with his arms holding me tight. With him by my side, there were no nightmares, no bad memories, no worries. In our little white house, I had found the peace I so desperately sought after Daddy died.

Turning onto our street, I saw he was home and unloading something from the back of the truck. I pulled into the driveway next to him.

"So much for a surprise dinner. Why are you home during daylight hours, mister?" I retrieved the cake and potatoes from the back seat, then walked around the car to meet him.

"I hoped to beat *you* home. Looks like we ruined both our surprises." He leaned over the items in my hands and gave me a kiss.

"What do you have back there?" I nodded toward the truck.

"You didn't see it?" he asked, moving to stand in my line of vision.

"No..."

He placed his hands on my shoulders and spun me toward the porch. "Go inside. I'll get the rest of the groceries. No peeking!"

"Fine, *I guess.*"

He pinched my leg, just below my ass cheek, as I headed toward the porch. I turned and gave a playful glare.

"I said no peeking!"

"I'm not peeking, sheesh!"

Entering the house, I moved toward the kitchen to place the groceries on the table, but it was covered from one end to the other in potted plants of all shapes and sizes. There were ferns, a peace lily, orchids, spider plants, and others I couldn't even name.

"What in the world?" I laughed and turned toward the door as Glen entered, carrying the other bags.

"Happy anniversary," he said with a smile.

Setting the cake and potatoes on the counter, I said, "Did you buy out the whole nursery?"

"Close to it." He placed the bags on the floor and moved toward me, wrapping his arms around my waist and clasping his hands behind my back. "I figured you'd appreciate them more than cut flowers."

"Well, you were right. I love them."

He pulled my face into his and kissed me in that way he did that still took my breath away.

After freeing my lips from his, I said, "You'll have to help me hang them in the windows. A shelf or two may even be required. I'm afraid you just made a lot of extra work for yourself."

"When have I ever been afraid of work? Speaking of, I've got one more thing to do. Go take a bath, then we'll cook together." He planted one more peck on my lips, then disappeared through the front door.

Soaking in the tub, and just as Catherine's ghost appears to Heathcliff in *Wuthering Heights*, Glen pushed open the door and entered.

"All done?" I asked.

He kneeled beside the tub, grabbing the wash rag I'd hung over the faucet. "Not even close," he said, submerging it in the bubbles.

"I meant with the surprise."

"Oh that—yeah, that's done." He smirked and glided the rag over my belly.

"Then we should get started with dinner or we'll never eat." I leaned forward and pulled out the drain plug.

"Nuh-uh," he said, holding the towel open wide, waiting to wrap me in its warmth. "Dinner can wait."

After traveling from bathtub to bed—and thoroughly enjoying *dessert* before dinner—the setting sun filled the room with a peachy-orange light as we laid together, legs entwined.

"Can I see my surprise *now?*" I asked while tracing circles on his bare chest.

He looked out the window. "Now is the perfect time," he answered, pulling on his underwear and jeans. "Come on, before we miss it!"

"Miss what?" I climbed out of bed and moved to the bathroom for my clothes.

"You'll see if you hurry up!"

When we were both dressed, he took my hand and pulled me through the living room and to the front door.

"I hope you don't think it's too cheesy or cliché," he said, turning to look at me.

"And if I do?"

"Too bad." Grinning, he opened the door and pulled me through it.

I looked to the right but saw nothing out of the ordinary. Then I looked left, and my eyes landed on a wooden porch swing hanging from the roof.

It was painted black, with silver chains, and a floral-print pillow rested in each corner.

"Oh, it's beautiful!" I walked toward the swing and ran my fingers along the smooth-sanded wood of the armrest. "Why would I think it's cliché?"

"Well, you know...everybody in the south has a porch swing of some sort. You like it?"

"I love it." I took his hand and pulled him over to sit side-by-side on the swing. Turning sideways, I draped my legs across his lap. "Wow, look at that sunset."

"Yup. Good thing we didn't miss it," he said, massaging my bare feet with both hands. "I love you, Cat. Now and forever. More today than I did yesterday, and I don't even know how that's possible." He looked at me with eyes so intense, it felt like my insides had gone molten.

And we never did get around to making dinner.

———◆———

On a still-warm Tuesday in mid-September, I offered Glen a glass of champagne when he arrived home from work.

"Champagne?" he asked as he pulled off his boots. "What are we celebrating?" He leaned back in the armchair and spread his legs wide.

I carried the glasses to the living room, sat on his lap, and handed him one. "To the new general manager of the Asher IGA." I clinked my glass with his and took a sip.

"That is worth celebrating!" He took a drink, then rested the glass on his knee. "Congratulations, Cat. Now you can be the one bringing home the bacon."

"I work at a grocery store. I'm always the one bringing home the bacon."

He laughed, took another drink, and said, "Let's go somewhere nice for dinner."

"Or..."

"Or?" His mischievous eyes darted to mine, dirty thoughts on full display within them.

"We could make a baby."

His whole body went stiff, then he softened with a laugh. "You're not serious."

"I am."

"Shouldn't we wait till those paychecks start rollin' in, babe?"

"Well, last I checked, it takes nine months to make a baby."

"But...Cat, even with a promotion, we couldn't pay a babysitter. You'd have to quit work, and we'd bring in less than we are now."

"Or Mama, Janine, and Aunt Kitty will help. We'd be lucky if we ever saw her, I think."

"Her?" he asked with a grin.

"Yes, her. You know your truck is a her, and I know our baby is a her."

"The baby that doesn't exist yet?"

"Correct. Doesn't matter though. I still know."

He gave a loud laugh and took another sip. "*How* do you know?"

"Same way I knew my life was forever changed the first time you showed up at my house."

"What? You never told me that." He looked bewildered.

"Liza always thought I was psychic, but I don't think that's the right word. I only ever know things...*feel* things...about myself. It's more of a—an intuition."

"Interesting. Well, I think we'd be crazy to go there, Cat. We'd be...twenty years old."

"And? Both our mamas were twenty when we were born. Are you out of excuses yet?" I snuggled into his neck and kissed behind his ear.

"It appears I am." He took my glass, leaned forward, and set both on the table. Hooking one arm behind me and the other under my knees, he stood and carried me to the bedroom.

It was November 17th—Glen's birthday, and also the day I would forever remember as being the day I learned I was pregnant.

I went off the pill the night we decided to try for a baby, but still, October's period came and went. When November's never arrived, I drove to the next town and purchased an at-home pregnancy test promising *never-before-seen accuracy* and *results in forty-five minutes*. When I got home, I hid it, and made a decision: If my period still hadn't come by Glen's birthday, I would take the test.

Then I lived the longest four days of my life.

When I woke on the 17th, I rolled over to find Glen's side of the bed empty, only vaguely remembering his goodbye kiss. Then I bolted upright in bed, squeezed my eyes shut, and thought, *this is it*.

Traveling between the side of the tub and the vanity to check the results, while watching the minutes tick by on the kitchen timer, I realized that tiny chemistry experiment would determine my *entire future*.

Twenty-two more minutes.

Sixteen more minutes.

Eleven more minutes.

Pure torture is what it was. I vowed to check one more time, then not again until the timer dinged.

I stood, moved back to the counter, and looked.

"Is that liquid...*changing colors?*" I dropped to my knees for a better look. *Oh my God.*

I stood, clapped my hand over my mouth, and screamed. I ran into the bedroom, jumped up and down on the bed, and screamed some more. Then I flopped onto my back and brought my hands to my stomach.

All my hopes and dreams had come true. I was nervous, terrified, and...a million other emotions I couldn't even name.

I was going to be a mom. And Glen was going to be a dad.

We were having a baby.

———— ✦ ————

"You're serious?" Glen asked, setting his soda on the kitchen counter.

"Why would I joke about such a thing? Yes, I'm serious!"

"I'm going to be...a dad?" His eyes grew wide as he looked down at my belly.

I couldn't tell by his reaction if he was happy or completely freaked out. "You're going to be a dad. Happy birthday?"

"Oh my God, Cat!" He lifted me from the ground, spinning circles in the kitchen as I giggled. When he sat me down, he dropped to his knees, lifted my shirt, and kissed my stomach again and again. "I just—I can't—" He looked up at me with tear-filled eyes.

"Why are you crying, dummy? It's a happy day."

"The best birthday of my life!" He stood, lifting me into the air again, squeezing me so tight I could barely breathe.

"Glen—" I managed to say, even with a lack of oxygen.

"Sorry." He sat me down again, pulled me in close, and kissed me like I'd never been kissed before.

It was a kiss of joy, pride, and protection. Of hope, fear, and surprise. A kiss filled with every emotion I had experienced, but couldn't name, since 8:32 that morning when that liquid changed colors, and that baby changed our lives.

NOW

I've told Jenna most of it, only sparing a few details. No child needs to know the specifics of the first time her parents had sex, after all.

"Wow. I knew GiGi took Grandpa Philip's death hard, but I didn't know *how* hard. That's terrible. It must've been awful for you."

I nod. "It was awful for all of us."

"And his dad had *two* families? That's...insane."

I nod again, knowing she hasn't even heard the worst of it yet.

Jenna leans forward with her elbows on her knees and looks at me. "So, it wasn't love at first sight, but you really loved him."

"Yes, I did, but it's important to me that you understand this isn't a love story, Jenna. This is a...*life* story. There's so much more to it and frankly, I'm not sure I can do it justice in telling it."

She gives me a curious look, like she's wondering if I'm reconsidering telling her anything at all.

"But I'm going to try," I say.

She nods and stares off into the distance.

"If you still want to hear it, that is."

"Yeah, I do. Sorry, I guess I'm still hung up on the *you loved him* part. I always thought you just kind of *tolerated* him."

I sigh because that breaks my heart. "I should have been more open with you, but I wanted to protect you. My emotions were—all over the place."

"Did you think I needed to be protected? Because it would've been nice to have a little more...*emotional freedom* in our house, I think."

"What do you mean?"

"Just that things were always very straightforward—go to work, go to school, do homework, do chores. There wasn't a lot of room for much else."

I stand and move toward the kitchen, looking for wine.

"It's above the fridge," Jenna says, as she stands and follows me.

"I think I was afraid of showing any sort of weakness. When Daddy died, I was *full* of emotions, and it made me feel so vulnerable. And we were so busy...there wasn't a lot of time for fun, or long heart-to-hearts. I'm glad you got a lot of that with other people in your life, though."

She smiles. "I was pretty lucky, overall, I think."

"Well, as we've both learned...it takes a village."

1984

14

BENTWOOD & ALARM BELLS

On August 23rd, Jenna Elizabeth Lewis was born. As she took her first breaths, Glen looked to the window, and said, "I think the clouds just parted. This little girl has brought the sunshine!"

Cradling Jenna in her arms, Mama cried and said, "She looks just like Philip," damn near refusing to give her back.

At home, I rocked her in the same bentwood chair Mama once rocked me, watching clouds pass out the window and listening to her gentle breaths. I heard the front door open and close quietly. Looking at the clock, I realized I'd held her through a full two-hour nap.

Glen's footsteps traveled our way, then he leaned against the doorframe. Crossing his arms, he gave a closed-mouthed, satisfied smile.

"Hey," I whispered.

"Hey."

I expected him to greet me with a kiss, but he stayed where he was, continuing to smile.

"What is it?" I asked.

He shook his head. "I still can't believe this is real." Making his way over, he kissed each of us on the forehead.

"She's real alright. Changed fifteen poopy diapers today that prove it." I stood, placing her in his arms. "I'm gonna shower. She'll probably wake soon."

He pulled her close. "I brought dinner whenever you're ready."

"I'm starving. I'll make it quick."

Moments later, I worked conditioner through my hair, feeling so damn grateful. When Daddy died, my life was upended, and it felt like it could never be set right. But Glen unburied me when I was emotionally six feet underground, right alongside my dad. He helped Mama, without ever being asked, and he let me cry when I mourned the loss of the *old her*, too. He encouraged me through senior year, even when Asher High was the last place I wanted to be and he, above anyone else, had been the proudest of everything I'd accomplished since.

And in that shower, I realized that the way he looked at me when I held Jenna set my soul on fire. I thought I was in love before, but it turned out *there was so much more room for love.*

Our period of newborn bliss lasted four weeks.

After that, Jenna cried nearly every minute she was awake, and it was impossible to get her to sleep. Her eyes transformed from glistening and wonder-filled to red-rimmed, sunken, and exhausted. She was physically and emotionally spent. We all were.

I moved the phone from left ear to right, to better hear Mama. "Say that again, Mama. I couldn't hear you."

"Does she still not like baths?" Mama asked.

"She hates them."

"Well, give her one anyway. Then feed her and go for a drive."

"But she hates that stupid bucket seat, too. It won't work."

"If it doesn't work, come here. You can rest while I tend to her."

I shifted Jenna's position to ease the pins and needles in my left arm. "Okay."

"Good luck," Mama said.

Just as I hung up, Glen walked through the door. "Not *again.*"

"No, this is one long episode. I wish it were *again*. Mama says bathe her, feed her, and put her in the car. See if she'll fall asleep that way." I moved toward Jenna's room to retrieve a clean sleeper and a diaper.

When I passed the living room again, Glen was on the sofa with his head buried in his hands. Looking up, he said, "Want me to do it?"

He'd been awake since 4:30, worked all day, and was even more tired than I was. He came home at lunch hoping to grab a nap, but it was a wasted effort.

"Can you pack bottles and diapers? If she doesn't fall asleep, I'll go to Mama's."

"Okay," he answered, standing from the sofa.

I turned on the bathroom heater and filled the sink with warm water, bouncing Jenna in my arms. Then, I forced a bath she didn't want, and my head felt like it would explode from the sound of her screams echoing off tile. When finished, I dressed her and moved to the rocker.

Glen brought a bottle. She drank an ounce and a half, then cried again, refusing more.

Standing from his kneeling position, Glen paced the room.

"Guess we're going for a drive. You should get some sleep," I said.

"Okay," he answered, in a tone of defeat.

⸺ ◈ ⸺

After an hour of driving in circles, I turned the car toward Mama's. Just as I entered the neighborhood, the crying subsided, and Jenna slept. I pulled into the driveway, not daring to move her from the car, but hoping I could get some sleep of my own. Just as my eyes closed, she cried again.

Damnit all to hell!

I drove for another twenty minutes before she fell asleep once more. Then I kept driving—at times, holding my eyelids open with my fingers just to stay awake.

As I passed the closed-up shops on Main Street, I was envious that their employees were relaxing at home, as I burned gas we couldn't afford, trying not to doze off and crash into a building or tree.

They don't know how lucky they are.

Immediately, I felt guilty because I knew how lucky I was too, even if things were hard in that moment. I knew it wouldn't be that way forever.

When I pulled into our driveway, Jenna was still sleeping. Then five minutes later, she wasn't. I let loose a heavy sigh and shut off the engine. Entering the house, I found Glen asleep on the sofa. He woke when I shut the door.

"No luck?" he said as he sat upright.

I shook my head. "At least she isn't crying." I sat next to him, holding her in the bend of my elbow.

He placed an arm around my shoulders, and I scootched closer, resting my head against him. Staring into Jenna's eyes, wishing there were some magic words I could whisper that would make her sleep...to *really* sleep...I'd never felt so helpless. I stared and stared, noticing how little she seemed to even blink, as my eyelids grew heavy.

I dozed off and when I came to again, she was still wide awake.

"Can you take her? I have to pee," I said to Glen, who appeared lost in thought.

"Hmm? Oh, yeah." He scooped her up and the moment he did, she cried. He looked at me with such frustration and pain in his eyes, it left me unsure of what to say or do.

"I'll just be a minute."

Glen paced the living room, bouncing and *shhh'ing*, but she still cried. When I returned, he placed her in my arms, then disappeared into the bedroom.

By 3:00 in the morning, I'd managed to feed her half a bottle and get her into her crib. I slid into bed beside Glen, as he lay on his back with an arm over his eyes.

"I don't know how to do this," he said. "I don't know how *you* do it. How *do* you do it?"

I turned toward him, resting my head on his chest. "I don't know either. Clearly."

He pulled his arm from his face and turned his eyes toward me. I couldn't see them, but I could feel them. "I'm serious, Cat. Why doesn't she like me? Why can't I calm her like you do?"

I sighed, turned onto my back, and closed my eyes. "Neither of us know what we're doing." I stopped short of adding that I'd wondered a million times why my super-powered instincts didn't extend to knowing how to calm my own baby. "Everyone says she'll outgrow it. She won't be a newborn forever."

He was quiet for a long time, then just as I started drifting off to sleep, I heard—or maybe dreamed—that he said, "I'm not meant to be a dad, Cat."

October came and went, and Jenna still cried. Glen's hours stretched longer and longer, despite the autumn days growing shorter. When he was home, he was quiet. Distant.

I'd gone back to work and as much as it killed me to leave Jenna, I was thankful for the break—which made me feel guilty for feeling that way.

"I've almost got everything packed," Janine said when I arrived after my shift. "Oh! I wanted to show you something she seems to like."

Jenna had just finished eating, so Janine took her from me. She turned her onto her stomach, laid her on her forearm, and patted her back. "Tried every position to force a burp, but she just cried. Then I tried this, and well—she doesn't hate it—and eventually, it works."

Jenna belched, and Janine shrugged her shoulders. "See?"

It was the first time I'd seen Jenna burp without screaming since she was a month old. "How did you think to do that?" I asked as Janine placed her back into my arms.

"I remembered doing it with Glen." She handed me the diaper bag. "Maybe she's just gassy. Try cycling her legs after she eats."

"Thanks, Janine. See you tomorrow?"

"Yup. See you tomorrow."

When we got home, Jenna was crying before we even got out of the car. She wasn't hungry, had just been burped, and had a clean diaper. There was no reason for her to be pissed at the world—she just *was*.

Entering the house with a baby in one arm and my purse and diaper bag on the other, Glen attempted to take the bags, but I gave him Jenna instead.

He'd barely seen her lately. He needed to *hold* her.

I kissed him on the cheek. "I'm going to shower. She's been fed and changed."

"Okay, but—" He stared with wide eyes asking, *how do I make her happy?*

"Just hold her. Talk to her. Shake a rattle to give her something to focus on. She's going to cry no matter what, and I just need to get clean. I'll be quick."

He nodded, turned her upright, then bounced her gently as he paced the room.

I showered and dressed to the sound of escalating screams. Exiting the bathroom, Glen handed her to me, then moved to the kitchen for a beer.

I laid her on her back, grasped her feet, and moved them in a circular motion, like riding a bicycle.

Please let Janine be right.

Glen returned, collapsing into the armchair.

As I pumped her legs, her screams softened into a totally normal new-born cry, then into whimpers. A moment later, she was quiet, and her eyes grew heavy. I offered a pacifier, and for the first time in a long time, she was calm enough to accept. Her eyes closed as I picked her up.

"How'd you—" Glen looked at me like I'd walked on water.

I moved to Jenna's room and sucked in a breath, hoping she didn't cry again when I laid her down. Placing her in the crib, I slid my hands out from beneath her and stood stock-still, expecting the worst. Instead, she turned her head to the side and slept.

Tiptoeing out of the room, I pulled the door closed. When I returned to the living room, it was empty.

"Glen?"

I heard his truck start, then he was gone.

It was 5:00 in the morning, the week before Christmas. I'd just fed Jenna and gotten her back to sleep, and I was wide awake.

I hardly saw Glen anymore. He stopped at the bar after work, came home at all hours, and crashed on the sofa. Then, he was gone again in the morning. As much as I didn't want to admit that maybe Liza was right, I wondered if it was really the bar he spent so much time in, or if he was somewhere else...*with* someone else.

Opening the cabinet, I reached for a coffee mug and gasped.

Oh, God...please don't let it be Ally Monroe.

I gave my head a shake and poured my coffee, just as Glen exited the bathroom and appeared for breakfast. I grabbed a second mug and poured his too.

"You're up early." He reached for a bowl and the box of Raisin Bran.

"Couldn't sleep." I added cream to both mugs, returned it to the refrigerator, and sat.

When he joined me, he stared at his bowl, unable to even look at me.

"Glen, what's going on?"

He continued staring at the empty dish. "I don't know, Cat."

"Can we maybe try to figure it out?"

Leaning back in his chair, he crossed his arms, his gaze never leaving that bowl. "I didn't tell you the whole truth about my dad."

I waited for him to continue.

"He was a drunk with a gambling problem. He was mean, abusive, and knew just where to leave the marks, so they wouldn't be noticed. He never touched Mom—only me and Robin, my sister. Doesn't mean he was nice to Mom, though. With her, it was all about mind games, control."

"Shit, Glen." I reached over, placing a hand on his shoulder.

He poured his cereal, then moved to the fridge for milk.

"And your mom stayed with him?"

He shook his head as he poured. "I never told her."

"Jesus, Glen, for how long? How long did she not know? Why didn't you tell her?"

And how had I never sensed there was more to his story?

"It started when I was eight—as far as I can remember—and ended right before we moved here. The first few times it happened, he cried and begged forgiveness. He promised he'd never do it again and asked me never to tell. So, I didn't. And I knew she needed him. She needed his money and his—comfort—I guess. She loved him. And like I said, he never laid a hand on her." He sat, checked the time on his watch, and took a bite.

"You were...seventeen...and he was still hitting you?"

He gave a little, weary laugh. "I gave it back just as good as I got that time. Pretty sure that's the reason I never saw him again. I told Mom about it on the drive here."

"I—I don't know what to say. I'm so sorry."

"Nothing for you to be sorry for, Cat," he said as he took another bite.

"Why have you never told me this before?"

Leaning forward with elbows on the table, he rubbed his temples. "Because I thought it didn't matter and I don't know...I didn't want you to feel sorry for me or pity me, because I thought I was fine." He checked his watch again.

It was time for him to leave for work, but I had a burning question I needed an answer to.

"What's got you thinking about all this now? What does it have to do with—anything?"

Turning his face to me for the first time since he sat at the table, he looked me dead in the eyes and said, "Because I hurt her, Catherine."

My heart skipped a beat. "What do you mean you hurt her?"

"You had gone to the store. She started crying, and I couldn't soothe her. I tried everything. I wore a damn path in the living room, back and forth, back and forth. Then, I just stopped. Held her out in front of me at arm's length, one hand on either side of her chest. She screamed louder...and louder...and suddenly it was like I snapped out of a dream. I laid her on the couch, unbuttoned her sleeper, and there they were: two giant, red handprints on either side of her." He sniffed and wiped away a tear. "I hurt her, Cat. I squeezed her until she screamed and...I hurt her."

It didn't make any sense.

"I bathe her every night. If you'd hurt her, I would've noticed."

"They were there, Cat. My hands. They were there."

"She's a fair-skinned baby. Even the gentlest of touches leaves her skin red for a moment. Then it goes away. You didn't hurt her."

"Even if that's true, does it matter?"

"What?"

"Doesn't the fact I think I *could've* hurt her ring any alarm bells for you? Because it sure as hell does for me." He stood, grabbed his cap and keys from the counter, and took a step toward the living room.

I came to my feet, stopped him, and placed my hands on either side of his face. "You didn't hurt her. You are not your dad. I've never seen you lose your temper, even once. You'd *never* hurt her."

Shaking his head, he said, "I *felt* it—that *rage*. And I recognized it as *him* as soon as it happened." He took a step around me, then turned back to face me. "What is it they say about the apple not falling far from the tree? I've never thought I was like him before, but there's something about becoming a dad—that's changed *everything*."

"Of course it has...for me too, Glen, but we'll get through it. Maybe we should talk to someone...I don't know, maybe Mama's pastor?"

"We don't even go to church, and I'm not sure what good it would do, anyway."

"It's worth a shot."

"I don't know, Cat." He bent the bill of his cap between his hands, then placed it on his head. "I've got to go. See you after work."

15

FALLEN APPLES & CRYSTAL BALLS

Three days later, the pastor stopped by for coffee. Glen didn't talk much, so the conversation that was meant to be between the two of them became one between the pastor and me. Glen sat like a child in a parent-teacher conference, and I focused on answering the pastor's questions honestly, while being respectful of Glen's feelings and experiences. It felt like walking a tightrope.

After the pastor left, Glen picked up one of the two brochures he left behind. "Anger management? Do you think I have anger management problems, Cat?"

I didn't hesitate to say, "No, I don't."

"And this one—" He picked up the second brochure. "Infant care basics." Opening it, he skimmed the highlights. "Feeding, bathing, nail care...I'd say we've figured all that out already, wouldn't you?"

I nodded my head.

"So?" he asked.

"So what?"

"We tried the pastor. What do we do now?"

The silence between us was thick and charged—like how it felt outside when a wall cloud formed, and nobody knew if—or where—the funnel would drop. I didn't have an answer for him then, and as I drove to Mama's for advice, I still didn't.

I knocked on Mama's door at 5:45, knowing I had to pick up Jenna at Janine's by 6:30. Mama opened the door and waved me inside. I followed her to the kitchen table, where she had a pot of coffee waiting.

"I can't drink coffee this late in the day, Mama. You know that," I said, pulling out my chair.

"All right. More for me." She poured herself a cup and took a sip. "So, why the impromptu visit?" She was still wearing her uniform, which made me feel bad for dropping by on short notice after she'd just worked a full day at the hospital. I could see in her eyes that she was tired.

"Well, it's Glen. He's—going through something, and I'm not sure what to do."

"What sort of something?" Mama asked, taking another drink.

"I'm not sure how much he'd appreciate me sharing, to be honest—"

"Catherine, are you here for advice or not?"

I sighed and stood to fetch a glass of water. "Well, his dad was not a good person. Glen says he was—abusive."

Mama looked up with surprised eyes.

"I think Jenna has triggered some bad memories, or...some fear about being a dad."

Mama motioned for me to re-take my seat, so I did.

"What kind of abuse?" she asked.

"He hit him."

"Once?"

"No—" I cleared my throat of the blockage that was making it hard to breathe, much less speak. "For years."

"Oh boy," Mama said.

"Yeah." I took a drink of water and looked out the window. Then I turned back to her. "The pastor came by, but it didn't help. Glen kind of froze up and didn't talk much. He left some brochures, which were—"

"Not helpful," Mama said.

"Not at all."

"So, how is this affecting things?"

"He's been distant, quiet, not really holding her much. He's working longer hours, going to the bar after work—we don't see him much anymore."

Mama nodded.

"And he said—he said he hurt her." I caught the look of shock and anger come across Mama's face, so I continued quickly. "But he didn't! I know he didn't. He said he held her too tight and noticed handprints on her sides afterward, but I gave her a bath that night and there was nothing. I tried explaining that she's just fair-skinned; that she turns red easily and a few minutes later, it's gone."

Mama nodded again. "That's true."

"But he either doesn't believe me, or he's freaked out by it still. It's like he doesn't trust himself to be around her."

"Have you ever seen him get violent? Has he ever hurt you, Catherine?"

"No, never. There was the fight with Bo at the bonfire all those years ago, but Bo instigated that. It wasn't an angry reaction to anything."

"Hmm—" Mama said. "It sounds like the *fear* of it all is what's getting to him. Will he be the sort of father his dad was to him? Or will he make his own way?"

"He said *the apple doesn't fall far from the tree*."

"Sometimes that's true, but I would think the fact he's aware of the possibility and worried about it *being* true is a good sign, right?"

"I hope so. But what do I *do*, Mama?"

She was quiet for a moment, then said, "Do you think he'd see a psychiatrist? Try to get to the bottom of the problem?"

My first instinct was to laugh out loud, but I only said, "It was hard enough to convince him to meet with the pastor."

"Figured as much," Mama replied. "Then I suppose you do your best to keep him involved. Keep trying to get him to talk." She placed a hand on mine. "But you'll also have to accept that not all fathers are like yours,

Catherine. Many are quiet and distant with their kids. They work long days, come home, eat, shower, and go to bed. And for some families, that's a blessing."

"For families with dads like Glen's."

"Yup."

"I wish I had a crystal ball to look into, so I'd know how it all turns out."

It was the first time in my life I'd wished I really had psychic powers.

"Time will tell, child. In the meantime, watch him *like a hawk* when he's around that baby."

At Janine's, I pushed the door open and entered with a, "Hello, I'm here!"

"In my room," she called back.

When I entered, she was doing her makeup while Jenna lay on her back in the playpen, swinging a small stuffed bunny with one hand. I gave Janine a peck on the cheek.

"How was she?" I asked as I picked up my cooing, drool-soaked baby.

"Great! I think she's finally finding her way out of it. She slept fine, ate fine. I see a lot more sleep in your future." She smiled and reached for her perfume.

"Thank God," I answered. "Hi, baby girl. You had a good day, did you?" I hugged Jenna close. "Let's hope we can keep that up at home, huh?"

Janine turned on her stool to face me. "How was work?"

"Long, but fine. Now, to head home and make dinner."

"Mm-hmm. I remember those days. Working, keeping up with the house, tendin' to a baby. I'd say I miss them, but I'm not sure I do." She gave a little laugh.

"I hope you know how much I appreciate you keeping her when Mama and Aunt Kitty can't," I said.

"Oh, none of that. She's my grandbaby, Catherine." She stood, moved to us, and pinched Jenna's cheek. "My little companion."

I placed Jenna back in the playpen and began gathering her things.

How did Janine do it, mostly alone? How did she manage a relationship with a man who was only a part-time father? How did she continue loving him when he only allowed her to have a small *part* of him?

"Can I ask you something?" I said.

"Sure." She moved back to the mirror to check her face.

"How did you do it? I mean, Glen's dad didn't live with you all the time, right?"

Janine paused with her lipstick tube halfway to her mouth. Then she turned to me. "No, he didn't. It wasn't easy."

"Was he a good dad?" I knew the answer, but couldn't think of another way to venture into the conversation.

Janine sighed and re-took her seat. "He was when he was...and he wasn't when he wasn't. What's this about, Catherine? Is everything okay?"

I sat in the chair by the window, my eyes set on Jenna inside the playpen. "It's just that Glen is having some trouble."

"What kind of trouble?"

"He's—I don't really know. I think Jenna has brought something up for him—some feelings about his dad." I looked directly at her, unsure if I should have a conversation about our relationship with my husband's mother, but knowing that if anyone could help, it was her. She'd been through it herself.

"Oh. I'm sorry to hear that. I'd hoped—" She looked down at her feet, clasping her hands in her lap. "I'd hoped he could skip it."

"Skip it?"

"Glen's dad was intoxicating. I'd never met anyone who could turn on the charm like that man, and I've met no one like him since. He made you feel like you were the only person in the room, and when he loved, he loved *big*. But he had his demons—alcohol, money...women. The same demons his own father battled."

"I see," I said.

"Growing up like that can leave a mark, and one of two things usually happens. Either you vow to do everything the exact opposite way they did, by learning what *not* to do, I guess—or you carry your scars a bit differently and they never really heal. When they don't heal, it becomes cyclical. Glen's dad never healed."

"You're saying—"

"I'm saying it's a bit of a curse. I feel like people don't take the importance of childhood as seriously as they should. What happens to you then—when the people you love and trust continuously let you down—it affects how you're formed, as a person. Then you affect your children in similar ways...and on and on."

"Did you know that when you were in the middle of it?"

"You're asking if I knew my child would grow up to fight the same demons? Why I stayed with the man if I knew?"

"That's not what I meant, I just—"

"No, you're smart for asking. It's a good question, given the predicament you've found yourself in." She smoothed her pleated skirt. "No, I didn't know. I think you have an advantage I didn't have."

"So—what do I do?"

"I can't tell you what to do. I *can* tell you how it usually plays out; give you a heads-up, so you'll know what could come...what to look for."

I waited for her to go on.

"The natural progression is an increasingly short temper—bursts of anger you don't feel you deserve—then heavier drinking, and longer periods of time when they don't come home. It's a survival mechanism. They pull back to survive...to avoid the guilt and helplessness they feel at being unable to change.

"Glen's not a violent person, so I don't think you have anything to worry about there. He is, however, very critical of himself. He dissects his every move and if he feels he's made a wrong one, he'll withdraw. He may go quiet on you, start spending more time everywhere else but home. But he also has a taste for the bottle...and somewhat of a roving eye."

I sucked in a breath and felt tears forming that I didn't want to let loose.

"But I have a feeling you know all of this."

I gave a brief nod and lowered my head as a tear rolled down my cheek.

"You'll have to set boundaries, Catherine. What can you accept and where do you draw the line? Make sure he understands those boundaries and hold your ground when he toes the line...because he will. If you don't, you'll keep pushing those boundaries further and further out and then...well, that's when you lose yourself. And no woman with a child can afford to lose *herself*."

"Is there anything I can do to help him? I don't think he'll consider any kind of therapy, or that we could afford it if he did."

"No, he won't do therapy." She began packing makeup into her purse. "Best advice I can give is to set those boundaries, then just love him. I do think you can love a good man through it—to the other side of it—and unlike his father, Glen *is* a good man. But you're going to have to figure out what price you're willing to pay to try, and at what price it becomes too much."

I stood as she zipped her bag and turned toward the door. "Thank you," I said.

"Come talk to me anytime, Catherine. I'm always here. Can you lock up on your way out?"

"Yes, ma'am."

"Love you," she said.

"Love you too."

Two days later, it was Christmas Eve. Jenna slept while I sat curled up on the sofa under a blanket, holding a mug of hot cocoa between my hands. I watched and sipped as Glen laid presents under the Christmas tree.

After placing the last one, he moved to the kitchen and came back with a glass of whiskey. It wasn't the first of the evening, and as he sat next to me with a sigh, I smelled its sweet scent on his breath.

He wrapped an arm around me and pulled me in close. Together, we stared at the glowing Christmas tree, lost in our own thoughts.

A memory surfaced. I was eleven. I'd gone downstairs for a glass of water and caught Daddy stacking presents beneath the tree. I'd figured out the whole Santa thing a couple years prior, but there was something about seeing him in the act that made me cry.

Daddy placed a finger to his lips, a gentle reminder not to wake Bo. Then he smiled, took me by the hand, and led me to the kitchen. Removing the Santa hat from his head, he placed it on mine, then slid the plate of cookies we'd left for Santa across the table, gesturing for me to take one. I did. Then he poured two glasses of milk, sat with me, and handed me another cookie.

I didn't know that five years later, Daddy would die in December, and Christmas would never be the same again.

A tear rolled down my cheek, and I raised my hand to wipe it.

Glen squeezed my shoulder and said, "You okay?"

I nodded. "Yeah. I just miss him—my dad."

"Christmas must be hard for you."

"It's not my favorite," I said.

"Is there anything I can do?"

It felt like a loaded question, even if he didn't intend it to be.

I turned my face to him, noticing his deep blue eyes appeared almost black in the dark room. I wanted to ask him a million questions; to dig into his mind to understand what was happening inside it; to figure out what we needed to do. I couldn't follow Janine's advice and think about boundaries. All I could think was...how could we fix it? How could we make him better, before boundaries even needed to be set? I didn't want boundaries between us. I wanted nothing between us.

But I couldn't form the questions, so I said, "Glen, I need you to try."

He looked down at his drink, understanding exactly what I meant. "I am trying, Cat."

"I lost my dad as a kid and it's something I think will affect me forever." I didn't add that he, too, had an experience with his dad that would likely affect him forever. "I don't want that for Jenna. She deserves two parents; to make the wonderful memories all kids should have. She needs her dad."

He nodded. "I am trying. And I'll keep trying, okay?" He tilted my head up to look me in the eyes.

"Okay."

A few minutes later, he went to the kitchen for a refill. On his way back, he stopped and leaned against the archway to the living room. He brought the glass to his lips, then held his hand out towards me, like he was asking me to dance.

"What?" I asked.

He waved his fingers, beckoning.

I made my way over and he placed his arms around my waist, pulling me in closer. I leaned my head against his chest.

"When was the last time you stared at the stars?" he asked.

I looked up to see his face, and he smiled.

Taking my hand in his, he led me to the back porch. Placing his glass on the railing, he spun me around, so I faced away from him, and pulled me in close. With his arms wrapped tight around my shoulders, crossed in front of my chest, he said, "Look up."

When I did, I saw a magnificent, pitch-black sky with stars so bright they didn't even look real.

God, I've missed this.

Glen swayed from side to side as we stared at the sky, swaying me along with him.

"Are we dancing under the stars?" I asked.

"Mm-hmm."

"But there's no music."

"We make our own music, Cat. Always have, always will."

1985

16

SWEET TEA & TRAGEDY

By January, Jenna regularly slept and ate just as well as before, and it was like we could all *breathe* again. Then, two weeks later, I picked her up from Aunt Kitty's, and she warned Jenna was teething. I was terrified.

Things were just getting back to normal. Since Jenna had stopped screaming around the clock, Glen looked like the weight of the world had lifted from his shoulders. He stopped going to the bar. He talked to her, sang to her, played with her. And Lord, help me, but we couldn't keep our hands off each other.

It made me wonder: Who was that man? Or maybe the better question was, who was the man who, for so long, avoided being left alone in the same room as his daughter? They were like...two different people.

Did this mean when things got hard, he'd slide right back into *that person* again? Or did it mean he'd found his way through to the other side, as Janine said he might?

I didn't know, and it pissed me off that the only answer I could come up with was the one I despised the most: *Only time would tell.*

When school let out for spring break in March, Aunt Kitty called, offering to keep Jenna even on my days off. I was hesitant, but she convinced me that having a bit of time to myself would be a good thing.

Just as we hung up, Glen arrived home from work. It was the same routine as every other day: a low, sing-songy whistle to announce his arrival, a wink, boots off, then padding in socked feet to meet us. Kisses all around.

"Figured we could get burgers or something tonight, if that's all right. I need to shop." I dipped a spoon into a jar of sweet potato baby food and attempted to sneak it into Jenna's mouth. She turned her head, spreading the orange puree from mouth to ear.

"As long as it's not...whatever that is." He bent low to get a look at the label. "Guessing it's not as tasty as your mom's sweet potato casserole?"

"I don't know, actually." Lifting the jar, I decided *what the heck*, and tried a spoonful. "Oh, *God!*"

"Why would you do that?" Glen doubled over in laughter, then straightened himself up and fetched a glass of water.

"It's just sweet potatoes! How could it be so bad?" I chugged the water. "Oh, but it is *so* bad!" I unbuckled Jenna and pulled her from the bouncer. "Mama's so sorry, baby. Never again, okay? *Bleh*, that's going to haunt me in my dreams!"

The phone rang. I took another large gulp of water, then answered it. "Hello?"

"Can I speak with Glen, please?" Her voice was low and gruff, almost a whisper.

"May I tell him who's calling?"

"It's Robin."

"Robin?" I turned to face Glen, who'd gone white as a sheet.

"Yes," she answered.

I lowered the phone, then held it out to Glen. "I think—I think it's your sister."

He stared for a moment, frozen in shock. He'd only mentioned his sister a handful of times. As far as I knew, he hadn't seen or spoken to her since his dad left. It had been three years.

I covered the mouthpiece as best I could with one hand. "Do you want to talk to her?"

He nodded and took the phone. "Robbi?"

Jenna grew fussy, so I moved her to my other hip, bouncing her in place. "Hi," he said.

I could only hear one side of the conversation, and I wondered if I should give him privacy, but the lost look in his eyes told me to stay put.

"I'm good. Yeah, Mom's fine, too." … "Where are you?" … "Still in Chicago? Uh-huh, okay." He paced the kitchen. "No, I haven't spoken to him since—well, since he left." … "That was Catherine, my wife. Yes, I'm married. Crazy, right?" … "You are? Wow, congratulations. Babies are—" … "What do you mean?" … "Robbi, are you okay? Have you taken something?" … "Robbi—" He stopped pacing and stood up straight and tall. The muscles in his jaw twitched as he clenched his mouth tight. "Don't say that. You don't know that. Hey—are you okay?"

His eyes darted to Jenna. Then a second later, there was a loud *pop!* that even I could hear.

Glen jerked the phone away from his ear. "*Shit!*" He raised it to the other ear. "Robbi! Talk to me. Tell me *exactly* where you are...Robin!"

He turned to me, mouth gaping wide, tears streaming down his face, still holding the phone to his ear.

I couldn't wrap my brain around what had just happened.

What was *that?*

"Glen, what—"

He dropped the phone and took off running for the door. "Do *not* hang up that phone!" he yelled on his way out.

Jenna cried, reaching after Glen, who was long gone.

The phone dangled from the cradle, hung on the wall.

I picked it up. "Robin?"

But Robin didn't answer.

⸻ ✦ ⸻

Glen didn't come home until almost 1:00 in the morning. When he entered, still in the socked feet he rushed away in, his eyes were red and puffy, and his hands shook.

"Hey—are you okay?" I asked when I met him at the door.

He walked to the kitchen, picked up the dangling phone, then closed his eyes and placed it back on the cradle. Propping his forearm on the wall, he leaned his head against it.

I moved to where he stood, placing a hand on his shoulder. "What happened?"

He shook his head, still leaning on his arm. "They couldn't trace it."

"What?"

"They couldn't trace the call."

"What does that mean?"

He stood upright and pulled a beer from the fridge. "They don't know where she is. I filed a report, and they sent it to Chicago PD, but they'll never find her. She's gone."

"You don't know that."

"That was a gunshot, Catherine. She's gone."

No, she wouldn't...

But I didn't know Robin. Maybe she *would.*

"Would your dad know where she is? Or...her mom must know. They'll find her."

"They'll still be too late. She's gone." He brought a hand to his head, rubbing his temples, breathing deep to hold back the tears.

"I'm so sorry. Why would she do it?"

He sat at the table and took a long chug of beer. When he set the bottle down, it was half empty. I took the seat next to him and leaned my head on his shoulder.

"She was pregnant," he said. "Her last words were, *I can't be a mother. People like us are not meant to be parents.*"

I gasped. "My God, that's terrible…Why would she say that?"

He took another deep breath. "Because it's true, Cat. Every word she said was true."

For two days, Glen barely left the kitchen as he waited for the phone to ring. He paced, drank, and stared—into his glass, at the ceiling, the floor, out the window. Then, when he grew tired, he laid his head on the table and slept—ten minutes here, fifteen there.

He hadn't mentioned going to Chicago, but I knew it was on his mind. When Mama's pipes broke, he helped. When she needed her car battery replaced, he did it. When her floor melted to the turkey pan, he fixed it. He didn't feel right about himself if he couldn't help, and I knew if anyone could find Robin, it was Glen.

Which is why I packed his bag that morning.

"I'm going to pick up Jenna from Aunt Kitty's," I said. "Do you need anything while I'm out?"

"No," he answered, still staring through the window. "Cat—do you think it would be crazy for me to go up there?"

"No, and I already packed your bag."

He turned to face me. "You did?"

I nodded. "Will you fly or drive?"

"Drive. We don't have money for a ticket. Maybe it'll clear my head."

I nodded again. "When will you go?"

"As soon as I can. I need to let Uncle Rudy know I'll be out from work for a while."

"Tomorrow, okay? You need a good night's rest...and to sober up before making that long drive."

"Cat, I'm fine," he protested.

I gave him that look that said, *I'm the wife and I know best.*

"Fine, tomorrow. Early."

⁕

Neither of us slept much. Every time I closed my eyes, I heard that *pop!* just as loudly as when it happened, and judging by how Glen kept startling awake, he heard it too.

It was incredibly disturbing—and heartbreaking—to witness someone end their life, even over the phone. She was someone's baby, someone's sister—*Glen's* sister. I couldn't even look at Jenna without bursting into tears and I had a sudden, increasing urge to call Bo.

After dropping Jenna at Aunt Kitty's the next day—a quick in and out, so she wouldn't notice anything was wrong—I returned home, sat at the table, and stared at the phone. Glen left around 5:00 in the morning and wouldn't call for several hours yet.

Sitting at that table, a million horrible thoughts rushed through my mind: That *pop!* I'd never forget; Glen, on that long drive; Bo, working at the same metal factory Daddy did; Jenna, sleeping all alone.

Anything could happen to any of them.

I walked over, picked up the phone, and dialed Bo.

"Hello?" It was his girlfriend.

"Hey, Stacey. It's Catherine. Is Bo around?"

"Yeah, hold on."

"Hello?" Bo said.

"Hey, I—uh—just wanted to see how you were doing."

"*Okay?*" His voice was skeptical.

"It's been a while, ya know. That's all."

"Yeah, I guess."

There was an awkward silence I felt I needed to fill.

"Glen's sister died."

"Oh, shit. That sucks. I'm sorry."

I'm sorry? It was probably the first time Bo had said those words in his life.

I knew Stacey was good for him.

"It's been rough. Glen went to Chicago."

I heard Stacey say something in the background.

"Yeah, yeah, okay," Bo said to her. "Look, Stacey's asking if you guys wanna come over for dinner."

I heard her say something more.

"Next weekend," he added.

A dinner invitation? What the hell?

"To your apartment?" I only asked because I'd never seen it.

"Yes, *to our apartment.* It's not a white house on a hill or anything, but it's still suitable for eating in."

"I'll ask Glen, but I don't know if he'll be up for it."

"All right, whatever. I gotta go."

"Okay. Bye, Bo."

When Glen called that night to let me know he made it, I breathed a massive sigh of relief. For three days after, I called into work because I couldn't bear the thought of being away when he called again.

Standing in the shower after putting Jenna down for the night, I watched the water swirl round the drain, attempting to empty my brain of all thought. Then I heard something. I shut off the water, listened, and heard it again.

Shit! The phone!

I wrapped myself up in a towel and flung open the bathroom door. Running through the house, I slid on wet feet when turning into the kitchen to answer it.

"Hello?"

"Cat, it's me. They found her."

I wasn't sure what to say. Should I ask where? How?

"She shot herself in the chest. She had roommates, but when the cops arrived, she was alone. They had come, grabbed their drugs and money, and left."

"They saw her, and didn't call the police?"

"Cops think they were afraid to report it. Thought they'd be suspects or go to jail for the drugs. They took off."

"Poor Robin." I wiped the tears from my face. "Are you okay? I mean, I know you're not okay, but...are you?"

He breathed deep, in and out. "I don't know."

I asked the only other questions I could muster. "What happens now? When will you be home?"

"Her mom is having her cremated. She doesn't want a service. So, I'll leave tomorrow."

"Okay," I whispered.

"Are *you* okay?" he asked.

"Me? I'm—I don't know either. I just want you home."

"Well, I'll see you tomorrow. I'm going to get some sleep now."

"Okay. I love you."

"I love you too."

He made it home around 9:00. When he walked through the door, he dropped his bag, and hugged me...then hugged me some more. He didn't want food, just a shower and his own bed.

Lying next to him, so glad to have him home, I wondered what he'd been through since he left. I thought about how hard it must've been, and I cried when I wondered how we were supposed to just *live our lives* after going through something of such magnitude. It felt like we were forever changed.

He slept till 10:00 the next morning, kissed Jenna, then went to work. I called the store to let them know I'd be back the next day, too.

Back to business as usual.

But it wasn't the same. When Glen came home, he went straight to bed. The next day, too. The day after that, he didn't come home until early morning. He showered, then left for work again.

"He needs time, Catherine," Janine said when I dared to discuss it.

"He's been through hell and back, Catherine," Mama said, when I brought it up to her.

So, I waited...and waited.

"It's been three months. What do I do?" I asked Janine, one afternoon in June.

She poured a glass of sweet tea and brought it over. "That depends. What is it that bothers you most?"

"Not knowing where he is, when he'll be home, or if he's okay." The sound of that gunshot still haunted me in the dark, and I worried Glen would be next; that he'd do something that couldn't be undone.

"Do you remember the conversation we had about boundaries?"

I nodded.

"I think it's time you set some."

When Glen came home a couple days later, I was ready.

"Hey," I said from the table as he opened a bottle of beer.

He nodded, then took a drink.

"Can we talk?" I asked.

He pulled out the chair across from me and sat.

"I'm worried about you, Glen."

He sighed and looked out the window.

"I think we need to talk to somebody. We could start with our family doctor and see where he thinks we should go from there."

He stared at me without blinking.

"Don't you think we should?"

"We? Or just me, Cat?"

"However you want to do it, together or separate."

"No," he answered, firmly.

"Glen, I'm scared for you."

He took another drink. "Did I ever try to tell you how to feel about your dad's death?"

"No—of course not."

"Then, do you think you can maybe return the favor?" His voice wasn't angry or accusatory at all. He was asking for space to grieve, in his own way.

"I'm not trying to tell you how to feel. I would—I would never. But I am worried."

"I'll be fine." He stood and tossed the empty bottle into the trash. Then he grabbed a full one from the fridge and moved toward the front door.

"Glen—"

He opened the door.

"Glen!"

He turned to face me.

"You can't stay out all night anymore. It makes me worry too much."

"I think I can do what I want, Cat."

The words, the tone—lit a fire inside of me. One I'd felt with Bo, Mama, and Liza a million times, but never with Glen. Then I remembered Janine saying he would resist any boundaries I put in place—at least at first.

I took a deep breath and said, "No, you can't. You have a family. You don't get to choose not to come home."

For a moment, anger flashed within his eyes, then it turned into something else. Something softer.

"Okay," he said with his hand still on the doorknob.

"Okay?"

"Yeah." He walked out the door, closing it behind him.

Slowly, I began to see tiny glimpses of the Glen I loved returning to me. He still grieved, but he no longer ran away to do it out of sight. It wasn't a perfect life we were living, but he was home, and that was all I could ask for. My twenty-first birthday passed without much celebration, but for Jenna's first birthday in August, we had a small party at Mama's. Of course, Aunt Kitty brought cake.

That was the day Bo announced Stacey was pregnant. The look of surprise on Mama's face had us all on edge—unsure how to respond—but then she looked at Stacey and smiled. From there, it was all *congratulations*, hugs, and tears—mostly Aunt Kitty's.

Mama made a proclamation instituting a standing Sunday night dinner at her house. To which Bo and Uncle Charlie groaned, Aunt Kitty clapped with joy, Stacey beamed, and I looked to Glen—who stared at the toes of his boots, lost in his own mind.

1986

17

EGGSHELLS & CIGARETTES

I couldn't shake the feeling I was walking on eggshells again, only it was Glen I tried not to crush, rather than Mama. Mostly, he was fine. Not great, but fine. Every so often, though, he'd start drinking more, conversing less, and eventually he'd disappear.

When he came home again, I'd remind him it was unacceptable, and he'd nod, apologize, and correct himself. It was like he needed that reminder...like it pulled him back from the edge of a cliff.

However, a week before the first anniversary of Robin's death, he began spiraling—fast. I saw it in the way he looked at Jenna; in the way he *didn't* look at me; in his refusal to join us for Sunday night dinner; in the drinking; the short fuse; the not coming home.

Twice that week, I asked Janine for advice. Both times, she said, "Anniversaries are hard, Catherine. Just do your best."

What does that even mean?

I was so tired.

I was tired of managing our house and family like a single parent; of slinking past him in the hallway as he avoided my eyes, my touch; of worrying; of the up-and-down rollercoaster ride of Glen's emotions.

And I was tired of the guilt I felt for *being* tired of his emotions.

Jenna was nineteen months old. She'd started walking, talking in her own little way, and learned new, exciting, wonderful things every day. But he was missing it. Even when he was there and it was happening right before his eyes, he was missing it, and it broke my heart.

⸺◆⸺

In April, Stacey and Bo became parents. They had a baby boy and named him Philip, after our dad. My brother was almost in tears when he told us and for the first time, I realized that Bo really missed him, too.

Bo was different after that. He took to being a daddy like a duck takes to water. He doted on that little boy…anticipated his every need. I—and everyone around us, I think—could see it made Glen uncomfortable.

Philip fascinated Jenna. She thought he was her own personal baby doll. She kicked and screamed whenever it was time to leave him, wanting to bring him home with us, like he was a toy that belonged only to her.

I couldn't get enough of him. His eyes were a pale brown, almost gold—just like his mama's—and he had a tiny freckle on one cheek, right where a dimple might someday form. He was a sleepy baby who didn't have a care in the world as far as who held him, so long as he was being held. For me, it was love at first sight, and it made my heart ache.

"You're a natural, ya know," Stacey said as I snuggled him close.

"Well, I've had lots of practice." I smiled and nodded toward Jenna, who played on the floor at my feet.

"No, it's not just that," Stacey replied. "Were you around a lot of babies growing up?"

"Mama is an only child. No cousins for us."

"Ah, that's right. Well, I don't know what it is, but you look like you're made for this. It's, uh—taken a bit of getting used to, for me."

"Well, hopefully he'll continue to be his sweet self and not put you through what this one put us through." I nodded again toward Jenna. "She was a handful once the colic set in."

"God, I hope so," Stacey said with a laugh. "I don't think I could do it!"

I smiled, thinking back on how hard it was, but also acknowledging that it was worth it, and I'd do it all over again—in a heartbeat.

"Are you two planning to have another?" Stacey asked.

I looked down at the small, warm bundle in my arms, then gave a subtle shake of my head. "No, I don't think so." I'd come to terms with the idea that Jenna would be my only child—even with being just twenty-two years old and knowing I still had so much love to give—but something about saying it out loud ripped my heart in two.

"She's a lucky little girl, then. Won't have to fight anyone for attention!" Stacey stood from the sofa and moved toward the kitchen. "I'm going to see if Bo's got the grill fired up yet. Be right back."

A few minutes later, Glen walked through the back door and into the living room. He saw me rocking baby Philip, with Jenna playing on the carpet next to me, and stopped in his tracks. Then he lowered his head and lifted a hand, rubbing his temples with two fingers.

He looked up with glossy eyes and crossed the room. Dropping to his knees, he took one of my hands in his. "I'm sorry, Cat," he said, with a shake of his head. "I'm so sorry."

"What are you sorry for?"

He looked back down at Philip and said, "You deserve so much more. And I'm sorry."

"Glen—"

He stood, squeezed my hand, then turned toward the kitchen again.

"I don't need more, Glen. I just need *you*...and *her*. That's all I need."

When he faced me again, there was no denying the tears in his eyes. He opened his mouth like he had something to say, then closed it again, and walked away.

Glen didn't come home for nearly a week after that. I was so sick with worry, it felt like I didn't sleep a wink the whole time he was gone. But when he finally walked through the door, it took two seconds for all that worry to transform into pure rage.

"Where the hell have you been?" I screamed as I tossed a pot into the sink.

He didn't answer.

"Glen!"

He still didn't answer.

"You can't just show up here after being gone almost a week, then say nothing. Where *were* you? Why didn't you call?"

He pulled a pack of cigarettes from his pocket, walked out the back door, and lit one on the porch.

I followed him out, slamming the screen door behind me. "You smoke now?"

He nodded.

I stood there for a moment, with no idea what to say. "Well, hell, give me one!"

He cocked his head when he looked at me, trying to figure out if I was serious. Then, he pulled a cigarette halfway out of the pack and held it out for me to take.

I slid it from its package with two fingers and placed it between my lips. He flicked the lighter, and I leaned in. I took a long drag, then seated myself on the top step to take another.

He looked at me, confused.

"Daddy smoked. I may have bummed a few," I explained.

His lips turned upward in a tiny, nearly imperceptible sign of amusement as he sat on the step next to me.

"Are you going to speak?" I asked him.

He twirled the cigarette between his fingers. "I stayed with a friend for a few days."

"A friend?" My brain flooded with potential images of this *friend*. All of them had boobs.

"A guy from work."

I let that sink in, then said, "Yeah, okay. Sure," not even trying to hide what I suspected.

"Cat, his name is Leo, and he's married. They have three kids. He lets me stay in the room over his garage sometimes."

"Why? Why do you do that? Is it so hard to come home to your own family? I don't understand!"

"I don't understand it either, Catherine! If I did, I'd be fixed, wouldn't I? I don't—I just—Cat, I'm really messed up." He dropped his head and held it between his hands. "I think I need help," he said, without looking up.

Jesus Christ. Took him long enough.

I placed a hand on his back, rubbing a circle around his shoulder blade. "Okay. Then we'll find help."

"Who?"

"I'll call Mama. She'll know what to do."

<hr>

The next week, Glen started therapy. He seemed optimistic about it, and I was happy, because he was once again coming home.

It lasted two months.

"What do you mean, you're not going anymore?" I asked.

"It's just not—it's not helping," he said. "When does the help come? When do I feel better?"

Having never been to therapy myself, I didn't have an answer. "I don't know, but you can't get better if you don't go."

He sighed and sat on the sofa. "Maybe I won't get better. Maybe I can't be fixed, Cat. I don't think this is going to work."

Something about the way he said it threw up a red flag. "*What* isn't going to work?"

He looked up at me for what felt like the longest moment of my life. "I think maybe I should move out."

In an instant, it was like all the oxygen had gone up in flames. I moved to the armchair and sat. "You can't do that."

"I think it would be for the best—for all of us."

"No—you can't. You can't just leave! How would that make anything better? She needs you!" I gestured wildly toward Jenna's room, where she slept, oblivious to her parents discussing a breakup of her family before she had even seen her second birthday. "She needs her daddy! I—I needed *my* daddy—and I need *you*. You can't—you can't leave us like he left me! Glen I—" The room spun, and I felt the world growing smaller and smaller.

Where had all the oxygen gone?

"Shh, Cat—Look at me," he said. "Look at me."

I refocused my eyes and saw him down on one knee, gripping both my hands in his. I didn't know how he even got there. But I looked at him, and I burst into tears.

He leaned forward, and I buried my face in his shoulder. "You can't leave me. You can't leave *her*. She needs her daddy...she—she needs her daddy," I mumbled, sobbing into his neck.

"Shh—okay. Okay." He held me tighter.

"Swear to me, Glen. Swear you'll never leave us."

"I swear. Catherine, I swear to God. I'll never leave you. I won't."

⸻ ◆ ⸻

Jenna's birthday passed. Halloween, Thanksgiving, and Christmas too. Through it all, I was terrified out of my mind. I woke every day, wondering if it were the day everything would all go to hell. If it were the day he would leave and never come back.

It wasn't anything Glen did that made me feel that way. He was there. He was attentive. He was Jenna's favorite playmate. Somehow, he'd dug deep and found what he needed to power through, but I couldn't trust it.

I couldn't allow myself to believe it was real. I lived in a state of paralyzing anxiety and constant hyper-awareness, just waiting for the other shoe to drop.

Glen could sense it. "I'm right here, Cat," he would say, whenever he saw it written across my face. "I'm right here." Again and again, he offered a reassurance I never felt. Until one day when he took my face in his hands and said, "Until you tell me to go, with crystal-clear words that could mean nothing else, I'm not going anywhere."

And that was it. That's what it took for it to sink in. I needed not just reassurance, but a sense of being in control. Once I had that, it finally clicked.

He wouldn't leave unless I told him to.

I don't know why I believed it, when it could have been an empty promise, just as the others could have been, but I did. I let my guard down, opening myself up to him all over again.

And it was the most wonderful three months of my life.

1987-1995

18

LIPSTICK & PORCH SWINGS

With the second anniversary of Robin's passing, it all fell apart again. It was the same sad story, just a different day.

Two months later, Mama asked, "What time do you want to get together for Mother's Day?" through the phone.

"Maybe 1:00?"

"I'll let Kitty know. Bo, Stacey, and the kids will be here by then, too."

Stacey had her second baby the week before, making the two boys almost exactly one year apart, just like Bo and me.

"What do you mean *by then?*" I asked.

"He lost his job and fell behind on rent." Mama sighed. "They're staying here for a while."

"That's some pretty shitty timing for them. With a newborn?"

"I'd say getting laid off is pretty shitty, no matter the timing."

Jenna called for me from the other room.

"I have to go, Mama. See you Sunday."

"Yeah, see you then."

I hung up as Jenna entered the kitchen, hugging her blonde-haired, blue-eyed Pillow People. She sat at my feet to play.

She'd be three years old in a few months, and it was astonishing how magical she really was. She was smart, possessing an innate ability to sense the feelings of others. When I was happy or excited, she fed off that energy, and she was happy and excited too. When I was sad, she absorbed my sadness as her own, without even knowing why. She'd curl up under a blanket and watch cartoons for hours or disappear to her room and flip through picture books, alone on the floor.

Someday, I knew she'd have to harness that superpower; to learn to distinguish which feelings were hers and which were free-floating, environmental emotions that weren't hers to bear. Until then, all I could do was keep a handle on my own feelings, to not cast a burden her little heart didn't deserve. It was exhausting and terrifying. I was so afraid I wouldn't get it right.

I reached down and stroked her hair. "You want to go to the park today, love?"

"Yes!" she answered, jumping up from the floor. "Daddy too?"

My heart sank. "Daddy's still on his work trip, but we can get ice cream!"

Daddy wasn't on a work trip. It was simply the story I told her each time he disappeared.

She bounced up and down, her face lighting up with a smile—*his smile*.

"Let's go then. First, we have to potty, okay?"

She nodded and ran toward the bathroom.

As I stood to follow, I searched the kitchen and living room for any sign of him and found nothing. No pair of old dirty boots, no cigarette cartons, no empty beer cans in sight. It was like he no longer existed.

But I knew he was out there somewhere.

My heart could still feel him.

⋅•◦•⋅

On Sunday we went to Mama's for Mother's Day lunch. After Aunt Kitty and Uncle Charlie left, Jenna played with Philip, Bo and Stacey snuck upstairs for far too long, and Mama and I sat at the table sipping coffee.

"Is everything all right?" Mama asked with hands clasped around her mug.

I pulled my eyes from the window to meet hers. "Yeah, fine."

She cleared her throat and took a sip. "I'm disappointed Glen's not here for Mother's Day."

I looked down into my mug. "Me too."

"What are you going to do?"

"About what?"

"About...*him*. It's not fair for you to live like this. You're young and still have so much life to live."

"Jenna is my life, Mama."

"Yes, but it's not fair to her either, is it? She misses him. Whenever she stops asking about him, he shows back up, and it starts all over again."

I sighed because she was right, and Jenna didn't deserve it. When he *was* home, though, he was so great with her, at first. I saw how he looked at her, and it was clear he was head over heels for that little girl, but then...his eyes would change, and he'd start drifting away from us again.

Taking a drink of my coffee, I said, "I know it's not fair to her, but there's not much I can do about it."

"You could leave him."

She said it so bluntly, so matter of fact, that it took me by surprise. "No, I couldn't. Even if I could, where would we go?"

"Here, of course."

"You have a full house, and if I do anything, it'll be something I can do on my own. I'm grown and I have a child. It's my job to take care of us, Mama, not yours."

She nodded. "Had a feeling it would come down to that. You're a lot like me, in that sense. But you saw where that got me, once upon a time."

I took another drink as the memories came rushing back. It was then I realized that not only could I never put that burden on Mama, but I would rather be anywhere else than back in her house. There were too many memories there—of Daddy, of the crazy Mama he left behind, of falling madly in love with Glen...

And I missed him—or the old him I sometimes saw—and if there was a chance that version of him could ever return to me for good, I'd hope, pray, and wait. For Jenna's sake, and my own.

"Well, you'll figure it out," Mama said as she stood. "You always do."

A week later, I sat on the porch swing watching the neighborhood bicycle gang do wheelies in the cul-de-sac, spotlit by a single streetlight.

I gulped down the last swig of wine in my glass and returned to the kitchen for a refill. Grabbing the bottle, I stepped back onto the porch as headlights beamed down the street and a familiar sound echoed.

My heart skipped a beat as he pulled into the driveway.

Act cool, Catherine.

I re-took my seat, placed the bottle on the porch at my feet, and set the swing in motion. Cutting the engine, he sat in the truck for a moment, then stepped out and made his way toward me.

"Cat," he said, climbing the steps.

"Glen," I replied, with a sip from my glass.

He gave the doorknob a turn.

"Mother's Day was last week," I said, staring at the sky.

"Happy Mother's Day, Cat."

"You should've been here. Jenna misses you."

He brought his hand to his forehead, rubbing between his eyes.

"I miss you too," I added.

Ignoring me, he reached for the doorknob again.

"Can you come sit? Please?" I held out my wine glass as incentive.

Tears sprung to my eyes as he went inside, and as I wiped them away with my free hand, I found comfort in the rocking of the swing.

The door opened again, and Glen appeared, holding a beer. He sat next to me, brought it to his lips, and took a long chug. My eyes shifted to his mouth and neck, and I watched the muscles work there as he swallowed it down.

God, I missed him. And I was so stupid for it.

"Where'd you go this time?" I asked, not beating around the bush.

He took another drink, offering no answer.

"Well, okay, then. Good talk." I stood and walked toward the door. "I'm going to bed. You can take the sofa."

⸺⬥⸺

He'd been home two weeks. It took a few days, but eventually he relaxed, became more talkative, and even joined us on our after-dinner walks around the neighborhood. It was hard to go on like everything was fine, but he was *there,* slowly getting back to himself again. So, though it was hard, I found it even harder to ruin the good by bringing up the bad.

It was my day off, which meant it was also laundry day. As I placed clothes inside the barrel, I dropped a few. When I picked them up, a hot pink scrunchie fell to the floor.

I took a deep breath and continued filling the washer.

When I was done, I retrieved the scrunchie and walked to our bathroom. Opening the cabinet under the sink, I pulled out the tube of lipstick I'd hidden there the previous week—the day I drove Glen's truck to the post office because my car needed gas.

Staring at the scrunchie in one hand and the lipstick in the other, I knew what I *should* feel, but something didn't seem right. I pulled the top off the lipstick and froze in place at what I saw: It hadn't been used.

I placed two fingers inside the scrunchie and stretched it wide, gauging the resistance. It was new, too.

Jenna appeared, still in pajamas. "Park, Mama?" she asked.

I shoved the items into my pocket and stood. "I've got a better idea. How about we go see Grandma Janine?"

"What do you think it means?" I asked Janine.

"You're sure they're new?"

"The lipstick definitely is, and I know what a well-loved scrunchie looks like. Maybe it's not new, but it hasn't been used much, if at all."

Jenna played in the back yard while we kept watch from the porch.

"Hmm," Janine said, pulling her sunglasses from the top of her head back to her eyes.

"Look, Janine, I'm not completely obtuse, okay? I knew when I married him something like this could happen. I had plenty of warning from—well, everyone."

She turned her face to me but didn't speak.

"But I married him, anyway. I loved him, and I still do. But this—this doesn't make any sense."

Shaking her head, she said, "No, it doesn't. Unless—" She pulled her sunglasses back to the top of her head and looked directly at me.

"What?"

"Maybe he bought them, and he wanted you to find them."

"Why would he do that?"

"I don't know, Catherine, but if that's what he did, then the most logical assumption is that he's trying to push you away."

Suddenly, I felt dizzy.

I won't leave unless you tell me to go, he'd said.

"Does that seem like something he would do? *Could do?*" I couldn't fathom it. It was so underhanded, so scheming.

"Catherine, you need to talk to your husband."

Janine offered to keep Jenna that night, so I let her. Then I waited for Glen on the porch. When he arrived, he climbed the steps, sat next to me, and kissed my cheek.

"I think we need to talk," I said, pulling the lipstick and scrunchie from my pocket.

He gave them a look, then set his eyes on the house across the street.

"Whose are these, Glen?"

He didn't speak. Seemingly holding his breath, the vein in his neck twitched as his blood raced.

"Did you buy them yourself?"

His face jerked to mine and it was full of surprise, or maybe disbelief. "Why would I buy them, Cat?"

"I don't know. You tell me." I took his hand in mine, lacing our fingers together.

We sat in silence for a long while before I said, "Glen, talk to me. Why did you want me to find these things?"

His shoulders dropped. "I thought if you found them, you'd—" He didn't finish the sentence.

"What? Leave? Kick you out? File for divorce?"

At the word *divorce*, his panicked eyes found mine.

"Is that what you want? A divorce?" I asked.

"No, it's not what I *want*."

"Then what is this about? What *do* you want?"

He didn't answer.

"Look, I know you didn't have a typical upbringing—with how your dad lived and all. So, I get that maybe you're not looking for *typical* either. I think maybe you want more."

His eyes searched mine, trying to understand.

"You've been through so much, Glen. We both have. But I love you, and I'm not going anywhere."

He stared off into the distance again.

"You don't have to push me away. I understand you have a life away from us and that somehow, it makes you happy. I'll never ask what you do when you're not here, but I want you here more, and I want you to be *happy* when you are. I want *us* to be happy when we're together."

He stood, shaking his head. Pulling his keys from his pocket, he walked back to his truck and drove away.

⸺ ⬦ ⸺

Two days later, I was at the end of the sort of day that leaves you mentally and physically drained. My feet were on fire, my hair a disheveled heap on top of my head, and I'd sweated through my uniform—twice. I was ready to go home and see Jenna. Janine had kept her at our house that day while hers was being repainted, and I was grateful for not having the additional stop to make on the way home.

I hadn't seen Glen since I gave him the go-ahead to do whatever he damn well pleased, and I couldn't make sense of it. If it was about a *roving eye*, as Janine had put it, shouldn't he be happy? Wouldn't any man like that be happy, being given the green light by their wife to see whoever he wanted to see? Be with whoever he wanted to be with?

I still couldn't believe I'd said it—that I outright gave him permission. It happened fast, with no thought. It wasn't surprising, though, because it was how I'd always felt. I told Liza so in *high school*.

I would rather have him in my life in that unconventional way than to not have him at all, and Jenna deserved two parents—two *happy* parents. If that was what it took to give her a happy father, then so be it. It wasn't like it hadn't been done before—I lived through the 70s, for crying out loud. I was young, but I had eyes and ears and watched TV. I saw how some people lived.

And it was just *sex*.

"I'm out of here, Chris. Don't forget I have tomorrow off." My stomach growled, reminding me I never took my lunch break.

"Enjoy your day off," he said, punching my timecard for me.

Outside, I was greeted by June summer air so stiff, you'd think you may need a butcher knife to cut through to the other side. My tennis shoes *squelched* on the semi-solid, newly paved blacktop as I crossed the parking lot.

As I dug through my purse for keys, my fingers landed on something hard and sticky—a discarded lollipop. *Trash* and *purse* were synonymous to Jenna, apparently. I tossed it back into the bag, located the keys to unlock my door, and climbed into the driver's seat.

"Jesus!" If it was hot outside, it was an inferno inside that car. I started the engine, rolled down the windows, and cranked up the air conditioning, knowing it would only blow hot air the whole way home.

Peeling my legs from the vinyl seat, I settled in, turned up the radio, and drove homeward. I'd worked six days straight and ached to spend time with my baby girl. We'd have a simple dinner, then go for our evening walk, have a bath, and I might even have enough energy for bedtime stories, knowing I didn't have to work in the morning and do it all over again.

As I pulled into the neighborhood, the intro of Whitesnake's "Here I Go Again" played. I cranked up the radio as the drumbeat hit. Pounding my hands on the wheel like I was the one playing the drums, I stopped when I saw it wasn't Janine's car in the driveway, but Glen's truck. She must have left when he got there.

When I parked, I saw them.

"What the *hell?*"

No. No, no, no.

That was *not* Ally Monroe, sitting on *my* swing, with one leg draped over my husband's lap, and the other dangling off the side and wrapped around his. I gave my head a shake. Surely, I was hallucinating from damn near working myself to death on an empty stomach.

It wasn't real.

He would never bring that woman to my house and put her on the front porch for the world to see.

It couldn't be real.

When he flicked his cigarette and stared me dead in the eyes through the windshield, I knew it was real, and I also knew that it was over. It was *all* over.

19

ZINNIAS & NUTJOBS

He knew she bullied me; that she was why I lost all my friends and became an outcast. He knew what she did after that day in the doctor's office, the lies she spread about being with him after we got together, and that she continued trying to be with him afterward. *He knew.*

And he knew she was someone I could never turn a blind eye to.

Clear as day, in my mind, I heard: *Guess I'm letting him push me away, after all.*

A loud *thunk* at the back of the car pulled my attention long enough to see the neighbor boy retrieving a basketball. He grinned through the window, then returned to his mama. Her eyes bounced between my car and my porch, as she whispered to another neighbor who had left the comfort of her own porch to join her.

Who the hell did Ally think she was? Sitting there with him...*like she belonged there.*

"Oh, God—Jenna!" I threw open the car door and stepped out with it still running and that song still blasting. Climbing the steps, I couldn't put any of the words in my head into a sentence worthy of what I was feeling. They stared but made no effort to separate. Ally just sat there, twirling her hair, smacking her bubble gum.

From the car, that song screamed at me to *make up my mind...to stop wasting my time!* I made it to the door as Glen snuffed out his cigarette in my potted plant.

Jenna was watching TV in the living room. I picked her up and hugged her tight, with tears streaming down both cheeks.

God, what happened in my house? What did she hear? What did she see?

"Help Mama pack a bag. We're gonna go see GiGi."

In her room, I said, "Only two toys, love. Can you get your toothbrush?"

She nodded and ran for the bathroom while I packed her duffel bag, placed her blanket on top, and zipped it shut.

"Toothbrush, Mama." She handed it over, and I shoved it into a side pocket.

"Now let's pack my bag." I led her down the hallway to our room. When finished packing, I said, "That's everything. You ready?"

She gave a nod. I held both bags in one hand and took her hand with the other as we walked out onto the porch.

Son of a bitch hadn't even budged.

The anger—*pure rage*—inside me was one I'd never felt. Even with everything I'd been through, none of it compared to *this*: the anger I felt when he'd deliberately made a fool of me and didn't care who knew it. When, of all the women he could have chosen, he chose *her*.

And still, the words wouldn't come.

I dropped Jenna's hand, plucked the cigarette butt out of my zinnias, tossed it at his feet, and scooped up the pot. "Keep your damn cigarettes out of my plants," is all I managed to say, as I nudged Jenna toward the car with my knee.

I looked up at them once as we left, and they still hadn't moved.

Still didn't give a damn.

⸻⦿⸻

I flipped the rearview mirror up so Jenna couldn't see my face and drove to Mama's house. Once there, I parked and pulled Jenna from her seat.

Grabbing her bag and my plant, I kicked the door closed as Mama appeared on the porch with a mixing bowl in her hands.

"I didn't know y'all were comin'," she said. "You staying for dinner?"

"She is. I'm not," I answered, as we climbed the steps.

Mama set the bowl on a table. "Are you okay?"

"I'm fine. Can Jenna stay for a while?"

"Of course, but—what happened?"

"I can't get into it now. I have to go." I sat the bag and plant on the porch.

"Come inside. I'll make coffee." She picked up the bowl and moved toward the door.

"I can't stay."

"Sure, you can. I have a king-sized bed and only sleep on a third of it. Plenty of room."

I hadn't told her a thing, but still, she knew.

"*No*, Mama."

Her eyes were full of questions, and it killed me, but I couldn't stay there. Not with Bo there, while that woman was on my porch, when I knew the whole town would discuss what happened at every social function for months. I needed to get away; to disappear.

"I don't understand," Mama said.

"Take her, please. I'll be back for her, but I don't know when. I need to find somewhere we can start over, Mama. *Please.*" My attempt to stall the tears had failed. My insides were all twisted up, and I swear I could feel every bit of physical pain it brought.

"I can't let you go like this. Come inside, child. We'll figure something out, but you can't go anywhere like this." Mama took my hand, attempting to pull me inside.

"Mama, *listen* to me! I'll figure it out on my own. Just take care of her while I do it...*please!*"

I felt a squeeze around my leg and looked down. Jenna clung to me, looking up with worry—or confusion—on her face, and I couldn't take it.

I bent down and wrapped her in my arms. Then I pulled back to see her. "You're going to stay with GiGi for a while, okay, baby? Your cousins are here! It'll be like a sleepover every night. Doesn't that sound fun?"

She looked as devastated as I felt.

"Mama loves you, and I'll be back real soon, okay?" A tear ran down my face, landing near her purple jelly shoe. Pulling her in for one final, long hug, I stood and faced Mama again. "I'll call you."

"Catherine—" she said, but I was already gone.

I drove to the bank, closed out our joint account, and left with a white envelope containing $817.00. Pulling into the gas station, I filled the tank. That was $10.80—gone.

Starting the car, I drove to the parking lot exit, stopped, and stared.

Where could I go?

A car honked behind me, so I turned onto Main Street, still trying to figure out where I'd go and what I'd do when I got there—all while crying the saddest tears of my life, and picturing Jenna's sweet face.

I missed her so much already.

When I came to the highway, I pulled onto the shoulder. One sign pointed north and the other south, toward Mobile/Pensacola. Like something from a dream, I remembered what she looked like the first time we took her to the beach: sun-kissed shoulders and nose, sand in her hair, ice cream trailing down her chin.

I entered the highway and traveled south.

The sun was setting behind puffy, white clouds when I arrived in Pensacola. Exiting the highway, I took the bridge to the beach. The gulf came into view as the sun hit the horizon, making the ripples on the emerald-green water glitter.

Climbing out of the car, I made my way to the parking lot's edge. When I stepped onto the powdery, white sand, it felt like the world shifted and everyone in it came untethered and floated off into space.

Now, it was just me.

I sat at the water's edge until the sky grew black and the tide came in. Listening to the waves crash on the shore, all the other noises of the world ceased to exist. I knew I should still be fuming, but all I felt was a hole in my heart where Jenna should be.

I shouldn't have left her. She should be here with me.

But I couldn't have brought her. I had to find a job, a place to live, day care or a babysitter. I couldn't do that with her there, and I knew it. So, I stood, dusted the sand from my legs, looked to the sky, and prayed to whoever could hear me:

Help me bring my girl home, to a new place where no one knows us, and we can start something new. Where we can be happy, just the two of us. It's all we need.

I walked back to the car and headed inland in search of a cheap hotel.

The next morning, I opted for a stale bagel and warm cream cheese from the hotel's breakfast bar, rather than eating elsewhere. The money wouldn't last forever, and I needed to find a job before I'd seen the last of it.

"Excuse me," I said to the desk clerk. "Do you sell newspapers?"

"Right around the corner," she answered.

"Thank you."

I located the machine and paid a quarter for a paper. Returning to my seat in the breakfast room, I scanned classifieds, making note of anything I could be qualified for. Then, I set out to find a job.

Five hours later, exhausted from running all over Pensacola searching for addresses that meant nothing to me, I had been told repeatedly that the positions were filled. College students out for summer break had taken every job. And I was nearly out of gas.

I pulled into a gas station, spent another $11.00 I couldn't afford, then drove back to the hotel. "Is there a pay phone?" I asked the clerk. "I didn't see one outside."

"No pay phone, but you're welcome to use the phone in your room."

"For long-distance calls?"

"The long-distance fees and surcharges will be added to your bill, but yes."

That wasn't something I could afford.

"Okay, thanks. I'll find a pay phone tomorrow."

"Okay then. Enjoy your evening!"

Entering my room, which smelled of stale salt water and deep-fried fish, I had an intense realization: *It would never work.*

I had no job, no home, and no Jenna.

What was I thinking?

I kicked off my shoes and curled up under the covers. Then, I cried myself to sleep, praying that somehow a miracle would find me, and I could make it on my own.

Even after two weeks, I still had no job. I was down to $518, even though all I'd paid for was the hotel, gas, a load at the laundry mat, and the occasional call to Mama and Jenna. I ate one meal a day—the free one at the hotel—and my clothes looked no different on me than they did on the hanger. Staring at myself in the mirror, I thought, *I wouldn't hire this bum either.*

Snap out of it, Catherine, and go find a damn job.

I grabbed my bag and headed to the last option available to me: the grocery store, which placed an ad in the morning paper for a cashier. If that didn't work, I'd have to move to the next town and start over. Or worse, admit defeat and head back to Asher. The grocery store had to work.

Entering the store, I spotted the customer service desk to the left. I straightened my shirt and approached the counter.

"How can I help you this morning?" the man asked with a smile. He was short, middle-aged, and had a bald spot right on the top of his head. Giant glasses covered most of his face, but beneath them were kind eyes.

"I saw an ad for a cashier. I'd like to apply," I answered.

"Do you have experience?"

"Yes, sir. I worked at IGA for six years. I was store manager there for almost four."

"Store manager? And you're applying for cashier?"

"Yes, sir. I'll take anything."

He looked up from his paperwork and said, "Fill this out." Reaching for a clipboard, he placed an application on top, then handed me a pen.

"Thank you. Um—do you know when the person you hire could start?"

"Right away."

"Okay, thank you."

I completed the form using the hotel address and phone number. When I returned the clipboard, he gave it a once-over.

"Can you start tomorrow?"

"Yes!" I yelled, without intending to. "Today even."

"Tomorrow's fine. What size shirt will you need?"

"Medium, please." I looked down at the one I was currently swimming in. "Actually, a small would work."

"Let me see what I have." He moved into a back room, reappearing a moment later. "It's a medium. I don't have small."

"No problem. Thank you."

"Your name is Catherine?"

"Yes, sir."

"Your experience at IGA is impressive. You've done nearly everything, it looks like."

"Yes, sir."

"We should have a management position available in the fall. If everything goes well, you should put in for it."

I felt myself smile for the first time in weeks. "Thank you—uh, sir."

"I'm Walter," he said.

"Thank you, again. You don't know what this means to me."

"See you tomorrow, Catherine."

Suddenly, I felt it: a minuscule ember of hope.

A week later, I stood in front of the breakroom bulletin board, scanning flyers and sticky notes. I worked a day and a half to pay for every night at the hotel: My time there was limited. I needed a roommate.

"What'cha lookin' for?" Tina asked as she entered the room, fluffing her bottle-blonde hair. She was younger—probably eighteen or nineteen—and oozed immaturity. She had a weird vibe I couldn't quite figure out, so I'd kept my distance.

"I need to find a roommate. I'm getting tired of living in a hotel."

"Hotels are hella expensive!" She took a candy bar, placing no cash into the jar we were supposed to use on the honor system. "My boyfriend just moved out, if you're interested."

"Seriously?" I took a step closer, then stopped when she took a step back.

"You got any pets?" she asked.

"No pets."

"Kids?"

"Uh, yes—"

"Sorry, no kids. I can't do kids."

"No, she's with my mom for now. I don't have any kids *with* me."

"But she will be, eventually?"

"Well, yeah—"

"Nope. No kids." She tossed her wrapper in the trash and turned toward the door.

"Wait! I hear you. No kids."

She looked me up and down. "How *old* are you?"

"Twenty-three. Why?"

"Yeah, you look it. That's okay though, you can buy the beer. What time do you get off?"

"At 6:00."

"Me too. Give me a ride home and I'll show you the place."

"Okay, yeah."

"Still—no kids."

"Got it."

⟶ ◦ ⟵

Tina's apartment was on the wrong side of the tracks, literally. It was downright scary after dark. However, there was a spare room, a refrigerator and stove, and it was way cheaper than the hotel.

"Do you cook?" she asked.

"Yeah, I cook."

"Well, then you're hired."

"I'm what?"

"As the apartment chef! You're hired. I don't cook."

"I can move in?"

"Yup."

I jumped up and down a little and wanted to hug her to death, but she looked terrified by my excitement, so I refrained. "Thank you! How long is the lease?"

"There's about nine months left, I guess. We'll take the ex off and put you on. I do this about every six months, so the landlady's used to it."

"You do what every six months?"

"Cycle through boyfriends or roommates. You know how it goes."

I'd been in the same house with the same person for five years, and definitely didn't *know how it goes*, but that wasn't what she wanted to hear. So, I said, "Yeah, I do."

"Guess I'll see you at work tomorrow, then. Oh, hey! Can you pick me up?"

"It's kind of in the opposite direction, but sure."

"Great. 9:30?"

"See you at 9:30."

I left feeling both ecstatic and full of dread because I knew it was a huge mistake. She was crazy; a total nutjob. I apparently had six months before a new boyfriend replaced me, and she didn't cook or have her own car. I could never bring Jenna there, so that meant six months to get that promotion, save all I could, find my own place, and settle in with enough money left to drive back to Asher, get Jenna, drive back, and hire childcare.

It was impossible. And six months without Jenna, on top of how long I'd already been without her?

I thought I might just die.

20

NAKED WOMEN & FEVER-DREAMS

Tina and I worked the same shifts, so we could ride together. She was a bit of a dingbat, was totally flakey, and had *really* sketchy friends...but she also took night classes and seemed to have some semblance of ambition. There could be worse roommates.

Rolling over in bed, I pulled the covers over my face.

It was Jenna's birthday. I worked in an hour, and all I wanted was to stay under those blankets and never emerge, but I knew I couldn't.

With a groan, I tossed the blankets aside and headed to work. Stopping at the pay phone outside the store, I pulled coins from my pocket and called Mama.

"Hello?"

"Hi, Mama. Is she awake?"

"Yes." Mama called for Jenna. "Here she is."

"Hello?" Jenna said in a sleepy voice.

"Hi, baby. Happy birthday!"

"Mama!"

"Have you had a good birthday so far? Did GiGi make you pancakes?"

"She's cooking. They have chocolate chips."

"I love chocolate chip pancakes! I bet Aunt Kitty will make you a chocolate cake, too!"

"Yup."

It was quiet for a moment, and I wasn't sure what to say next. I wanted to say I'd be home to eat that cake with her, that I had a gigantic gift for her...that I'd *be there*.

My heart pounded as I cried. God, how I wished I could go just one day without tears.

"Well, you're going to have the *best* day," I said. "I wish I could be there, but I'm working so hard to get us a nice home so you can come to the beach. Won't that be fun?"

"Yeah."

"Pancakes are ready!" I heard Mama say.

"You better go eat those pancakes before they get cold."

"Okay, bye."

"Bye, baby. I love you!"

"Love you."

A second later, Mama was back on the line. "How are things?"

"I'm working, and no longer living in a hotel, so better."

"Good. Do you know how much longer? She misses you."

"I miss her too."

So much.

Checking my watch, I said, "I'm going to be late. I have to go," avoiding her other question.

"Okay, but I still think you should come home."

"I know, and you're probably right, but I have to try. Mama, I'm trying."

"All right. Call if you need anything."

"I will. Love you."

"Love you too."

September and October passed, the promotion never came, and I started to worry. Then, worry turned to despair, and from there it got worse.

I missed Jenna so much I physically felt sick. My stomach ached most of the day, every day. I'd had a headache for a month, and nothing helped. The weight I'd hoped to regain hadn't come, and my savings hadn't grown like I needed it to. I wanted to crawl into my tiny closet and never emerge again, but I had places to be.

"You'll have to find a ride to work. I got squeezed in for an appointment, so I called in." I grabbed my bag and headed toward the door.

"Fine. I'll call in too," Tina replied, not looking up from the latest copy of the *National Enquirer*, spread across her lap.

"What do you mean you'll call in too?"

"I don't feel like workin' anyway. I'll blame it on cramps or somethin'."

Tina had called in a lot lately, and I hadn't seen her heading to school much either. It would be surprising if our arrangement lasted three months, let alone six. The thought made my head spin.

<hr>

The lady across from me was older than Mama and Aunt Kitty together, and I wasn't convinced she'd heard me correctly. So, I asked again, "What do you mean I don't qualify?"

"You don't qualify. I'm sorry," she answered.

"How can I not qualify?"

"There are criteria to qualify for assistance, and you don't meet them."

"I work for minimum wage. I have a daughter. Did you list her as a dependent?" I leaned forward, peeking at the paperwork.

"Mrs. Lewis, she doesn't live with you. You're also married, so your husband's income must be considered. You have a roommate who helps with expenses, and you have a job. You don't qualify."

"Let me get this straight: You *can't* count my daughter as a dependent, because she doesn't live with me yet, but you *can* count my husband's income, even though he doesn't live with me either?"

"I know it's confusing." She leaned forward, clasped her hands, and lowered her voice. "I didn't say this—but get a divorce, get custody, and lose the roommate. Then, come back and see me."

"But that's crazy! How do I file for divorce if I have no money? How do I bring her here if I can't feed her or pay for childcare? How do I afford rent without a roommate? It doesn't make sense!"

"I'm sorry, Mrs. Lewis. I am."

I left the office in tears. Then I went to work even though I called in, because any hope of help had been crushed. I was alone, and I would continue to be alone. There was no help. No light at the end of the tunnel, as far as the eye could see.

◦

Approaching the apartment, I heard music and laughter, and caught the sweet scent of marijuana. The door was ajar and pushed right open.

"*What the hell?*" I exclaimed.

Tina sat on the lap of a shirtless man, and across from her, another woman straddled a second shirtless man. As I recovered from *that* shock, a naked woman walked from Tina's room to the living room, carrying a joint in one hand and a beer in the other.

I spun around, closing my eyes. "Tina!"

"Oh, Catherine, relax. It's only a little fun. You want a drink?"

"No! Don't you have class?" I asked, with my back still turned.

"I'm done with school. Or rather, school is done with me," she said.

I turned to face her, but regretted it, and turned again. "You dropped out?"

"Got kicked out. Lost my financial aid because my grades weren't so hot, and when I couldn't make payment, they gave me the boot. Good riddance, really. I hated that place."

I moved toward my room, stopping in the doorway. "Will you be at work tomorrow? Walter's asking."

"Tell Walter he can go to hell." Her reply was met by laughter from her friends.

Shutting the door, I placed my back against it and slid to the floor. My chest tightened. Then the sobs came. I cried for hours, and the whole time, it was Jenna's face I saw.

No promotion, no assistance, and soon to be no roommate and no apartment. I've failed you, baby girl...and I'm so, so sorry.

When Tina moved out, I applied for assistance again, only to be told it still wasn't enough. Less than a week later, a banging on the apartment door startled me from sleep. Wrapping myself in the blanket, I answered it.

"Mrs. Gilmore, hi," I said, squinting against the sun.

"Is Tina available?"

"She isn't here."

"Then I'll leave these with you."

I took the stack of papers and saw *EVICTION NOTICE* typed across the top. "Eviction?"

"You're two months behind on rent. You need to vacate by end of week."

"We paid our rent, Mrs. Gilmore." I pulled the blanket tighter, shielding myself from the cold November wind sweeping through the breezeway.

"I'm sorry, but you haven't." She turned to leave.

"I don't understand! I gave Tina my half, and she said she paid it! Mrs. Gilmore, please!"

Turning again, she walked back to me. "Let this be a lesson, okay? Choose your friends—your roommates—wisely. Be careful who you trust. You have through Sunday." She gave a pat on my shoulder, then walked away.

Sunday night, I gave one last look at the place that was supposed to be the first building block of a new life. Jenna would never have lived there, but the arrangement was supposed to help me start moving in the right direction. Somehow, though, I let it slip through my fingers.

I was a grown woman. I worked. I was responsible.

It shouldn't be so damn hard.

Throwing my bag into the backseat, I left that old apartment behind. As I drove back to the hotel, I was heartbroken and panic-stricken, because I was going backwards—one giant step at a time. And with no savings and no promotion, I couldn't stay in the hotel long. Soon, I'd have to admit I'd failed…Soon, I'd have to go home.

I had enough money to pay for the hotel room for five days. When I checked out, I had nowhere to go.

"Are you hiring?" I asked the clerk. "I'm usually off work by 6:00, but I could take an earlier shift. I could work till 11:00, or later. Maybe I could work in exchange for a room?"

"I'm sorry, no. We minimize during the off-season. We'll have openings in March." She handed me my change with a smile.

Then the college kids would poach all the jobs, just like before.

"Yeah, okay. Thanks." I shoved the money into my pocket and headed to my car.

As I drove, I looked for a church, hoping someone could point me to a shelter, but all the parking lots were empty. Continuing to drive as the sun set, I eventually ended up at the beach. I parked and walked out to sit on the sand.

I didn't know what to do.

The tightness I'd felt in my chest for days had only grown worse, and this time when it struck, I coughed. Then I coughed again, and I couldn't make it stop. I straightened my back and tried taking deep breaths, but each time I did, the coughing returned. A stiff breeze came off the water, my hair flew into my face, and a chill ran through me, feeling like it cut right down to the bones.

Pulling my jacket tight, I moved back to the car. I started the engine, turned up the heater, and listened to music until the world grew dark. When my eyes began to close, I locked the doors, turned off the car, and climbed into the back seat.

———◆———

I slept in my car at the beach for weeks, showering at a truck stop near the highway. The cough lingered, and when I showed up to work after Thanksgiving, I burned with fever.

"You look terrible!" Walter said upon seeing me.

"I have a cold, but I'm fine."

"Clock out and go home."

What home?

"I can work, really. I'm fine."

Please don't make me leave. I need money and a place to stay warm.

He placed a hand on my forehead. "You're burning up. Get some rest. Don't come back until that fever's gone."

"Walter—"

The look on his face let me know I wouldn't win.

"Okay." I grabbed my things and left.

The only place I could think of going was the library, so I turned in its direction. When I got there, I watched as mothers led children into the building. It made me sad, but it was the babies that really got to me. When moms pulled tiny infants from car seats, rested them on their chests, and covered them with warm blankets, I cried in big, uneven sobs. With the sobbing came the coughing, and shooting pains in my chest, ribs, and back.

I couldn't go in. They'd take one look at me, grab their kids, and run for the hills. I knew, because it's what I would do. Starting the car, I returned to the beach, where I locked the doors, and fell into a fever-dreamed sleep. I woke once after dark, turned the car on for heat, then dozed off once more.

The next time I came to, I'd yet to open my eyes but had a feeling I wasn't alone; that I was being watched. Frozen still from fear, I lifted one eyelid enough to see without making it obvious—then I lost it.

I screamed like I'd never screamed before, coughed, then screamed some more.

I was going to die. And no one would even know where to find me.

He hunched over the window, hands cupped on either side of his face, trying to see inside. He wore gloves with no fingers, a dark hood over his head, and had missing teeth. The beard on his face hung to his chest, with God-knows-what clinging to it, and all I could do was scream.

Then, he *banged*. He pounded on the roof of the car, the window, the back windshield. When I looked up at his face again, he grinned.

Holy shit, holy shit!

Scrambling into the front seat, I shoved the shifter into drive and pressed the gas pedal to the floor, crying and coughing, and thinking, *maybe I should just let him kill me.*

I drove in circles for hours. Every stop light made me feel like a sitting duck. When the sun rose, I was low on gas and falling asleep at the wheel. Turning toward work, I parked and watched as the first employees arrived.

There was Pete...and Margo. Jenny. Hector.

I knew them. They were safe. I was safe.

I let my eyes close, and slept.

⸻❖⸻

The next time I woke, it was *by* the banging, and I screamed and flailed like the man was inside the car and I was fighting for my life.

"Catherine!" he screamed.

How did he know my name?

I tumbled into the front seat, ready to make a second escape.

"Catherine!" he said again.

I turned toward him, eyes pinched closed, afraid to open them.

"Catherine, it's Walter! Look at me."

I opened my eyes, and the relief I felt was instant. Then, it was like I'd been ripped apart at the seams and all my insides had fallen out. I collapsed onto the steering wheel, cried, and screamed.

"Open the door." Walter tapped on the window.

Don't tap. Don't bang. Please.

"Open it, Catherine, or I'll call the police."

I looked up and saw his worried face, which was nothing like the man who'd grinned at me in the dark. I unlocked the door.

Walter yanked it wide open, leaned in, and wrapped both arms around my shoulders, which brought on the hysterics all over again.

"What happened? Are you okay?"

When I didn't answer, he asked again.

"I'm okay," I said.

"You're not hurt?"

"No." Another fit of coughing took hold, and I doubled over in pain.

"You need a doctor."

"Don't have money for a doctor."

"Why are you sleeping in your car?" He looked genuinely concerned, and it was the first time anyone had looked at me like they gave a damn since I moved to that place.

"Had nowhere else to go," I whispered.

He squatted and took my hand. "You don't have any money at all?"

I shook my head *no*.

He stood again, pulled two twenties from his wallet, and held it out for me to take. "It's not a lot, but it's enough to get home."

"Home?" I was unsure of what he meant.

"Yes, home, *with your kid*." He gave a nod, encouraging me to take it.

But I didn't need encouragement. I'd never been so ready, so relieved in my life. "Thank you," I said, accepting the money.

"If you start feeling too bad, find a hospital. You don't look too good."

I nodded.

"It's been nice knowing you, Catherine," he said. Then he shut the door.

21

LITTLE BOATS & BEER CANS

I shoved the car in park, climbed out, and ran toward the porch. When I hit the top step, Mama opened the door.

"Where is she?" I tried to shove past her to get inside.

"Oh no, child." She pushed me back.

"Mama—" The coughing came on quickly and violently and *I couldn't breathe.*

"You need a doctor. Get in the car."

"Mama...I need...to see her!" I struggled to get the words out, gasping for air.

"Not like that, you don't. Let's go. I'll drive."

"Mama, *please!*"

"Catherine, you're sick. You look like hell and you're gonna scare her to death...or get her sick, too. *Get in the car.*"

I took one backwards step down the stairs.

Mama nodded. "I'll be right there. Go on."

I continued down the stairs and entered the car, keeping my eyes on the door—hoping for just a *glimpse* of her.

Mama exited the house with her purse, climbed into the driver's seat, and took me to the hospital without a word.

Hours later, I stared at pastel-striped wallpaper as the doctor provided diagnoses of pneumonia, dehydration, gastritis, and malnutrition. At the word *malnutrition,* Mama inhaled sharply and turned my face to hers.

"What hell have you put yourself through, Catherine?" Her chin quivered as she fought to hold back tears.

I turned back to the wallpaper as the doctor offered a treatment plan.

"Thank you, doctor," Mama said.

He left the room, handing the chart to a nurse in the hall.

"I want to see her, Mama. I came all this way to—" I sat up straight when the coughing started again.

"Shh—come on, rest." Mama pushed me back onto the pillow. "We'll bust you out of here soon enough."

The door burst open, and Liza appeared. "Oh my *God*," she said when she saw me.

"Liza? How—" I didn't finish my sentence before she cut me off.

"Bo called. What the hell happened to you?" she asked.

The door swung open again, and a nurse entered. "Laurel, you know we only allow one visitor at a time." She nodded in exasperation toward Liza.

"Yeah, yeah. I'll step out for a bit." Mama squeezed my hand, then left.

"Are you okay?" Liza asked, as she took Mama's seat.

I nodded.

"What happened?"

"I can't get into it all right now, Liza. I'm so tired."

She grabbed a tissue from the bedside table and dabbed her eyes. "I always knew that man would kill you, but I didn't think he'd *literally* kill you."

"It's not his fault. Not directly, anyway. I have myself to blame for this."

She looked at me hard, trying to piece together what I've left unsaid.

"Why are you here, Liza? It's been—years."

She lowered her head, then looked back up at me. "I'm here because I'm your best friend. No number of years or arguments will ever end that, and you know it."

I nodded, because she was right. No matter how furious I may be at Liza, no matter the reason, she was still *my* Liza. And I couldn't be mad at her for trying to protect me, because she was right then too. She somehow knew Glen and I would never work out and she tried to tell me.

Why don't I ever listen?

"Where've you been?" I asked, leaning my head back against the pillow and closing my eyes.

"Oh, ya know, here and there. Pensacola at first, then Savannah, Atlanta, Birmingham...basically mooching off every friend and family member I've ever had." She took my hand and gave it a squeeze. "But I'm not going anywhere, ever again. It's you and me now...Bonnie and Clyde."

⸺◈⸺

Between the coughing, nurses checking vitals and changing IV bags, breathing treatments, meals I couldn't eat, and doctor follow-ups, I got little sleep.

"I've sent Bo to Kitty's. I'll get your room ready and makeup his for Jenna, since you're contagious," Mama said.

"Thank you."

"For what?" She waved her hand like it was no big deal.

"For not sending Jenna to Aunt Kitty's, too. I know you want to."

She sighed, picked up my hand, and gave it a squeeze. "I'd send myself to Kitty's if I could. This is *bad*. You get that, right? I'm afraid to think—" She dropped her gaze for a moment, then looked back up at me. "You were *blue*, Catherine. Do you know what that means?"

"That it's bad?"

She gave a half-hearted laugh. "Let's just say I'm glad you came home when you did."

"Me too, Mama."

⸺◈⸺

After two nights in the hospital, Mama and Liza helped me climb the porch steps.

"Is she here?" I asked between breaths.

"She's at Kitty's till we get you settled," Mama answered.

Inside, they guided me to the sofa. I focused on catching my breath while Mama went upstairs, returning with a transfer belt.

"I have to wear that?"

"Yup." She fastened the belt around my waist. "Ready?"

I nodded, and she and Liza helped me up and over to the stairs.

"You put a chair at the top, Mama? Seriously?"

"You'll be thankful for that chair in a minute, you'll see. Use the handrail and lead with your right foot."

We took each step nice and slow. Liza was to my left and Mama stood behind me as I climbed the stairs by putting my right foot on top, then bringing the left up to meet it. Six stairs up, I paused, and Mama gripped the belt tighter.

"You okay?" she asked.

"Fine. Just need a breath."

When I'd had a moment, Mama said, "All right, let's go. We're halfway there."

"Like Bon Jovi," Liza said.

"What?" Mama was confused.

"Nothing, Mama," I said with a wheeze.

Once I'd made it to my room and settled into bed, Mama turned the channel dial on the TV, searching for something suitable. She stopped on *The Price Is Right*. "You're all set. I'll make soup. Chicken noodle?"

"Yeah, but easy on the chicken...and the noodles," I answered.

"So I'm assuming carrots and celery are out?"

"Please."

"Chicken *broth* coming right up." She turned toward the door, then paused. "After you've eaten and taken a nap, I'll have Kitty bring Jenna home, okay?"

I nodded and smiled. "Okay."

Liza stayed a few minutes longer, then left me to nap. When she closed the door behind her, I pulled the blanket to my chin and stuffed my arms beneath it, feeling like I'd never be warm again. I shuddered and pulled the blanket to my nose.

Would Jenna even remember me? It had been six months...and she was only three.

I felt a warm tear slide down my frozen face, wiped it away, and watched a little blue-haired old lady spin the Big Wheel.

When Mama entered again, she carried soup in one hand, and held Jenna's little fingers with the other. For a moment, it felt like a dream.

"Jenna?" I asked in a voice that cracked.

"Mama!" She wiggled free from my mother, ran toward the bed, and threw her arms over my legs.

"Hi, baby! I've sure missed you!" Placing a hand upon her back, I pulled her closer to my face. I wanted to look at her, smell her, hug her, and never let her go.

"Not too close," Mama warned as she set the bowl of soup on the nightstand.

"Can I hug her at least?" There was a tinge of disrespect in the question, which I knew Mama didn't deserve.

"Keep your head turned." She pointed a finger, letting me know she was serious.

"Come here and give Mama a hug," I said.

Jenna gave that smile I'd missed so much, then climbed onto the bed, laying herself over me and squeezing my neck tight.

I thought my heart would explode.

I fought so hard to not let her see me cry. My chest jerked in a jagged, unnatural rhythm as I fought to hold the emotions in...and struggled for air. I kissed Jenna's hair, then nodded to Mama, who lifted her from the bed and set her back on her own two feet. Then the coughing began, and I turned my head away. "Take her...Mama, take her."

Mama grasped Jenna's hand again, then said to her, "Okay, we'll come back and visit a bit more before bedtime. Let's take a bath."

"With the little boats?" Jenna asked.

"Yes, of course, with the boats!" Mama answered.

Jenna followed Mama through the door. I heard water running in the bathroom and the two of them chatting, though I couldn't make out their words. All I knew was, she was there, and I was there, and I swore to God I'd never, ever be without her again.

<hr>

"Why do I still feel like I've been bulldozed?" I asked as Mama poured me a glass of juice.

"Because you were damn near dead less than two weeks ago, Catherine. Give it time."

I sighed because I didn't want to give it time. I wanted to go on a walk with my daughter, take her to the park, push her in a swing. I wanted to be the one giving her baths and cooking her meals. "You should tell Bo and Stacey to come home. Aunt Kitty and Uncle Charlie must be losing their minds."

"You wouldn't get much rest with everyone here. We'll give it a few more days."

"Mama—"

"Hmm?"

"You're not hoping they'll realize they need to find their own place and never end up coming back here, are ya?" I grinned to let her know I was onto her.

"They found jobs months ago! There's no reason to stay here now, aside from it's just *easier* to have someone do all your cleanin' and cookin' and child rearin' for ya, than it is to do it yourself!" Mama emphasized every verb by throwing her hands into the air. Then she flopped into a chair.

I smiled and sipped my orange juice. "I'll be out of your hair too, soon as I can."

"That's not what I meant. You have a reason to be here. You need to rest until you're back on your feet. And where would you go?"

I set the juice on the table and inspected the tiny bubbles clinging to the inside of the glass. "I think there's only one place I can go."

"You don't mean—" Mama looked at me like I belonged in a straitjacket.

"Where else? Clearly, I can't make it on my own. Not yet, anyway."

"You cannot go back to that man."

"I'm not going back to *him*. I'm going back to a home with electricity, running water, and food. A home that Jenna knows. A place we can be together and safe. It won't be forever, Mama. I'll get my old job back and when the time is right, we'll move on."

"I can't believe what I'm hearing."

"I don't have a lot of options, do I?"

"You could stay *here*."

"Yeah, but with Bo here, it wouldn't last long. Besides, I need to do it on my own."

"But if you're going back to him, you're not doing it on your own, are you?"

Ouch.

"I'll work, save money, and when I'm able to, we'll leave. It's the same thing I tried for in Pensacola, only it's here...with Jenna. Don't you see?"

"I suppose," she said with a shake of her head. "I can't decide if you have more courage and smarts than I've ever had, or if you're seriously lacking...on both counts."

"Well, I guess we'll find out."

⁌❍⁍

After I'd weaseled my way back into a job at IGA and opened a new checking account—only in my name—I told Liza my plan. She yelled, like she always did, but eventually came to see my side of things.

"Well, like you said, it won't be forever. I'll get my own place, and you can live with me. It's about time I moved out of my parents' house anyway, don't you think?" she asked with a grin.

"Liza, you don't even like kids. Why on Earth would you offer to live with one?"

"I never said I don't like kids!"

"Yes, you did."

"No, I said I didn't *want* kids. I'm totally cool with being the fun aunt. That's perfect for me, actually."

"It won't feel so perfect when you realize she lives there, and you can't just send her home when you're tired of her."

She waved her hand to shoo away the thought. "Nah, it'll be *fine*," she said. "So, when are you doing it? Moving back?"

"I'm going to drive by there on my way home."

"And what? Ask his permission?"

"It's not about permission. It's about...ground rules."

"Oh, yeah, because he's been so good at respecting those, right?"

She had a point, of course, but I knew it would all be different. As much as I loved him, I *hated* him, and it was no longer about trying to keep him focused, happy, and present. All my concern for his well-being went out the window the day he brought Ally Monroe to my house.

All that was left was me and Jenna, and it was all I would ever need.

———◆———

After leaving Liza's, I drove to our neighborhood. Turning the corner onto our street, I saw his truck and pulled into the driveway next to it. Taking a deep breath, I climbed out, gently closed the door, then tiptoed up the steps. One peek through the window on the door, and the hair on my arms stood on end. He was *right there.*

I entered quickly, before I lost the nerve.

He sat sprawled across the sofa, surrounded by piles of clothes, empty beer cans, old TV dinner trays, and fast-food trash. When he looked at me, his eyes grew wide. "Catherine," he said. "You're back?"

I nodded.

He stared for a moment, then looked down at his hands.

"Glen—" I said, but he didn't answer. I moved to stand between him and the TV.

He drank from a near-empty bottle of beer and stared me dead in the eyes, without blinking.

"We need to talk," I said.

He turned off the TV.

"I'm bringing Jenna home. Tonight."

"Here?"

"Yes, here. This is her home."

"Cat, I don't think that's a good idea."

"Why not?"

"Because—you *left.*"

"And that was *my fault?*" I asked, but he didn't answer. So, I took a deep breath and refocused. "Look—I'll cook, clean, do the shopping, and take care of Jenna. We'll be roommates. Nothing more. You can continue doing whatever you want with whoever you want, but I have a couple of stipulations."

"Stipulations?"

"When you're here, you sleep on the sofa. And you will never bring anyone to this house again, *ever*. You'll also find your women in the next town over, or the next county, even. No one from Asher. I have to live here and raise a daughter here, Glen."

He stood and moved to the kitchen, pulled another beer from the refrigerator, then fell back onto the sofa. "Okay."

⋯⋯◆⋯⋯

When Mama brought Jenna home, Glen was gone. He stayed long enough to clean up the trash and wrangle his dirty clothes into the hamper, then he left. He didn't ask questions or make demands. He walked softly, eyes cast down, determined.

Determined to do what?

"Mama, come play!" Jenna took my hand and pulled me to her bedroom, which still looked the same as it did the day we left. Her bedding was still crumpled in such a way that I could see where she placed her hands to push the blankets off when she woke that day.

My eyes filled with tears, which quickly coursed down my cheeks.

It was all such a waste of time.

She ran to her toy chest and started digging. Then, she held a naked Barbie doll with matted hair up in the air, in triumph. "Here you go." She held it out for me to take.

"Thank you. I think she needs clothes and a hairbrush. Do you have those?"

She turned back to the chest and continued to dig.

What a miracle she is.

She was the product of two people who were completely unafraid—of anything. We had each other, and that's all we needed. She was the living embodiment of everything we once were; everything that was good.

How did it all go so wrong?

I heard the front door close, so I made my way to the living room as Jenna continued searching through her toys. Glen was in the kitchen, emptying grocery bags onto the table.

"You went to the store?" I asked, puzzled.

He nodded.

Eggs, bread, fruit, lunch meat, carrots, cereal, milk, juice...and more.

"Does she still like these?" He held a package of strawberry wafers up for me to see.

"She does, but—I planned to shop in the morning."

He didn't respond as he set to putting things away. I picked up the milk and eggs and placed them in the refrigerator. We moved around each other like some sort of dance, each of us knowing the exact next step to take to avoid coming too close to the other.

It was a dance that was so different from any we'd danced before. It was *charged*, in a completely new way, and it made me sad.

When finished, he flattened the paper bags, then placed them under the sink. He looked at me for a moment, as if he had something to say, but no words came. Then, he grabbed his keys from the counter, and he was gone.

22

EPIC LOVE & PLASTIC REINDEER

The next morning, Glen called.

"Can we talk?" he asked.

I glanced over at Jenna eating breakfast at the table. "No," I answered.

"Catherine, please. I owe you an explanation."

"Only if I want one."

"Cat—"

I wondered, *what sort of explanation could he possibly give?*

Pure curiosity got the better of me. "Fine. Come by at noon. I'll take Jenna to Mama's."

"Okay. Thank you."

I hung up without a reply.

He arrived five minutes late and found me on the porch, wrapped in a blanket, watching the neighbors across the street. The parents were putting up last-minute Christmas decorations as the kids rode tricycles in the driveway. It was so perfect, it made my heart hurt.

Glen climbed the steps and gestured to the empty end of the swing. "Can I sit?"

"You hung the swing," I said, thinking that what I'd really like to do with that swing was *burn it.*

"Christmas is in four days, and I have nothing to put under the tree." I gestured to the neighbors as they worked. "Or a tree," I added, speaking aloud to myself, more than to him.

"I'll pick one up."

I pulled the blanket tighter around my shoulders. "Why are you here?"

"Because we need to talk."

"So, talk."

He was quiet for a moment, then said, "I'm sorry, Cat."

I pulled my eyes from the plastic reindeer the neighbors were erecting to see him reach for me. I pulled my hand away and folded both together in my lap. "You're *sorry?*"

"I am. But it's not what you think—not what I made you to believe."

"I don't *think* anything. I *know* you brought *her* here, to my house, and sat her on my swing. I gave you all the leeway you could have ever asked for Glen, but you—"

He leaned forward, placed his elbows on his knees, and stared at the toes of his boots.

"Why did it have to be Ally?"

"Because it was the only way I could set you free," he whispered, without hesitation.

"What does that even mean?"

He took a deep breath, then said, "Catherine, I never knew things would be like this. I didn't know that having a baby would—pull me apart. If I had known, I would've never done it."

I gasped and dug my fingernails into the back of my hand, restraining myself from knocking the man smooth out. "It's a little late to be having second thoughts about a baby, Glen."

"That's what I'm saying. There were no second thoughts. None. I wanted it just as much as you did. I just didn't know—there was no way I *could've* known—everything that would happen after. It's all related to my dad somehow, Cat. And Robin. I don't understand it entirely, but I understand enough to know that it is."

"So, okay, you didn't know you had *daddy issues*—"

"Catherine—"

"What? That's what this is, right? I'm tired of dancing around it, Glen. Your emotions, your issues...they're not mine to bear or protect anymore. I can't be responsible for everything that you're feeling anymore. I can't. I won't."

He nodded. "I never meant for you to be the one to bear them in the first place, Cat."

"Well, when you love someone, that's what you do. But I can't do it anymore. I can't...*love* you anymore, Glen. It almost killed me. I almost *died* in Pensacola. Do you get that?"

He looked at me with such shock on his face that the old me would've felt guilty for phrasing it the way I did, but this new me? The new me *didn't care*. I was tired of hiding it all from him; of always putting his fragile state ahead of my own.

"What happened in Pensacola?"

I focused my eyes back on the family across the street. "What happened with Ally Monroe?"

"Nothing happened with Ally."

I laughed so loud, it took even me by surprise. "You don't expect me to believe that?"

"No, I don't, but it's the truth. I brought her here because I knew it was the only way you would ever leave. I couldn't leave *you*, Cat. I saw what that would do to you the day I dared to even mention it. You had to choose it for yourself."

I scoffed as I stood from the swing and pulled the blanket tighter. "You wanted so badly to be rid of me that you staged the whole thing? Whatever that was? It was a—a what? A ruse?"

"Not because I wanted to be rid of you. Never." He leaned his head into his hand, then ran that hand down his face. "Because I wanted to rid you of—me."

I stood still for a moment, absorbing what it all meant. "God, you're even more screwed up than I could have ever imagined. And you know what really bothers me? That I didn't see or feel it coming. I was blindsided by some idiotic plan you hatched to—to—"

He looked up at me then. "So, you believe me? It's the truth, Cat. There have been no other women. You believe me, right?"

I shook my head. "It doesn't matter if I believe you. You win. I'm done. Just...keep the lights on and food on the table, and I'll never ask for anything more. As soon as I'm able, we'll be out of your hair and you can...drown yourself at the bottom of a bottle, for all I care."

———◆———

I communicated via the refrigerator—posting bills that needed to be paid, work schedules, babysitter arrangements, lists of chores that needed doing, weekly dinner menus.

To my surprise, he responded. He left cash or checks on the counter for the bills and made tiny "G's" next to the days I worked that didn't have an "M", "J", "K", or "L" next to it. Meaning, he was home to watch Jenna when Mama, Janine, Aunt Kitty, or Liza couldn't. It didn't happen often, but when it did, he was there.

He crossed out each chore as he completed them, and he placed checkmarks on the dinner menu as a way of letting me know what days he would be home. Over time, I started leaving notes, asking him to pick up milk or new swim goggles for Jenna. He fulfilled every request.

It wasn't an ideal life, but it was easy. We kept our distance. He spent time with Jenna when he felt he could, and I was freed from the constant worrying and shouldering of his demons. And I think he was free, too—no longer consumed by expectations he could never meet.

We carried on that way for two years before the heaviness lifted. Then, we became comfortable sitting in the same room again. I read novels or tended to my plants while he strummed an acoustic guitar—a hobby he picked up somewhere around the one-year mark.

I knew never to expect him to be around in March—particularly during the week of Robin's passing—and made sure I could handle everything on my own during those times.

And in a strange twist of fate I never saw coming, something else happened: We became friends.

We started laughing together again. It was all very surreal, but also so very comfortable. There were no expectations of romance or sex. There were no arguments over the past. We'd moved on; shifted into something new. It reminded me of when Glen told me in high school that his dad had two families. He'd said, "It was a weird, messed up arrangement, but it worked for them." In a way, we had found an arrangement that worked for us, too.

The townsfolk chattered, of course—always curious about what went on behind closed doors at the Lewis house. But Glen kept his promise. If there were ever any other women, he found them outside of Asher. It didn't stop the rumors, but it made them easier to bear.

Six more years went by in a flash. I was too busy to even notice them slipping away. I worked, went to secretarial school, started a new job at the library, managed our home, and raised Jenna. Glen worked, found some sort of therapy in playing in a garage band, got a handle on the drinking, and gave Jenna as much of a daddy as he could. It wasn't until Jenna met a new friend at school that I realized yet another change was on the horizon.

Michelle was cute as a button, and too bright for her age. They were eleven, playing Nintendo and snacking on Fruit Roll-Ups, when Michelle noticed the pile of blankets folded on the end of the sofa.

"Who sleeps there?" she asked.

"My dad," Jenna replied as she jerked her arms to jump over some turtle-looking thing in *Super Mario Bros.*

"That's weird. Married people sleep together in the same bed."

"Huh?" Jenna asked as she hit something and shrunk to tiny Mario.

"Married people sleep *together*."

"Well, not all of them, I guess," Jenna said.

"Do you even know what being married *means?* It means they have sex."

My heart skipped a beat, and I felt my face flush. I rinsed the bowl I'd just washed and placed it on the drying rack as I listened.

"Eww, gross!" Jenna shrieked. "I don't want to think about that—*eww!*"

That made me chuckle.

"They all do it. How do you think *you* got here?" Michelle said. "Well, they *should*. Are they even married if they don't have sex?"

At that, I clicked off the TV, and asked them to go ride bikes.

That day opened a whole can of worms for Jenna. She had questions. It started with the obvious: *Why does Daddy sleep on the couch? Why does he work so much? Why does he leave for so long?*

Then, they got complicated: *Why don't you ever go on dates? Why don't you ever hug or kiss? Do you love him? Does he love you? Does he love me?* It was that last one that prompted a conversation with Glen.

"Jenna's starting to ask a lot of questions," I said one evening while she was at Michelle's.

"What kind of questions?" He hit play on a cassette he'd loaded into the stereo.

"She's starting to notice we're not a *typical* family."

He glanced toward me, then cocked his head.

"She wants to know why you're only sometimes here...why you sleep on the couch. She asked why we don't go on dates or show affection—that sort of thing."

"Oh—" He sat in the chair and leaned back, placing both palms on his thighs. "What did you say?"

"I explained things away as best I could, but she'll keep asking. I can make excuses for us all day, but she's too smart. She'll eventually see right through them."

He nodded. "So, what do we do?"

I'd been thinking about it since the day I overheard that conversation between Jenna and Michelle. I'd gone back and forth over what the best plan of action would be, but the bottom line was that the whole *roommate* arrangement was supposed to be temporary. It was meant to last only until I could take care of us myself. I had saved enough—started making enough—years ago, and he was still there.

What confused everything was how easily it *worked*; how easily we became *friends*. We were comfortable together in our new roles. He came and went as he pleased, and I never had to worry about a thing. Jenna had her daddy. Even if he was only a part-time one, she still *had* him, and that was important to me. I couldn't rob her of that if things were fine how they were. Now, though, Jenna was getting older. Someday, she'd have relationships of her own, and she needed to know what that should look like.

"Do you still feel the same way about—being a dad? It's been a while since we've talked about it, so—I don't know where your head's at these days."

He sat up straight, then leaned forward on his knees. "This—what we've been doing—works because I keep my distance, Cat. I know myself well enough to know that I can't get too close. I can't—risk getting too close."

"What do you think will happen? Because you think you can't be a dad to her, but you're *doing* it. You're here. You spend time with her. She knows you. She loves you. You're literally *being* her dad by tricking your brain into thinking you're not. It's...bizarre."

"Maybe so, but it's like—I'm a babysitter. Babysitters are supposed to be fun, kind, and caring. They're not around enough—they don't get *close* enough—to damage. Parents have such intimate access to their kids. It's so easy for them to screw 'em up, and I don't want to hurt her, Cat."

"But you love her. Babysitters don't always love the kids they care for. You're so much more to her than that, and you know it."

He nodded his head. "I do love her. Of course I do."

"Well, right now, she sees a friendly relationship between her parents—which is great—but she's also learning that marriage is...devoid of romantic love and affection. We're not setting the example I'd like her to emulate when looking for her own partner someday. She needs to know that love can be so much more."

"The kind of love we used to have for each other."

"Yeah," I answered, meeting his eyes. "I wish she could've witnessed that kind of love. That kind of love is epic...once in a lifetime."

"I wish things could've been different for us, Cat."

"I know. Me too."

"I do still love you, ya know. The only reason that epic, once in a lifetime love isn't still there is because I fight so damn hard every day to fend it off. Which probably means it isn't gone at all, in reality." He removed his cap and scratched his head. "What a trip it all is. Really. Who could make sense of it?"

"I think maybe a good therapist could," I said with a little smile.

He smiled too. "Yeah. Maybe."

"So, just so I understand, you think you could still love me...*really* love me...but you don't let yourself, because you still don't think you could be a dad to Jenna. Even though you *are* a dad to Jenna."

"I guess, but also—" He put his cap back on and pulled the bill down over his eyes. "I can't love you that way because you no longer love me, and I'm pretty sure that would kill me, Cat."

I was stunned...because the reality was, he was wrong. I'd told him I no longer loved him, but it was never true. I'd hoped that by saying it, we'd both come to believe it, but it had been eight years since I came back, and the words I'd said that day were no truer now than they were then. It was a lie I'd hoped would become a truth. And it never did.

A week later, Glen moved in with Janine. Before he left, he asked, "How will you explain it to her?"

"I suppose I'll tell her it just didn't work out; that we were too different."

He opened the door to his truck. "Tell her anything you want. Tell her I cheated. She'll hear rumors anyway, if she hasn't already. It's the most believable thing. Just don't tell her the truth. She doesn't deserve that burden."

I knew what he meant—that she didn't deserve to spend her life knowing her father left because she had the audacity to be born. It wasn't anything she did, but it would haunt her, nonetheless.

"Okay," I said.

He pulled me in for a hug. It was the first time we'd touched in what felt like a whole lifetime, and it brought forth excruciating memories of every time he'd held me before. It reminded me how it was once so *normal.* It made me sad, and angry, that I'd taken it all for granted.

I told Jenna exactly what I said I would—that we were just too different, and it was time we went our separate ways. She came to me a week later, recounting rumors she'd heard at school. I tried convincing her they weren't true, but she was putting things together—the lack of affection, the sleeping arrangements—and she believed what she wanted to believe.

And because it was less destructive for her than the truth, I let her.

23

FAIRY TALES & FIRE ANTS

A few days after Glen left, the phone rang.

"Hello?"

"Catherine, it's Janine. What the hell is going on?"

"Uh—you haven't spoken to Glen?"

"He won't talk. He goes to work, comes home, and goes to bed."

"Is he drinking?"

"Nothing too extreme, no. A few beer bottles in the trash, but nothing like before."

I let out a sigh of relief. "Well, that's good, at least."

"Why is he *here*, Catherine?"

I twirled the cord around my fingers and checked around the corner for Jenna. She was locked away in her room, blasting some yodeling song she kept playing over and over. The Cranberries, I think?

"He moved out," I said. "Jenna started asking questions, and he still felt like he...couldn't be who we need him to be. So, we decided it was time."

"Oh...I'm so sorry," Janine said. "How are you holding up?"

"I'm okay. It was a fine conversation. No drama. We both know it's for the best."

I heard Janine sigh through the line. "He still loves you, Catherine."

"I know."

"And you still love him."

"I know that too."

She sniffed, trying to hold back tears. "Your story isn't over yet. You'll see."

I didn't respond to that, but if I had, it would've been to say, "Well, it sure as hell feels over to me."

———————

A month or so later, Liza said, "I hear he's moving to Montgomery," as she grabbed a bag of Bugles and pulled it open.

"For a big work project. I think it's temporary," I answered.

"And if it's not?"

I stared, trying to figure out her point. "Then, I guess he'll move to Montgomery. What?"

"You've been with that man, in some form or another, since you were seventeen. He can't just move away without you having some sort of feelings about it." She shoved a Bugle into her mouth.

"Of course I have feelings about it, Liza."

"Well? What are they?"

Conflicted, that's what.

"I'm mostly sad. I feel like this has all been some kind of fairy tale gone wrong. I wish my fairy godmother would show up and wave a wand—give us a chance to go back and do it all over," I said.

"Would you do it over? The only way it would be different is if you never got pregnant."

"Liza!"

"Am I wrong? That's the issue here, right?"

"Then maybe I would've tried harder to find someplace else to live after Pensacola. I think staying close to him, even as friends, makes it all so much harder now."

"Because you never got to stop loving him."

I looked at her, trying to decipher if that was meant as a matter-of-fact statement, or if she was judging me for it. All I saw in her face was truth. "I thought I'd stopped loving him—for a while at least. It didn't last long, in the grand scheme of things."

She nodded, popped another Bugle, then said, "You're right."

"Huh?"

"It is like a fairy tale. Only it's one of those dark, depressing ones without a happy ending. The ones meant to teach us something."

"*Grimms'?*"

"Yeah, that's it. What do you think you were supposed to learn?"

"I don't know, Liza."

I really didn't know.

⸙

Once Glen settled in Montgomery to lead a team for a new neighborhood development project, we arranged for him to take Jenna for a day trip. It was meant to be a few hours at the planetarium, then lunch, and a movie.

She was home by noon.

"What happened?" I asked after she'd stormed off to her room.

He looked down the road like he was eager to be on it, driving away. "I don't know. We walked around the museum, but she didn't talk much. I don't think she wanted to be there."

"So, you just brought her home? You had a full day planned!"

"No, I asked where she wanted to go for lunch. She said she wasn't hungry, mumbled something about this all being *so weird*, then said she wanted to go home."

"Did you try convincing her otherwise? She's just a kid—"

"Of course I did, but she wasn't interested, Cat."

I sat on the top porch step to think. He sat next to me.

"Well, it was just the first try. I'll talk to her, and we'll try again. She'll come around," I said.

"I don't want to force her to do anything she doesn't want to do."

"I don't either, but I have a feeling this is about what she heard at school. She thinks you were unfaithful. I should have talked to her—denied it—but she never asked. I only know because I overheard her and Michelle talking. I should've talked to her then."

"If her thinking I'm a terrible person is the best way to explain all this, then that's what we go along with. She can't know I left because of her, Cat. She just can't."

"You didn't leave because of her. You left because of *you*." I don't know which of us I'm trying to convince. It's a line I've told myself, over and over...because if I felt it was truly about *her*, rather than *him*, I'd never forgive him.

"And maybe someday she'll understand that, but she's just a kid, remember?"

I lowered my head and watched a trail of fire ants cross from one side of the sidewalk to the other. "Okay. I'll think of something."

He leaned over, put an arm around my shoulder, then used his free hand to turn my face to his. "We make our own music, Cat. Remember? Even if we make it up as we go along."

I nodded.

He stood, walked over to the garage door, and lifted it.

"What are you doing?" I asked.

"Getting some bait for those ants."

⸻◆⸻

After he left, I knocked on Jenna's door. I couldn't hear music, so I knew she was listening with headphones. I pushed the door open and found her doing just that, while flipping through an old issue of *Tiger Beat*. She looked up when I entered, then flipped another page.

I sat on the floor next to her and gestured for her to remove the headphones. When she did, I said, "So...do you want to tell me what happened?"

She flipped another page.

"Jenna, I know this is all new. It's not easy for any of us, you know."

She ripped out a full-page image of Jared Leto, dressed as Jordan Catalano.

"You like him, huh?" I asked.

She rolled her eyes. "He's okay."

"Will you tell me what happened? Why did you want to come home?"

She let out a huge sigh. "It was just weird, Mama. I wasn't having fun, and you told me if I'm ever anywhere that I'm not having fun, to come home."

"That's true," I said. "Do you have any idea what made it feel weird?"

She shrugged.

"Jenna, I know you've heard things about your dad at school—about why he left."

She looked up at me cautiously, like she was afraid I would tell her something she didn't want to hear.

"I won't go into the details because—well, it's grown-up stuff—but your dad is a good person. I have no bad feelings toward him, and if *you* do, I think we should talk about them."

It took her a moment to formulate a response. "He's a good person? He didn't do anything...awful?"

The look on her face begged for brutal honesty, and for a moment, I considered giving it to her. But no, she didn't need the truth—not all of it, anyway. "He is. And he loves you, Jenna. I know he wasn't around all the time—"

"Yeah, like never," she said.

"It wasn't *never*. And it doesn't mean he doesn't love you. I hope you know that."

She took a moment to process that, then picked her headphones up again, looking at me to ask if it was okay.

"All right. Guess I'll go make lunch. Grilled cheese?"

She nodded and went back to her music.

Their next endeavor was simpler, more brief—pizza at Nico's. She came home smiling that day, so we planned another. Eventually, he started driving in once a month to spend the day with her, and things seemed to be headed in the right direction.

When he dropped her off one Sunday, after a fishing trip to the lake, he said, "Hey, you remember those schedules you used to tack up on the fridge? With her school things? Plays and stuff?"

"Yeah, I remember."

"Could you start sending me that info? She said she has some track thing next weekend and—well, if I'd known—I would have driven in then, instead of today."

Well, hot damn.

"Sure, I can do that," I said with a half-smile.

"What are you smirking at, woman?"

"I wasn't smirking. No smirk here." I felt the smile spread across my face.

"I just want to know, okay? If I can make it to things, I will. No big deal."

"Yeah, okay. No big deal."

He went to the track meet that weekend. Then, the next month, he came in for another. The first time, Jenna was excited to see him. The second, she wasn't.

As the two of us drove to Dairy Queen for ice cream afterward, I asked, "What's going on, Jenna? Why do you seem upset that your dad came in for the meet?"

"I don't know. Guess I just didn't want to see him."

"Did something happen? Did he upset you somehow?"

She shook her head.

"Then what is it?"

She looked out the window. "They all talk, Mama."

"Who? The kids at school?"

"Yeah."

"Well, who cares what they think, huh? They don't know us. They don't know *him*."

She turned to face me. "When will they ever *stop* talking? Do you know what it's like to have the whole school whispering about crap that isn't even true?"

Oh, boy, did I ever.

"Actually, I do, but I've learned that people only talk about it until there's something newer or more interesting to gossip about."

She gave me a distrustful glance, clearly thinking I was a million years old and clueless.

We enjoyed our ice cream, went home, and I called Glen. After explaining what happened, we decided we'd ask Jenna if it was okay for him to go to future events. If she said no, we'd respect that. Easy enough.

Sometimes she said, *okay*. Others, she said, *sure, but can he kinda keep away a bit?* And occasionally, she said, *not this time, Mama.*

The sixth-grade Christmas play was one instance when she said he could come, but she wanted him to keep his distance. The thought of all those faces on stage having direct eyes on her father in the front row made her uncomfortable.

I sat in the front row, though. In fact, with Liza, Mama, Aunt Kitty, and Janine sitting with me, we took up *most* of the front row—and not one of us felt bad about it. With five disposable cameras clicking and winding every time she moved, we were the most annoying people in the room, and we didn't feel bad about that either.

Just as Jenna stepped forward to recite her monologue, I had a sudden feeling I was being watched. I snapped a picture of her standing at the microphone, dressed as a wise man, then looked over my right shoulder. I scanned the rows of seats, turned back for another picture, then looked for him again.

He was there; I knew it.

Jenna returned to the risers. Another wise man approached the microphone, and I turned to look one more time. I didn't even bother searching to my left. I felt him on the right.

Then I found him, standing at the very back, leaning against the wall with his arms crossed. When we made eye contact, a crooked grin appeared across his lips, and he raised a hand to the bill of his cap, saying *hello* from across the crowded room.

It gave me goosebumps—and I love/hated him for it.

I thought that over time Jenna would start letting Glen sit up front when he joined us in public; would start letting him be seen. In reality, it went the other way, until eventually he stood at the back by default. Every time, I *felt* him before I saw him—always standing or sitting off to the right, and always with that grin. And every time, it brought *goosebumps*.

It didn't dawn on me until much later that if he was always on my right, that meant he was finding me first, and positioning himself so that I'd always know where to look for him. It was sweet, and so very *Glen*.

There was only one time he didn't show up to something I felt for sure he would attend. He'd gotten stuck in traffic, which left me waiting...waiting...waiting for the charge in the air I always felt when he was near. I kept looking over my shoulder, wondering why I couldn't *feel* him, but I soon learned there was nothing wrong with my *Glen-radar*—he simply wasn't there.

The disappointment I felt was unexpected, and the hate I threw at myself for *feeling* disappointed was biting and harsh. I tried to determine which response was from the real me: the one who felt disappointed, or the one who was angry at myself for feeling that way.

In the end, it didn't matter, because I didn't like the person I was in either case—not one bit.

NOW

"**Y**ou said you didn't know her," Jenna says.

"Who?"

"When you first told me about the woman on the porch, you said you'd never seen her before."

I know the conversation she means...the one we had when she came to Asher two years ago after leaving her family behind, convinced they were better off without her. There were a lot of things I kept from her in that conversation...and a lot of untruths, too.

"I've told no one who it was except Liza."

"Why?"

"It's painful, Jenna, and I didn't think that woman would ever leave Asher. It was just better if no one knew it was her."

"Is she still there now?"

"No. She moved away a year or so ago, thank God. She was a realtor, ya know. Her face haunted every corner in town for over a decade. Also, I have to come clean with you about that conversation."

She looks at me with squinty eyes, trying to understand what I mean.

"I wasn't completely honest with you then. At that point, I thought I would go to my grave with you never knowing the truth about what really happened between your dad and me. So, I told the same old story I've told you your whole life. And I'm sorry for that."

"You mean letting me believe he cheated on you?"

"Yeah, that's the big one. Also, I left out the fact that we became friends after we moved back home. It took a while, but it happened. We weren't just two miserable people forced to live together, Jenna. It worked for us. Everything I've told you tonight is the truth." I bring my hands to my lap and wait for her anger to come.

But it doesn't. Instead, she brings her wine glass to her lips, and says, "So...*I'm* the reason he left?"

"Is that what you took away from all that? Because maybe I didn't do a good job of explaining..." I search her eyes for some sign that she *gets it*.

Please, God, let her get it.

"You were happy and in love until I came along, then it all went to shit."

"No—see, this is why I went along with the whole *he was a cheater* thing. I never wanted you to think it was you, because it wasn't. It was *him*. He was so screwed up by everything he'd been through. You being born just brought it all to the surface."

"No, I get that," she says.

"You do?"

"Of course, Mama. I, of all people, have a pretty good understanding of how becoming a parent can mess with your mind, don't you think?"

I nod, because she's right. She's been through it herself.

"Then why did you say it was because of you?" I ask her. "If you understand, how could you say that?"

"No, what I meant was...if I hadn't been born, you guys would've been fine, and that blows my mind. I thought there was more to it—you know, the other women, the drinking. I didn't realize you were happy together; that you really loved each other. That's all. God, it's just so—*tragic*."

"That's a little dramatic, don't you think? I mean, no one died. We all survived, didn't we?"

"Yeah, you survived, but have you ever been happy? *Really* happy?"

The question feels like a dagger to the heart.

"I've—yeah. I was happy raising you. Everything I did, everything I worked for—was for you. You were the only thing in my life that mattered. Jenna, it's like you're an actual piece of my heart that's been removed and left to find its own way in the world. I *hate* that. If I could move you back into my house and keep you there forever, I would. So, yes, I've been happy. Being your mama makes me happy. I didn't need anything else."

"I get that, too," she says.

"I know you do, because you love your kids. You're a great mom, Jenna."

She gives a little nod. "So, we're up to what...seventh grade? I don't remember seeing Daddy much after that."

"Well, that was mostly your doing. You were too busy with friends by then to want to spend time with your lame parents. But he was still around."

"He was?"

"More than you knew."

1996

24

GOOD TREES & GOOD SALESMEN

Jenna spent her afternoons on the track or hanging out with Michelle, who was also on the team. They were practically joined at the hip. They reminded me of Liza and myself, and I loved that for her. Every girl needs one truly great friend, who's more like a sister than anything, and Jenna had found hers in Michelle.

My life was pretty bland, but too busy to be boring. I mostly worked and did my best to hold everything together. I spent time with Liza, joined Mama, Bo, & Stacey for Sunday dinners, and sometimes offered an extra pair of hands to Mama's church group when they needed them. Nothing earth-shattering or life-changing ever seemed to happen, and I liked it that way. I'd had enough excitement to last a lifetime.

It was on a Saturday in May that Glen showed up unexpectedly at my door.

"What are you doing here?" I asked.

"Mom has a raccoon problem."

"A raccoon problem?"

"In the attic. I've been up there banging on pots and pans, trying to scare Mama Raccoon away, and hoping she takes her babies with her." He took off his cap, smiled, and shook his head.

That made me laugh. "Well, come in. Have a beer."

He followed me to the kitchen. "Wow, your plants are doing well." He gestured toward the dozens of plants hanging in the windows and sitting on the shelves he'd built.

"Yeah, they're damn needy, though." I grabbed two cans of beer from the fridge and opened them as we sat at the table.

What I didn't say was that I would never let those plants die. Whenever they took a turn for the worse, I propagated them; created new ones from the old. They were a relic from another life that I just couldn't let go of.

"I figured while I was here taking care of Mom's chore list, I'd see if you have anything that needs to be done around here." He took a deep swig of beer.

"You don't have to do that. I manage okay."

"But I want to. Come on, surely there's something."

It was technically still his house, too.

We bought it just before Jenna was born, when the landlord's wife finally gave him the green light to sell.

"I guess you could get rid of the old stump in the back yard. The tree died a while back, then fell down after a storm. I had someone come out to cut it down, but they wouldn't dig up the stump."

"The old elm?"

"Yeah."

"That's too bad. That was a good tree."

I burst out in laughter. "A good tree?"

He laughed too. "It was probably a hundred years old—or older!"

"Jeez, when did you become such an old man?"

"I'm old because I care about trees?"

"No, you're old because you say *that was a good tree*. Do you also yell at the neighbor kids to *get off the grass?*"

He chuckled at that. "All right, whatever you say. But if I'm old, you are too."

I gestured toward the plants all around us. "I've always been old."

He laughed. "Well, you've always been an old soul, at least."

"Wise beyond my years, right?"

"Mmm-hmm. So, come on, let's go take a look." He stood and moved toward the back door.

He made quick work of that dead stump. Then, he pointed out that the old single-pane windows needed replacing. A few weeks later, he was back to oversee the delivery and installation.

"This must've cost a fortune," I said.

"It needed to be done. Will help with your power bill, too." He stooped to pick up a piece of trash in the yard, walked over to the garbage can, and dropped it inside. As he approached me again, he said, "So, I have an opportunity, and I'd like your advice."

"What sort of opportunity?"

"A work thing. There's a lot of business to be had in Montgomery. Lots of development happening in the suburbs. Uncle Rudy thinks we should open a branch of the business there, but he wants nothing to do with it. Says he's plenty busy here. It would be mine, Cat."

His eyes were hopeful and excited, but I saw a bit of uncertainty in them, too.

"Could you manage it? The admin side of things would be new for you, right?"

"Yeah, that's what I'm worried about. I've always been the one getting my hands dirty. I don't know the first thing about hiring people, payroll, taxes..."

"You'd need an office manager to keep things in line. If you found the right person, I have no doubt you could do it." I smiled as I remembered him once saying, *I'll make something of myself someday, Cat. You'll see.* "It's exciting, really."

"It is, isn't it? And I'm thinking...we spend so much money sourcing materials from our supplier: brick, stone, sand, fill dirt. Maybe there's benefit to cutting out the middleman." He grew more confident, more animated, as he spoke. "We'd sell by the truckload, direct to developers and homeowners, and get the materials for our own projects at cost. And, looking long term, I could bring in a landscape architect and start doing that too. The first thing that happens after we finish a job is landscaping. Why not get in on that?"

I nodded and smiled. He had it all planned out, and if he wanted it, I knew he'd make it happen. "I think you should do it."

"You do? I'd have no idea where to start."

"Talk to Uncle Rudy. Let him help you build a business case. He'll know the legalities, the paperwork, the financing. Then hire an office manager. You'll need someone good, with lots of experience. You can't skimp on salary."

He nodded. "You really think I can do it?"

"I really do."

Glen left that day and drove straight to Uncle Rudy's. Three months later, he had his own business, and three months after that, he ordered his first delivery of raw materials and purchased a dump truck. He was on track to add landscaping services to the business within a year.

I was so proud of him, but it had all gotten me thinking about my own plans for the future. He was growing—as a person, as a businessman—and I was...stagnant.

The thought didn't stick around long, though. There was little time for daydreaming about the future when I was neck-deep in the present.

Shortly after Jenna's twelfth birthday, she met a boy. His name was Tyler and I'll be damned if he didn't have a remarkable resemblance to Jared Leto.

I overheard Jenna and Michelle talking about him on more than one occasion after school. Their shrieks and giggles made me smile. My beautiful, sweet daughter had her first crush, which was hard to process, given that it seemed like I'd just been changing her diapers, spoon-feeding her sweet potatoes, and washing her hair.

When was the last time I washed her hair?

It seemed cruel that the last time had come and gone without even realizing it was the last time. With tears in my eyes, I picked up the phone and dialed Glen.

"Hello?"

"Hey, it's me." I cleared my throat of all the emotion stuck inside it.

"What's wrong, Cat?"

"How do you know something's wrong?"

"I can hear it in your voice."

I sighed and walked with the cordless phone to sit at the table. "From three words?"

"Yup."

"Fine. I'm just—a little sad today, is all."

"What about?"

"Jenna's growing up on us, and I don't like it."

The sigh came from him this time. "*You* don't like it? I've missed most of it."

I wanted to point out that his absence was his own doing, but held my tongue.

"So, what happened?" he asked.

"She has her first crush."

"Oh, shit. Who?"

"His name is Tyler. I don't know much about him yet. I will say one thing: Our girl has good taste. He's the spitting image of a young Jordan Catalano."

"Who?"

"Jared Leto, the actor."

"I have no idea who that is, Cat."

"Well, do yourself a favor and don't look him up. It'll only make you feel worse."

Two days later, the phone rang.

"That boy is trouble," Glen said.

"What boy?"

"The one Jenna's—uh, Tyler."

"How do you know he's trouble?" I smiled, because I knew where the conversation was headed.

"I watched a re-run of the show!"

"Glen!" I laughed out loud. "I told you not to!"

"Well, I couldn't help it. I had to see."

"And your opinion of a boy you've never met is that he's trouble because he looks like an actor you don't know?"

"I don't have to know him. He's trouble, plain and simple."

"Well, I guess we'll see. There's a school dance next weekend and the girls are going with him and a couple of his buddies," I said. "We're taking them to Waffle House before."

"Like a *date?*"

"No, not a date. She's twelve!"

"Well, stick close. Maybe chaperone or something."

"I'm not chaperoning the dance—*Jesus.*"

"Catherine!"

"What? She's growing up, Glen. We can't stop it."

"I know, but—I just—"

"What?"

"I've missed so much. I'm *missing* so much. And I miss—*you*."

I gasped, louder than I should have. I missed him too, but I'd never say it…but he did. Knowing better than to open the can of worms on that conversation, I said, "I have to go, Glen. Talk to you later?"

"Yeah, okay. Bye, Cat."

"Goodbye."

Jenna's dance came and went, and I decided I liked Tyler. He brought her a tiny corsage of pink roses, slipped it onto her wrist while holding her fingers, and smiled. At dinner, he was polite, funny, and quite—charming. The only thing that worried me was that he seemed so much older than he was. He reminded me of Glen.

After the dance, Jenna, Michelle, and Tyler became three peas in a pod. It got me thinking about what Jenna envisioned her future to look like, which then got me thinking about how I envisioned mine after meeting Glen at seventeen. I compared what I'd hoped for to the life I was living, and it brought on a kind of sadness I hadn't expected. I was in a dark place of longing—for the past, for what could have been, for some sort of future that was happy and free from feeling like I was stuck *in-between*.

The next week at work, our head librarian retired. Another took her place, but it left an opening that needed to be filled.

"You'd make an excellent librarian," a co-worker said over sack lunches in the break room.

"College never fit into my life, sadly. Maybe someday." I took a sip of my Coke.

"College never fits into anyone's life, but people do it anyway. If you want it, you have to just go for it. There will never be a good time."

Those words haunted me for days. They induced vivid daydreams of what it would be like. I saw myself carrying books, making friends, studying by a lamp late at night while Jenna slept. I couldn't get it out of my mind.

So, I drove to the nearest college, forty-five minutes away. I felt so old, walking by all the twenty-somethings rushing to class. I found my way to the admin office, picked up a few pamphlets, and as I turned to leave, heard a voice address me from behind the desk.

"Can I help you?" she asked.

"Just looking for some information, thank you." I held up the pamphlets to show I'd found what I came for.

"Do you have any questions?"

"Oh," I said with a laugh. "A million, but I don't want to take up your time."

"It's not a bother. That's what they pay me for." She smiled and motioned toward a table.

I joined her there and folded my hands in my lap.

"What are you interested in studying?" she asked, crossing her legs to get comfortable.

"I work in a library, and I've always loved books. I think maybe I'd like to be a librarian."

She nodded. "You need a master's degree for that."

"I do?"

"Yup."

"Oh." My shoulders slumped as all hope drained away.

"But you have to start somewhere. If you don't start, you'll never achieve it, right?"

"But I'm thirty-two years old. I work full time, and I have a twelve-year-old daughter. My husband, well, he's—"

"And?"

"Excuse me?"

"You'd be one of our older students, but you wouldn't be the only one. We have a program for working students like you, and counselors who help you through every step. What it all comes down to is, where do you see yourself in six years, if you don't try?"

Oh, she's a good salesman.

"How would I pay for it?" I asked.

"You could apply for grants. There are also various types of student loans. Some aren't paid back until after graduation." She stood. "I'll get you the applications, and an admission application, too."

I left there with everything I needed to *do* something with my life. It was exhilarating and terrifying all at the same time. I had no idea how I could make it work, but that woman in the office made it seem so easy. I wanted to believe her. I wanted to believe in *myself*.

When I left for Pensacola, the only thing I wanted was to stand on my own two feet. When I came back and moved into our house again, I planned to save money in order to eventually leave Glen, and make it happen on my own in Asher. All of that washed away, though, when Glen and I fell into a new routine—a new friendship—and I gave up. I was comfortable and lost sight of what I really wanted. Since he left, I'd managed just fine on my own, and I was proud of that, but I still didn't feel like I'd become who I was meant to be.

A mile from home, I made a U-turn and drove straight to Mama's.

⸻ ◆ ⸻

"So, what's up?" Mama asked as she brought over two cups of coffee.

Of course she knew something was up. I didn't just stop by in the middle of the week for nothing.

"Well, you know I don't like asking for more help than I have to—"

She looked at me with curious eyes as she took a sip.

"—but I think I want to go to school."

Mama lowered her mug and continued to stare. "For what?"

"I want to be a librarian. I'd need a master's degree, but I figured I could at least get started on a bachelor's program. It may take me longer than most, but I—I think I can do it."

"Really? Well, isn't that somethin'?" She took another sip. "So, what do you need from me? Money?"

"No, I'll apply for financial aid; take out a loan if I need to. I just need some after-school help with Jenna. She's old enough to stay on her own, but I hate to think of her *being* alone that much. I want her to have hot meals with people she loves, not cereal in a dark, empty house."

Like the cereal-for-dinner I often had after Daddy died and Mama started working nights.

"How can you afford to cut back at work?"

"I have some savings, and there are night and weekend classes. I'll have to change my work schedule a bit, but the library's open till 9:00, so I'll figure it out."

"I'd have to adjust my work hours too, so the sooner you let me know the schedule, the better. But I think we can make it happen."

"You do?" I felt a rush of relief. "Thank you!" I stood and gave her a hug, then grabbed the coffeepot and topped off her cup.

"You're welcome, child. And for what it's worth, I'm proud of you."

"You are?"

"Of course. It's not easy to leave your comfort zone and take a chance on something unknown. Makes me proud."

"Thank you, Mama."

"You're welcome. Now, you better go get our girl."

"Okay. See you Sunday?"

"See you Sunday."

When my acceptance letter came in December, I called Glen with the good news. That afternoon, he sent flowers.

"Thank you for the flowers," I said through the phone.

"You earned them. I'm proud of you," he said, softly strumming his guitar.

"Well, I haven't done anything yet."

"Sure you have. You've decided to go after something you want. Your life has been so much about worrying about everyone else for so long—your mom, Jenna, me. It's brave, what you're doing. You should be proud of that."

"What if I can't do it?"

"You'll find a way, Cat. You always do."

1997

25

GLOWING AMBER & HOPPING FENCES

On a frigid Monday in January, I forced my way toward the front doors of the school, huddled beneath an umbrella as sleet fell from the sky in sheets.

"Let me get that!" A man appeared at my right, pulling the door open for us both to enter.

Once inside, I shook my umbrella over the weather mat and said, "Thanks," as I closed it.

"No problem. Hey, do you know where C-12 is? I haven't had a class in this building before."

I looked up to find the most gorgeous head of jet-black hair and the brightest brown eyes I'd ever seen in my life.

They're like glowing amber.

"No, sorry. I'm new," I answered, unable to look away.

"I have a map here somewhere. I'll find it. Thanks anyway." He squatted, unzipped his backpack, and dug around inside it.

I made it halfway down the hall, then spotted a large-scale map of the campus hanging on the wall. I turned back toward him and said, "Hey, found the map!"

He smiled, and hurried my way.

In the weeks that followed, we chatted briefly when we saw each other between classes. I learned his name was Martin. He was thirty-four, a business major, and was graduating in May. After that, he'd move to New Orleans for culinary school.

One evening, shortly after Valentine's Day, Martin asked, "Vending machine coffee?" as he held a paper cup out for me to take. Followed by, "Would you like to get a *real* coffee sometime?"

I wasn't sure how to answer. Was he asking as a friend? Or more? Regardless, when was the right time to tell him—or anyone like him—that I was married, but not *really* married?

"Wow, there's a lot going on in that brain of yours," he said with a laugh.

I laughed too, and said, "Yeah."

He has no idea.

"Let me try again: Would you like to have a *friendly* cup of coffee with me, somewhere it's prepared and served by actual humans, and maybe smells a bit better than whatever moldy/rubbery thing they've got going on in this building?"

Was I that transparent? He must think I'm a total weirdo.

Rather than confirming just how weird I was by declining the invitation, I said, "Sure, I'd like that."

He smiled, pulled a piece of paper from his bag, and scribbled a number.

It took me twelve days to find the courage to call, but when I did, we agreed on a time and place to meet for that coffee. Fifteen minutes into our friendly coffee date, I told him about Glen, before I lost the nerve.

"It's weird, I know...that I'm married, but we're not together," I said.

"A bit, yeah. But I suppose lots of couples separate, right?"

"Yeah, I guess so. My priority right now is keeping Jenna safe and happy until she graduates and moves on to whatever comes next."

"And then you'll...also move on to whatever comes next?" he asked.

"I suppose. Or at least consider it."

"That's a long time to put your life on hold."

"Is it? It's been so long already. What's six more years?"

"Not to sound harsh, but why don't you just divorce?"

It was a question I'd asked myself a million times.

"It's complicated. I want him to still be in her life."

"Most divorced parents still have their kids in their life."

"Yeah, but Glen is...well, it's a long story. I just don't want to push him away. Not while Jenna's still young."

How could I explain that Glen lived in constant fear of not being good enough for her? That he was one life crisis or binge drinking episode away from disappearing for months on end? That I was afraid someday he'd disappear and never come back?

That as much as I wanted to pretend it was all about Jenna, my deepest fear was not having him in *my* life, in some form or another?

Martin leaned forward. "Catherine, I'm going to be very direct with my next question, and you're going to wonder if I'm asking it for my own personal interest. The answer is *yes,* I am."

"Okay?"

"Are you saying you're not interested in dating for at least the next *six years?*" He locked those amber eyes with mine, and I felt lost within them.

I took a deep breath, caught my eyes wandering down to his full lips, then forced them back up again. Then I said something that took even me by surprise. "I mean, I wouldn't say no to a burger...or a beer."

He smiled. "How about a burger *and* a beer?"

"Even better."

⚬

We saw each other twice a week outside of school—sometimes more. I refused to call whatever it was we were doing *dating,* but we both knew it was. Our first kiss was outside the movie theater after seeing *Fools Rush In.*

And it was...*okay.*

What I enjoyed most about the kiss had nothing to do with sparks or butterflies, but the feeling of being in someone's arms again. Glen and I cut all physical relations after Pensacola. There were times after those first two years passed, when we shared the sofa while watching TV, or he placed a hand on my shoulder when maneuvering around me in the kitchen, but other than that, I hadn't been touched—hadn't been held or kissed—in ten years. You don't realize how much you miss that until something like a surprise kiss happens, and it's thrust upon you again—at least, I didn't.

I'd never been with anyone but Glen, so to say I was hesitant, nervous, anxious, and conflicted about getting physical with Martin would be an understatement. But our time together had an expiration date, and that somehow made it easier.

The first time he held me...really held me...was in my living room as we watched *Dazed And Confused* because all the new releases at Blockbuster were snatched up quick on a small-town Friday night. Jenna was at Mama's and when he pulled me down to sit between his legs, then gently tugged my shoulders back to rest against him, it was the first time I'd been pressed against a man in a decade.

Two minutes was all it took for my defenses to crumble. My shoulders lowered, my jaw slackened, my fists unclenched, and a tear slid down my cheek. He felt the change just as much as I did.

Moving his lips to my ear, he said, "You're far too wonderful to spend your life not being told just *how* wonderful you are." Then, he held me tighter as the final credits rolled up the screen, and a decade of tears rolled down my face.

For weeks, Martin held me...and did a lot of other things I very much enjoyed. We never had *actual* sex though. There was something about being that intimate with him that just didn't feel right; I couldn't bring myself to do it.

Regardless, it was an experience I never knew I needed, and it opened my heart in a way I could have never expected. Not for *love*, but for *touch* and *connection*. I no longer jumped out of my skin when bumped into at the grocery store, or when Jenna surprised me from behind with a tap on the shoulder. The world felt a tiny bit kinder—less threatening—and I remembered what it felt like to be wrapped up tight in someone else; to be cared for and protected.

Through it all, though, I found myself counting down the days until he'd leave for New Orleans. Partly because it made me so sad to think of losing him, but also because I was ready to let him go. He never said so directly, but Martin wanted much more from me than I was ready to give.

"So, it's like exposure therapy?" Liza asked after I explained the situation to her in my kitchen.

"What's that?"

"Exposure to whatever it is you're afraid of—in small doses—until you're not afraid of it anymore. For you, that's physical touch and emotional connection, apparently."

"That's a thing?"

"Yeah, it's a thing. Do you live under a rock?"

"Does it work?"

"I don't know, you tell me." She stared at me for a moment, but I offered no reply. Then, she stood and waved for me to follow. "Anyway, come with me. I have a surprise."

I followed her outside and across the yard. She stuck a foot on the wooden cross-plank on the back fence, swung her legs over, then jumped down.

"Liza, what the hell?"

"Come on, just do it!"

"Thirty-two-year-old women don't hop fences, Liza!" I said, placing my foot on the plank anyway.

"Oh, come on. We're not old ladies yet."

When I landed on the other side, she led me between the two houses backing up to mine. Rounding the corner of the house on the right, she stepped onto the porch, pulling a key from her pocket.

"You *didn't*—" I said in disbelief.

"They're not side-by-side, but close enough, right? We'll put in a gate!" She unlocked the door and stepped inside.

"How did you do this?"

"It's rented. Daddy co-signed the lease."

"*Oh my God!* You live here?"

She nodded her head and smiled. "We finally did it!"

"We've talked about this since we were—what, eight years old?"

"Younger than that, I think. Now, call Glen and ask him about that gate."

"I can't. Not now."

"Why not?"

"It's March, Liza."

"Right. Well, soon then."

Even Liza knew better than to ask anything of Glen in March.

Glen took Jenna to the movies a couple weeks later. While in town, he stopped at the hardware store for all the things required to build a gate.

"I still can't believe Liza moved next door," he said, unloading the truck.

"Not technically next door."

"Close enough. I don't think you could be rid of that woman if you wanted to."

That stung, because I had lost Liza before—twice. And I hoped to God it never happened again.

He noticed the thoughts swimming behind my eyes. "Hey, Cat, I'm sorry. I didn't mean to drudge up bad memories." He stepped toward me. "She's a good friend. I'm glad you have her."

"Me too," I said. "Do you—have anyone?" As soon as I said it, I realized how he might take it: that I was maybe asking if he was *seeing* anyone. "I mean, any good friends?"

"Not really." He turned back to the truck bed. "Been pretty busy growing the business and coming here when I can." He pulled a long piece of wood across the tailgate and stood it on end, holding it with one hand and shutting the tailgate with the other.

"I'm glad you come here to see Jenna and help your mom, but if you need time to do other things, I can hire someone to take care of stuff around here. I told you that before."

It came out sounding a bit angry, and maybe I was angry. Maybe I thought he blamed me for his lack of a social life, and I knew I didn't deserve that—because I *had* told him I could handle things on my own, and I could.

"Catherine, I'm here because I want to be here. And I don't just come to see Jenna and my mom." He rested the wood on his shoulder and moved toward the back yard.

An hour later, Liza ran through the new gap in the fence and up to my porch, hair flying wild. "He's putting in a gate!" she said as she hugged me.

"Looks that way." I glanced at Glen, bent over a sawhorse with a power saw in his hand.

Liza followed the direction of my eyes, looked back to me again, then back to Glen. "*Oh no*," she said.

"What?"

"Don't *look* at him that way, Catherine!"

"What way? You're crazy, Liza."

"No, no, I'm not. You have only ever looked at one person that way and he happens to be standing in your back yard, all hot and sweaty, and...gorgeous. How is he still so gorgeous, anyway? It's been like fifteen years, for crying out loud!"

"It's unfair, isn't it?" I said dreamily, still staring at the man in my yard.

"It's because he's a man. Men have room to age gracefully. We're somehow meant to find the *elixir of life*."

I turned toward the house and entered the kitchen.

Liza followed me. "Don't think we're done talking about...all *that*."

"There's nothing to talk about. We're separated and have been for a long time."

The truth of it was, Martin had woken something inside of me, and with Glen so close, I could remember *everything*. What it felt like when he held me. How right it was. The way my spine tingled when he kissed me.

"Oh, shit, you're blushing!" Liza yelled.

I turned toward the sink for a glass of water because I was blushing. I could feel it, and it was the first time it had happened in a long time.

"Catherine, I hate to ask, but what are you feeling right now? What are you thinking?"

Turning to face her, I said, "I don't know. I'm confused. I think Martin has me all confused."

"Because you like him?"

"Of course I like him, but that's not it."

"Well, then, what is it? You're not...feeling some kinda way about—" She looked through the screen door, then back to me again. "Oh, Catherine..."

"I've always felt for him, you know that. It's never gone away. It doesn't matter though, does it? He's still—messed up. It doesn't matter."

I turned to rinse my glass as Glen walked through the door. "Hey, can I get some of that?"

I refilled the glass and handed it over. Then, I left the kitchen and yelled to Jenna as I walked to her room, "You ready? Don't forget your toothbrush!"

I stopped for Chinese takeout after dropping off Jenna for her sleepover at Michelle's. When I got home, Liza was gone, as I knew she would be. Glen was still there though, hanging the gate he'd built. The sun was low, but hot, and somewhere along the way, he'd shed his shirt.

Lord, help me.

He climbed the steps a half hour later, tugging his tee shirt over his head as I placed plates on the kitchen table.

"I grabbed enough for you, if you wanna wash up," I said as he entered.

"Yeah, thanks." He washed his hands at the sink, splashed water on his face, and dried himself with the kitchen towel. Then, he joined me at the table.

"So, how's school?" he asked, scooping fried rice onto his plate.

"Uh—it's hard to juggle, but it's good."

"How many hours are you taking?"

"Just two classes, so six hours. Wanted to ease my way into it."

"Smart," he said. "Have you made any friends?"

I stood and took two sodas from the fridge. "Yeah, a couple," I said as I returned to my seat. "One of them—his name is Martin—I've grown close to."

I wasn't sure why I brought up Martin, other than because it felt like the right thing to do. We weren't *together*, but I'd grown closer to him than anyone else, and that seemed like something Glen should know.

He paused with his fork halfway to his mouth, then rested it on the edge of his plate. "Oh, I see."

"It's not what you're thinking. He's been so kind to me, but it feels—"

"Weird?"

"I was going to say, *pointless.*"

He leaned back in his chair and crossed his arms over his chest. "You can do whatever you want, Cat. That's been the arrangement since Pensacola, hasn't it?"

I nodded. "I know, but it's not—that's not what I want. Not with Martin."

He picked up his fork and poked at his chicken.

"Have you—done whatever you want?" I asked.

His eyes flicked up to mine as he set his fork down again. "Are you asking if I've been with anyone?"

"Yes." There was no sense beating around the bush. We were so far beyond that—*years* beyond that.

"No."

"No?"

"No," he said again. "I guess I've felt the same way—that it would be pointless. If I can't be the man you need me to be, Cat; a man you could love—then I don't want it. I don't want anyone."

"Well, that doesn't seem fair. Just because we're not a good match doesn't mean you couldn't find a better match with someone else."

He shook his head. "We *are* a good match, Catherine. The best match. I'll never find that again—not in a million lifetimes—but I want you to be happy. So, if this *Martin* makes you happy, then you should give it a chance."

I couldn't believe it, and it made me both sad and furious. All I'd ever wanted was *this man*...for us to be a family. He'd told me repeatedly that it couldn't happen; that he was broken. Yet there he sat, professing undying love, and that he'd never want anyone else.

It was too much.

"Well, what I meant by *pointless* is that he's moving away soon. He graduates next month."

"Oh. I'm sorry to hear that, I guess." He sat upright again and went back to his food.

The shift in body language was almost comical. I couldn't help but smile at the transparency of it.

"What are you grinnin' for?" he asked.

"It's just that you don't seem too sorry about it."

"All cards on the table?"

"Always."

"I'm not sorry *Martin's* moving away. Not one bit."

"But we're free to do whatever we want?" I asked with a smirk.

"Of course. Doesn't mean I have to like it."

26

ROCKY ROAD & REGRET

The semester ended, and it led to a long, lonely, boring summer.

Martin had moved to New Orleans—with a sweet goodbye that left me a bit sad, but not heartbroken. Liza was with her cousin in Pensacola for the season, Jenna was in and out of the house (but mostly out) with Tyler and Michelle, and I hadn't signed up for summer classes. It was actually so long, lonely, and boring that I looked forward to Mama's Sunday night dinners.

Then, the Friday before school started, Jenna traveled to Destin with Michelle's family for one final summer getaway. It was that night, after a half bottle of wine on the front porch, that I grew *tired* of being lonely. So, I picked up the phone and called Glen.

"Hello?" he answered, groggy from sleep.

"Did I wake you? It's only 9:00, old man."

"Waking up at 4:30 in the morning will do that to ya," he said.

"Right. Sorry. I can let you go..."

"No, Cat, it's fine. Fell asleep on the couch watching the weather. What's up?"

"I don't know. Had nothing better to do, so I thought you could keep me company."

"No Friday night movie?"

"Nope. Liza's in Pensacola and Jenna's in Destin."

"Who'd she go to Destin with?"

"Michelle, of course."

"Of course. Michelle really is her Liza, ya know."

"I know," I said with a smile.

"How much have you had to drink?"

"What? How did you—"

"I can sense the nostalgic smile, and you only ever smile like that when you're drinking, Cat."

"Oh, *give me a break*...you cannot!" I grabbed the bottle and topped off my glass.

"Glug, glug, glug—" he said. "I can hear you pouring it."

That made me laugh out loud, and I was grateful for it. It felt so good to laugh. I pulled my legs up beneath me on the swing and settled in. "It's been a hell of a summer. I deserve a bottle of wine on the porch, thank you."

"Hmm," he said in what sounded like a tone of agreement. "You're doing a great job with it all, ya know."

"Am I? Doesn't always feel that way."

"You are. It's not easy working full time, raising a teenager, going to school, keeping that old house in shape—you're really something amazing, Cat."

I didn't feel amazing. I felt exhausted and restless from treading water and getting nowhere fast. With a sigh, I took a sip, and said, "Then pour a glass and raise a toast in my honor, why don't ya?"

There was no reply and for a moment, I thought we'd lost the connection. "You there?"

"I have a better idea."

"What?"

"You go take a long bath and I'll bring pizza."

My heart skipped a beat as every red flag in the world seemed to materialize inside my brain all at once.

He couldn't be serious.

"I already ate," I answered, trying my best to stay cool.

"Ice cream then."

"Glen, what—"

"Shh, Cat. Just say *okay*."

I wanted to say, *that sounds like a terrible idea.* I wanted to remind him he was two hours away and it would be damn near midnight before he got there. I wanted to flat out tell him, *hell no*, and end the conversation...

But did I? Is that what I wanted?

What I wanted was to not be alone.

"Cat?"

I took the largest gulp of wine I'd taken in my life, and said, "Rocky Road."

"As if I'd dare bring anything else. On my way."

"Okay," I said in a near-whisper.

"And Cat?"

"Yeah?"

"Leave the porch light on."

⁕

I took that bath, and after much deliberation, decided it didn't mean a damn thing if I shaved my legs while I was in there. I usually shaved in the bath, right? *No big deal.*

Just as I pulled my wet hair up into a loose knot on the top of my head and slipped into a pair of lightweight pajama bottoms and an old t-shirt, I heard the front door creak open, then close.

I smoothed moisturizer over my face and neck, sprayed deodorant under each arm, then moved to the living room, where Glen stood, holding a tub of ice cream.

"How was the drive?" I asked, leading him toward the kitchen.

"Not bad. No traffic this time of night." He pulled bowls from the cabinet like he still lived there, then reached into the drawer for the ice cream scooper. I sat at the table, because clearly, he had it under control.

When he brought the bowls and spoons to the table, I dug in. "Nothing ever tastes as good as the first bite," I said, savoring it.

He watched me for a moment, then asked, "Is everything okay?"

"Yeah, why?"

"Just...on the phone, you sounded like you could use some company."

I nodded, because yes, I was craving company. I just didn't know when I called him that it would turn into...a midnight rendezvous. "Like I said, it's been a rough summer."

"In what way?"

"Everything just went from super busy to...not, I guess. Jenna and Liza have been gone most of the summer. I didn't take any classes. Martin's gone." I stirred the melting ice cream in my bowl. "It feels like everyone made their connections to far-off, exciting places, and I'm riding the bus alone." I scooped another bite. "But not the fun bus," I said, pointing my spoon at him for emphasis. "I'm stuck on the one that just goes in circles around town. That bus stops at like...the post office and the grocery store." I gave a grin, hoping to convey that I wasn't looking for any sort of deep discussion about it; that I was okay.

He reached across the table and briefly rested his palm on my cheek. "You're not alone, Cat."

"I know. Sorry for all the whining. It's just been a bit lonely, is all. Jenna will be back on Sunday, then Liza shortly after. I should really soak up the peace and quiet while I can."

He removed his baseball cap, scratched his head, and smiled as he tossed the cap on the table.

And all I could think was, *God, he's a handsome man.* Followed by, *nope.*

It was time for the man to go.

"So, uh—thanks for driving all the way out here. You didn't have to do that." I stood, collected our bowls, and carried them to the sink.

As I rinsed them, I felt a warm breath on my neck as his arms wrapped around my waist. It had been a long time since I'd forgotten how to breathe, but I suddenly remembered exactly what it felt like.

I turned to face him, slowly, feeling a bit dizzy by how quickly it had all escalated. He hadn't touched me *like that* or stood *that close* in…a whole decade.

"A late-night drive and Rocky Road won't buy you sex, ya know," I said, looking up into those deep blue eyes.

Everything within me shouted, *look away!* But then I wondered, *what if I didn't?* What if I chose *not* to follow my gut?

A slow smile spread across his whole face. "I'm only here because you sounded like you could use a friend. In fact, no matter *how* hard you try to seduce me with your—" He leaned in close and breathed in deep. "—jasmine-scented hair and dewy, post-bubble bath skin, I *won't* have sex with you." When he leaned in again, he whispered right into my ear. "Might as well get that idea out of your filthy, gorgeous little head—right now."

I shoved him away with two hands on two solid pectorals. "Oh, get *over* yourself," I said with a laugh.

He smiled. "I mean it. Keep your mitts off me, woman. Control yourself." He turned and walked toward the door.

"Where are you going?"

"Home. I made you feel better, right? My job here is done." He placed a hand on the doorknob, paused, then gave me a cocky grin over his shoulder. "*Or—*"

"Or what?"

"We could go to the lake."

"Still just as many stars as ever," I said, looking up into the heavens.

"No matter how much everything changes, this place always remains the same." He pointed to a shooting star. "See?"

I reached for the cooler, pulled out a can of beer, and handed it to him. Then, I grabbed one for myself. He stared at his for a moment before popping the top.

"I assumed you wanted one," I said. "You don't have to drink it if you don't."

"I'm good, Cat."

"You sure?"

"Yes. I'm in a good place. For now, at least, I'm in control of the beer, not the other way around."

"That's good to hear. But what moves you from a good place to a...bad one?"

He crossed his legs at the ankles, holding himself up with one arm and grasping the can in his other hand. "Everything, I guess."

"Like?"

"Literally *everything*. Work is stressful at times. I've never ran a business before. I don't know what I'm doing."

I waited for him to go on because I knew it wasn't just work that drove him to drink.

"And Uncle Rudy's not doing so great. He's on blood pressure meds, but they can't get it under control. It's affecting his kidneys now."

"Oh, I didn't know. Janine hasn't mentioned anything."

"I don't know what I'll do if he retires. I'm barely keeping the Montgomery branch alive. There's no way I could handle both."

"I thought business was good in Montgomery?"

"It is. The problem is that I don't know how to run it all efficiently. I'm a *laborer*. I'm made for getting my hands dirty, not sitting behind a desk, barking orders."

I turned my eyes from the water to see the profile of his face, silhouetted by the moonlight. He was still my Glen. He'd do anything to fix everything that was broken, but he only knew how to fix with his hands, his back—with hard, manual work.

"You'll figure it out, Glen."

He took a long drink of beer. "I will—eventually. I promised you I'd make something of myself one day, Cat, and I'm going to do it."

I lifted my face to the stars, then squeezed my eyes shut as a tear rolled down my cheek.

How could he not see that learning to manage a business wouldn't make him who he was meant to be? That there was so much more work to be done? I knew he was a good man. I'd always known it. But he was meant for more. *We* were meant for more.

"What else?" I asked.

"Hmm?"

"What else drives you to drink—in the unhealthy way?"

"I think you know the answer to that."

"Me? Jenna?"

"I have so much regret. So much damn regret."

"We all do. It's one of the terrible things about being human," I said.

"What do you regret?"

"I regret not seeing through the whole *Ally on the porch* thing. I should have known it wasn't what it looked like, and I should have—I don't know—kicked her ass, sent her on her way, and stayed to talk about it."

"There isn't a woman alive who would've reacted that way, Cat."

"I should've never gone to Pensacola. I should have—done literally anything else. I also regret not realizing how much your dad hurt you. If I'd known, we could've talked about it—before deciding to have a baby."

"I wasn't exactly forthcoming. How could you have known?"

I turned to look out over the water. "I'm so angry about how it all turned out. For a long time, I felt nothing at all. I was just—numb. Now that I actually *feel* again, I wish I could turn it all back off. The anger is too much."

"Yeah, me too."

"Tell me what it's like for you. When you think about your dad, when you hit rock bottom, what is it like?"

"Shit, Catherine—" He sat up straight, pulling his knees in and resting his arms on them. Then, he turned to look at me as if asking, *do you really want to know?*

I nodded my answer to his unspoken question.

"It's not anger, for starters. It's *homicidal rage*. If I could track him down and kill him with no one ever knowing, I would. Wouldn't think twice about it."

"You wouldn't."

"I would."

Even in the near-dark, in the shadows, I could sense the seriousness in the look he sent my way, and it made the hair on the back of my neck stand on end.

"Do you know what it's like to wake in the middle of the night, with your drunken father standing over your bed? To lie motionless, because if he knows you're awake, you're done for? To hear him walk down the hall and do the same thing to your sister? To hear her screams because she didn't have the sense to keep her eyes shut? Robbi was always begging for a fight. She never knew when to play dumb, to hide. She wanted to prove she could take it...that he couldn't hurt her. But he did. He always did."

My heart hurt. There were no words.

"After we moved here, I shrugged it off. I made myself believe that it wasn't so bad; wasn't that abnormal. That lots of kids had asshole parents, ya know? I was fine. Mom and I were happy. I met you, I had football and work, and friends—I was fine. But then Jenna was born, and it all came back. I was so scared. I knew I'd never hurt her like he hurt us, but there are so many ways to hurt a child...I just couldn't do it.

"Then Robbi—well, Robbi called after all those years just to kill herself while I was on the line." He pulled a cigarette from the pack lying on the grass, then flicked a lighter. His face glowed amber by its light just long enough for me to see him close his eyes as he took the first long drag.

"I'll *never* forgive her for that. She said she was pregnant, then she said *we weren't meant to be parents,* then she killed herself. All while you stood there holding the most beautiful baby I'd ever laid eyes on. A baby that was *mine.*" He wiped away a tear, then turned to face me. "I'm so sorry, Cat. You had no idea what you were getting yourself into, and you didn't deserve it. I'm so sorry."

I scooted closer, swung my legs over his lap, and hugged his neck. Then he cried.

"You have done the best you could. Maybe you weren't around as much as some dads, but you were around a hell of a lot more than many others. You've done the best you could."

He snubbed his cigarette in the grass, wrapped his arms around me, and squeezed tight. "I miss you so much. Sometimes, I think I hear your voice, but it's always just some stranger in the crowd. Or I think I see you from behind, but it's never you. When I close my eyes, I see you. I'm always wondering what you're doing, where you are, if you're happy. I don't think I'll ever be happy again, Cat, but I want you to be...I'd do anything just to know you were happy.

"I thought it would get easier; that with time, I could move on. But it's been two years since I moved out, and it's not easier. It's like there's a wound I'd hoped would heal, but it's only healed on the outside. Inside, it's—festering. I don't know what to do. I don't know how to—not love you, Cat."

Burying my face in his neck and my hand in his hair, I held him tight, not knowing how to respond to all the feelings he'd just dumped in my lap. It hit too close to home, because all of it was true. I felt it, too.

I still loved him. I'd never stopped loving him. Even when I was so angry with him about Ally that I could have burned our house down with him inside it, I still loved him, and I didn't know how to make that kind of love go away.

"Take me home, Glen."

His eyes searched mine by the moonlight, trying to determine if I was angry or upset. Then, he simply said, "Okay."

I slid my legs off his lap, then he stood and offered a hand. Pulling me to my feet, he said, "I'm sorry, Cat."

"Enough of that. I love you, Glen Lewis. I always have. And we've always made our own music; done things our own way, right?"

He let out a long, slow breath as he held himself intact. "We have."

"Then take me home. Hold me. Love me."

"I don't know if I can do that, Catherine. I don't know if I could ever let go if I did."

Wrapping my arms around his neck, I rested my head on his shoulder, and said, "Then we'll have to learn how. It's the best we're gonna get."

He pulled back to see my face, and asked, "Can I kiss you, Cat?"

I nodded, then stood on my toes to reach him.

It was a kiss that felt so open and raw, and for a moment, every kiss I'd shared with Martin flashed through my mind, melding into what felt like a memory of one, singular kiss. At the time, I thought Martin's kiss was okay—great, even—but when Glen's lips touched mine, I realized why kissing Martin had only left me feeling hollow.

It was because his kiss was the wrong shape, the wrong size. Martin's kiss didn't fill the void inside me...and, instincts be damned, I'd just been reminded that Glen's did, and always had.

NOW

J enna scratches her head as she says, "So, you had a one-night-stand...with your own husband?"

"Not exactly. More like a four-year secret affair with my own husband."

"Mama!" The look on her face tells me she's shocked, and maybe even a tiny bit repulsed.

They never do really grow up, do they?

They're always still just your kids—disgusted by the idea of their parents ever having had a sex life.

"There were a lot worse things I could have done, Jenna. Having sex with your spouse is pretty low on the sin spectrum, I think."

She leans back in her seat. "Did you ever—was I ever—was I *there?*"

"He lived two hours away! It's not like he was just poppin' in for a quickie after you went to sleep."

"Oh, *God!* Never say that word again, okay?" She turns her head away, like she can't even look me in the eye.

I laugh as I stand and head toward the bathroom. When I return, she's hugging a pillow to her chest, gnawing on her fingernails.

"Well?" I ask, knowing she has questions or something more she wants to say.

"Give me a minute," she answers.

I wait, because if there's one thing I know about my daughter, it's that you don't push her to talk before she's ready.

"Okay. It makes sense. When I think about it, it makes sense," she says.

I nod.

"And I *really* like Martin."

That makes me smile. "Yeah, me too."

"Whatever happened to him?"

"A man like that doesn't stay single for long. He was married within a year," I say with a smile.

"Good for him," she replies with a smile of her own. "But how did it end—with Daddy? You said four years, so that would've been when I was seventeen?"

"That's right," I reply.

"Well, who called it off?"

"I did."

She gasps. "No way."

"What do you mean, *no way?* You don't think I could ever have the backbone to stand up for myself?"

"No, Mama. Of course that's not it. I just—I guess I still have some belief that he was a runner. I mean, come on, how many times did he come and go when he lived with us? He did whatever he wanted."

"Because that was our arrangement. God, Jenna, are you listening at all?"

"I'm listening!"

"Allowing him that freedom—to come home when he felt he could and to go away when he needed to—is what kept him in your life for so long. He needed that space to breathe, because he was lost, Jenna. Broken. And I needed to be free of feeling like I was responsible for him. Allowing him to come and go did those things...for both of us."

"I get it, okay? I get it." She runs a hand through her hair, then hugs the pillow tighter. "So why did it end?"

"Because it had to."

"Could you be a bit less vague, please?"

I reached for the wine bottle and topped off her glass. "Because in 2001, it was me who broke."

2001

27

GOODBYE BLUES & COFFEE BEANS

We carried on in secret, with Glen always parking elsewhere in the neighborhood and arriving through the back gate. And he always brought his guitar. He'd play old songs I'd forgotten about, new songs I didn't even know, and sometimes, he'd strum absentmindedly while we talked.

We knew we couldn't be together in a real way: I'd set boundaries for how much of his emotional wellbeing I'd take responsibility for years ago. Glen had his own set of boundaries—regarding how much he could and couldn't risk with Jenna.

But just as much as we couldn't be together, we also couldn't be apart. All those years after Pensacola, we were roommates—strictly platonic. As weird as that may seem to other people, it worked for us because *we were together*, and the world felt calmer, safer, more sensical when we were together—whether sex was involved or not. Neither of us could let go.

By Jenna's junior year, she had switched from track to cross country (alongside Michelle) and was working at Blockbuster (also with Michelle). Whatever one of them did, the other did too. Glen saw her less and less as her life became increasingly centered on her friends—particularly Tyler. They never dated, that I knew of, but there was something significant there, nonetheless.

In mid-March, she spent the week of spring break at Michelle's, and Glen spent three blissful days and nights with me. He was never himself in

March, but it had become clear that he handled the anniversary of Robin's passing better when he was with me than when he wasn't.

On his last night, as we laid twisted together under the sheets, I listened to the slow rhythm of his breath as he drifted off to sleep. It was 2:00 in the morning, and I knew we had just over two more hours together in our perfect cocoon.

Two hours wasn't enough.

Forever would never be enough.

I couldn't sleep, and when he opened his eyes at 4:27, I smiled.

"It's freaky how you do that," I said.

"Do what?" he mumbled in that sleepy, raspy voice.

"Just wake up, like you've got some sort of built-in alarm clock."

"Hmm," he said, raising one arm up and resting it beneath his head. "I've woken up at the same time for twenty years, Cat. I'm my own damn rooster."

I gave a tiny laugh at that, because it *was* funny, but I was too tired to offer more.

"Why are you awake?" He stroked my hair away from my face.

"Couldn't sleep."

"Ah. You've got the goodbye blues."

I sucked in a deep breath, then let it out slowly, as I felt tears well up behind my closed eyelids. "Yeah, guess I do."

"Me too." He brought the arm out from under his head, slipped it behind my neck, and pulled me in close. "But...I do have to go."

"Not yet. Stay until the sunrise."

"What? No, I can't, you know that. Sneak in, sneak out."

"Screw the nosey neighbors. Stay."

He slid his arm out from under my neck, sat up on the edge of the bed, then stood.

My heart sank—he was leaving.

He moved to the bedroom window, drawing back the curtains. Then he raised the blinds. Returning to bed, he slid his arm right back under my neck and said, "What are you crying for, woman? You know I can't say no to you."

I tilted my face toward his. "We still have a couple hours before sunrise, though."

"What should we do with our time?"

I slid my hand across his chest, then down to the angled muscles at his hips.

"I like where your head's at," he said, with a slight tug of my hair.

"What do you mean? Waffles? 'Cause that's where my head's at. I'm starving."

In one quick motion, he flipped me onto my back and straddled my hips. As he leaned in close, he whispered, "Sure, babe. *Later.*"

In early May, I stood at the bursar's desk at school, going over student loan repayment schedules and wishing I would've at least grabbed something from the Hardee's drive through on the way there. I was lightheaded, short of breath, and a nervous wreck.

Graduation was in four weeks.

It felt silly going through the motions of graduation when I was thirty-seven years old and everyone around me was...*not.* But I'd worked so hard that I didn't care if it was silly. I *wanted* the cap and gown, the senior pictures, the ring, the announcements. I wasn't planning to invite anyone outside our small family, but it was important to me, just the same.

I was even excited for the graduation party Mama decided to host at her house after the ceremony—which meant I tolerated the twice a day phone calls to ask about what food I'd like, who I'd like to invite, whether I wanted red or white wine (the answer was both), and on and on.

After picking up my cap and gown, I set out to meet Liza at the bakery for brunch. It shared space with the bookshop, which made it my favorite spot in Asher, aside from the library. That day, though, when I entered, the cozy, wonderful scent of fresh-ground coffee beans was overwhelming...damn near sickeningly so.

That's when I knew I was pregnant.

Liza was people-watching from a two-person bistro table by the front window. Just as the realization hit me, she turned her head, and her eyes met mine. I opened my mouth to say something, though I didn't know what. She was by my side before I'd even closed it again.

"Hey, are you sick? Do you need to sit down?" she asked.

I pulled out the closest chair and flopped into it, still staring at Liza.

"Do you have food poisoning or something? You're like—you're *gray*."

Looking around, I spotted at least three people who I either knew directly or through Mama. It was not a safe space to have a mental breakdown. "I, uh—I need to go home."

She nodded. "Can you drive?"

"Of course I can drive, Liza."

"Well, I'm just sayin'—you look—"

"Terrible. I get it."

"I'll follow you," she replied.

Once we were on the sidewalk and moving toward the parking lot, I leaned in close to Liza and whispered, "I need a pregnancy test."

She stopped dead in her tracks.

I turned to face her. "Can you pick one up?"

She closed the distance between us and took my hands in hers. "No need. I have a whole stockpile at home."

My face must have given away my surprised/not-surprised reaction to that statement.

"What? I told you, I'm not having any babies. I keep an eye on my shit." She pushed the button at the crosswalk, and we waited for the signal to cross. "How late are you?"

"I'm not sure. I've been so preoccupied with finals and graduation, I just sorta lost track of everything else. I haven't even thought about my period in...well, I don't know how long."

Liza looped her arm through mine as we crossed the street. "But you're on the pill, right?"

I nodded.

"Then it's probably just stress. It's thrown your cycle off. Let's not get ahead of ourselves, okay?"

I nodded again, but inwardly, I *screamed*.

I knew, without a doubt, that I was pregnant and within the hour, Liza knew it, too.

◆

"What are you going to do?" Liza asked as we rocked in the swing.

"I don't know."

"I'm assuming it's Glen's?"

I threw her a wicked glare.

"Just making sure, jeez," she said. "You two have had this weird arrangement for years. For all I know, it very well could be someone else's."

"Don't you think I'd tell you if there was someone else?"

"I don't know. You still haven't come clean about Martin."

"That's because I've told you a thousand times that Martin and I never slept together."

"Okay, *okay*. You're sticking to the *we just fooled around* bit. Got it." Her attention went to a dog barking somewhere in a back yard down the street, then she looked back at me. "Will you tell Glen?"

"I need to figure out how I feel about it first; decide what to do." I pulled my legs up and crossed them beneath me. "It's so unfair."

"Which part?"

"I wanted another baby more than anything when Jenna was little. I wanted so bad for her to have a little brother or sister. Bo and I haven't always been close, but as kids, we were best friends. I wanted that for her so much. And man, do I miss what it feels like having a baby resting on my chest...in my arms. That little scrunch they do when you pick them up..."

Liza placed her hand on my knee and gave a squeeze.

"If this would've happened back then, there'd be nothing to think about. But now—Jenna's a year from graduation, Liza. That age difference is *insane*. Can you imagine?"

"No, I for sure cannot."

"Just when she's ready to fly the coop, I'd what? Start over? Just the idea of it is exhausting. I'm not twenty-years-old anymore. I don't have the same energy...or patience. And *God*, what would I even *tell* people?"

"I think *people* should be the least of your concerns. You need to figure out what *you* want. You can worry about people later. Or don't worry about them at all. That's my vote."

"I wish it were that easy."

"I mean, it could be. I've never given a damn what people in this town thought about anything, have I?"

"No, you haven't, but I'm not like you. We're not the same."

She nodded and pulled her hand back to her lap. "Well, we can stay here as long as you want. We can talk, or not talk. Whatever you want to do."

My legs were falling asleep, so I unfolded them, placing both feet back on the porch. "I will either have this baby and place it with a family who will love it, or..."

"Or?"

"Hop back on the merry-go-round."

"No third option for you?" Liza asked.

"No. I couldn't do that. I'd spend the rest of my life thinking…wondering…regretting. I know myself, and I don't think I would survive it. I'm not strong enough."

Liza took my hand again. "Catherine, you're the strongest person I know. I understand what you're saying—the reasoning. I get it, and I support it. But I won't let you think of yourself as weak. You've never been weak, ever. Well, aside from a soft spot for a certain tall, handsome man…and really, who could blame you for that?" She squeezed my hand tight and smiled.

"Thank you, Liza…for everything. I don't know what I'd do without you."

"Well, luckily, you won't ever need to find out. It's you and me till the end, remember?"

I laid my head on her shoulder and set the swing in motion. "Bonnie and Clyde."

Liza went with me to the doctor the following week, where they drew blood to confirm the pregnancy. I was told to come back in three weeks for an ultrasound, which, in my best-guess, would put me between twelve and thirteen weeks pregnant. It would also be just two days after graduation.

"Why is it that every time you graduate, you're hiding some big, life-changing secret? An elopement, a pregnancy—" Liza asked as she cut into her spinach enchilada.

I gasped. "*Oh, God,* what do you think it will be after I finish my master's?"

"Maybe you'll decide you're sick of it all and become a nun?"

I dipped a tortilla chip in queso, then held it up to Liza's fork as a toast. "Cheers to that."

Just as I popped the bite into my mouth, Liza's eyes flicked up to someone behind me, and I felt a hand on my shoulder.

"Janine! Hi!" I stood and wrapped her in a hug.

"Hello, ladies. Enjoying your lunch?" Janine asked with a smile.

Liza slurped her drink. "Best margaritas in the county," she said with another slurp.

"Have one for me. Tequila and meds don't mix." She made a silly frowny face, then turned to me. "Have you spoken to my son? He's coming in tomorrow to do some work for Rudy. He's shorthanded this week."

"No, but—ask him to come see me while he's here, okay?"

Liza's eyes darted back and forth between me and Janine.

"Sure," Janine said. "Well, I'll leave you two to it. Come see me soon, Catherine."

I nodded. "See you soon."

After Janine picked up her takeout order and exited the restaurant, Liza looked to me with an *I'm glad I'm not you* face. "Looks like you're going to have to figure this out sooner rather than later."

"Yup. Especially now that *she* knows."

"What do you mean she knows? It was a one-minute conversation."

"It's not the length of conversation that matters, Liza."

"Not everyone has a gift like yours, ya know."

I sighed in exasperation. "I'm not psychic, for cryin' out loud! You know what? Never mind. It doesn't matter. I've decided what I'm going to do."

Liza leaned forward and took another sip through her straw, without touching the massive, frozen goblet in front of her. "Yeah?" she asked, still gripping the straw between her teeth.

"I'm having a baby."

"Well, that part's a given."

"And I'm keeping it."

"Oh, *shit.*" Liza leaned back in her seat and crossed her arms. "Well, all right then. When do we get to go shopping?"

—◆—

The next day after work, I kicked off my shoes and laid on the couch, exhausted. I'd forgotten how much the first trimester wipes you out. I closed my eyes, thinking I just needed a fifteen-minute nap before Jenna got home from school. Fifteen minutes wouldn't hurt anything, right?

When I woke again, it was to the sound of a knock on the door. I sat up straight, shook my head a little to clear the grogginess, then stood to answer it.

"Hey," Glen said.

"Hey." I rubbed my eyes and opened the door wider for him to enter. "I heard you were in town. How's Uncle Rudy?"

"He's good. Hangin' in there. But how are you? Are you sick?" He stepped close and took my head in his hands.

"Not sick, exactly, no."

His face contorted in that way it does when he's worried. "Mom said you wanted to see me."

"Sit. I'll bring you a beer," I answered.

"I'll get it." He turned toward the kitchen.

I picked my usual spot on the sofa and pulled a throw blanket up over my legs. He returned from the kitchen and offered me one of the two bottles in his hand, which I declined. Then he sat in the chair, pulled off his work boots, and took a sip.

"There's no subtle way to say this," I said as he took another drink. "Glen—I'm pregnant."

All at once, he choked, stood, spewed a mouthful of beer across the living room, coughed, and asked, "What did you just say?"

"You heard me correctly."

"What? How? I mean—*whoa*, Catherine." He sat back down in the chair, his eyes never leaving mine.

"Yeah. Whoa." I pulled the blanket up higher, over my chest. "And I'm pretty sure your mom knows."

"How would she?"

"I saw her yesterday. I don't know for sure that she does, but mamas have a certain sense about these things. I've avoided mine since I found out, for that very reason."

"When *did* you find out?" he asked. "Why didn't you call me?"

"Last week. I needed to let it sink in a bit before I told you. This is—a lot to wrap my head around."

"Cat, don't take this the wrong way, but is it mine?"

I felt my face grow hot and my ears rang.

"Yes, I'm sure," I answered as calmly as I could muster.

He leaned forward, with both elbows on his knees, and hands clasped between them. "Wow, okay. Well, do you want to talk about it now, or do you need a bit more time?"

"I could ask you the same thing."

"Me? No, I don't need time. I'm sick of wasting time, Cat."

He stood, crossed over to the sofa, kneeled in front of me, and took my hands. "No more wasting time. We didn't plan for this, but it's happening. Jenna's nearly grown, Cat, and I've wasted all of it. I won't do that again. I want to be a dad—a *real* dad—to this baby. If you'll let me."

28

BROKEN MEN & SHATTERED DREAMS

I pulled my hands free from his. "You're not serious."

"When you said I was being a father by somehow convincing myself I wasn't, you were right. I'm tired of hiding from it, and I'm not scared anymore. I want us to be a family. I can do it—I *know* I can."

When contemplating all the possible ways this conversation could go, I never imagined it would go like this...and it made me furious.

"I think you need to leave," I said.

"Isn't this what you want? What we both want?"

"Do you think it's what *Jenna* would want, Glen?"

He looked so confused that it both made me pity him and want to murder him on the spot. I threw the blanket off my lap, stood, and walked to the door. Opening it, I motioned for him to leave.

"Talk to me, Cat," he said when he stood. "Help me understand."

I didn't want to help him understand. The fact he was so blind to it only made me angrier.

How could he not get it?

"For Jenna's entire life, you've kept your distance because you were so afraid of hurting her. Now, she's nearly grown, and you feel like *you can do it?* Not with her though...no, with a *new* baby. That one, you can be a dad to, the way Jenna always wished you would've done for her. The way *I've* always wished you would've done for her!"

"That's not what I meant—"

"I know it wasn't, because you're too damn dumb to see it, but it *is* the truth." I motioned again for him to leave.

"Don't make me go. Let's talk about this. I'm sorry if I—"

"I don't want your apologies. You can't push your daughter away her whole life because you were broken, then be the dad she never had to her sibling. I won't let you do it."

"Then what do you want from me, Cat?"

I'd assumed Glen's role in the baby's life would be the same as it was in Jenna's. Now, I wasn't sure I even wanted that. He didn't *get it*, and that only made me see *red*.

Then, it hit me: He would never get it. As long as he was broken, he'd never understand how not to break my babies...how not to break me.

"I want you to leave. Other than that, I don't want a damn thing."

—◦—

For three weeks, I held myself together as best I could. My emotions ranged from excitement at the thought of holding a baby of my own again, of watching them grow, and learn, and shine...to crying in desperation for it all to be a dream.

Then, on the Tuesday before graduation, Liza and I went out to dinner. Afterward, while window shopping and ducking into stores to snag things Liza just had to have, I spotted something *I* had to have.

"What's that?" Liza asked.

"Goodnight Moon." I held the book to my chest. "It was Jenna's favorite. We read it so much when she was little that the cover came right off. I kept it, but—"

"You're thinking baby deserves a new book."

"Yeah." My hand went instinctively to my belly.

Liza saw, then looked me in the eye, trying to determine what I was feeling.

"I never thought I'd be in this position, Liza, but—I'm not scared anymore. I'm just—so damn happy."

She smiled, grabbed my hand, and led me to the checkout counter.

Walking toward the parking lot afterward, I clutched the book to my chest and said, "I told Glen."

"Was he an ass about it?"

"Not in the way you would expect." We came to the car, so I leaned against it, still clutching the book. "He said he was ready to be a dad to this baby—that he could do it."

Liza looked at me, confused. "That's a good thing, isn't it?"

"It would be if he'd ever once said the same thing about Jenna. It's not fair, Liza! How would that make her feel?"

"It's been seventeen years. People change. If he's ready, doesn't that mean he's ready to be who Jenna needs him to be too?"

I shook my head. "She's off to college in a year. It's too little, too late."

"Kids don't stop needing their fathers just because they grow up. She'll always need her daddy, Catherine."

I looked down at my toes, remembering all the times I'd cried in the dark because I was a grown woman who still needed her daddy. How many times had I thought that I would give anything for one more hug? One more conversation? One more goodnight kiss on the forehead?

"Come on, let's go home." Liza opened my door. "We'll stop at the Piggly for snacks."

"Rocky Road. And salt and vinegar potato chips," I said.

"Yup. ETA: five minutes."

Over the course of two days, Glen's number appeared on the caller ID fourteen times. On the fifteenth, I picked up.

"Hello?"

"Hey," he replied.

There was a long, uncomfortable silence on the line.

"Did you need something?"

"Don't be like that, Cat, please. We need to talk."

"About what?"

"Catherine!" His voice was one of a man at his wit's end—a man who'd run out of patience for any sort of games.

"Fine," I said.

"I'm at Mom's. Can I come over?"

"No."

He sighed. "How are you feeling?"

"A bit crampy, but okay." Truth was, I'd been crampy for days and had started spotting that morning. I'd scheduled a doctor appointment for the next day.

"And...otherwise?"

I gave a sigh of my own. "Glen, I'm fine. I'm happy...and excited. I wasn't sure if I ever would be, but I am."

"That's great, Cat."

Silence again.

"Have you told your mom?" he asked.

"No. Have you?"

"Of course not, and I won't until you're ready. She's acting weird, though. Like she—"

"Knows?"

"Yeah."

After another long pause, he asked, "So, what do we do? What do you need from me?"

It was the question I'd been dreading, but I knew the answer. I'd known it since the day he said he wanted us to become a real family for this baby.

"I don't want you to do anything. I'll raise this baby on my own, just like I mostly did with Jenna, and they will feel just as loved by their mama as Jenna always has. I don't want—or need—you to do anything. In fact, I'd prefer it if you didn't."

"What does that mean?"

"It means you should continue to be a part of Jenna's life, but you can't call here anymore. I'll get her a cell phone and send you the number. She's heading off to college in a year, so you're in the home stretch, right? Then, you'll be free."

"I don't want to be free, Catherine. I want us to be a family."

"You still don't get it?"

"Get *what?* I understand you're upset that I've never been the person you wanted me to be for Jenna, but God, Catherine, can't I just have your permission to *start* trying to be that person? How do I ever become him if you won't let me try?"

"You don't just flip a switch and become a whole new person, and you know that. It takes time and work. You need to do the work, and I'm about to have a baby to worry about, and care for, and love. I don't have it in me to do that and also hold your hand while you get your shit together, Glen. I don't."

"So, what are you saying?"

"I'm saying, I'm done. I wish you all the best, but I can't do this anymore. Please don't call here again."

"Cat, please don't do this. I love you. I *need* you. I don't like the person I am when I'm not with you. Catherine, please—"

"And you don't see a problem with that? You shouldn't need me in your life to be the person you want to be...to *like* yourself. I can't be your crutch forever, and you can't always be mine."

"But—"

"Glen, I'm begging you to get the help you need. Do whatever's necessary to find happiness with yourself, with your life. Go look for that man you always said you'd become. And if you find him...you better also come find me, because...well, I'm gonna want to meet him."

"Catherine—"

"Goodbye, Glen." I hung up the phone.

As I stood, walked to the kitchen, and placed the phone on the dock, my heart pounded hard and fast.

What have I done?

Leaning against the counter, I forced myself to take deep breaths.

Had I really just evicted him from my life, after twenty years of loving him? Twenty years of hoping for him, praying for him, begging the universe to help him, heal him, make him whole?

Two decades of memories flashed through my mind. The good and the bad all bled into one another until I couldn't tell them apart; until they all coexisted in a single moment.

I grew dizzy as my heart pounded and my chest ached. The whole kitchen was a blur, like some obscure impressionist painting. Struggling to make sense of it—to decipher what was a light bulb, a cabinet pull, a faucet handle—I realized I couldn't *see* anything.

Then, I turned toward the windows, and the painting shifted to various shades of green.

My plants.

I found the shape of leaves of ivy; fragile petals of an orchid; fronds of a fern. I ran my fingers along them. The more I touched them, smelled them, looked for them—the more I found. My heartbeat slowed as tears ran down my cheeks.

I squeezed between the dining chairs and the shelves of plants in the windows, touching them, seeing them all...one by one. As I came around the end of the table to the ones hanging across the front window, I bumped into something and heard a crash.

My peace lily.

Pot, roots, and stems...broken.

She was one of the plants Glen gave me for our first anniversary—one of the few that had survived all those years, despite the odds. I'd saved her from certain death more times than I could remember. Every time, I'd felt heartbroken at the thought of losing her, but seeing her in pieces on the floor, I felt—nothing.

I scanned the shelves until I found another he gave me that day. Picking it up with both hands, I threw it down hard against the tile. Clay pieces and potting soil scattered everywhere.

I still felt nothing.

Seizing another pot, I threw that one too. Then another, and another.

I counted them as I threw them...*five, six, seven.* Wiping the hair out of my face, I gave a blood-curdling scream and threw two more.

Ten, eleven, twelve...

I screamed, and threw plants, again and again—ones given to me by Mama, Jenna, and Aunt Kitty, too—I sobbed and grieved for them, but I couldn't stop. I didn't know how to make myself stop.

Then, it felt like I'd been zapped by lightning in my belly. I doubled over in real, physical pain, with eyes clenched tight. When I opened them, I saw red as the world spun.

Blood. And pain.

So much pain.

Gripping the countertop, I moved to the phone and dialed Liza with soil-covered hands.

"Hey, you wanna do dinner?" she asked when she answered.

"Liza—help."

It was the only two words I managed to say before falling unconscious to the floor.

I woke in a hospital room with no memory of Liza coming to the house, the paramedics, the ambulance. I was foggy and confused.

"What happened?" I asked Liza.

She took my hand in hers. "Maybe I should get the doctor."

"Liza—what happened?"

She took a deep breath and said, "You had an ectopic pregnancy. It means the baby implanted in your fallopian tube."

"I know what it means."

She nodded. "It burst, Catherine."

I stared at the ceiling tiles.

"They had to remove the tube. I'm afraid—" Her voice cracked, and she paused.

"I lost the baby."

"I'm so sorry."

I turned to face her. "Okay."

"Okay?"

"What else am I supposed to say?"

She dropped her head into her hands. "Catherine, I—"

"Shh. I'll be fine. Shh." I stroked her hair. The truth was that I wasn't fine, and I didn't know if I ever would be again, but that was my pain to bear—not Liza's. "Where's Jenna?"

She wiped tears from her face. "I called Blockbuster. She's there till 9:00. I didn't tell her anything. Just asked her what movie she wanted to see on Friday."

"Have you told Mama?"

She shook her head. "No."

"Can you call her? I can't—I just can't be the one to say it."

"Of course. Uh—how much do you want her to know?"

"Tell her everything. Then ask her what we should tell Jenna. She can't know the truth, and she should stay with Mama until I'm back on my feet."

"Are you sure you don't want to tell Jenna?"

"It's all over now. There's no sense in telling her anything."

"Okay," she replied. "Okay."

Mama said to tell Jenna it was a cyst, so that's what we did. Graduation came and went, but I missed it. There was no graduation party at Mama's either.

On my second day home, I stared at the mess of plants, pots, and soil covering my kitchen. Liza asked if she could clean it up, and I tried to determine if I cared enough to salvage what plants I could—if it would cause more pain to do so, or to let them go.

Ultimately, I gave Liza the go-ahead, then retreated to my room to cry and sleep. For three days, Liza brought food to my bedside and laid next to me as we watched TV.

"Catherine," she said on that third day. "You're going to have to step foot into your kitchen at some point."

I changed the channel. "Not yet."

"Okay," she said as she stood. "Need anything?"

"No, thank you."

She closed the door behind her as she moved to the kitchen to warm a can of soup for my dinner.

A week or so later, after Liza left to run errands, the doorbell rang. I covered my head with my pillow to drown out the sound, but there was no use. For twenty minutes, it rang and rang, until I thought I'd lose my damn mind.

I threw the covers off and made my way down the hall. "Whoever you are, you better be dyin'!"

When I opened the door, I found Liza, holding a peace lily in one arm and a wriggling basket in the other.

"Thought I'd have to ring all night!" she said.

"What are you ringin' for in the first place?"

"To get you out of that room!"

The basket jerked in her hand, then whimpered.

"Liza—"

She smiled. "This is to re-start your collection." She held the plant out for me to take. "And this is because you need something to take care of in the meantime." She pulled the lid back on the basket and a tiny golden head poked up and tilted to one side.

"You bought me a *dog?*"

"Fostered. If you two don't get along, we can take her back, but she's sweet as pie and you're gonna love her." Liza pulled the puppy from the basket and handed her over to me.

I stood on the porch with a plant in one arm and a soft, warm ball of fur in the other. The puppy wriggled, placed two paws on my shoulder, then licked the whole side of my face.

Liza giggled. "See? The sweetest."

I turned toward the door and walked inside. "Liza?"

"Yeah?"

"Never give me an animal again, okay?"

"Okay. But you love her, right?"

I sat on the sofa and snuggled that little dog tight. "Yeah. I think I do."

⸻◆⸻

We named her Goldie, and she became my second pillar of strength alongside Liza. Once I gave Mama the okay to stop by, she became my third. Then came Aunt Kitty, and eventually, Jenna came home too. I leaned on all of them in different ways. I knew nothing but time would ease the pain but having them buzzing in and out of my house all day, every day, sure helped.

I needed the noise. I got too lost in my head in the quiet, which wasn't a safe place to be. In the silence, I sobbed for my baby and shot angry prayers through the ether, not knowing if they were reaching the ears of anyone who cared.

It was in one of those too-quiet afternoons that it felt like I plummeted all the way to the bottom of—what? Grief? Sorrow? Self-pity? Anger?

All of the above.

It was the day I grew the angriest I'd ever been at God—or at least, at the God that Mama raised us to believe only wanted *good things* for His children. If that were true, how could He have let me lose my daddy at sixteen? My best friend immediately after? My mom and brother in the way that I did? The man I loved—or at least, the man he once was? And now, my *baby?*

No good and kind God would ever let one person lose so much, then expect them to keep living as if their world hadn't crashed down around them, time and time again. What had I done to deserve such penance? To live in constant fear of someone else I loved disappearing in the blink of an eye?

Nothing.

That's when I decided I was done living in fear of whatever undeserved punishment some unknown God would arbitrarily decide to send my way. The problem, though, was that the opposite of fear was faith. And when you don't have faith to replace fear, what's left to stand in its place?

I didn't know, so the only answer that made any sense to me was a bleak one: To cast away the hope with the fear.

If you never hope for anything, you can't fear never getting it. If you don't wish for a happy ending, you can't be crushed when one doesn't come. If you don't open your heart to possibility, you can't be disappointed when the possibilities never arise.

I picked up the phone and called Glen.

"Hey," he said.

"I lost the baby."

"*What?*"

"And I want a divorce."

NOW

“Whoa,” Jenna says. “You were—*pregnant?*”

I nod.

“And your fallopian tube *burst?*”

“Yes.”

“Oh my God. Mama—people *die* from that!”

“Yes, Jenna. I’m aware.”

“It all makes so much sense.”

“What does?”

“I knew something wasn’t right. The way GiGi, Aunt Kitty, and Aunt Liza never left you alone after that. How they all seemed to be in some sort of *mourning*. God, Mama, I thought you had cancer or something! I was terrified!”

My heart skips a beat. “Oh, honey. Why didn’t you talk to one of us?”

“Would it have done any good? You were all lying to me about...everything. What good would it have done?”

“You were seventeen.”

“I was old *enough*.”

I drop my head in pure shame. “You’re right.”

“You didn’t tell me the truth because then you would have had to tell me the truth about all of it, and that was too hard for you.”

I nod as a tear slides down my cheek.

“Why didn’t you tell me later?”

This is something I've asked myself many times, and every time, I've told myself it was better to just let sleeping dogs lie...but now, I see it for what it was—cowardice.

"I should have, I know. But Jenna, I spent so much of my life trying to protect you, and to tell you everything you knew about your family was a lie—well, I didn't realize until too late that it would be impossible to do, because I didn't have the courage to do it. It was all just so—messed up. It was never how I intended to live my life. It's like Daddy died and everything took a massive detour...it all went left somehow."

"So, why tell me now?"

I place my half-full wine glass on the coffee table and reach for the glass of water next to it. Stealing a glance at the clock, I see it's 2:00 in the morning. "Do you think we can finish this tomorrow, hon? It's pretty late."

"Nope. I'd never be able to sleep, and I doubt you would either."

That's the truth.

"Forget the last question. Just...keep going. What happened next?"

"Well, he let me go."

"The divorce. I remember that. It was in January of my senior year, right?"

"Yes."

"What pushed you to do it then, as opposed to all the other times it would have made sense to?"

"Because, as I said, losing the baby broke me. I lost all hope, and I was tired of caring so much. I wanted to be free of it all. I wanted him to heal and have a happy life, but I couldn't be a part of it anymore."

"But you still loved him," she says.

"Yes. I always loved him, and he always loved me. The divorce nearly killed him."

Her eyes flick to mine and take hold.

"He spiraled, hard. I only knew what I heard from Janine, but it was enough. When she told me how bad the drinking got...how he nearly lost his business…how he was living in bars and his truck again…I couldn't take it anymore. I asked her not to tell me anything else. I didn't want to know. It broke my heart. It took everything I had to not pick up the phone and try to bring him back to reality, but I knew I couldn't. If I did, we'd be in the same place all over again, and that wasn't healthy for either of us. I was done spending my life trying to save a man who didn't want to be saved. He needed to sort it out on his own."

She stares, waiting for me to go on.

"Then you graduated high school, got that scholarship here in Texas, and I wasn't doing so good myself. It was like I'd lost my life's purpose when you left. I felt both immensely proud, and like I'd been…set adrift."

"Mama—"

"*But*—I realized I could either sit around and wallow, or I could do something with myself. And since the divorce was finalized and the school no longer needed to consider Glen's income for financial aid, I was able to start grad school. I threw myself into it and found—not a replacement purpose—but an additional purpose, I guess. From there, everything got better."

"Did you ever hear from him after that?"

"When we signed the divorce papers, he asked if we could stay in touch—if we could still be in each other's lives in some way—and I told him again that I didn't want to see him or talk to him until he got the help he needed. I made no promise to spend my life waiting around for him or anything, and I didn't. But I knew that if he ever found his way to the other side, I'd just want to tell him how proud I was of him.

"Which brings me to the answer to your previous question." I take a deep breath and say, "I'm telling you now, because…well, because he's back."

"He's back?"

"Yes, Jenna. Your daddy is back."

ONE WEEK PRIOR

(June, 2021)

29

SOUTHERN SINGLES & BUTTERED BISCUITS

The library doors slid open, and I entered with a deep breath and a smile. The library was my favorite place in the world.

"I thought you were going to be late," Patrick said, vacating my seat behind the circulation desk.

"I'm never late." Stuffing my bag under the countertop, I adjusted the chair to my height and logged him out of the computer.

"Coffee?" he asked.

"Yes, please."

He disappeared to the break room and just as I hit the enter key to login, my phone buzzed inside my purse. I retrieved it and saw that it was Liza. Denying the call, I shot her a text saying, "I'll call on my lunch break."

"Let's get our hair done after work," was her reply.

"I'll call on my lunch break!" I searched for the eyeroll emoji, knowing she was *actually* rolling her eyes at how long it was taking me to reply. I added it and hit send.

Patrick returned, placing a steaming mug of coffee on the desk. "Here you go, boss." He pulled out the chair next to me and sat.

"Thank you. And quit calling me that." I blew on my coffee and took a careful sip.

"But you are the boss. I still don't understand why you choose to work here and not in that cushy office reserved for the head librarian."

"I like being where the people are. The people are the best part about the library—aside from the books, of course."

"Well, of course." He smiled that broad, beautiful, perfect smile.

Patrick almost made me wish my daughter wasn't a happily married mother of three, living eight-hundred miles away. He was adorable, in a bookish sort of way, possessing the most gorgeous hazel eyes behind trendy black frames.

Those tailored pants of his weren't horrible to look at either.

I felt myself blush and turned back to my screen.

"I told you I won't break up your daughter's happy home." He sent a sideways glance in my direction.

"I have no idea what you're talking about." I took another sip of coffee, stifling a smile.

"Have you downloaded that dating app yet?" he asked.

"Yes, I downloaded it—only so you'd quit asking me if I did."

He gave a laugh and said, "Found anyone worth swiping right for?"

The truth of it was, I'd downloaded the app and created a login, but hadn't opened it since. I couldn't let Patrick know that though, so I said, "No. Not one."

"Keep swiping. Sometimes it takes a while to separate the wheat from the chaff."

"If you say so." I grabbed my mug of coffee and set out to find literally anywhere else to be.

<hr>

"So, what are we doing today?" The stylist ran both hands through my hair, tousling it in the back.

"Just a trim and a root cover-up." I hooked a finger under the neck of the smock, attempting to pull it loose, but it wouldn't budge. "Can I get some slack here, please?"

"You should do something different. You've had the same long layers for a decade. Maybe try a shag? They're popular again, ya know," Liza said.

"Ooh, you'd look great with a shag," the stylist piped in as she loosened the smock.

"A shag? If I wanted to look sixteen again, I'd be at a plastic surgeon's office, not a hair salon."

Liza gasped. "Oh my God, you did have a shag!" She doubled over in laughter in the seat next to me. "We were cool once upon a time, weren't we?"

"Were?"

"Well, I'm still cool. Don't know about you." She gave me a once over and shrugged her shoulders.

"I'm going to mix the color. You two play nice." The stylist disappeared to the back and Liza sent another disapproving look in my direction.

"Will you at least let her dermaplane your face?" she asked.

"What's wrong with my face?"

"Nothing...if your intent is to grow a full beard by Labor Day."

"Liza!"

"I mean, if that's what you're into, go for it. You do you."

"You want to *shave my face?*"

"Dermaplane it. There's a difference. You can tell yourself it's all about *exfoliation.*"

"You're obnoxious, and I don't know why we're still friends." I ran my fingers along my chin, noticed the stubble, and my face grew hot.

"Because *somebody* has to tell you," she mumbled under her breath.

Maybe I *was* overdue for a good plucking session. So what? I was a fifty-seven-year-old, happily single woman and I didn't give a damn if other people felt uncomfortable with someone else's body hair.

Liza could suck it.

The stylist returned and began pulling cold dye through the hair at the crown of my head. I watched in the mirror as she worked, then my eyes turned to my own face. Fine lines flanked the corners of my eyes, and three deep creases ran the length of my forehead.

God, when did those happen?

I felt myself growing warm all over again.

"You know what? Let's do it," I said.

"The shag?" the stylist asked, with entirely too much enthusiasm.

"God, no! Shave me."

"Shave?" Now she was completely confused.

"She means dermaplane. No one's pulling a Britney Spears here," Liza clarified. "And yay!" She clapped her hands like a five-year-old who'd been promised ice cream.

"Liza—"

"Hmm?"

"Shut up."

***

"I don't think my face has been this smooth since I was a toddler. It feels weird," I said, running my fingers along my jawline.

"You look amazing—all glowy and gorgeous." Liza pushed the menu off to the side.

"Am I going to have to shave every day before work now?"

She gave an amused laugh. "Not every day. It will grow back, but no worse than before, and you can buy a kit and do it at home for maintenance."

"Maintenance? Like a car?"

"Yes, *just* like a car." She rolled her eyes.

The server came to take our order, we requested the usual, then she went on her way.

"So, I have a confession," I said.

"Is it juicy? You never give me anything juicy." She took a sip of lemon water.

"I joined one of those dating apps."

"You *what?*" She choked a bit on her drink, or at least made a convincing show of pretending to do so. "Why would *you* join a dating app? Has some lucky guy re-awakened the long-dormant butterflies?"

"Butterflies! Really? Post-menopausal women don't get butterflies, Liza. I think it's impossible for us to have feelings much deeper than the occasional rage we feel when someone steals our Diet Coke out of the fridge at work."

"I don't think that's true, and I don't think you do either."

"Well, things didn't turn out great last time I was butterfly-filled, and I don't want to go down that road again. I only downloaded the app because Patrick won't get off my back about it."

"Ooh, how is Patrick? Just as hot and hunky as ever?" she asked with a devilish grin.

"Still fifteen years too young for you. I told you, I will not set you two up. I have to work with the man!"

"So? I'm just lookin' for a bit of fun, Catherine."

"Exactly. And when the fun runs out, I'd be the one stuck with the leftover awkwardness. Maybe if you ever decide to get serious, I'll think about it."

"Psh," she said with a wave of her hand. "You know that will never happen. I like being alone, dating around, being free to do whatever I want."

"How is it possible you are still the same person you were at seventeen? You always said you'd never get married or have kids. How did you know that at such a young age?"

"I knew who I was pretty early on, I guess."

"If only we could all be so lucky."

"So, have you found anyone interesting?" Liza asked.

"What?"

"On the app."

"Oh, God, no. I haven't even looked."

"Well, it's not exactly a terrible idea…"

"No way, Liza. I am happy with my life."

"Yeah, yeah, with your dog and your books and your trashy late-night TV. I know."

"You say it like it's such a terrible thing. I like my life…just the way it is!"

"Okay, I get that. But you did date around for a while after you…worked through the aftermath of the whole Glen thing. So, you *were* interested."

"And then I realized I was happier alone, and that was that."

"You don't feel like maybe you're just—I don't know—settling for being alone because you're afraid to let anyone in?"

"Do *you* feel like *you're* settling for dating around because *you're* afraid to let anyone in?"

She leaned back in her seat and gave me a hard stare. "All right. Touché."

"Here we are, two burgers with fries. Anything else I can get you?" The server set the plates and a bottle of ketchup on the table.

"No, thank you." I answered her. "This looks great."

She nodded and moved on.

Liza poked at her food with an unsure face.

"What's the matter?" I asked.

"Nothing. You just—got all up in my head. Now I'm wondering if I really want this burger, or if I'm just settling for it because we were afraid the four-star Indian restaurant next door would keep us up all night with indigestion."

"You done, Liza?"

"I suppose."

"The burger is fine."

"Hmm," she replied, squirting ketchup onto her plate.

"What does *hmm* mean?"

"All I know is, we went from *great* to *fine*. And now I want Indian food."

On Sunday, I knocked twice on Mama's door, then entered to find her in the kitchen. The air was thick with the comforting scent of a casserole in the oven and the lights were dimmed, just the way she liked them.

"I brought salad," I said, setting the bowl on the table. "Are the others coming?"

"They'll all be late, of course, but yes. Why is it that no one can arrive anywhere on time these days? It's *rude*." Mama pulled her frizzy gray hair over one shoulder as she moved the salad to the fridge. Then she turned to me. "Wine?"

"Sounds good." I pulled out my usual chair at the table and took a seat.

"You could get the glasses, at least," Mama said with a toss of her hands. The woman was seventy-seven years old, and still hadn't lost her ability to tell you just how she felt in as few words as possible.

"Yeah, okay. I'm on it." I retrieved five wine glasses from the hutch in the formal dining room. When I returned, Mama gripped the twist-off cap of a wine bottle and struggled to open it. I knew better than to ask if she needed help.

For so many years, when I was all wrapped up in a secret affair with Glen, I skipped our Sunday night dinners. I don't know if I was afraid Mama would see right through me and figure it all out, or if I was embarrassed or ashamed, but I distanced myself from her, Aunt Kitty, Bo, and Stacey—and now it made me sad for all the time that I missed. Now, I never took a Sunday night dinner for granted.

"There! That one was a bugger." She gave two of the glasses a healthy pour, then sat at the table. "Did Jenna call you this morning?"

"Yes. We didn't talk long, but she seems to be doing okay." I took a sip of the dry white wine Mama chose to go with our chicken casserole.

"She's knee-deep in planning Ryan's birthday party. It was all cakes, and party favors, RSVPs, and whatnot."

I nodded, to show I was listening, but I was also busy trying to decide what picture to include on my *Southern Singles* dating profile…if I decided to actually try the stupid app, that is.

"What's so interesting that your head's only half-in our conversation?" Mama asked.

"Uh—nothing. Sorry." I set the phone face-down on the table.

"Catherine…"

Shit…busted.

"It's…kind of funny, actually. My co-worker's been bugging me to try this dating app. I got so tired of being pestered about it, I joined."

"You did what now?"

"Joined a dating app. Just to see what it was about and get him off my back. Nothing serious."

She laughed. "Is that how people meet people nowadays? Your generation is so strange."

I grabbed the bottle of wine from the counter and topped off our glasses, because clearly the serving Mama poured into them wasn't enough. "Well, it's not my generation. I'm a bit old for it, to be honest."

"Well, took you long enough. Good luck."

"Took me long enough to—wait, what?"

"Can't say I agree that an app on your phone is the right way to go about it, but I'm all for you having a bit of fun. It's been too long since you've had any fun, Catherine."

"But I'm not even using it. I only told you because it was funny. And I've had…*fun,* Mama."

"With who?" She looked at me with eyebrows raised. "Never mind, I don't want to know."

Jesus, discussing my sex life with my mother was not on my Sunday night dinner BINGO card.

"I'll ask around at church. One of those ol' biddies has to have a single son who's worth a damn." Mama took the casserole out of the oven.

I came to my feet and crossed over to where she stood. "Mama! You can't go tellin' the whole women's group that I'm—"

"Can't tell who what?" Aunt Kitty asked.

I turned to see her standing near the front door with a covered dish in her hands.

"Catherine's ready to have her biscuit buttered," Mama said.

"Mama!" I moved back to the table and collapsed into the chair.

Aunt Kitty laughed as she set the dish on the counter. "Is that so? My, my—"

The door opened again as Bo and Stacey entered with shopping bags.

"Well, good for you, Catherine," Aunt Kitty said. "I'd say it's about time."

"Why does everyone keep saying that? I haven't just escaped the convent, ya know. Good Lord—"

"About time for what?" Stacey asked as she and Bo started emptying bags.

"Oh, no—I'm not doing this. I'll be on the porch." I picked up my wine glass and exited through the front door to the sound of Mama and Aunt Kitty busting a gut in the kitchen.

30

NOT-MENOPAUSE & UNEASY FEELINGS

Monday morning at work, I was still stewing over the humiliation of the previous night's family dinner. How was it possible for southern mamas to have such a knack for embarrassing the shit out of their children, no matter how old they were? And I was one of them! Did I do it to Jenna, too? God, I hoped not.

"You all right?" Patrick rounded the corner of the desk and took his seat.

"Yes, why?"

"You seem preoccupied. Those girls have been giggling quite loudly for ten minutes and I haven't seen one pointed glare." He nodded toward a group of homeschoolers gathered in the corner.

"Hadn't noticed."

"Exactly. So, what gives?"

I was desperate to give no mention of my mother-inflicted humiliation and to avoid any conversation revolving around my personal life. Before I realized what was about to come out of my mouth, I said, "Are you seeing anyone?"

He looked at me as if to say, *God, woman...please don't ask me out,* and without warning, I was *on fire*. It started in my face, traveled down to my neck, my armpits, then to the backs of my knees.

"Oh, no—Patrick, that's not what I meant." I fanned my face with my hand. "God, it's hot in here, right? I'll check the thermostat." I flew out of my seat and headed to the break room, even though the thermostat wasn't in the break room, and I had no idea why I'd gone in there.

Then I saw the refrigerator. I rushed over, flung open the freezer door, stuck my head inside, and spent a solid minute wishing I could teleport through it.

Patrick cleared his throat behind me. "Catherine?" he said softly.

I closed the freezer door and turned to face him, but my glasses had fogged up and I couldn't see a thing. I removed them and wiped the lenses with the bottom of my shirt. "Just checking to see if I left anything in there for lunch. Did you need something?"

"Yes. I need you to explain yourself." He laughed, but gently. "Look, I know you're not coming on to me. We've been friends a long time, and I like to think I can read a room."

"Okay, God, I'm sorry. That was weird." I put my glasses on again.

"Yes, that was weird," he said with a smile.

"I only asked because...well, Liza kind of...likes you."

There. Liza had been successfully thrown under the bus, which was my original intention before I put my head in the freezer. Only now, I remembered, I'd been trying to *avoid* setting Liza up with Patrick.

Damnit all to hell.

"Liza? Really?" He looked surprised, but in no way similar to the surprise that was on his face when he thought *I* was the one who was interested.

I wasn't sure how to take that.

"If you're seeing someone, I can—"

"No—I'm not seeing anyone, actually."

Well, shit.

"Thanks for letting me know, I guess." He turned toward the door, paused, then faced me again. "In the spirit of making things weird—I can't help but notice—well, my friend is a doctor who specializes in hormone replacement for women who, uh—"

"Who what?"

"Who, you know, are dealing with menopause."

"*Oh my God*, Patrick! This isn't menopause!" I said, gesturing to my sweaty pits. "That ship sailed years ago...this is just your standard, run-of-the-mill mortification!"

"Oh! Okay then." He turned toward the door again as his cheeks grew pink. "I was just trying to be a good friend. Sorry, Catherine." He ducked out of the break room quickly.

And I shoved my head back into the freezer.

⚬

At home after work and errands, I was greeted as I always was by a warm fuzzball circling my ankles.

"Hello, Beezus!" I bent to stroke her soft coat. "When are you ever going to bark *hello* back or catch a case of the zoomies, huh? Maybe tear up a shoe or two? You're entirely too well behaved." I crossed to the sofa and flopped. Beezus joined me. "Maybe it's time we found you a Ramona, to shake things up around here. Or maybe a Picky-Picky?" She rested her head on my leg, and I scratched between her ears.

I never thought I was a dog person, but when Liza brought Goldie into my life, I knew I was. We had eleven sweet years together and after she passed, it took a year for me to come around to getting another. I considered Beezus to be her baby sister.

The toilet flushed down the hall and I damn near jumped out of my skin.

"I still can't believe you named that dog Beezus." Liza came around the corner, wiping her hands on her jeans. "Such a dorky librarian thing to do."

"Liza, you scared the hell out of me! If you don't start letting me know when you're walking over, I'm going to change the locks." I nudged Beezus from my lap and headed to the kitchen.

"That might mean something if you ever locked the doors." She sat at the island I'd had installed in a remodel several years back. "So, what are we doing this weekend?"

"It's Monday, Liza."

"So?"

"So...I can't think about the weekend yet. And I don't know if I want to do anything anyway. I think I'll just Netflix and chill." I moved to the wine cabinet and perused my choices.

Liza let out a loud, booming laugh.

"What's so funny?"

"*Netflix and chill* isn't something you do alone. Or...I mean, I guess you *could—*"

"What are you on about?" I chose a deep red malbec and got to work on the cork.

"Google it," she answered. "Or, here—" She typed away on her phone, then held it up for me to see.

"Aw, hell. No wonder Patrick looked at me funny."

Liza doubled over in laughter again.

"I'm glad you find my humiliation so amusing." I poured our glasses. "I've had enough of it over the past two days to keep you going for the rest of your life, I imagine."

She sat up straight on her barstool again. "What do you mean? There's *more?*"

"Wouldn't you like to know?" I took a sip and sat next to her.

I refused to tell her about my interaction with Patrick. I wouldn't encourage that in any way. He knew now that she liked him, and it was up to them to sort the rest out.

God, I hoped they didn't sort it out.

"Liza, something's up."

"Hmm?" she asked as she sipped.

"It's been a weird couple of days. Everything's been *off*. I feel so...on edge, like I can't relax. Like something big is about to happen."

"Ooh, it's the gift!" Her eyes were wide and excited.

"As I've said a million times, I don't have psychic powers."

"You do! I don't know why you deny it." She took another drink. "You should try out my tarot deck."

"And now, we're done. Time to go, Liza." I shooed her toward the back door.

"But what do you think it could be this time? What are you sensing? I'm telling you—the cards could help!"

I nudged her onto the porch.

"Call me when you figure it out!" She held her wine glass up high in the air as she descended the steps and crossed the yard.

After Liza left, I ate a frozen burrito, washed my face, brushed my teeth, and watered my plants. Then, I climbed into bed with a book in my hands and Beezus at my feet. But as hard as I tried, I couldn't focus on the words.

What could it be?

The last time I had this feeling, Jenna showed up in Asher, teetering on the edge of death.

God, what if it was Jenna?

I texted her, "Just checking in. Everything okay?"

A few minutes later, I received her reply. "Doing great. Thank you for checking on me. Love you."

I sighed as I clutched the phone to my chest. Then a second wave of fear came over me.

If it wasn't Jenna, there was only one other person it could be.

—◆—

The next morning, I called Janine, but got her voicemail.

"Janine, it's Catherine. Can you call me, please? Talk to you soon." I hung up and saw a tiny head bob over the top of the circulation desk.

"Hello, Lucas." I pulled a sticker from the drawer and slid it within his reach.

His chubby little fingers felt around and snatched hold of it, then he ran away.

Looking up, I spotted his mama in the kids' play area. I gave a wave and a smile as my phone rang.

"Janine, hi! Thanks for calling me back."

"Of course. What do you need, hon?"

"Just checking in to see how you're doing. It's been a while."

"That's sweet. I'm doing well. And you?"

"I'm great. Staying busy with work, ya know."

"Of course."

"Do you know if—I know I rarely ask about Glen—but do you know if he's doing okay?"

She was quiet for a moment, then she said, "Yes, he's fine."

"Are you sure? Have you spoken with him recently?"

"What's this about, Catherine?"

"I've had a strange feeling lately, that's all."

"I see. Well, I spoke with him over the weekend. He's just fine."

Thank God.

I may not have seen or spoken to the man in twenty years, but I still cared for him; still wanted him to be well and happy. "Okay then. Thank you," I said.

"All right, hon. Keep in touch, okay?"

"I will. Thanks again."

"Any time."

When my lunch break arrived, I wandered around town, unsure what to do with myself. Liza was working reception at a dental office a county over, since she couldn't find anyone to fill it for her temp agency, which she'd launched after working a few years at another service in town. Both forms of work suited her: She enjoyed not being tied down to one position day in and day out, and she loved sitting behind a desk, telling people what to do.

I chose a to-go sushi roll for lunch and moved to the park at the town square. It was full of young moms with children on picnic blankets, in pop-up chairs, and on every bench. As I looked for a place to sit, a commotion on the south end caught my attention. A mother with two young children stood from a bench as her oldest launched himself face-down onto the grass.

Ah, Logan. I'd recognize that meltdown anywhere.

I also knew that meant it was nap time, and she'd be scooping him up in her free hand any second. I moved in their direction, intent on being the first to reach the empty bench they would leave behind.

As I anticipated, she picked Logan up around the waist and headed to her car, with him kicking and crying the whole way. I sat on the vacated bench and pried the plastic top off the sushi container. As I mixed wasabi into the soy sauce, which I knew I'd regret later, a low rumble echoed off the buildings surrounding the square. Glancing around for its source, I saw nothing out of the ordinary, so I added a bit more wasabi.

A moment later, that low rumble was back, and I deduced it was someone stopped at the traffic light who was now again creeping through town, on their way to somewhere far more interesting.

As I took the first bite of my California roll, the rumble grew louder, but it wasn't the cover-your-ears kind of rumble often heard around town as the teens flew by in their obnoxious trucks with doubly-obnoxious, cheap exhaust tips. No, this was a *real* truck—V8, with an actual carbureted engine. I hadn't heard a truck that sounded like that since—

No, it couldn't be.

I stood and spun circles, trying to determine where it came from, still holding the sushi container as the pea-green soy/wasabi mixture spilled over its sides.

Janine would've told me if he was in town...wouldn't she?

Then, I saw it.

Matte black, chrome wheels and bumper, a tall figure in a backwards baseball cap in the driver's seat, and an arm I'd know anywhere, resting on the open window. Hell, I'd know *that truck* anywhere, even if it was army-green the last time I saw it.

And suddenly I knew what that anxious feeling was all about—why, for days, it had felt like I stood at the edge of something truly earth-shattering.

Because I was.

Because Glen had come home.

I'd never ran so fast in my life. I couldn't imagine what folks must've thought, watching an old woman hoof it like she was late for curfew. Ducking down an alley, I pulled out my phone.

"Liza! Answer the damn phone! He's here! Why is he here? Call me back!"

Call me back, Liza, I prayed.

The phone rang and her name popped up on the screen.

"Liza!"

"Why are you calling me in the middle of the day?"

"Didn't you check your voicemail?"

"Who checks *voicemail?*"

"He's here!"

"Who?"

I took a deep breath and shoved down a sudden, intense need to vomit. "Glen. *Glen's here!* Who else would I be talking about, Liza?"

"So? It's not the first time he's visited his mom. What's the big deal?"

"Janine's always given me a heads up when he's come into town, so I could do my best to avoid seeing him, Liza. I just talked to her this morning, and she said nothing about him being here...and this feels...different. I need you to pick me up. I can't walk back to work with him rumbling around."

"Rumbling?"

"Just come get me!"

"You want me to drive a half hour to pick you up and drop you off two minutes up the road?"

"Yes!"

"You've lost your damn mind. Where are you?"

"Between Sticky's and The Tavern, in the alley. Hurry!"

"Keep your panties on. I'm on my way."

⸻◆⸻

I spent the rest of my shift making excuses to keep myself away from the front desk. When I ran out of things to do, I hid away in my office, which drew more than one suspicious glance from Patrick. I realized he probably thought I was avoiding him due to our previous mortifying encounter, but that was a problem for another day.

At 4:00, I gave up and went home early. Once there, I tried reading, watching TV, and tossing a ball to Beezus in the back yard, but none of it eased the anxiety I felt in my gut.

Why would he come after all the time that had passed? After a few years, I assumed he'd either sorted himself out and felt no need to make contact, or that he never would sort himself out, and I'd never hear from him again. Either way, I gave up on the possibility of that man ever stepping foot on my porch again.

I glanced down at my mom-jeans and flowery, ruffled sleeve shirt. Running my hands around my waist, which was considerably thicker than it was when he last saw me, heat rose to my face.

Why did I even care?

He was twenty years older too, right? Surely, he wasn't still *Glen Lewis.* Surely, he was *Old Man Lewis,* or some other insulting moniker gifted to him by the young and beautiful.

I suddenly found myself wishing I hadn't avoided him so well over the years...at least, if I'd seen him in passing, I'd know what I was in for now.

There was a tap on the back door...and I fought the urge to run right out the front.

When I opened it though, there he stood on the second step, just as gorgeous as ever with a full salt and pepper beard, skin somewhat sun-worn, and tiny crow's feet near the eyes. Different, but still as beautiful—as heart-melting—as the last time I saw him.

"Hello, Cat," he said with a smile.

I had no words.

And I never thought I'd feel so glad to have shaved my face.

"I parked on the next street. Wasn't sure if you'd want me coming through the front. Hope that's okay," he said.

I nodded, perhaps a little too vigorously. "Yeah, it's fine."

He climbed the last step to stand on the porch. "Missed me?"

My whole body felt numb, like it wasn't me standing there, but a proxy. Then, I looked into his eyes and all anxiety melted away, replaced by pure joy and an all-encompassing hope that maybe somehow, the man standing before me had found his peace, at last.

But hope was unnecessary, because I knew he had. I could see it all over his face.

"Of course I missed you, dumbass. What took you so long?" I smiled, and he matched it with a crooked grin.

"It's been quite the ride, Cat. A wild, terrifying, and...really hard ride."

"But you made it," I said, bringing my hand to his cheek.

He placed his hand on mine and said, "Yeah, I made it."

31

SMALL TALK & PERFECT STORMS

"You've remodeled," he said as he pulled out a stool.

"Yeah, eventually, storage became more important than seating for six. Look, Cabinets!" I opened one to show him.

"Who was your contractor?"

"Bradly Brothers."

"They do great work."

"Yeah, I think so." I ran my hand along the smooth countertop, wondering why we were chit-chatting when there was so much to talk about that really mattered.

I pulled a beer from the fridge. "Drink?"

"Just a Coke for me, thanks."

I looked around the fridge door to see his face. "You sure?"

"Positive."

I swapped the beer for two cans of Coke and settled on the stool next to him.

"Thanks," he said, popping the top on his, as I popped mine. "I like the glasses."

"What?"

He pointed to my face.

"Oh," I said, removing them and placing them on the counter. "Since I last saw you, I've started wearing glasses, then switched to contacts. These are for blue light. Sometimes I forget to take them off after work."

He nodded and then we sat in what felt like a very long, uncomfortable silence.

"So—" we both said at the same time.

I laughed and looked down at my drink. "What brings you to town?"

He fidgeted with the tab on his can. "Honestly?"

"Preferably, yeah."

"Okay, well—you."

I sucked in a breath. "Me?"

"Yeah, Cat. You."

I cleared my throat and self-consciously smoothed my shirt. "Okay. So, why did you want to see me?" I tried so hard to pretend like we were discussing Jenna's next cross country meet, or whether it was time to replace the water heater.

"Maybe I should have called first. I was going to, but I was afraid—"

"No, it's fine, Glen. I'm just surprised. I spoke with Janine this morning and she didn't mention you were in town."

"I didn't tell her I was coming."

"Why not?"

"Because I wasn't coming to see her this time, Cat. I told you why I'm here."

"Oh."

"I'm sorry this is weird," he said. "I hoped we could just—catch up."

"Catch up?"

"Yeah."

"How do two people catch up after twenty years?"

"Well, clearly, neither of us is very good with small talk," he said with a smile. "So, I guess we get right to it, starting at the beginning."

"Okay. You go first."

He picked up his Coke, stood, and held out his hand. I took it and followed him to the living room. Once we were settled on the sofa, he turned toward me and brushed the hair from my face. "Still so beautiful," he said.

Heat rose to my cheeks, and I looked away. "You're stalling."

"Right." He pulled his hand back to his lap. "Well, I gather that Mom told you I went to a dark place after the divorce."

I nodded.

"First thing I did was go to the liquor store. I don't know how I survived. I drank and smoked so much that I was never hungry, so I barely ate. I lost a lot of weight, ended up in the hospital more than once, and came very close to losing my business. I just didn't care anymore, about anything. I barely went to work. My office manager quit, and I couldn't be bothered to hire another. When my project managers threatened to walk out, I finally came around and hired someone. She saved my business. I'll always be grateful to her for that."

He reached out and took my hand. "I don't consider myself a weak man, Cat, but hearing you say you never wanted to see me again showed me just how weak I really was."

"For the record, I didn't say *never*."

"No, but what you asked me to do sure made it feel like never. I didn't think I could do it. So, I drank. And I'm sure you remember about the girls in high school...before you and I were together?"

"Yeah," I said, though I wished I didn't.

"My therapist helped me realize that after my dad left, and because of all the times he'd left us prior—because he lived between two families—and because he chose that family over ours, I had major abandonment issues. The girls I was with before you...it was because I craved the attention. I needed it, to feel like I was worth something. I needed to feel *chosen;* to know I could be loved.

"Then I met you, and I knew I had, in truth, been chosen—in the best possible, most real way. But after you ended things, it all came back. I didn't realize it then, but I thought I'd been abandoned again. I thought I'd never be good enough for anyone; that no one would ever choose me and mean it. So, I went right back to that attention-seeking frame of mind."

"This is your way of telling me you slept around?"

He sniggered and said, "Yeah, pretty much."

"Were you ever serious with anyone? I mean, I imagine you were—or maybe you *are*." The thought of it twisted my stomach into knots.

"There was a roommate who became a girlfriend, so we sorta lived together by default for a while, but no. You?"

"I've dated off and on, but nothing serious."

"Why is that? You're so—worthy of love, Cat. I hate to think you've been alone all this time."

My insides were doing funny things I didn't recognize, while my brain still screamed to *be cool*.

"Oh, I don't know," I said. "I was so focused on Jenna, school, work. And to be honest, I'd had enough drama and heartbreak for a lifetime. I never wanted to be married again or to get serious with anyone. I was over it. Plus, Liza takes up a lot of my time. Not to mention Goldie and Beezus—"

"Who?"

"My pups. Liza gave me Goldie after I lost the baby and murdered my plants. She said I needed something to take care of, and with Jenna leaving in a year, and you leaving too—well, she was right."

"You murdered your plants?" His eyes grew wide as he looked toward the kitchen windows.

"That's a whole 'nother story, and as you can see, I've since replenished."

"And the dogs? Tell me you didn't murder them, too?"

"Goldie died of natural causes, thank you very much. But now I have Beezus." I gave a little whistle and said, "Beezie—come to Mama."

A very long moment later, she rounded the corner and plopped down on top of my feet.

"Not very lively, is she?" he said with a tilt of his head.

I scooped her up. "Nah, but she's perfect just the way she is." Snuggling her close, I scratched between her ears.

"Catherine?"

"Hmm?"

"I know we have a lot to cover here, but I hope—assuming you don't still think I'm a broken dumbass in the end—that I'm not too late. Please tell me I'm not too late."

I looked up from Beezus, right into Glen's deep blue eyes. "I don't know."

"Oh. Okay, well—" He rubbed his palms on the knees of his jeans like he felt completely dejected, or like he was about to stand and leave.

It reminded me so much of that night on Mama's couch when he first told me he liked me and asked if I liked him, too.

I placed my hand on his. "I may not know now, but if you'll stay and tell me more...maybe we'll find out."

⚬

"So, therapy, huh?" I pulled my legs up beneath me on the sofa.

"Yup. But first, AA."

"Really?" Now I understood why he declined the beer.

"Losing a business and living on the brink of bankruptcy has a way of changing your perspective."

"I imagine so."

"It took six months before I could commit, but my sponsor encouraged me to go to every meeting, to listen to the others speak. More than once, I showed up reeking of alcohol...or still drunk. Eventually, though, it sank in."

"That's great. How long has it been?"

"Seventeen years, three months, and—some number of days," he said.

"You haven't had a drink in *seventeen years?*" Having asked it in an inappropriate tone of surprise, I course-corrected. "I mean—that's not just *great*. That's amazing!"

He laughed and said, "Thank you, Cat."

"Then therapy came next?"

"Well, there was some overlap, and they continue to overlap still—the therapy sessions and the AA meetings, I mean."

"You still go to both?"

"Pretty sure I always will. My therapist could buy a house or two with the money I've sent his way so far, I'm sure. Not to mention the money I threw at others before I found one I clicked with. The first few were all about talk therapy. I tried it for a while, but God, there's only so much I could listen to myself talk! Every time I left, I'd sit in the car, trying to determine what I'd learned, and rarely came up with anything."

"What did the last therapist do differently? What worked for you?"

"We still do talk therapy—and I understand how useful it is now—but after the third or fourth session, he recommended we also try EMDR. Later, we added tapping. I've even done hypnosis and acupuncture."

"I don't know what half those things are."

He smiled and hung his head. "I wish I didn't have the need to know either, but all of it together is what saved me."

"I went to therapy for a while, too."

"You did?"

"Yeah. Jenna showed up here a couple years ago, in rough shape. I told her she should find a therapist. Then, I realized how hypocritical that was, because I probably needed one too. So, I went. Turns out, I have abandonment issues of my own. And trust issues, and poverty trauma and PTSD from what happened in Pensacola...I'm a whole stew of issues."

"You've been through a lot, Cat." He gave my knee a squeeze. "Is Jenna okay? I send her a birthday card every year, but I rarely hear anything back."

"She was dealing with pretty serious depression, but she's better now, I think. She's always been sensitive and an overthinker, ya know. She gets so far into her own head, she loses sight of the real world. I'm afraid she'll struggle with that her whole life."

"Do you think that has anything to do with how she was raised? With—at the risk of sounding self-centered—me?" he asked.

"Maybe...somewhat? Though I'd say her personality was pretty well formed from birth."

"God, the colic!" he said with a laugh. "That was terrible."

"I thought I would lose my mind then, but it wasn't just that. Even as a preschooler, she was moody. I think she was depressed before she knew what depressed *meant*. I wish I would've done something more to help her as a teenager, but she was always so busy, and she had a way of making it look like everything was okay as long as she was busy. I should've gotten more involved."

"I'm sure you did all you could. You always do."

Did I though?

I shook away the thought and refocused on Glen, who stared at me with piercing, peaceful eyes.

"Do you realize your trauma caused you to latch on to me, and mine caused me to latch on to you?" I asked.

Now his eyes were confused, like he was trying to map it out in his head.

"You were looking for someone to choose you over everyone else, and I was looking for someone who I thought would never turn their back on me—or die. Someone who felt solid and could provide some sort of safety, away from the madness of my mother and brother."

I saw the moment the dots connected in his brain.

"Holy shit," he said.

"Yeah."

"We were the perfect storm."

Simultaneously, we both leaned back, folded our hands, and stared at the wall.

———◆———

"Are you hungry?" I asked. "I can order pizza."

"I could eat."

I dialed Nico's and placed a delivery order. Twenty minutes later, Glen tipped the driver and carried the boxes to the kitchen.

"So, what else have you learned in therapy?" I asked, as I placed slices onto paper plates.

He took his and sat at the island. "You ask like it's so easy to talk about."

"Oh, no…I know it isn't. Sorry. You know I've always wanted to know as much as I could, as fast as I could. That hasn't changed." I pulled two paper towels off the roll and sat next to him.

"You never did have much patience," he said with a wink.

Oh, God…not the wink!

He took a bite, then wiped his mouth with the napkin. "Have you heard of complex-PTSD?"

"No, I haven't."

"It usually arises in children who've experienced trauma or abuse. Many people don't realize they have it until later in life."

"Do you?"

"Yeah. My dad beat us for years, Cat. I thought I was good at compartmentalizing it—tucking it away in its own little box—and that it didn't affect me, but it did."

"Of course it did."

"I've learned that the C-PTSD is likely why I turn to alcohol, sex, and even working too much when things get hard. It's my way of avoiding the stress and pain." He set his pizza slice on his plate and turned toward me. "And also why I was so afraid to be a real father to Jenna."

I gasped in surprise, having not expected the conversation to turn in that direction so soon.

"I was afraid of becoming my father, which, I think you sensed. But it wasn't just about the possibility of hurting her physically, it was about being afraid I would let her down...that I could never be enough...that I would break her, like I had been broken. So, even though I didn't know exactly what it was all about, I knew I had to keep my distance. I just wish—God, I wish I knew then all that I know now."

"You think you would have felt differently if you had?"

"No, but I would've responded to it differently, that's for sure. I've come to terms with who I am, Cat, but no matter how much I learn about myself, how much healing takes place, those feelings are a part of me. Only now I can recognize them for what they are. They don't scare me anymore because I know what to do when they arise. Does that make sense?"

I nodded. "Jenna's said something similar since starting her own therapy."

He took another bite of pizza and said, "Hey, whatever happened to that boy she was so crazy about? Tyler."

"Hell if I know," I said, taking another bite myself. "They continued with whatever it was they had, even after she went to college. Then she met Andrew and quit Tyler cold-turkey. I see him around now and then. I still don't think he's gotten over it. What I don't get, is if that's the case, how did it end up the way it did? Why were they always so afraid to let go of each other, but also afraid of *being* together?"

He let out a sharp, loud laugh.

"What?"

"I'm no therapist, but—don't they sound a bit like us?"

It took me a second to process the words. "Oh, shit."

He smiled. "But she's happy with Andrew, right?"

"She is."

"Then it appears our girl figured out what she wanted a lot sooner than we did. She's smarter and braver than the both of us put together."

"Yeah, I guess so."

"And your mom and Bo, I assume they're doing okay?"

"Bo and Stacey are married. Their kids are grown and all doing well. He and Stacey seem happy. And Mama's just as infuriating as ever, but I love her for it."

He smiled as he stood and grabbed another slice for each of us. "Time marches on, I guess."

"It does. Which makes me wonder...if you've been going to therapy and AA all these years, why are you just now coming to see me?"

He took a bite and said, "My dad died a few months back."

"Oh. Do I say *I'm sorry?* Or..."

"No, we still weren't close. My aunt found Mom's number and called with news he was sick. Mom called me, and after thinking on it, I went to Chicago to see him."

"That must've been difficult."

"It was, and it wasn't. I've worked hard to let go of as much anger as I could, so I wasn't super emotional when I saw him. The worst part was looking at him and seeing *myself.* Or at least, the me I could've been. He was dying of liver failure and full of nothing but regret."

"Did he apologize?"

"Not in any direct way, no. He may have been full of regrets, but he was still an asshole."

"That's too bad."

"Yeah. Anyway, I never reached out to you before, because in AA they tell us we shouldn't, if doing so could cause harm. I was afraid of interrupting the life you'd built and doing more harm than good. It felt selfish to risk it. But after seeing my dad dying and hearing all the things he wished he'd done differently, I had to take the chance. So, I asked Mom how you were and if she thought it would be harmful to you if I reached out. And, well, here I am."

I placed my pizza back on the plate. "I'm glad you came," I said with a squeeze of his hand.

"Me too, Cat. Me too."

32

HYPOCRITES & HEATHENS

"**Y**our turn," he said after we'd finished eating and moved back to the sofa.

"What do you want to know?"

He thought for a beat, then said, "Did it make you sad—the divorce? Or were you so ready to be rid of me by then that you were just...I don't know...relieved?"

"Glen!" The fact that he'd even asked that question shook me to my core.

"I'm just trying to piece together the whole picture, Cat."

"I don't—I don't even know where to start in describing what that did to me."

He looked at me with such intensity that I had to look away.

"You were *everything* to me. You saved me when no one else could. When my dad died, and my whole world went to shit—"

"I told you a long time ago, that you saved yourself, Cat."

"I know, and there's some truth to that, but I needed *someone*, after losing *everyone*, and you—well, you were the only one brave enough to stick around. When I let you go—when we divorced—I was lost. I didn't know how to function in a world without you, and I hated myself for it because it made me feel like a total hypocrite."

"Hypocrite? *How?*"

"Because I told you there was something wrong with you if—if you didn't even like yourself without me around...and there I was, feeling lost, alone, and afraid without *you*. I missed you with my whole heart—just as much as I'd ever loved you with my whole heart—and I hated myself for it. And then I hated myself for the hypocrisy of it all."

He shifted in his seat so his whole body faced me, then reached up and wiped a tear from my cheek. "What else?"

The question made me realize how little we'd covered and how much there was still left to say. It made my heart race and panic swell within me, because it didn't feel like we'd ever *get it all out*.

"One thing at a time, Cat," he said, reading my mind.

"After I lost the baby, and after...letting you go, I realized my whole life was built on fear. I was afraid of being alone, of losing someone else I loved, of what everyone else thought of me, of not being able to support myself and Jenna, of her depression, of—you never finding peace. And I just couldn't do it anymore. I gave up the fear."

"You just—gave up the fear? How does one do that?" he asked, perplexed.

"By giving up everything."

He tilted his head to the side as he tried to understand.

"I just—went numb. I'd been through it before, so I knew what it was. It was a choice I made in order to survive. But when you're numb, you don't just lose the fear. You lose everything. I had no faith, no hope. Nothing. Have you ever experienced that before? The numbness?"

"No, I don't think so. Well, maybe when I drank myself into oblivion—but even then, I wasn't completely numb. It took the edge off the pain, but I knew it was still there. What brought you back around, Cat?"

I laughed at the question because the answer was so ridiculous. "Believe it or not, it was Mama's church group."

"*What?*" He let out a booming laugh of his own. "I'm sorry, maybe that's not supposed to be funny," he said, trying to hide a grin behind his hand.

"I laughed first. Because it *is* funny."

"How did that even happen? Did the sky finally open up and rain fire, or what?"

"Stop it! You make me sound like such a heathen!"

"*Well?*" he said, with a shrug of his shoulders, like my being a heathen was kind of a given.

"Are we being serious here or not?" Even as I said it, trying to bring us back to a respectable conversation, I couldn't get the words out without a laugh.

"Oh, sorry. Yes, totally," he answered, with a mock-serious face.

"Okay, *well*—I'd gone with her before that, ya know, when they needed extra volunteers for things, but I was never a regular."

"Right," he said, still trying not to laugh.

"And I guess Mama saw me all depressed, and spiraling, and numb, and well...you know Mama."

He nodded.

"So, she said there was some big event coming up, and they'd never be ready on time, and blah blah blah. I don't even remember what it was now, but you know how she is. She made it seem like it was just so *dire* and she *needed* me."

"Of course."

"I ended up helping at that event and then, of course, there was another *dire emergency*, so I helped with that one too...before I knew it, I was there every week, *saving the world!*"

He shook his head and laughed.

"It was all so obvious that it was just...endearing, you know?"

"You're saying your heart grew three sizes that day?"

"*Shut up!*" I grabbed a pillow and threw it at his face.

He was doubled over in laughter now, and I had no idea how to go on.

"We're talking about my innermost turmoil here, ya asshole!"

"Oh my God, Cat...you're gonna kill me. I'm not a young man anymore, babe—" He cried with laughter—actual tears streamed down his face.

"God, you're an ass."

"What's the—what's the rest of the story? Come on, I want to know."

"I'm done. You can...take yourself on back to Montgomery, or wherever it is you came from."

He breathed in deep, pulled a hand down his face, then let the air out slowly, re-centering himself in the present. "Okay, I'm good. Please, Catherine, do go on." One more little chuckle escaped, but then he sat nice and polite, waiting for the rest of the story.

"Bottom line is...I realized that faith, and hope, and miracles, and divine intervention...aren't necessarily all so divine."

Now I had his attention.

"Those women, with their endless acts of kindness...and cheeky wit...and nonsensical snark—they made me realize I didn't need a sea to part, or to witness a burning bush to believe in something great. Because they were performing little miracles every day. They were bringing food to people who had nothing to eat; just leaving it on doorsteps and disappearing without a trace. They left cash in mailboxes when people didn't have gas to get to work. They babysat children they didn't even know, so moms could take an hour to themselves. Everything they did was a small miracle—a blessing—for someone who needed it. They made me realize that maybe God *wasn't* so far away that he couldn't be bothered to intervene in all the shit I'd been through. Maybe *I* just wasn't close enough to God."

"Meaning?"

"I couldn't see the miracles, couldn't receive the blessings, because I wasn't close enough to the miracle workers. I was—staring up into the sky, looking in the wrong place the whole time."

"What an amazing way to see the world," he said with a squeeze of my hand.

"Are you still making fun of me?"

"No, Cat. Not at all."

"Do you still play guitar?"

"I do."

"Did you bring it?"

"Goes with me everywhere."

"Do you think you could—"

Before I even finished the sentence, he was out of his seat and through the back door. He returned a few minutes later with the guitar, sat, and started strumming.

"'Dust In the Wind'?" I asked when the song ended.

He nodded and went right into the next one.

A half hour later, he paused and stretched his fingers.

"You okay?" I asked.

"Yeah, they just don't work as well as they used to," he answered with a tiny smile, while shaking his hand. "So, tell me about those," he said, laying the guitar next to the sofa and gesturing to the plants in the kitchen.

I took a deep breath, unsure how much to tell him. "I was upset and I kind of—smashed them."

He stared, waiting for me to go on, but I didn't.

"That doesn't sound like the complete story," he said.

"It was just after I told you I didn't want you in the baby's life."

"Oh. I see."

"It was an accident. At least, the first one was. The other thirty-seven, not so much."

"You know how many there were?"

"Counted them as I smashed them because...I'm neurotic. Anyway, there's something else you should know about that day."

"Hmm?"

"I had been cramping off and on for days."

"Yeah, the miscarriage."

"It wasn't just a miscarriage, Glen. It was an ectopic pregnancy, and it ruptured my fallopian tube—while I stood right there." I nodded toward the place I stood when I lost our baby.

"Oh my God, Catherine."

"One second I was smashing pots, and the next I was doubled over in pain, covered in blood. I still have nightmares about it. That was one of the worst days of my life. I was due to have an ultrasound a few days later, but of course, I never had one. Sometimes, I've wondered if I had not worked myself up, tossing potted plants around my kitchen, if I would've made it to that ultrasound—at least then I'd have a picture. I don't even have a picture." I picked at my nails as the tears came.

"There's no way to know, Cat." He placed an arm around my shoulders. "And you can't live your life with *what-ifs*."

I knew he was right, because I'd given up on the *what-ifs* a long time ago. This one, though, had stuck with me.

"Wanna know my biggest *what-ifs?* The ones that took the longest to bury?" he asked.

I turned my face to see his.

"I wondered, what if I'd told my mom that my dad hit us? What if I'd taken Robin and ran away to get help? What if I'd tried harder to find her after he left? What if I'd stayed in touch with her after moving here? Or asked her to move here too, after she turned eighteen? Maybe—if I'd done more—she'd still be alive."

"Glen, you can't—"

"Shh, Catherine. I know. It took a lot of work, but I know now. I'm only telling you because...well, I've been buried beneath the *what-ifs*, too. It's hard to let them go, but once you do, it's like you can finally breathe."

I nodded, then burst into tears.

He stood, pulled me up from the sofa, and held me while I cried over—and let go of—the last of my *what-ifs*.

"Cat—" he said, pulling my face up to his. "Please tell me now that I'm not too late."

All I could think, in that moment, was *I would've waited my whole life for you*. But I didn't want to say so, unless I knew it was true.

Is that what I'd been doing for twenty years? Waiting for him?

No, I didn't think so. What I'd been waiting for was the moment I knew I'd become a whole person, on my own, and that I liked the person I'd grown to be. That moment had come for me, years ago, and I'd been satisfied—happy even.

What I'd *hoped* for, though, was that he could do the same. And somehow, against all odds, after I'd given up any hope that the day would come...there he was: standing before me, pleading for me to give him another chance; a chance to get to know the man he'd become.

I took his face in my hands. "No, you're not too late. I love you. I've always loved you."

He wrapped his arms tight around my body, pulled my head into his chest, and kissed the top of it. Then, he held me.

And he hasn't let me go since.

NOW

"**I** thought you said this wasn't a love story. I was not expecting a love story, Mama!" Jenna pulls a tissue from the box and blows her nose.

"Well, it's not *just* a love story," I say with a shrug.

"What are you even doing here?" she asks. "You could've told me all this over the phone! You're leaving...tomorrow...and going back home to that man before he...disappears again."

"Jenna—"

She picks up her phone and starts tapping away. "Look, there's a flight at 11:40."

"Jenna—"

"Let's call the airline and see if you can get it switched."

"Jenna!"

She looks up from her phone and I see tears streaming down her cheeks.

"He's not disappearing this time."

Her lip quivers as she says, "He's not?"

I shake my head and smile.

"You're sure?"

"Positive."

She gives a quick nod.

"And I'd like to see my grandbabies for more than ten minutes while I'm here, if that's okay with you."

She nods again. "Okay." Pulling another tissue from the box, she says, "And for what it's worth, Tyler was never my—*Glen.*"

"He wasn't?"

"No. Tyler and I—we never were in sync, timing wise. The stars never aligned for us in any way that made sense, and it doesn't matter. I'm grateful for it. Andrew is—well, he's maddeningly perfect." She gives a little laugh. "Okay, maybe not perfect, but perfect for me. I don't have any *what-ifs* about Tyler, Mama."

I give a sigh of relief, then hope it was discreet enough that she hasn't recognized it as such. "Okay." As I stand, I pull her up with me and wrap her in a tight hug. "Should we get some sleep now?"

She nods, and we take ourselves to bed.

33

INDIAN FOOD & SEEING STARS

I t's raining cats and dogs when Glen picks me up from the airport two days later. He holds an umbrella over us as we walk to the short-term parking garage.

"So, how did it go?" he asks, stepping over a puddle.

"Well, I think." I scoot in closer, wrapping my arm around his waist. "She wanted to put me on a plane the next morning. Said I needed to get back home quick before you left again."

He looks at me with deep creases etched between his eyebrows. "That sure doesn't make it seem like it went well, Cat."

I laugh once and say, "Okay, maybe that wasn't the best anecdote to start off with."

"Maybe not," he replies.

"She's fine, Glen, with all of it. She's a smart, grounded woman who's been through hell herself. She understands that life isn't always easy or fair, and that sometimes we become a million different versions of ourselves before we ever find the one that fits. She gets it, and she's happy for me...for us."

He nods as we step under the cover of the parking garage, collapses the umbrella, and turns to face me. "So, what do we do now?"

"I think we start living the life we always wanted," I say with a smile.

"Does that mean I get to take you home and carry you to bed?" There's a twinkle in his eyes I haven't seen in a very, very long time.

"Yeah, I think it does."

"Okay, but first...can I—"

"Glen, if you ask if you can kiss me, I'm gonna smack you."

He smiles wide and proud. "Fair enough." Spinning his cap from front to back, he lifts me from the ground and kisses me like it's the first time, all over again.

⚛

Back at work on Monday, I'm pulling books from the drop box when Liza saunters through the doors.

"So, where are we going?" she asks, as she leans on the counter and checks her nails.

"I'm having lunch with Glen today. I thought I told you," I answer.

Patrick sneaks a look up toward us both, waiting to see how this plays out.

"No, you never told me! I drove clear across town, Catherine!" Liza crosses her arms and makes a pouty face.

"Oh, heavens! I didn't know you made a ten-minute drive, Liza. That changes everything!"

"Can I at least tag along? A girl's gotta eat, and I don't like eating alone."

Tossing my hands into the air, I say, "Yes, you can tag along, jeez."

She flashes a huge grin, then turns to Patrick. "What about you? Do you eat?"

"Uh—yes?" He's said it like he's unsure if it's the correct answer.

"Good. You'll join us too. Let's get Mexican. I feel like a margarita."

⚛

To my surprise, Liza behaved herself at lunch with Patrick. There wasn't a single batted eyelash, flirtatious comment, or gaze held too long. Sitting in my kitchen after work, I ask her about it.

"I didn't realize I was supposed to flirt with him. I was there for the food and drinks. Their margaritas really are the best in Asher," she answers.

"I just thought, as much as you've talked about how good looking he is, you would've used the opportunity to your advantage."

"Every time I mention him, you call me an old lady!"

"I do not!"

She gives me that over-dramatic look she does when she's thinking, *oh, really?*

"Okay, maybe I tease a bit about the age difference, but when has that ever bothered you?"

"It doesn't bother me, but it does make me think maybe you've told him I was interested and he, well...isn't."

"He said no such thing."

"Wait—you told him?"

I nod.

"And he doesn't think I'm just an annoying, dried-up old lady?"

"Not that I'm aware of, no. Liza, if you like him, just ask him out."

She twirls her hair around her finger. "Kinda already did."

"*What?*"

"Slipped him my number under the table."

"Of course you did."

On Thursday, Liza shows up at the library around noon.

"Do we have lunch plans?" I ask.

"I don't know if *you* have lunch plans, but *I* sure do," she answers with a smile, just as Patrick exits the break room.

"Hey, Liza. Let me just log out real quick." He leans over his computer, closes a few tabs, then logs out.

I get a good look of Patrick's rear end as he's leaned over the desk, then shoot Liza an *all right then* face.

She blushes as she smiles.

"Where are you two headed?" I ask.

"Tandoor," Patrick answers. "Want us to bring you back something?"

"Indian food? Not burgers?" I ask Liza.

"We're just gonna...try it out," she answers with a knowing grin.

"All right then. You two have fun. I brought my lunch," I say.

"We plan to," Liza says as Patrick moves out from behind the desk. She threads her arm around his and says, "See ya later!" as they go on their way.

When Patrick returns an hour and a half later, he pulls out his chair, sits, and stares at the blank computer monitor.

"Patrick? You okay there, bud?"

He turns to face me, leans back in his seat, and folds his arms across his chest. "That woman—Liza—she's really something, isn't she?"

I give a loud, single laugh, then cover my mouth when several heads turn my way. "If you only knew."

⁕

I take Beezus with me to Sunday night dinner, hoping she'll provide the emotional support I need to tell Mama about Glen. When I open the car door, Beezus runs to the porch, tail wagging a hundred miles an hour.

Jeez, she's never that excited to see me, and I'm the one who feeds her.

I climb the steps with wine and frozen breadsticks in a tote bag and knock on the door.

"In the kitchen!" Mama yells from inside.

I take that as permission to enter and push open the door. Beezus runs straight to Mama's ankles.

"Beezus! What a nice surprise! Always love it when my grandbabies come to visit," Mama says, stooping low to pet her fur.

I set my things on the table. "Good to see you too, Mama."

She laughs, crosses over to me, and gives a little hug. "And you too, of course."

I pull the wine and bread from the tote. "Do you want this chilled?"

"Put it in the freezer for a bit. That'll be good enough," she answers. "Bo and Stacey had something *more important* to do tonight, and Kitty's not coming either. She has a thing at the school. I swear, anytime they need something, she's the first to sign up."

"She enjoys it, Mama. I think she misses those crazy kids since she retired from teaching." I place the wine in the freezer.

"Yeah, yeah, I know. It's no skin off my back, but I hate for her to miss pasta night. It's her favorite. Maybe you can drop off a plate for her on your way home?"

"I can do that."

Out of nowhere, I have a crazy thought, but it's one I can't believe I've never had before. "Mama, have you and Aunt Kitty ever considered being roommates?"

"*What?*" She turns to me, disbelief written all across her face.

"You both live alone, in homes that are entirely too big for you. You're at each other's houses almost every day. You do everything together: your morning walks, your grocery shopping and errands. Wouldn't it make more sense if one of you sold a house, and you moved in together? Half the housework! Wouldn't that be a dream?"

"She's my best friend, Catherine, but I still need my space. We'd kill each other." She turns back to the stove and gives the noodles a stir.

"You guys have been surprisingly civil lately. Maybe you're mellowing in your old age." I mean it as a joke, but Mama's face tells me she hasn't received it as such.

"Nobody's mellowing. Trust me," she replies as she turns back to the stove. "So, I hear you've been spending time with Glen."

Mama's never been one who worried much about tactful segues.

"Yes, I have."

"Well, what's that about?"

"If we talk about this, can you...I don't know...promise to keep an open mind?"

She places a lid on the sauce, wipes her hands on a towel, then moves to the table. She takes a seat and gestures for me to do the same. "I promise I will try. But you also know that if I have an opinion, I'm gonna give it."

"Yes, that I know." I pull out the chair and sit. "We've been reconnecting; getting to know each other again."

"*Okay...*" Mama says, clearly biting her tongue.

"It's been a long time, Mama. We've both changed—and grown."

She nods.

"I won't get into specifics, but we were both so young and broken when we met. And now...we're not."

"You're not?"

"Well, no. I mean—what? Do you think I'm broken?"

"It's not you I'm worried about," she answers.

"Like I said, it's been a long time. He's gone through a lot of therapy, he's been sober seventeen years, he's—" I drift off, mid-sentence, because I can't find the right words to describe the transformation that man has undergone.

"He's what?" she asks.

"He's finally...well, I won't say he's the Glen I once knew, because he's not. He's someone entirely different. He's had a hard time of it, but he's finally happy, Mama."

"And are you happy?"

"I am. I found my peace a long time ago, and I've been happy with my life for a long time, too. But damn if I don't feel the happiest I've felt in—I can't even remember. It feels like—like we're finally ready for each other. I love him, Mama. I've always loved him."

She breathes in real deep, then lets it out slow. "Well, not that you've ever listened to me before, but you're fifty-seven years old, Catherine. You don't need my permission or advice to do anything. You know what's best for you."

I lean back in my seat, choosing to take that as a win.

The door flies open, and Aunt Kitty enters, waving a piece of paper around like she's swatting at a swarm of bees.

"Kitty! I thought you were volunteering at the school?"

"I'm not going! I'm too...too pissed off to be around children right now. They've sent another one, Laurel!" She stomps over to Mama and hands her the paper.

"What is it?" I ask.

"Hells bells, Kitty, isn't this like the fourth one?" Mama asks her.

"The fifth!" Aunt Kitty replies.

I lean across the table, trying to get a peek at the paper. "But...what is it?"

"Assholes!" Aunt Kitty yells as she pulls out a chair and flops into it.

"For months now, Kitty's been getting letters from a developer, wanting to buy her property."

"The nerve of them!" Aunt Kitty chimes in.

Aunt Kitty's property is over an acre and sits on the outskirts of town. For years, developers have slowly been gobbling up private property in the area and building townhouses and apartment buildings. I never thought about the possibility that one day it could be Aunt Kitty's house they tried to take.

Mama picks up the paper, pulls her glasses from the top of her head to her nose, and gives it another look. "Kitty, this is a lot of money. Significantly more than what was offered last time."

"I don't care how much it is! It's not about the money!" Aunt Kitty's face has gone flamingo pink.

"I'm just sayin' it might be time to consider it, is all." Mama sets the paper on the table.

"I have only ever lived in two houses in my life, Laurel. I went straight from my childhood home to my home with Charlie. It's not about the money, and I'm not considering it. Ever." Rising from her seat, Aunt Kitty moves to the freezer, retrieving the bottle of wine she somehow knew was inside it. "And I'm seventy-seven years old! Who wants to up and move from their home at seventy-seven? The nerve!"

Something about this conversation makes me feel like a kid eavesdropping on a grown-up discussion they aren't meant to be a part of, so I sit still and quiet.

"I get that, Kitty, I do. But do you want to spend the rest of your life fending off these vultures?"

"I'll tell them *no* on my deathbed," Aunt Kitty replies. "Have it carved on my tombstone, too."

Mama lets out a big sigh. "Okay, Kitty. I hear you. Okay."

The next day, I'm watering the front lawn as the sun sets, when Glen pulls into the driveway. I open the passenger door and say, "Hey! What are you doing here?"

"Wanna go for a ride?" he asks.

"Depends on where we're goin'. Paris? New York? London?"

"The lake," he replies with a grin.

I flip the lever on the hose nozzle to shut off the water, climb into the truck, and shut the door. "Think we'll see any shooting stars?"

"Depends on how long you want to stay." He reaches over, grips my thigh, and pulls me to the center of the bench seat.

I move one leg up and over the shifter as he leans in and plants a kiss on my temple.

"I'm too old to be riding in the middle of a bench seat, ya know."

He puts the truck in gear. "Humor me. At least this one time."

Sitting in the exact same spot I rode in all those years ago brings on a flood of memories—good and bad. "I can't believe you still have this old truck."

"Promised you I'd never get rid of it, didn't I?" he answers with wink and a smile. "And I've rebuilt practically every inch of it, so in reality, I'm not even sure it can be considered the same truck. But I tried my best." He squeezes my thigh again, then leaves his hand resting on my knee.

When we arrive at the lake, he parks in the same spot we always parked all those years ago. He opens his door, then offers his hand.

I slide across the seat to step out and see unfamiliar lights and shapes on the other side of the water. "Are those houses?"

"Yes. The county's zoned most of this as residential now and has been selling it off, piece by piece."

"They can't do that!"

"They can."

I pull my hand from his and head toward the shoreline. "Is that a—" I point toward a sign staked into the ground, unable to even say the words.

"A for-sale sign, yes."

There's a big red *SOLD* sticker plastered across the top.

"No! Who would—why would they—I don't understand!"

"It's all about the money, Cat, as most things are these days. These lots sell at a premium."

I sit in the grass, cross my legs underneath me, and feel a tear run down my cheek. "I can't believe it will be gone. It's our spot; our secret place." I wipe my face. "Those damn developers! They want Aunt Kitty's house, too! What has *happened* to the world?"

He sits behind me, placing one leg on either side of my hips. Then he wraps his arms around me and squeezes tight. "Catherine—"

I give a sniff.

"Cat?"

"Hmm?"

"I bought it. It's not going anywhere. It's ours."

Twisting around to see his face, I say, "You did what?"

"I bought it."

"You did not."

"I did."

I study his face, trying to determine if he really means it.

Oh my God, it's true.

"Glen!" I pull him in as close as I can, in my twisted position, placing my hands on either side of his face. Then, I kiss him.

When I let him go, he says, "And I'd say it was worth it."

"How did you—it must've cost a fortune!"

"A pretty penny, yes. But I'm selling the business in Montgomery, Cat. I'll run the Asher location full time, and it'll all come out in our favor in the end."

"I can't believe you did this. It's—" I can't even find the right words to say what it is.

"We don't have to do anything with it, if you don't want to. We can leave it just as it is and come here whenever we want, or we can build a house. I've found the perfect spot just up that hill." He points to the east.

I feel my smile grow from ear to ear. I didn't think I could ever be happier, but this feeling is something beyond *happy*. This is something you're only lucky enough to feel when your whole world shifts into place—a rare feeling I've had just three times before: when we were first married and moved into our house, when Jenna was born, and when I became a librarian.

"Do you remember the first time you brought me here?" I ask him.

"I remember everything, Cat."

"I was afraid of the dark, and you were afraid of the bugs."

He laughs and tightens his arms around me. "I'll never get used to them. Still blows my mind that those creepy things even exist."

I smile as he kisses my cheek.

"What do you mean you remember everything?" I ask.

"Every first. Every second. Every third. Every last. I remember it all. As much as I've tried to forget, it's all still there."

"You remember everything."

"I do."

"We've wasted so much time," I say.

"It wasn't wasted, Cat. We needed that time. We became different people in that time."

"I suppose. It's still stupid."

"Agreed." He stands, moves back to the truck, and turns on the music. When he returns, he pulls me up from the ground. "Cat, I'm so sorry."

"You don't need to—"

"No, listen to me. I know I couldn't help what happened to me or how it all...broke me, but that doesn't make me any less sorry for every bit of hurt, every tear, every scar on your heart, every ounce of faith you lost, every moment you ever doubted yourself, every hardship I caused...every goodbye. I'm sorry I was too scared and stubborn to get help sooner. I'm sorry it took my dad dying before I could come back to you. I'm sorry for every time I was too weak to stay...and for every time I was too weak to go. But the way I see it, we have twenty, maybe thirty years left on this earth, and I intend to spend every bit of it at this lake with you, if you'll have me."

There's a lump in my throat that's making it hard to breathe, much less speak, so all I can do is nod.

He leans in for a kiss and I close my eyes, unable to see the stars in the sky, but still seeing stars.

34

STOLEN THUNDER & NEW ADVENTURES

Six months later, it's Christmas, and I'm waiting on Mama's porch for Jenna, Andrew, and the kids to arrive.

The day is cold, crisp, and sunny, par for the course for December in southern Alabama. The smell of barbecue is in the air, as one of Mama's neighbors smoke meat for their holiday meal. I hear children giggling throughout the neighborhood as they enjoy their new bikes, skateboards, and basketball hoops, and it makes me eager for my own babies to arrive.

"You know, waiting out here isn't gonna make them arrive any sooner," Mama says when she joins me on the porch.

"Yes, I know. I'm just anxious. I hate that they have to make that long drive to get here."

"But they're in town, aren't they? They've got ten minutes of travel time from the hotel, max. Come on inside and get yourself some snacks."

"No, I think I'll wait here."

"All right, suit yourself." Mama waves me off, then re-enters the house.

Just as she shuts the door, I see it: Jenna's minivan turning the corner at the end of the street. I'm up and out of my seat in a flash, jogging toward the end of the driveway, waving my arms like I'm guiding them down a runway.

Andrew pulls in and parks, while Jenna and the kids wave from all windows.

"Hey, Mama," Jenna says as she opens the car door and climbs out.

I wrap her in a tight hug. "Hey, baby. How was your trip?"

"It was fine. The kids all had their food and drinks and electronics, so it was the easiest trip yet. Sorry we couldn't make it at Thanksgiving as usual. Just couldn't work it out after coming to see you and Daddy for two weeks in August."

"You're here now, so all is forgiven." I give her a peck on the cheek, then pull the handle to open the back sliding door. "Look at you three! You've grown up on me!" I say to my grandkids in the back.

"Grandma!" Audrey yells as she jumps out and gives me a big hug.

I squeeze her tight as Ryan and Noah climb out after her, carrying gifts wrapped in bright paper, covered in reindeer and snowmen.

"Ooh, Ryan, I hope those are for me!" I say, pinching his little cheek.

"Yup. There's some for Grandpa and GiGi too!" he replies.

"*Grandpa!* Oh, he's going to love being reminded that you guys call him that," I say with a laugh and a glance toward Jenna.

She smiles as Andrew comes around the front of the car and gives me a kiss on the cheek.

"Good to see you again, Catherine," Andrew says.

"Yes, you too. Let's get inside and warm up."

The kids run for the front door with Noah trailing behind, yelling, "Wait for me!"

Jenna slides her arm through mine. "Is Daddy here?" she asks, as we move toward the porch.

"Yup. Inside helping Mama with the ham."

"And Aunt Kitty?"

"Of course."

"Uncle Bo and Aunt Stacey?"

"On their way. Aunt Liza, Patrick, and Janine will be here, too."

"Hard to believe Aunt Liza's kept Patrick around this long," Jenna says.

"She seems to really like him. Says *he's her lobster*. I'll be damned if I know what that means."

Jenna laughs so loud, it makes my ear ring. "It's a *Friends* reference, Mama. You really should watch that show."

"Hmm, maybe when I retire."

She gives a full, bright smile as we climb the old wooden steps and enter the house.

"There she is!" Aunt Kitty says as she pounces on Jenna.

Glen looks up from the oven with that same full, bright smile Jenna just let go of.

And it feels like my heart will simply burst.

Two hours later, *Miracle on 34th Street* plays on the TV in the living room while we sit, gathered around Mama's formal dining room table. With seating for twelve and fourteen people here, we've had to pull in two dining chairs from the kitchen to make room for everyone. It's the first time in a long time that Daddy's spot at the table has been filled for a holiday dinner, and it makes me so grateful, I could cry.

Mama sits in Daddy's place now, looking like a proud mother hen, observing her little chicks, one by one. When her eyes meet mine, I smile, then look away. The last thing I want is to embarrass Mama by catching her being sentimental at her own dining table.

We're passing serving bowls of mashed potatoes, green bean casserole, stuffing, and cranberry sauce around as Glen cuts slices of ham to add to each plate. Just as Jenna hands me the potatoes, Mama asks, "So how's the house coming along? Have you chosen a spot to build on yet?"

Glen glances over at Mama as he continues to cut. "Yes, ma'am—right on top of a beautiful hill overlooking the whole lake. The plans should be finished up by next week."

Mama nods. "Can't wait to see it once it's built. From what I've seen of the plans so far, it's going to be gorgeous."

Janine looks to me with a smile. She's so very proud of her son, and ecstatic to have him back in Asher year-round.

"And you're headed back to Montgomery soon, right?" Mama asks Glen.

"Just for two or three weeks while we close on the sale of the business. Part of the deal is that I hang around for a bit to help the new folks get settled. I should be back by February. It'll be a relief to just have the Asher location to manage, that's for sure." Glen places the knife on the serving platter and takes his seat.

"I bet," Mama says. Then she turns to Liza. "You're not having dinner with your family today?"

"We are," Liza answers. "And Patrick's too, so forgive us if we're light eaters." She turns to Patrick and smiles. "Actually, we have some news as well."

My eyes dart to Liza.

No way she's getting married.

"Liza, maybe not now," Patrick says under his breath.

"What? They're family." She smiles as she addresses the room in general. "We're going to Europe...for a whole year!"

"Oh, that sounds wonderful!" Aunt Kitty says.

"You're—what?" I ask.

"Surprise!" Liza tells me. "Isn't it exciting? He's going to write a book—historical fiction—so we're going to travel England, Scotland, Ireland, and Wales for research. Maybe Germany. Can you believe it?"

"Liza—how can...how can you leave your business for a year?" I ask.

"My manager has it all covered. She does most of the work anyway," she answers, flippantly.

I turn to Patrick. "Did you put in notice that I haven't seen?"

"Uh—not yet. I was planning to do that on Monday, Catherine." He turns to Liza. "I told you this wasn't the right time. She deserved to know first, Liza, because she's my boss. And your best friend."

Liza looks confused for a moment, then it's like it hits her all at once. "Oh, God. You're right." She looks at me as she says, "I'm so sorry. I'm just so excited and couldn't hold it in. I'm an idiot."

Out of the corner of my eye, I see Mama giving me a face saying, *do the right thing, Catherine.*

So, I offer a smile and say, "It's fine, Liza. Took me by surprise, but it's fine. I'm happy for you."

Liza positively beams with happiness.

"When do you leave?" I ask.

"January 12th," she answers, leaning into Patrick.

"If that's too soon, we can push it back," he says.

"I'll make do. And you'll still have your job when you get back. You know I could never replace you."

He smiles. "Thank you. That means a lot."

"Well, if we're tellin' news—" Bo says, as we all turn our eyes to him. "We're also moving—to Huntsville."

It's quiet for a moment, then Stacey chimes in. "We want to be closer to the kids and grandkids. We've both just taken new jobs, and we've signed a lease on a house."

Mama nods again and says, "Good for you. When is this happening?"

"In January also," Bo answers.

"Well, all right then. Should we say grace?" Mama asks.

We bow our heads as she leads the prayer. "Heavenly Father, thank you for bringing us all here today. Thank you for this family, this food, our health, and our—happiness. In Your name we pray—Amen."

"Amen," is heard round the table, then the room is filled with the sound of silverware clanging and questions about where Liza and Patrick will go first, what side of town Bo and Stacey will live on, and when they plan to visit next.

When folks dig in for seconds, Mama clears her throat, and all eyes turn to her.

"Well, Kitty, I'm afraid the young'uns may have stolen our thunder," she says.

Aunt Kitty shrugs her shoulders and takes a sip of her wine.

"We have some news of our own," Mama says.

There's no way there's more.

Glen takes my hand beneath the table, like he knows something terrible is coming, and he's trying to anchor me in place.

"Kitty has sold her house," Mama says.

"To the developers?" I ask.

Aunt Kitty huffs as she leans back in her chair. "Bastards were gonna get it eventually anyway, so I figured I might as well take advantage of the offer." She picks up her napkin and dabs at her eyes.

"Aunt Kitty, I'm so sorry," I say.

"Thank you, hon, but I'm okay. I've made peace with it," she replies.

"So...since Kitty's loaded now, we're gettin' the hell out of Dodge," Mama says as she takes a bite.

I pause with my fork halfway to my mouth.

What the hell is happening?

"You're what? Where would you go? And *why?*" Bo asks.

"Florida," Mama and Aunt Kitty say, together.

"Pensacola?" I ask.

"Heavens, no. If I'm going to Florida, I'm going to *Florida*. Not lower Alabama," Mama replies. "We considered Tampa, but good Lord, so many people."

"And I can't do all those bridges," Aunt Kitty says with a terrified face.

"So, we decided on a little town near Sarasota," Mama says. "Found a condo in a nice retirement community. And to answer your last question, Bo: We're *going* because you lot have finally gotten yourselves to a point where we don't have to worry about you nonstop. Jenna's happy. Bo's happy. Catherine's happy. Liza's happy," she says, pointing her fork at each of us, in turn. "You're all settled. You don't need us anymore."

"And let's face it—we're not getting any younger," Aunt Kitty adds.

"And *also,* we're both pretty tired of this town," Mama says with a dramatic eyeroll. "It's time for something different. We'll be roommates, which I believe was your idea," she says, pointing her fork at me again, as she chews a piece of ham.

"I—uh—" I can't find the words. "Excuse me." I stand, place my napkin on the table, and head out the front door. Just as I sit on the top step, the door opens again, and Glen appears. "What the hell just happened in there, Glen?"

"Not anything I ever saw comin', that's for sure," he answers. "Are you okay?"

I take my time in answering. "I just need to sit with this for a bit."

"Okay," he says as he sits next to me.

"For someone who has *abandonment issues*—this is a lot. They've all been my support system for so long, I don't know how I'll get on without them. Any second now, it's going to hit me right in the face, and I just can't be in front of all of them when it does."

He nods. "We'll sit out here as long as you need, Cat."

I lean my head on his shoulder and wait, while a million thoughts whirl through my mind. I can see Mama and Aunt Kitty walking arm-in-arm on a beach, stooping low to collect seashells from the sand. I can picture Liza, posing in front of Big Ben and The Kelpies, or sipping coffee in a Marylebone High Street cafe. I envision Bo and Stacey having Sunday night dinners of their own, surrounded by the sweet family they've created. And while I'm picturing all of this, I also see Jenna and Andrew returning to Texas, living their best, chaotic life with my grandbabies, too...making memories they'll all have forever. None of it will be perfect for any of them, but *my God,* they'll be *living.*

A tear slides down my cheek as I struggle to name the emotions I'm feeling. Then, it hits me. I look up at Glen, who stares back with a patient expression, as he waits for me to figure it out.

"It's not coming," I say.

"What's not coming?"

"The fear, the hurt, the anger, the sadness…the *freak-out*—It's not com-ing."

He brings his hand to my face and wipes away a tear. "Then, what's all this, Cat?"

My God. It's happiness. It's—pure joy.

I laugh loud, and hard.

Glen cocks his head to the side and asks, "Have you lost your marbles, woman?"

"No! At least, I don't think so. Glen, I think—I think I'm *happy* for them. For all of them! I'm excited for everything they're all moving on to do! I thought for sure that the terrible feelings would come; that I would freak out; that I was going to lose it—and I didn't want them to see that happen, but—there's nothing but *joy*."

He pulls me up and hugs me tight. Then he leans back to look at me. "Let's go in there and tell them that, okay?"

Placing one hand on either side of his face, I say, "But you better not be in Montgomery any more than three weeks, ya hear? We have adventures of our own to get to."

"Yes, ma'am." He takes my hands in his. "Catherine Lewis?"

"Hmm?"

"Can I kiss you?"

"Will you *ever* stop askin' me that?"

Seizing me at the small of my back with one hand, while entwining the other in the hair at my neck, he says, "Never."

Looking for more from the Women of Asher?

Keep reading for a preview of Jenna's story
(Book 1 in the *Women of Asher* series, AVAILABLE NOW)!

Jenna Cartwright has run away from her family in a desperate bid to save—or end—her life.

Driven to despair by debilitating depression, loneliness, and anxiety, Jenna makes a panic-driven decision to leave her husband and young children behind.

Upon fleeing to her hometown of Asher, Alabama, Jenna searches for help from the generations of women she loves most. As she learns their long-held stories, Jenna struggles to untangle her own thoughts and emotions, while also grappling with the impossible decision of *what comes next.*

Can she find the strength and courage to return to her family, heal her soul, and form her own life-saving sisterhood? Or will she remain a hopeless runaway mother, trapped by a longing for an irreversible escape?

1. RAIN

What I wouldn't give to be the type of mom who remembers an umbrella and wears weather-appropriate shoes.

This morning, though, I was lucky to get everyone dressed and out of the house on time—or ten minutes late, which is "on time" enough, anyway. The weather was the least of my concerns.

"Are you ready to see Ms. Maggie and Henry?" I ask Noah while unbuckling my seat belt.

"Yup. Noah like Henry," he answers.

"Good. We have to hurry, though. Can we do that?"

He nods.

"All right, here we go!" I pull the hood of my fleece jacket up over my head, grab the diaper bag from the passenger side, then place it in the driver's seat as I step out of the car and shut the door. I push the button to open Noah's door and it slides back on its rails so slowly that for a moment, I wonder if it's broken.

I unbuckle Noah, place him on my hip, then push the button to close his door while opening mine again to grab the bag. As we begin the journey across the black parking lot river to the entrance of the coffee shop, there are no puddles to dodge. The whole lot is a greasy gazpacho of oily water, fast food trash, and fallen leaves. It covers the top of my running shoes and as I trudge forward, splashes my leggings clear up to the knees.

I step onto the sidewalk, under the cover of the awning perched above the door. Glancing through the glass, I see Maggie sitting with Henry. They're smiling and playing peek-a-boo as they wait for us to arrive.

I yank the hood off my head and set Noah to stand at my feet. Pulling the elastic from my ponytail, I shake out my hair and attempt to smooth it all back into place and re-tie it again. Taking Noah's hand, we move the one step needed to reach the handle. Just as I place my hand upon it, I'm hit right smack on top of the head by a giant, shockingly cold raindrop. Looking up, I see a gap about an inch wide between the back edge of the awning and the building. Another fat drop pelts me right between the eyes.

A frustrated growl escapes my lips as I dab the top of my head and my face with the sleeve of my jacket and take Noah's hand again.

"Are you going in?" someone asks from behind me.

I look over my shoulder to find a short, stocky man in a trench coat and tie, reaching around me for the door. I step to the right with Noah as he opens it for us, then my eyes meet Maggie's as we enter.

Maggie and I met several summers back while she was working at the local library. I had just two kids then—a two-year-old and a newborn. Dozing in and out of consciousness while sitting on the floor and leaning against the wall in the play area, I felt a tap on my shoulder. When I opened my eyes, I saw Maggie standing with a halo around her head—a literal halo cast from the building's fluorescent overhead lights.

That's when she told me I couldn't sleep in the library anymore. Then she offered me her name and phone number and directed me to call if I ever needed a babysitter—or a break.

We kept in touch and while Maggie and I don't see each other every day, or even every month, she's the closest thing I have to a real friend outside of those I left behind in Alabama so many years ago.

Regardless of that, though, there are still many days in which Maggie is a bit too much to bear—she's a person who is deliriously happy all the time. The glass is always half-full with Maggie and I can already sense how this coffee date is going to go. Particularly, that today is not a day in which I feel capable of placating Maggie's optimism, nor energized enough to try hopping onto her "good vibes only" train.

"Look at you!" she says, as we approach the table.

"I know, I know. But we're fine." I set Noah into the empty highchair next to Henry's, then tug off my rain-soaked fleece and Noah's equally soaked hoodie. I rub my upper arms for warmth—wishing I could do the same for my cold, wet feet.

Maggie's already ordered my black coffee as well as pastries and kolaches, so I take a careful sip, measuring just how late we are by how cold the coffee has become. *Still lukewarm, so not terribly late.* "Thanks for the coffee," I tell her.

"Of course. Seems like all I do these days is drink coffee, tea, hot cocoa—anything warm to take the edge off all this rain. Have you ever seen so much rain?" Maggie asks.

"Not here, I haven't. Weeks of it. It's just crazy."

"Are you guys going to the parade in San Antonio this weekend? I mean, if the weather cooperates for it?" Maggie blows on her latte, which is topped with a frothy, milky-white heart.

She, of course, thought to bring her umbrella and appears completely comfortable in a fuzzy, pastel pink sweater. A large, beautiful gold hair pin holds her perfectly un-perfect mom-bun in place and matching gold statement earrings dial up the look.

"I don't think so. I should probably work."

Billie Holiday croons one of my favorite songs in the background. I look down at my mug of coffee and close my eyes—just for a moment—to escape into the song's smooth chorus.

"Jenna, I don't know how you do it—stay home with three kids and work, too." She wipes a crumb from Henry's chin as he swipes the rest of his pastry off the table, sending crimson-red raspberry jam splattering across the impeccably clean black and white penny tile floor.

"Well, I don't always do it gracefully." I tear a kolache into small pieces with my fingers and place them, two at a time, in front of Noah.

"Grace or not, it's impressive. I consider it a good day if I've managed to shower," Maggie says with a chuckle.

"What? You still shower?"

"Girl—" She laughs.

"I didn't get the memo that a shower was a requirement for this coffee date, sorry."

"Stop it." She laughs again, but this time it's that uncomfortable one people give when you've said something that rings true, but they don't want to admit it.

I sweep a loose strand of hair that didn't make it back into my ponytail behind my ear. Why didn't I at least ditch the leggings and opt for real pants?

"Tell me about this new friend of yours. What's her name again?" Maggie asks.

"Bonnie," I say.

"Right. How did you meet her, anyway?" Maggie hands Henry another full-sized pastry—chocolate this time—and I'm tempted to set a timer to see how long before he throws this one on the floor, too.

"I saw her sitting on the park bench by St. Paul's a couple times, always alone. So, one day as I was walking by with Noah, I said hello and asked if she needed help. I assumed she was senile or lost."

"That wasn't the case?" she asks.

"Um, no. That woman hasn't needed saving a day in her life."

Bonnie's sweet, strong, and slightly stubborn by nature. She's not someone who could often, if ever, have been described as a 'damsel in distress.'

Maggie sips her latte with a petite little slurp. "And now, you guys—what—hang out?"

"Noah and I visit her once a week. Her house is gorgeous. She has hundreds of books—and these three giant, antique crystal chandeliers you'd have to see to believe."

"Sounds nice. I wish I had a place like that to escape to once a week. Though it seems a little *Tuesdays with Morrie*-ish to me."

That's not a similarity that's struck me before, but if Bonnie was willing and able to impart some sort of wisdom on how to find tangible happiness in life, I'd certainly listen.

"Well, she isn't sick that I'm aware of, and her stories are definitely way more risqué," I say with a raised eyebrow and a hint of a smirk, which catches me by surprise.

"Hmm—I might need to meet this lady," Maggie says with another slurp.

"No way, get your own old lady bestie!" I pretend to shoo her away and tear more tiny pieces of bread for Noah. He's not interested and shoves them both to the floor, so I hand him a milk cup instead.

Sneaking a peek at the clock on the wall, I can see I've only been at this table for twenty minutes. *God, how can time go so slow?*

"Is it weird that I have a 70-something year old friend?" I'm both trying to fill the time and genuinely interested in her answer.

"I don't think so. I think it's nice."

The bell jingles on the door as another set of moms enter with toddlers. All of them are wearing adorable, brightly patterned rain boots; the moms in plaid and polka dots and the kids in dinosaurs and unicorns. The moms pause in the doorway to shake out their umbrellas, while their kids run to a table on the other side of the room. Both mothers seem so happy and completely put-together—like two additional Maggies, copied and pasted into the coffee shop. As if one wasn't enough.

I look over at Noah's thin hoodie hanging on the back of the chair. A drop of water falls from the sleeve and lands in a tiny puddle on the floor.

What did the other two wear to school today? I can't even remember. I bet the moms sitting across from us remember what their kids are wearing—and have no similar concerns about whether they're sufficiently warm and dry.

"You haven't lived near your family since you moved to Texas for college, right? I imagine it gets lonely," Maggie says.

Lonely isn't quite the word I would use to describe it. *Disconnected* from everyone who knew me in what seems like a whole lifetime ago, maybe. *Wistful* for the Sunday night dinners that were once an annoying standing appointment in my ever-so-important teenage social calendar. Maybe somewhat *envious* for the time Mama and GiGi get to spend together, as they both grow older, and I'm 800 miles away—but certainly not *lonely*. Right?

"I guess Bonnie does remind me a lot of my GiGi." I pull my eyes back to our own table and pick at my scraggly nails while homing in on the doughy scent of fresh-baked bread escaping from the kitchen.

What is it they say? Name something you can see, touch, hear, smell, and taste, right? That's supposed to stop the anxiety spiral.

I can see amazing, caring mothers who have it all figured out. I can touch Noah's wet hoodie and know I've failed—again. I can hear friends having real, meaningful conversations. I can smell breads I used to love to bake. I can taste bitter coffee, which puckers the corners of my mouth and makes me crave the piping hot potion from my pot at home, complete with comfy clothes and no expectation of intelligent dialogue attached.

Wait—I don't think I'm doing this exercise right. *How many more minutes?*

Maggie, taking no notice of my increasing impulse to run right out of this coffee shop, continues taking her sweet time with her latte while filling me in on all the details of her mother-in-law's recent visit and the bake sale fundraiser at her church. Occasionally, she throws in a question about what my kids have been up to lately, to which I give the expected, socially acceptable answers and we move on.

She's trying. She really is. It's not her fault I can't connect with any of it today.

"Well, I hate to be the first to leave," she says, "but we have a dental appointment to get to." She starts packing up her things.

Thank God. I take her cue and begin packing our things, too. "No worries. It was good seeing you guys, though." I give Henry's hand a squeeze.

"Let's do this again soon, okay?"

"For sure. Soon." I stand and give her a hug, then she heads toward the exit with Henry on her hip, popping open an umbrella as she steps outside.

Tossing a cash tip onto the table, I scoop Noah up from his seat, throw the wet hoodie over his head, and beeline for the car.

On the way home, as Noah sings along to his favorite nursery rhymes, I struggle to keep the car between the yellow lines, which are barely visible through the pouring rain. I think of Maggie's sweet, oval face. I can't imagine she ever struggles with her kids, or her life, as I do with mine.

Does she also live with her head in the fog, waiting for a glimpse of the sunshine? I doubt it, and I'll damn sure never ask.

◆

Rocking Noah to sleep, cocooned together under his favorite blanket as the weather rages outside his window, I cling to his warm body and breathe him in.

I'm not much of a cuddler, but this is something of which I will never grow tired. Though I know from experience, he will one day grow plenty tired of being handled like a baby and what will I do then? There are no more children in my future: three is enough—and likely too many. Where, then, will I find my peace? It's not with joining the PTA or coaching a soccer team, I know that. This, this part right here, is where it all lies. All my eggs, in one withering basket, already worn thread-bare from the other two having outgrown the confines of my lap.

Noah lets out a heavy sigh, then his chest begins to rise and fall in a steady rhythm. I stand, lay him in his crib, brush the hair from his face, and stare.

What will I do, sweet Noah? How will I survive it?

A solitary tear rolls down my cheek and lands near his ear, darkening the red fire engine-themed bed sheet. I wipe my face and leave him be.

I emerge from the bedroom and head toward the kitchen in search of coffee. Saturdays are the one day a week when I can sleep-in and somehow, I dozed till after one in the afternoon.

"Good morning," I hear from the recliner in the living room.

Andrew's watching something on his tablet while Ryan and Audrey play peacefully on the computer in my office. Noah must be napping already. How does he get them to do that? How is it that just his presence brings calm to their crazy?

"Please wake me up at 11:00 on Saturdays, if I'm still asleep." I'm embarrassed for having wasted away so much of the day, even if it is my day to rest.

"Sure," he answers. "I figured I would just let you sleep until whenever." He runs his fingers through his hair, not even looking up from the tablet in his hand.

His well-intended reply bothers me, especially as I notice the fresh smell of dryer sheets escaping from under the laundry room door and I'm reminded I haven't done a load of laundry—or cooked a meal—in days.

It's not that I don't know these are things that need to be done. Of course I know, and I detest the guilt I feel at ignoring them, but somehow still can't seem to *do* them. These very basic things come at me like the nemeses in Audrey's video games. I throw up my right arm to deflect one, then the left to deflect another, praying I can somehow make it to safety before I'm buried beneath a pile of responsibilities I can't face.

Placing a bowl of one-minute oats and water into the microwave, I pour my coffee while it cooks. Outside the kitchen window, the rain is still falling, almost silently, creating a curtain through which not much at all can be seen. Heavy, but quiet at the same time. I sit at the table with my buttered oatmeal and black coffee and watch it fall.

This type of rain can be dangerous in these parts of Texas. The ground is so hard and dry, it can't readily accept the sheer volume of water released in the downpour. Flash flooding occurs, animals are lost, cars are swept from the road, and occasionally even small children are carried away in the current. But then, just as soon as it stops, the floodwaters seep into the ground, and the danger is gone.

It's never occurred to me before how much the transition from the dark days to the good is just like that—terrifying and deadly one moment, to checking the mail and washing the mud-covered cars the next.

Within a few hours, the rain dissipates and there isn't a dark cloud in the sky. The sun is shining bright, yet the rain still comes—sideways or at a diagonal. Audrey and Ryan love this kind of rain the most because there's no thunder or lightning and they know they're allowed to splash in it to their hearts' content. Despite my half-hearted objections and the cold, they grab their boots and jackets and they're on their way. They'll need baths when they come in and I'm so *tired*, but I let them go anyway.

I throw together a spaghetti dinner while they're outside and Noah plays upstairs.

"Can you call them in?" I ask Andrew.

"Sure. They're going to need baths."

"Yup." I don't look up from my pot. I am not interested in giving baths.

"Okay, I'll take care of it."

Andrew wrangles them inside and they're covered, head-to-toe, in mud which has now found its way onto his favorite gray sweatpants and bare feet. On my very best days, those are my favorite gray sweatpants too. On those days, I can't take my eyes off him. He looks so much like he did when we first met all those years ago, only somehow even better with age.

He guides them to the bathroom, proclaiming, "Don't touch anything!" about a thousand times along the way. Of course they touch everything, giggling as they go. I sigh, grab a wet towel and wipe clean the walls, the dining chairs, the countertops.

I hear water splash onto the tile floor in the bathroom down the hall.

"Oh, no, let's not splash out of the tub. You're going to make Mama super mad." Andrew's statement is met with giggles and more splashing. "No, really, keep it in the tub, you guys!"

Why does it have to be that they're going to make *me* super mad? I am not the only adult in this house.

Climbing the stairs, I find Noah playing in his room. "Hey, sweetie. Are you hungry? Let's go eat."

He stands, drops the toys from his hands, but hangs on to one red car.

"You want to take that one downstairs? Maybe he's hungry too."

"Yeah, hungry too," he replies.

As we make our way back downstairs and through the living room, Ryan cuts the corner from the hallway to the kitchen, sliding on wet feet.

"Ryan, don't—"

His legs come out from under him, sending him crashing to the floor with a thud. He screams.

I set Noah into the highchair, which he's almost outgrown, and move to Ryan.

"This is why we don't run in the house! Are you okay?"

He's crying and holding the back of his head.

"Let me see." I move his hands and feel a lump already beginning to form.

"What happened?" Andrew asks as he enters the kitchen. The front of his soaked tee-shirt clings to every muscle in such a way that I can see them move when he does.

"He slipped and hit his head. Why were his feet still wet?"

"Because he just got out of the bath."

"That's what a towel is for, Andrew!" I pull an ice pack from the freezer. "Here, sit down and keep this on your head." I hand the ice pack to Ryan. A bead of sweat rolls down my face, in a straight line from temple to jaw.

I should've just done the bath myself. No one can control whether a four-year-old remembers not to run in the house, but what can be controlled is whether they have wet feet when leaving through the bathroom door.

Audrey joins her brothers at the table. "What's for dinner?"

"Spaghetti," I answer, knowing exactly what will come next.

"I don't want spaghetti!" she screams.

Every single time.

My chest tightens and for a moment, I can't breathe. My first instinct is to lose it completely, but when I turn and see her waiting for my reply, I'm reminded it will do no good to give one. We've done this song and dance a million times and the ending is always the same.

Turning back to the stove, I pile pasta onto each of their plates, topping it with plain meat sauce with no trace of vegetables besides the tomatoes with which it's made. Luxuries such as bell peppers, onions, and mushrooms in the sauce left us the day she started solid foods. And crunchy peanut butter. And all ice cream that isn't red or pink.

They eat all they're going to eat and Andrew takes them upstairs to brush teeth and tuck them in. I clear the table of our plates, scrape their leftovers into Tupperware bowls, and attempt to attach a lid to one. It's too full and spaghetti sauce squirts all over my blouse and onto the floor.

"Son of a—" I pull a paper towel from the roll and wipe up the floor. The shirt, like so many in my closet, is a lost cause.

Wetting a clean rag, I move to the table, erasing their tomato-on-wood masterpieces from its top. As my hand runs over the indents made by years of pounding cutlery at the hands of tiny humans, I pause. I am both desperate for a break—an escape—and on the verge of tears for how fast they've grown.

"I'm going to hop in the shower and turn in early too," Andrew says as he returns downstairs, then disappears into our bedroom.

"Okay," I reply to no one, as he shuts the door.

I move to the sink, plunge my hands into the opalescent water, and wash the burned ring of spaghetti sauce from inside the shiny, silver pot—part of a set gifted to us at our wedding, back before dark days and good days, bumped heads, and pasta protests. As I scrub, a tiny, perfect bubble escapes the sink. I watch it float toward the ceiling, hit the can light, and pop.

After finishing in the kitchen and tucking Ryan back into bed twice, I hear the shower turn off and Andrew's bedside lamp click. I give it a while longer, then sneak into bed.

As I drift off to sleep, images of the kids joyfully splashing through the mud fill my head. Suddenly, I'm very aware of how much life resembles the sun-shower: It can be so beautiful and bright, but still, there's rain.

The Stories We Keep: Book 1 in the Women of Asher series, Available NOW.

YOUR REVIEW MATTERS

When We're Broken is an independently published novel. Your reviews through Amazon, Goodreads, and the retailer through which you purchased are meaningful and impactful. Please do take a moment to share your thoughts.

Thank you for supporting independent authors!

ACKNOWLEDGEMENTS

Thank you to my husband Michael for being my ever-present sounding board. A writer doesn't get through four versions of a story without someone who listens patiently as they work through it all out loud (at least this one doesn't), and I'm grateful for your willingness to always lend an ear...and a beer, when the situation calls for it (*Thank you, Linus*).

And Catherine's story wouldn't be what it is without the team of astoundingly insightful beta readers and sensitivity readers for it. Coco, Elisabeth, Connie, Jessica, and Gillian: Book by book, you're all making me a better writer, and I love you for it.

Esther, you are a dream to work with, and I will always be thankful for the beautiful covers you've created for these stories. I'm so glad—and so lucky(!)—to have been introduced to you.

Thank you to my third-grade teacher Mrs. Williams (whom the Asher High librarian is named for in this book), for inspiring my lifelong love of reading, and for helping little eight-year-old me feel less alone. The impact you've made on your students is real, and I am forever grateful for it.

And finally, thank you to every reader who's given these books a chance. The stories of the *Women of Asher* live loud, clear, and rent-free in my head, and I think there's a real possibility my sanity would be in question if I didn't have *you* to share them with.

ABOUT THE AUTHOR

Shawna Holly is an Okie who now lives outside of San Antonio, Texas, with her husband and three young kids. *When We're Broken* is her second novel, and the second in the *Women of Asher* series.

Prior to venturing into fiction writing, she served in the U.S. Air Force, worked as a government contractor, wrote a hyper-local blog focused on the beautiful Texas Hill Country, and owned a boutique web design and digital marketing firm (not all at once, of course).

When not writing, editing, publishing, or marketing, she can likely be found napping, over-caffeinating, taxiing her kids around town, procrastinating, or cheering at the baseball field.

Keep in touch at shawnaholly.com.

CONTENT WARNINGS

— Mild Profanity

— Death, Grief

— Physical Abuse (Off Page)

— Trauma, Mental Illness

— Teen Sex (Mild, Fade-to-Black)

— Suicide (Overheard, Non-Main Character)

— Substance Abuse

— Miscarriage

— Divorce/Estrangement